FROM SPRAWLING PLAINS TO MAJESTIC PEAKS,
THEIR LIVES TANGLED IN TRUST AND TREACHERY,
TRAGEDY AND HOPE. . . .

Iris—A beauty with hair as golden as the prairie grass and skin pale as the moon, she was bold in passion, steely in courage, constant in love. But she hardly knew what would be demanded of her as she rode with her new husband into an unknown land, a new era, and a whirlwind of danger.

Zack—The scar on his cheek mirrored the lifelong battle in his soul. Could his passion for one extraordinary woman heal his past? And could an unimaginable friendship change his future and that of a noble native people?

Strong Runner—Strong and swift, the magnificent warrior defended his beloved homeland with bravery, stealth, and a wisdom learned from the earth. But when his path crossed Zack's, did he dare believe that the desperate bluecoat's honor matched his own?

Morning Star—Strong Runner's wife knew firsthand the betrayal and violence of the settlers' brutal lust. But could she rise above the past and do what she must to save her husband, her children, her people?

Chase the Sun

Rosanne Bittner

Bantam Books
New York   Toronto   London   Sydney   Auckland

CHASE THE SUN

A Bantam Book / October 1995

ISBN 0-553-56995-3

Published simultaneously in the United States and Canada

Bantam Books are published by Bantam Books, a division of Bantam
Doubleday Dell Publishing Group, Inc. Its trademark, consisting of the
words "Bantam Books" and the portrayal of a rooster, is Registered in
U.S. Patent and Trademark Office and in other countries. Marca Reg-
istrada. Bantam Books, 1540 Broadway, New York, New York 10036.

PRINTED IN THE UNITED STATES OF AMERICA

RAD   0 9 8 7 6 5 4 3 2 1

For Dr. William Chandler,
neurosurgeon, University of Michigan
Hospital, Ann Arbor, Michigan,
from a new member of the
"Hole in the Head" gang.
Thanks for being one of the best
at what you do!

To my readers ...

The wind that howls through the rugged canyons and snow-capped mountains of America's West still speaks of the pain of settlers and Indians alike; of an era when two cultures clashed time and time again. Bringing them together in peace and harmony often proved as futile as chasing the sun, as did capturing a people as wild and free as nature itself. Those expected to contain our Native Americans and "chase the sun" were the U.S. soldiers, "bluecoats" the Indians often called them. This is the story of one soldier whose very soul was owned by the Indian spirit.

Of all recorded Indian uprisings, few tribes posed as bold and fearless a contest as the Nez Perce in America's Northwest, where approximately eight hundred men, women, and children fought against thousands of U.S. troops. Through some of the most rugged country in America, through mountains and passes so steep, they seemed impossible at times to master, this proud tribe, under the leadership of the now-famous Chief Joseph, confounded some of the best officers and Indian fighters the army could boast. Sometimes their 1300-mile, four-month journey took them south instead of north, in brilliant maneuvers to dodge the army. If not for the lack of food and proper clothing, and if the Nez Perce were not already weakened from loss of hope, they might have reached Canada . . . and if not for broken promises, they never would have tried to leave their beloved homeland in the first place.

This poignant flight makes up part of my story, and some of the major officers and Indian leaders mentioned actually existed. All locations and forts named in this story are real, and many events did happen, such as the attack on U.S. troops in Montana now called the "wagon box" fight, the massacre of eighty soldiers under Captain William Fetterman, the hanging of Indians at Fort Snelling, Minnesota, and the incident involving a young Nez Perce warrior called Wahlitits, which instigated the Nez Perces' flight to Canada. Any dialogue I have written involving historical characters is based on factual accounts of how these people reacted and behaved during these events.

All primary characters in this story are fictitious and purely the product of this author's imagination; however, there is no doubt that people just like them existed, and by the time I finish a story, they have become very real for me, as I hope they will for you. Certainly the spirits of those who settled this country, and those who gave up their beloved homeland for that settlement, live on forever. . . .

Come and chase me!

Try to catch me!

Can you catch the sun?

Can you capture the wind?

That is how easy it will be

To trap me.

Perhaps you will capture my body,

But you will never capture my spirit.

My spirit will live forever

In this land that is my home,

This land that will never belong to you.

Come and chase me!

Chase the sun, my enemy ... my friend ...

Chase the sun!

Part One

"*G*et yourselves up now, kids. It's time for chores."

Zack Myers rubbed his sleepy eyes. His father's voice was like an alarm clock, every morning, five A.M., and he never disobeyed the command. John Myers was a stern but gentle and loving man, a man who had worked hard to settle this piece of land in Kansas. Not a day went by that Zack's father didn't say, "This place will be worth something someday, and you kids will get it all. Out here a man can have all the land he wants. If he's willing to work it, he can have an empire."

Zack touched the end of his cold nose. He hated having to crawl out of a warm bed on such a chilly morning, but his father had a dream, and Zack loved helping the man realize that dream. Most of all, he liked the pride he felt when his father complimented him on work well done. Just the day before he had told Zack that some grown men probably couldn't keep up with him.

Zack shivered, thinking that if it was this cold up here in the loft, it must really be cold below. The fire in the fireplace must have gone out overnight. Usually the loft stayed warm the longest, and he was glad that was where he slept. He sat up and pulled a flannel shirt over his long-sleeved underwear, then forced himself out of bed, quickly visiting his personal chamber pot in the corner before pulling on thick woolen pants. He rinsed his mouth at a washstand and listened to familiar morning sounds as he finished dressing and pulled on socks and leather shoes.

"You too, Emily," his mother was saying. "Get out of that cot and get dressed. Help me with breakfast so your father and brother can get to their chores. You will need to gather more eggs after breakfast. You and I have some baking to do."

"But Miss Nancy doesn't want to get up yet," Emily complained.

"Then leave her in the bed and quit making excuses. Get up and get dressed."

Zack snickered. "I think you should make Miss Nancy get up too," he teased, referring to Emily's rag doll.

"You leave Miss Nancy alone!" Emily yelled back.

"No raised voices, either of you," John Myers ordered. "Get yourselves to the breakfast table quickly."

Zack giggled at the way his seven-year-old sister defended her doll as though it were a real person. She lost it once down the well and had cried herself sick. Zack's father had tied a rope around Zack and lowered him into the well to fish around for the doll until he finally found it. It had been a frightening experience for Zack, but he knew how much his sister loved that stupid doll. Since then he had become Emily's hero, a big brother who had braved that dark, scary hole in the earth to save Miss Nancy.

Being her hero hadn't changed the fact that Zack still thought of her as a terrible pest, nor did it change his resentment of her for being so spoiled. Why did girls get more privileges than boys? Yes, she had chores, but at least Emily's chores were mostly inside, away from the rain and snow and cold winds of winter, and from the beastly hot sun of summer, except when it was time to hang the wash. He didn't envy his sister or mother on washday. It was an all-day project that left his mother bone tired, her knuckles raw.

He finished tying his boots and grabbed his wool jacket, then climbed down a wooden ladder to the room below, where his father had rekindled a fire in the stone fireplace. The family's cabin was small, one main room with a tiny curtained-off area to the back, where John and Margaret Myers slept. Emily's little cot was placed near the fireplace.

Margaret often talked about the large home she had lived in back in Ohio before marrying Zack's father. "Four bedrooms we had," she would say longingly, "and a big parlor, a dining room and kitchen, and a big front porch." She always warned the children not to tell their father she had been talking about that big house. "It would hurt his feelings," she would tell them. "Right now this little cabin is the best he can do for us, but he's promised me that someday we'll have a big house of our own."

Zack often tried to picture that big house. He had never known anything but this little cabin. He didn't know anything about formal schooling either. That was another thing his mother often talked about. She'd gone to school with other children back in Ohio, and she seemed to think that book learning was very important. She had brought many of those books with her when she came to Kansas with her husband, and she used them now to teach Zack and Emily to read and write. Zack hated lesson time, hated having to sit still; but Emily loved it. Best of all, she enjoyed flaunting the fact she could read just as well, sometimes better than, her big brother.

"Sure can feel winter coming," Zack's father said as Zack sat down to the table, made by his father from cottonwood trees that were in abundance along the Smoky Hill River. The river was only a quarter of a mile north of their cabin, but Zack and Emily were forbidden to go there alone to play. Sometimes Indians used that river, and although so far the various tribes that frequented the area had given them no trouble, Zack's father did not trust them. "They're like wild animals," the man often warned. "Reach out to them, and they'll bite off your hand. Stories I've heard . . . I swear those painted savages sometimes torture and kill for the fun of it."

The orders were repeated often. If Indians showed up, they were to stay inside the cabin. If the Indians attacked, they should go into the root cellar through the trapdoor in the floor of the cabin. In the cellar was a hidden door that opened to a tunnel Zack and his father had spent weeks digging. It led to a nearby stand of trees, the escape hole hidden by flat boards covered with brush and rocks.

"I hope we never have to use it," Zack's mother often commented. Zack hoped so too, but he couldn't help thinking how exciting it would be if they did have to use it. He and Emily had begged to play in the tunnel, but their father would not allow it. It was simply too dirty and there was always the danger of a cave-in. But more important, someone might spot them coming out the other end, and their hidden escape route would be discovered.

"Eat plenty," Zack's mother said. She slapped several pancakes onto his plate. "It's cold today. Appetites are always bigger when it's cold."

"Thanks, Ma." Zack smoothed back his thick dark hair with his fingers. Cleanliness was another thing his mother insisted on, so he wouldn't tell her he hadn't washed his hands before coming to the breakfast table. There would be no getting out of it later after coming in from chores. He put fresh-churned butter on his pancakes, then added some honey. How his gentle, well-bred mother managed to brave beehives to gather that honey always surprised him; but she was willing to risk the pain of bee stings to bring some bit of pleasure to her husband and children.

Margaret Myers was a very pretty woman, slender and gracious. She had very dark hair that fell to her waist when it was undone, but Zack didn't see it that way often. She usually wore it rolled into a bun at the base of her neck. He looked like her in some ways, had her hair, her green eyes. Emily had her father's brown eyes, but her hair was also dark like her mother's. Their father's hair was lighter, and he had begun losing it early. He was thirty-six now and already half bald. He wore a wool hat on top of his head even in the house because he said it helped keep him warm.

"We'll surely get some more warm weather before winter truly arrives," Margaret said. She poured herself and her husband each a cup of coffee, then sat down at the table. "At least today the sun is out, and it still gets light fairly early. Before too long we'll be rising in the dark and it'll be dark again by the time chores are done."

"Just so Zack and I get in all the corn before the snow flies," his father answered. "There are still some potatoes left to dig too. First, Zack, I want you to go try to milk Jessie again."

Zack scowled. "She tried to kick me last time. She's been ornery ever since her calf died, Pa, you know that. Her milk's dried up on account of missing her calf."

"Don't talk about the calf," Emily pouted. "It makes me cry."

Zack cut into his pancakes. "Heck, Emily, it was two weeks ago. We'll hook Jessie up with Mr. Brady's bull again and she'll get another calf."

"Zack! Watch what you say!" Margaret said, looking embarrassed.

Zack reddened, not quite sure what was so wrong with talking about mating Jessie again. He'd gone with his father out to the pen when Jack Brady had brought his bull over several months earlier. His father had paid Brady for the use of the bull, and Zack had been allowed to watch when Jessie finally allowed the bull to mate with her. It was all just a part of farming and raising livestock, and to Zack, what had been done was no different from planting a crop. He wondered sometimes if that was how women got their babies, but he'd never been concerned enough about it to ask.

"He's just stating a fact, Margaret," John said. "We'll get another calf out of Jessie. She's a young cow."

Zack stared at his pancakes. It struck him only then that maybe that *was* how a woman got a baby. Somehow a man had to hook up with her. For a man to do something like that to a woman seemed incredibly naughty, and he could not begin to imagine his father doing that to his mother. Still, he and Emily had been born, and his mother had lost another baby a couple of years before. As decent as his father was, and as gracious and refined as his mother was, he figured there must be more to it than the man just putting himself in the woman. After all, they had to love each other first, so maybe that made it okay.

The conversation turned to other things, but Zack barely heard. He was too embarrassed to look at his mother again. He quickly finished his pancakes and excused himself from the table to put on his jacket. His father was saying something about Indian trouble somewhere, but he didn't pay attention. He pulled on his wool cap and walked outside to the barn. Before he reached the door he thought he heard an odd birdcall, a little trilling sound he'd never noticed before. He stopped and looked around, thinking to see an unusual bird, but there were none to be seen. He frowned in curiosity. Most birds had already flown south because of the coming winter, but then, there were still a few around. He figured this one was simply sitting someplace where he couldn't spot it.

He walked inside the barn and pulled up a stool beside Jessie. "Don't you try kicking me again, lady, or I'll kick you back," he warned.

Jessie mooed softly, turning her head to look at him. He wondered if a cow missed its dead baby the way a human mother would. His mother had mourned for weeks after losing that last baby. He reached for a bucket and set it under Jessie's udder. "Let's try again, Jessie. We need the milk. You had plenty right after you had that calf. Why'd you have to go and dry up on us?"

He pulled at a teat but got nothing. He tried another, then hesitated when he heard the odd birdcall again. The thought of Indians crossed his mind, but he ignored it. All the years they'd lived there, there had been no trouble with Indians. Some had come by a few times, wanting to trade something for food. His parents always obliged, trying to be friendly. He'd seen Arapaho, Cheyenne, Kiowa, and Pawnee, even knew how each tribe dressed a little differently. He was most afraid of the Pawnee, who were the most demanding when they came by, the least friendly.

He wished he could remember what his father had said about Indian trouble, which tribe was involved, what had happened. Still, whatever the trouble, it had to be old trouble. Things were probably better now. News spread slowly out here. Two days earlier a traveling preacher had come by, which thrilled his mother. The man had prayed with the family, and Margaret had insisted on singing some hymns together. She had also asked the preacher to pray over the little grave where her lost child was buried. After that, the preacher had walked off to talk alone with Zack's father.

Zack realized now it must have been the preacher who had brought news of Indian trouble. His father had probably not said much about it because he didn't want to alarm the rest of the family. Whatever the reason, the preacher's news couldn't have been recent. It took days to travel from one farm or town to another. Now there was even less fear of Indians, as more settlement in eastern and middle Kansas had chased most tribes farther west. Just this summer a new military post had been opened only a few miles away at the junction of the Republican and Smoky Hill rivers. Zack's father was overjoyed at the fact that soldiers now scouted the area often, checking with settlers to make sure they'd had no Indian problems. Things were much safer now.

Zack managed to get a little milk out of Jessie just as his father came into the barn to take out two of the draft horses. "I'm hitching a wagon and going to the cornfield," he told Zack. "Soon as you get what you can out of Jessie, clean out the stalls and then come out and help me pick. I'm hoping to have enough to be able to sell some to the soldiers at Fort Riley. Besides having a good supply for our own winter needs, I'll make a little profit this year." The man spoke the words proudly and led the horses outside to hitch them to a wagon.

Zack carried what milk he'd gotten out of Jessie to the house. His mother and Emily came back outside with him and walked to the henhouse to gather eggs while Zack returned to the barn to clean the stalls. Minutes later Emily came to the barn, clutching Miss Nancy.

"I thought you were going to let Miss Nancy stay in bed this morning," Zack said. He shoveled some horse manure into a wheelbarrow.

"She gets lonely without me," Emily answered.

Zack rolled his eyes. "When are you going to quit being such a baby?" he asked.

"I'm not a baby!" Emily scowled. "I got eight eggs all by myself this morning. That's the most I've ever found without Mama's help."

"I thought she went into the henhouse with you."

"She did, but she let me get the eggs all by myself." Emily raised her chin proudly. "I bet if you'd teach me how to milk Jessie, I'd get more milk from her than you do."

Zack shrugged. "I don't care. I wish you *would* learn to milk her. Then I wouldn't have to do it."

Emily glanced over at Jessie. "What did you mean about Mr. Brady's bull hooking up with Jessie? What does it have to do?"

"Never you mind. Why aren't you in the house with Ma? I thought you were supposed to help her bake."

"I am. She said I could come in here first."

"For what? Just to pester me with your questions?"

"No. Miss Nancy and I like to watch you work."

"Gee, thanks." Zack faced his little sister with a frown. "How about picking up a shovel and helping instead of watching?"

Emily walked over and patted Jessie's rump. "I don't have time. Mama said to take just a few minutes."

"You'd better get away from Jessie's rear. She's been a grump. She's liable to give you a good kick."

"Emily! Hurry inside now and help me."

Emily turned away at the sound of her mother's voice. "See? I told you I could stay only a minute."

"Just long enough to pester."

Emily stuck out her tongue, then turned and ran. Zack threw down his shovel and chased after her, and she screamed and laughed, clinging to Miss Nancy as she headed for the house. Then she stopped short, and Zack nearly ran into her. She stood staring toward the little overhang at the front door to the cabin, where her mother lay sprawled against the door, an arrow in her chest.

"Oh, no! Oh, no!" Zack exclaimed.

"Mama!" Emily screamed, finally finding her legs again. She ran toward her mother's body, screaming "Mama!" over and over.

Zack's thoughts raced in confusion. What should he do? At the same time Emily ran to her mother, he heard horrible screams coming from the cornfield. "Pa!" he groaned, horror and panic building in his heart. When he turned in the direction of the screams, he saw them, painted Indians making their way on foot toward the cabin, some already close. Zack realized they must have been hiding behind the buildings when he first came out to milk Jessie. Others must have been skulking in the cornfields.

Why! Why were they doing this! In the back of his mind he figured they must be Pawnee because their heads were shaved except for down the center, but it didn't matter what tribe they were. They had killed his mother with one quiet arrow. Now they were killing his father, making him suffer, and they would surely kill him and Emily! He ran toward Emily, but just as he reached her a warrior grabbed him, yanking him away. He began fighting wildly, kicking and punching, growling like a wild animal himself. He couldn't even see the man he fought. Rage made him blind. He could hear Emily screaming . . . and his mother. She was still alive! What were they doing to her?

Then there came a searing pain to the left side of his face. The Indian let him go and stepped back, grinning. He held a huge knife in his right hand, and Zack put a hand to his face, realizing that blood was pouring from the wound to his cheek. He stumbled back, turned to see another Indian scalping his little sister's limp body. Her head hung back oddly, and he could tell that it had been nearly cut off.

His eyes widened at the horror. Two other Indians hovered over his mother's body. She had been stripped naked, and one of them was doing that awful thing to her, that thing the bull had done to Jessie! He ran over and tried to push the Indian away, but another grabbed him and pulled him back. The rest of them stabbed his mother several times, then scalped her.

Zack bent over and vomited. He held his hand to his cheek to try to stop the bleeding, but blood seeped through his fingers. Was he next? What would they decide to do to him? It didn't really matter now. His whole family was dead. In a matter of minutes he had lost everything dear to him. A lovely, happy morning had turned to horror, and already he felt guilty that there hadn't been something he could do to stop this terrible thing. Let death come! He would welcome it!

The Indians turned on him then. Yes, they were Pawnee, and how he wished he had a way of killing every one of them! He stood still, waiting for the death blow, but one of them brought over a horse and motioned for him to get on it. Zack stood there confused for a moment, then realized they didn't mean to kill him at all. They aimed to take him away with them, and he was not about to go! He charged through them and headed for the house, expecting to be grabbed and killed, but they only laughed. He made it past his mother's and sister's bodies and into the house. He slammed and bolted the door, then slid down to the floor in a sudden torrent of tears.

Mother! Emily! Pa! This couldn't be happening! It just couldn't! He was having a bad dream, and he would wake up any minute. If not, the Indians would come try to break down his door. They would find a way to kill him slowly and painfully.

He waited, grabbing a towel from a nearby chair to hold it against his cheek. The terror of the moment helped him stop crying as his mind raced to determine what the warriors outside had in mind. Why hadn't they stopped him when he ran to the house? Why hadn't they killed him in the first place? They must be playing games. Perhaps they had decided that if he would not go with them, he was not worthy of taking at all. Now they *would* kill him!

He ran to the corner of the room, where his father kept a loaded gun. He grabbed it, wishing his father had kept his promise to teach him how to use the thing. There just hadn't been time. He ran to a window, poking the end of the rifle through a peephole in the inside shutters and breaking the glass with the barrel. To his surprise, he saw no Indians.

His body jerked in lingering sobs as he waited, watching, wondering. Then he heard a thumping sound against the side of the house, more on the roof. Soon he smelled smoke. He wiped his tears and blood with the sleeve of his jacket and stepped back from the window. Smoke filtered through a crack of the inner wall. So, they had decided to burn him alive inside the cabin.

The smoke grew worse, and he began to panic. It was only then he remembered the tunnel. He looked toward the door. "Damn all of you!" he sobbed. "I'll show you!" Quickly he opened the trapdoor and lowered himself into the cellar, keeping the rifle with him. He pulled open the hidden door to the tunnel, then closed it behind him. He waited a moment, forcing himself to stay calm. It was pitch-black, but he reminded himself that all he had to do was crawl through it to the other end and push his way out into the daylight. He just hoped no animals had found their way inside.

Shivering with terror and the horror of realizing his whole family was dead, he made his way through the tunnel. The odor of damp earth filled his nostrils, and more dirt spilled into his hair and eyes. Although the tunnel was only about fifty yards long, crawling through it without a lantern, his head filled with visions of his mutilated mother and sister, made the journey seem like forever. Finally he saw a little crack of light. He crawled faster, wondered how badly he was still bleeding. Somewhere along the way he had lost the towel.

He reached the light, waited there a minute. He heard nothing outside, no sound of horses' hooves, no voices. Cautiously he pushed on one of the boards, shoving away some of the brush above it that hid the tunnel exit. He slowly raised his head to look toward the cabin. It was engulfed in flames. The Indians danced around it, whooping and yipping in glee. The henhouse and barn were also on fire.

"You think you burned me up," he said quietly. "But you didn't! You *should* have killed me, cuz someday when I'm bigger I'll get you back for what you did!" He lowered himself back into the tunnel to wait, and again he burst into wretched sobs. "Mama! Pa! Emily!" he groaned. "I'll kill them! I promise! I'll kill them all!"

"My God! We're too late." Lieutenant-Colonel Howard Shaver rode toward the burned-out farm of John Myers. "This looks like it happened just a few hours ago. If we had come sooner to talk to Mr. Myers about that corn . . ."

"Damn!" Sergeant Norman Craig muttered as he rode alongside Shaver, coming to the bodies of Margaret Myers and her little girl. "How could they do this?"

Margaret lay naked and mutilated, her little girl beside her, both of them scalped. A rag doll lay near the girl. "Cover their bodies," Shaver told Sergeant Craig. Another soldier rode toward them then.

"We found Mr. Myers, sir," he reported, looking pale. "It's a terrible thing. Looks like he was tortured. He's out in the cornfield."

Shaver closed his eyes and sighed. "Get some men together for burial detail, Sergeant. There's already a grave out back. When we rode through here a month ago, Mr. Myers told me it belonged to a stillborn child. We'll bury the mother next to it, the little girl on the other side, the husband next to the girl." He opened misty eyes to look at the private who had ridden in to report about John Myers. "Any sign of the son?"

"No, sir. Maybe he burned in the fire, or the Indians might have taken him off with them. They sometimes take a boy child with them, try to make a warrior out of him."

"I'm aware of that, Private. I—" Lieutenant-Colonel Shaver stopped mid-sentence when he saw someone walking toward them from a strand of trees several yards away. "My God, it looks like the boy! How could he have survived!" He guided his horse closer to the approaching boy. "Come with me, Sergeant Craig!"

He was filthy, his jacket torn. There was an ugly cut on his left cheek, dried blood stuck to the side of his face, his neck, his clothing, his hands. His dark hair was mussed and caked with dirt, and he stood staring at them, looking dazed, a rifle in his hand. The look in the boy's eyes was astounding, for they were not the eyes of a boy. They were the eyes of a man, a man full of hatred and vengeance.

"They trapped me in the house," he told them. "I got out through a secret tunnel they didn't know about." The words were spoken flatly, coldly. "I tried to fight, tried to help my ma, my sister—"

"How old are you, son?" Shaver asked.

"Ten."

Shaver shook his head. "No ten-year-old boy could have stopped this, son. Don't blame yourself. Be glad you're alive and that they didn't drag you off with them."

Zack looked toward the blackened shell of the cabin where only hours before he awoke to the comfortable sounds of his parents' voices, his sister's whining, the pleasurable smell of breakfast cooking and a fresh fire in the fireplace. Now only that fireplace stood, smoke still wafting from the top of the chimney. He looked back up at the older soldier with chevrons of a round leaf on each sleeve. He remembered this man, had met him once at Fort Riley when he went there with his father to sell potatoes. The man seemed red all over, from his ruddy complexion to his orange-red hair and reddish-blond, bushy eyebrows. "How old do you have to be to join the army, sir?"

Shaver frowned. "Why do you ask that?"

Zack gripped the rifle tightly. "Because as soon as I'm old enough I'm gonna join, just so I can fight and kill Indians."

Shaver felt a pull at his heart when he saw the look in Zack Myers's eyes. Shaver had two children of his own. They lived back east with their mother and were about Zack's age. He could not imagine them having to witness the horror this young boy had witnessed today. "Maybe someday you will be a soldier, son, but our job is not to just kill Indians at random. Sometimes things happen that cause them to do what they did here today, but I agree it's unforgivable. When I see things like this, I want to kill them too. We will go after these hostiles. We'll try to see that they are punished."

Zack walked past them toward the house. "I'll do it myself someday," he answered.

Shaver dismounted and walked behind him to where Zack's mother and sister lay covered with blankets. "I'm Lieutenant-Colonel Shaver, son. We'll bury your family before we leave. Then we'll take you back to Fort Riley with us. We'll find you a home, don't worry about that."

Zack stared at the covered bodies. "It doesn't matter." He glanced up to see more soldiers riding in, a body draped over one of the horses. It, too, was covered with a blanket, but he knew it was his father. He also knew the man must have died a terrible death. "Nothing matters except getting old enough to fight Indians," he finished. He looked down at the other two bodies again, spotted the rag doll lying next to Emily. "Miss Nancy," he muttered, new tears coming. He knelt down and picked up the doll, holding it close for a moment before laying it on top of Emily's body. "Be sure you bury her doll with her. She'd want that. Emily gets lonely without Miss Nancy."

Another torrent of tears came, and again he vowed he would never, never forget this day, nor would he ever be able to kill enough Indians to make up for it. He hated them with a passion he never thought possible for any human being to feel.

"There's a dead cow in the barn debris," he heard a soldier telling Shaver. "If Myers had any horses, the Indians probably took them."

Jessie! Poor Jessie. Everything was gone. Gone! Everything except the hatred in Zack's soul. That would never go away.

2

June 1855

Morning Star snuck quietly through the dense stand of pine trees, her moccasined feet making no sound against the thick bed of fallen needles that carpeted the forest. She breathed deeply of the sweet scent of pine pitch, loved the smell of it. The same aroma filled her father's lodge from the pine branches beneath the blankets used for bedding.

She wondered at her secret fascination for Strong Runner. He had come to this little creek fed by the Walla Walla River, leading a few of his fine horses to water. Strong Runner was only sixteen, and already he had more horses of his own than many of the older warriors. Such wealth brought him great honor. He had a skill for catching and taming the wild ones. He had stolen two from a Blackfoot tribe when only thirteen. To steal horses from their old enemy was the greatest honor of all, but now Strong Runner had a new popularity among the Wallawalla Band of the Nez Perce. He had won four horses as prizes from other Nez Perce men who bet on him in foot races.

Strong Runner had certainly earned his name. His endurance in the foot races surpassed every other young man's, and always he made the run with a mouthful of water, spitting it out at the end of the race to prove he had run the entire race breathing only through his nose.

Morning Star hid herself in a cluster of rocks near the creek and watched him. Tonight Strong Runner would race again. Many would bet on him, including the white men who were there for the treaty council. She did not understand just exactly what all the meetings between her people and the white government men were about, except that the Nez Perce wanted to keep their hunting grounds, and make it clear they wanted no more whites settling in their lands. Chief James and Chief Joseph had counciled often with the blue-eyed men who had hair on their faces and wore heavy, dark clothing. They hoped this time the Great Father in the East would honor his promises. Many young warriors were growing restless and spoke of war, of using force to keep more whites out; but their older leaders believed in peace.

The meetings mattered little to her. What mattered was exploring this strange feeling that she had for Strong Runner. A ten-year-old girl was not supposed to even concern herself with boys his age.

She watched Strong Runner walk into the creek, petting and talking to the four horses he had brought there. He loved his horses, and seemed to understand them as though he were a horse too. She suspected he would use one of these in the horse races the following night. Even his horses were strong runners. Somehow Strong Runner was able to pull that running spirit from the horses and use it in his own body, or perhaps it was the other way around. Whatever the reason, he would be a rich man someday soon, for those who bet on him, whether it be a foot race or a horse race, usually gave him gifts when he won, a thank-you for bringing them riches through their bets.

Morning Star was not sure when these strange feelings had begun. It was simply something of which she was suddenly aware. Her father, Sits-In-Sun, often talked about Strong Runner, smiling about all the bets he had won on him, saying he could run like the wind. In the past several months he had begun inviting Strong Runner to their dwelling occasionally to eat with the family. He had mentioned once to her mother that someday Strong Runner would make a fine warrior and a fine husband for one of his daughters. Her father would even ask Strong Runner's advice sometimes about how he trained his horses to run so fast.

It was not often an older man asked a younger man for advice, and Strong Runner seemed honored at the gesture. He was always humble in his answers, showing Sits-In-Sun respect, asking questions of the older man in return. Morning Star suspected that was only to show his honor for Sits-In-Sun, to make sure her father did not think Strong Runner felt he was better or smarter than an honored elder.

Her eyes widened when Strong Runner removed his vest and weapons. His moccasins were already off because he stood in the water. Now he was removing his leggings, his medicine bag, his breechcloth! His shirt was already off, for it was a hot day. She studied his fine build, his muscles that rippled in beautiful rhythm when he ran. He reminded her of the handsome horses he owned, strong, powerful.

Even that part of him used for mating was similar to the male horse's. She knew about mating, and about how a man looked naked. She'd seen her brother, Two Owls, and other boys naked when they were little and played together. And a few times her mother and father's lovemaking had wakened her. Her mother had explained about men and women, where babies come from. A man had to plant that secret part of himself into a woman's secret part, and it was very special. A Nez Perce woman was expected never to do such a thing with a man until he was her husband. Otherwise she was considered dishonored, a disgrace to her family, not worthy of an honorable man.

Nez Perce women were not loose and did not take money and whiskey from other men in exchange for giving those men pleasure, not like the women of some other Indian tribes did. It was mostly white men who were willing to pay for them, and some Indian women even married white men. But Morning Star did not plan ever to marry one of those sickly, pale-faced men, most of whom seemed to talk out of both sides of their mouths. She would marry only a Nez Perce man, an honored one . . . like Strong Runner.

She watched him bathe, and the sight of him gave her stomach such flutters, made her ache all over. Were these feelings bad? Was she loose like those other women? Was something wrong with her to think about Strong Runner this way when she was only ten years old? She had a terrible need to be near him, always making excuses for just that. She looked forward to his visits with her father, made sure she was the one who handed him his food. She always tried to look pretty when he came, but it hurt so badly to realize he saw her as just a little girl.

Her father always hinted to Strong Runner how pretty his daughters were, but Morning Star feared that if he did decide to marry one of them, Strong Runner would pick White Bird, who was already an exotic beauty. Perhaps he would tire of waiting for either of them to be old enough and would marry someone else. If he did, she was sure she would die of a broken heart.

Besides his handsome looks, build, and his skill at running and at training horses, Strong Runner was also very smart. He was Christianized, due to his father and mother, who had been taught by missionaries during the time when most Nez Perces had turned to the white teachers who had come to their land to teach them a new way. Strong Runner's father had taught his son how to write things in the Nez Perce tongue, using white man's letters. He could also write things in the white man's tongue, and could speak it. Most of the missionaries were gone now, since the massacre of the white woman, Narcissa Whitman, and most of the other missionaries by the Cayuse Indians, leaving the *Waiilatpu* mission, where many had lived, abandoned.

The Cayuse were friends to the Nez Perce, but they were more warlike, and often the Nez Perce were blamed for bad things the Cayuse did. It wasn't fair, but the whites never seemed to care what was fair when it came to Indians. All were blamed for what one or a few did. They could not even tell one tribe from another half the time, so that many from several different tribes often suffered for the bad deeds of a few from another tribe.

She must not think about those things today. Today was her secret, special day. She had followed Strong Runner, thinking perhaps that by watching him alone with his horses she would discover some of his secrets to understanding their spirits, would learn how it was he ran so fast, how he handled his horses, things she might be able to take back to her father. Yes, that was why she was there, she told herself—to help her father, not because she could hardly bear to be away from Strong Runner, to take her gaze from him. She wished she understood why she felt this way, wished she could control these feelings, get rid of them. This was wrong for a ten-year-old girl. She must be very bad.

She started to leave, but then noticed a pretty but wild-looking Cayuse woman walking toward the creek, right down the pathway she would have to take to run away from there. Morning Star ducked low, hiding behind the cluster of rocks, waiting until the woman went by. She slowly looked up to see the woman approaching Strong Runner, catching him standing naked in the creek before he realized she was there. Wide-eyed, Morning Star watched as the woman asked Strong Runner in English if he would like some pleasure. Morning Star understood enough English to know what she said, and what it meant. The woman looked him over as though she were hungry and he was a delicious morsel, reached out, and touched his muscular chest.

Oh, those terrible Cayuse women! They had no morals! They were always after the single young Nez Perce men, who could not touch their own young women unless they were married to them. That did not seem to matter to some of the Cayuse women. The woman unloosed the ties on her tunic and let it fall. She stood there naked before Strong Runner, and he reached out and fondled one of her breasts, full breasts, something Morning Star did not have yet. Tears filled her eyes at the thought of how young and undeveloped she was. Strong Runner would never look at her the way he was looking at that Cayuse woman. The woman turned around and knelt to her knees, bending over and offering herself like a mare. She told him this was her gift to Strong Runner for winning a foot race the night before. She had won many beads and some cloth from another woman for her bet.

Strong Runner seemed hesitant, but that secret part of him grew big like a stud horse, and he went to his knees, positioning himself behind the Cayuse woman. She asked if he had ever been with a woman, and he replied that he had not, but that he needed to learn so he would someday know how to please his wife. He found his mark, and for the next several seconds he seemed lost in the Cayuse woman, grunting in rhythmic thrusts.

Morning Star's insides burned like fire, and her heart hurt so bad at seeing Strong Runner take his pleasure with someone else that she thought she might die. Her eyes teared so that the two figures became a blur, and she put her head down, struggling to keep her sobs silent. By the time she could clear her tears and look again, the Cayuse woman was bathing in the creek. She came out and put on her tunic. She walked to Strong Runner, licked his chest, then threw her head back and laughed.

"You are as good with a woman as you are at running and racing horses, my young warrior," she told him. "Win for me again, and I will visit you here again."

For the first time Morning Star found herself hoping Strong Runner would lose his race tonight. She hated this place, and hated that woman! A feeling of painful possessiveness filled her soul. Somehow she thought of Strong Runner as belonging to her. She sat down, unable to continue watching the woman flirt with Strong Runner, touch his body.

She heard the crack of a small branch nearby. The Cayuse woman must be leaving. She sat very silent and still, waiting, able to see the woman's head above the rocks as she went by. Suddenly a squirrel skittered across Morning Star's legs, startling her so that she let out a little gasp. The Cayuse woman turned and spotted her, and Morning Star wished she could crawl into a hole.

"Who are you! What are you doing here!" the older woman demanded. Her eyes widened with anger as she walked closer, but then she smiled. "You were watching, weren't you?" She laughed, calling out to Strong Runner. "There is a little girl here, one of your own people. I think she has been watching us!" She leaned closer. "Did you learn something, little one?" she snickered. "Someday a man will do that to you. Maybe it will even be Strong Runner, hmmm? Is that why you are here? To watch Strong Runner? I'll bet all you little Nez Perce girls dream about that fine warrior."

Morning Star was mortified. She had to get away before Strong Runner saw her! She jumped up and started to run, but the Cayuse woman caught her arm and whirled her around. Strong Runner was walking in their direction. She stared at him and he at her. What was that look in his eyes? Was he sorry she'd seen what they'd done? Was he angry she'd spied on him? Surprised? Embarrassed? Did he think her terribly bad? He was not laughing at her like the Cayuse woman did. In fact, he told the woman to let her go.

"I'm sorry, Strong Runner," Morning Star whimpered before running away. She flew through the pines, not noticing their sweet smell now, not caring about the great council and what might be decided there, not caring about the races. She knew only that she was devastated and humiliated. She would never live this down, and Strong Runner would never forgive her for what she'd done. Would he tell her father? She would be severely punished if he did. Others would find out. They would laugh at her, call her a bad girl.

And now Strong Runner would never look at her as something special, an innocent young woman whom he could perhaps marry someday. She had ruined it all with her curiosity, letting these confusing feelings for Strong Runner make her do something foolish. She ran until she thought her lungs would collapse, then fell into the grass a few yards from the main camp and cried. How would she ever face Strong Runner again?

Morning Star gathered with the rest of the crowd, staying close to her mother, Little Bear. The foot races would begin soon, and Morning Star hoped that if she mixed in with the crowd, Strong Runner would not notice her. Part of her almost hated him for doing what he did to the Cayuse woman, and for catching her watching. Still, she was at fault too. Her father would probably invite Strong Runner to eat with them again after the races, and she would have no choice but to face him. This was going to be a miserable evening.

Usually she loved these games. For the last two hours she had sat with her mother and other women, learning the gambling games they played with marbles and cards. The Nez Perces loved to gamble and to make bets on the racing games. The next night there would be horse races, but this evening . . . this evening she would watch Strong Runner again, study how his body moved when he ran, the way his muscles rippled, the way his long black hair flew in the breeze.

Little Bear bet on her own son, Two Owls, telling two other women she would give them beads and jewelry she had just won playing cards if Two Owls lost. The women gladly accepted the bet, placing their own bets on Strong Runner. Morning Star knew her brother could not possibly beat Strong Runner, but theirs was a loving family, and her mother would never bet against her own son. Little Bear was a gentle, generous, patient woman, and Morning Star wished she could talk to her about her feelings for Strong Runner, but she was too embarrassed. She was afraid her feelings and actions would disappoint her mother, whom she honored above anyone else she knew.

She walked away from the women to watch a group of white men who were also placing bets with each other and with some of the Nez Perce. There was something about them she did not like and did not trust. Her father had said that these men wanted the Nez Perces to promise to stop fighting with the Blackfoot Indians, their longtime enemies, and agree to stay within certain boundaries. In return they were being promised that no whites would come to settle inside those boundaries. Her father did not trust these powerful government men to make good on their promises, but the Nez Perces strived for peace above all else, and her father said they would probably sign this new treaty and try once more to cooperate with them.

A shot was fired, and the race began. Morning Star forced her way to the front to watch. Six young men dashed past, all of them about even, including Strong Runner's best friend, Little Eagle, and her own brother, Two Owls.

Morning Star knew what Strong Runner would do. He would hold back, saving his energy for one last burst of speed toward the end of the two-mile race. People yelled and cheered, and the white men mixed right in with the Indians, sharing the excitement. In moments like this it seemed they could always get along with the white men, but Morning Star knew there had been terrible problems in the past.

She smoothed back her hair, damp with perspiration. The day had been hot, and the evening had not brought its usual relief. She wondered if perhaps she thought too seriously about most things for someone her age. Her sister White Bird, a whole year older, didn't seem nearly as concerned with these things as she was, nor were any of her friends who were her age. None of them seemed interested in boys yet, or had mentioned having a fascination for any one young man in particular. They wanted only to play with their stick dolls. They did not seem concerned about problems with white settlers, or with any decisions that might be made at the council.

She had snuck close to the council lodges when the leaders of her people, her own father, Sits-In-Sun, as well as Chief James, Chief Joseph, Chief Lawyer and others met with the government men. In an effort to keep the peace among themselves and with the white man, the various clans of Nez Perces under their separate chiefs had decided to come together and act as one group. Morning Star had listened closely to everything they discussed. Things were nearly settled, but then Chief Looking-Glass had ridden in from a hunting trip, shouting that the Nez Perces should not sign the treaty too hastily. Now there would be more talks, and an ornery Looking-Glass was demanding more concessions from the white man's government.

She pondered all these things as the minutes passed. The runners had taken a pathway far into the nearby hills, and now, finally, they reappeared to the right. People began screaming and cheering. Morning Star knew she should cheer for her brother, but she could not help hoping Strong Runner was in front, and he was, closely followed by Jumping Wolf, a young man who was also very fast. Her brother was in third place.

Closer they came, muscles straining, bodies bathed in sweat, long hair flying, nostrils flaring. It was obvious Strong Runner had given that last burst of speed he always saved for this moment. He charged ahead, putting more and more room between himself and the others. Strong Runner dashed across the finish line to a roaring crowd. He went on, unable to stop quickly. He had to cool down, much the same as a horse that had been run hard needed to remain walking for a while before being allowed to rest.

Morning Star turned away as people rushed to congratulate the winners and pay off bets. The moment she dreaded was coming. Strong Runner would come to their tipi later. He would look at her with angry eyes, and she would be so embarrassed she would get sick to her stomach. She walked to her parents' large dwelling made of buffalo hides, wondering what it was like back when her people never lived a nomadic life. Her parents often talked of a time when the Nez Perces had few horses and lived in one place, living off the fish in rivers and lakes. They did not live in buffalo-skin lodges like they did now. They had lodges built of timbers, or lived in dugouts in the side of hills. But as they began to use horses more, they began to go farther away to hunt, and eventually they had begun to trade with nomadic tribes farther east, especially the Sioux. Migrating from one place to another to hunt and trade had changed their way of life, and had compelled them to start using tipis rather than permanent lodges.

She knew all of this from stories her father told, and stories her old grandmother used to tell before she died. That old way of life was mostly before the missionaries came to teach them new ways and a new religion. The trouble was, those missionaries and first white explorers had also brought strange, terrible diseases that had nearly destroyed the Indians. Many of the whites seemed immune to those diseases, and that was what angered the Indians. The Cayuse were convinced the whites were deliberately bringing these diseases to try to kill all the Indians, and that was why the Cayuse had murdered so many missionaries at the Whitman Mission eight years earlier.

It was that massacre that had brought out soldiers as well as more government men who had begun peace talks to better relations with the Indians. Few missionaries had ventured into Indian country since then, even though many of the Nez Perces still prayed and carried Bibles with them.

Morning Star hesitated. She could not find the courage to go inside the tipi, even though her mother passed by her with White Bird, telling Morning Star to come soon and help with the meal. "Your brother will be very hungry after that run," Little Bear said, "and Strong Runner will be joining us. He will be the hungriest of all."

And very angry, Morning Star thought with a pout. She walked over to sit on a nearby log, wondering what she was going to do, what Strong Runner would do or say. She felt like a stupid child, and that was probably exactly how Strong Runner thought of her.

"Hello, Morning Star."

Morning Star jumped at the words, and turned to see Strong Runner standing behind her. She felt heat coming to her face, and she could not find her voice. She had expected anger and accusations from this young man, but she got neither. He looked apologetic.

"I am sorry about what you saw today. Why were you there?"

Morning Star swallowed, tried to speak, but nothing came out. Her eyes began to tear.

"Do not be embarrassed," he told her. "You were curious. You did not know that woman would come there. I want you to know that I also did not know she was coming. What she did surprised me. I did not have time to think, and I could not help wondering what it was like. I hope you will not tell anyone what happened there."

Morning Star blinked in wonder. Here she had been afraid Strong Runner would tell her parents she had spied on him, had watched him mating with someone; but Strong Runner was afraid *she* would tell on *him*! "I . . . I would never tell," she answered, finally finding her voice. "I am also sorry. I . . . you are such a good runner, I thought if I followed you to the creek today, I would see what kind of magic you do to make you run so fast. I thought maybe you had gone there to pray or do something special that gave you power."

He grinned, a soft, beautiful smile that showed white, even teeth. Oh, he was so handsome!

"I went there only to water my horses. Sometimes I just like to go off and be alone. I know it is wrong to be with loose women like that one who came there. I know they sometimes have diseases. I am not going to do that again. I let myself be weak. I am going to pray about it."

Morning Star nodded. "I think I understand."

"Did you watch the races?"

She nodded again, her eyes wide with wonder. They were actually standing there, talking alone. This would be forbidden if she were older, and it hurt to think that he considered it all right because she was just a child. "I knew you would win."

He smiled more, looking embarrassed. He stepped closer then, holding out his hand to show her a beaded necklace with shells on it. "A Cayuse man gave it to me for winning the race. I like it very much. The shells tell of a time when we lived closer to the sea. I would like you to have it."

Morning Star looked up at him. "Me? Why?"

Their gazes held.

"Because you are special, and because you did not tell what you saw today."

Special? What did he mean by special? Was it just be-cause she was Sits-In-Sun's little girl? Or was it something more than that? She wanted to believe it was something more. "It is a nice gift, Strong Runner."

"I am glad you like it." He placed the necklace around her neck.

Morning Star trembled at his closeness. He smelled good, like fresh air and clean water. She realized he must have gone to the creek to wash away the perspiration before coming there. He took hold of her long hair and pulled it away so that the necklace fell properly around her neck. The touch of his fingers at the back of her neck gave her shivers.

"There. It is a little big on you now, but it is pretty . . . like you."

Pretty! He thought she was pretty! "Thank you, Strong Runner."

He nodded. "And I thank you."

Their gazes held a moment longer. "Someday you will be a pretty woman, gracious and honorable, like your mother."

He turned and walked away, and Morning Star stared af-ter him in disbelief. Had he really said those things? Did he mean he would wait for her to become a woman? If so, did that mean he would not take a wife, that perhaps he thought of her as someone he might want to marry someday?

This day of turmoil and embarrassment and fear had turned into something wonderful after all! She touched the seashells around her neck, feeling very special, and that's what Strong Runner had said she was . . . special.

3

DECEMBER 1862

*F*irst Lieutenant Zack Myers felt great relief at the accomplishments over the last few weeks of the campaign on which he had ridden with Colonel Henry Sibley. This was the first realization of revenge he had experienced since being assigned to duty at Fort Snelling, Minnesota. A sweeter justice would come when he watched the hanging of the Indians who were being herded ahead of the troops he commanded. He had always heard that Indians considered hanging the worst way to die—something about their spirits being choked off and being unable to reach their "happy hunting grounds" after death.

So be it. He felt no pity, nor did he care about the reasons behind what these Sioux had done. In his mind there had been no excuse for the fact that the Sioux had gone on a rampage of rape, raid, and murder. The full count was still not in, but so far it was estimated that at least four hundred settlers had died cruel deaths, and the numbers were still rising. Colonel Sibley had been assigned the task of finding the culprits, and Zack had had the pleasure of being a part of the mission.

"Must make you feel good helping bring in these hostiles,

doesn't it, Lieutenant?" The question came from Lieutenant-Colonel `Howard Shaver, the man responsible for his assignment there, and for helping Zack realize his dream of attending West Point.

"Yes, sir, it does."

"You've never quite gotten over that awful day your family was murdered, have you, son?"

Zack did not answer right away. He couldn't remember how many weeks or months it had taken for the nightmares to stop, dreams that left him shivering and sick. To this day he could not shake the terrible longing to see his sister and mother and father once more, just to be able to tell them he loved them, to try to explain that if he'd had the means to kill all those Pawnee that day, he would have. Somehow it had never seemed right that only he should have survived, and he had always wondered why.

"I was only ten years old, but it's still as clear as day to me, Colonel Shaver. The past twelve years have not softened the memory." Again he felt the numbness that came over him every time the massacre was reawakened for him. Part of him wanted to go back to the old farm, visit his family's graves, see what was left. He had never been able to bring himself to go, mostly out of fear of reliving what had happened there . . . little Emily with her throat slit, Miss Nancy lying beside her. . . . "I prefer not to talk about it, if you don't mind, sir."

"Yes, well, I can understand that. I'm sorry for bringing it up. I just worry about you harboring so much hatred."

Zack turned and looked at the man who rode beside him on a sturdy roan gelding. Shaver needed a big horse to carry his bulky frame, and the man had a big heart to match his size. He wondered how he could ever repay Shaver for all his help. He was a good man, the closest thing to a father Zack had had since his own father died so horribly. "You don't have to be sorry, sir," he answered. "I'm the one who's sorry for sounding rude."

"No, no. It was rude of *me* to mention it," Shaver answered. He removed his hat for a moment and ran a hand through his red hair, which now showed a generous amount of gray at the temples. "How about if we change the subject? Now that we've caught these hostiles, we can all relax a little.

There will be a hanging, you can be sure of that, and then there will probably be a celebration, perhaps a dance of some sort. Too bad Iris Gray can't be here. She must be quite a beauty by now."

"Sir?"

Shaver grinned. "Don't tell me you haven't heard some of the men talk about Colonel John Gray's daughter, Iris. She usually visits him every summer, wherever he is, but she didn't come this year because of the Indian trouble. I suppose since Colonel Gray is pretty well established in command of Fort Snelling, he'll still be here this coming summer, and I expect she'll visit then. I think she would be seventeen now. All the single officers were looking forward to her presence. Of course with the war back east, she may not even be able to come next year either." He sighed. "At any rate, I hope you will get the opportunity to meet her."

"I don't think that would do me much good, sir, considering her father is a colonel. I hear he comes from a wealthy family. He probably has a husband all picked out for his daughter, a doctor or a lawyer, or some soldier of higher ranking."

"Well, word is John Gray lost most of his inheritance when his parents died within a few months of each other. There were a lot of debts the family didn't know about, but I guess he's still pretty well off." He smiled at Zack, thinking what a handsome young man he'd turned out to be. "As far as whether she'd be interested in you, Zack Myers, you're as worthy a suitor as any other officer here. You're certainly at least worth a dance with the colonel's daughter. But since she won't be here, there are a couple of maids to officers' wives who will be allowed to come. They're pretty enough, young and available, as I am sure you and every other single man at the fort have already noticed. A young, handsome soldier like you ought to be able to garner a few dances with either of them."

Zack buttoned the top button of his army coat against a stinging wind. Minnesota was cruelly cold in winter, he'd discovered. For seven years after his family's slaughter, he'd been raised by Jacob Brown, a storekeeper who traded at Fort Riley and had been at the fort the day the soldiers brought him there. Brown had offered to take him in since he had a big family himself and said he thought that being surrounded by other children would help Zack recover from the shock of his loss. Winters could be cold in Kansas, but nothing like here in Minnesota . . . and nothing like the coldness in his own heart.

"I don't know about the handsome part, sir, but I don't really fit in with the other officers' social circles, even though I've been to West Point. I'm still just a Kansas farm boy with a background not much different from some of the rabble enlisted men. I'd be one of them, with no hope of promotion past sergeant, if not for you."

Shaver shook his head. "Nonsense. You fit in just fine. You may not have a wealthy background or a daddy who can pull strings in high places, but you earned your appointment to West Point from sheer determination. I saw the makings of a good officer in your eyes when you were ten years old. I'm just sorry I couldn't have kept you with me or sent you east to my wife at the time. I didn't think it fair to her, but if I'd known how cruel Jacob Brown was being to you, I'd have figured out something better for you."

Zack shrugged. "I didn't want to bother you with my problems. I'm just thankful for your visits during those years, and thankful you have a good friend in the Senate. I never could have made West Point without your help."

"Well, you proved yourself to everybody, high grades, an excellent record. I'm proud of you, Zack."

"Thank you, sir. And I'm proud to serve under you, glad they sent me here. When I heard you'd been transferred from Kansas, I put in a request for my first duty to be here. I guess my good record made me eligible to come here and train volunteers for the Civil War, even though I haven't even been in the war myself yet. I guess all they care about is my sharpshooting abilities. I don't know where I get them from. Handling a rifle just came natural to me."

"Well, your talent in that respect is badly needed. Most of these volunteers haven't held more than a hoe before joining the Union Army."

"I just hope they let me stay. I'd rather go after Indians than Confederates, if I may say so, sir."

Shaver grunted. "Be careful of your reasons for being here, Zack. Our duty isn't to kill Indians. Sometimes we're even supposed to *protect* Indians. We have to make sure whites abide by treaties that are signed, and there are times when the whites are harder to control than the Indians. The situation is going to get worse as more people come west, especially when this damn civil mess is over. Now that gold has been discovered in Montana, there's a big mess up there, again with these Sioux, just a different band. Right now the Sioux are winning, and maybe they have a right. That land was promised them in a valid treaty that the whites are now breaking. The army has its work cut out for the next few years, maybe ten or twenty. I don't see any solution in the foreseeable future, and there aren't enough of us out here for now to do the job right."

Zack squinted against the wind. "There were enough of us to bring in these hostiles."

Shaver grinned, fingering his thick red mustache. "We did manage that, didn't we? You just remember what I said about your reasons for joining up. I know how much you despise the Indians, and I can't blame you for it. Just don't let that hatred cause you to make poor decisions, Lieutenant. Letting personal feelings get in the way of smart decisions can cost you your rank. Besides that, hatred can eat a man up like a cancer."

The man rode ahead, and Zack watched him, always resenting any advice about Indians. He knew Shaver meant well. Maybe he was even a little bit right; but in his mind, no one truly understood the hatred that burned in his soul. He watched the Sioux who plodded along on foot ahead of the soldiers, many of them women and children. Most were not dressed warmly enough for this kind of weather, and a tiny part of Zack, the little boy in him that once cared about such things, wanted to feel sorry for the conditions under which these captives were being herded to Fort Snelling for trial. But the part of him who hated these people could feel no pity. Let them suffer. They were animals.

Because of people like these, the rest of his childhood had been miserable. All of Jacob Brown's children were older than he had been when he first lived there, and they picked on him constantly. It didn't take long for him to realize that the only reason Jacob had taken him in was to have another hand helping in his trading business. The man was cruel and abusive, and two of his sons had left home soon after Zack arrived, heading for California for the adventure. Zack couldn't blame them for running away from an unhappy home life. Not long after, one of the sisters got married and moved out. That left one brother and one sister, who along with Zack suffered Jacob Brown's strict discipline, often applied with a stinging willow whip.

Jacob put on a good show in public of being the good family man, which was why even Lieutenant-Colonel Shaver didn't know what was really going on whenever he visited Zack. People would often comment about how generous and Christian Jacob was, how good he was to take in the orphaned Zack Myers, whose family had been murdered by the wicked Pawnee. But behind closed doors Jacob was far from a loving father. Zack soon learned he was expected to work long days at his new father's store while the remaining brother helped the man with trading trips to farms and to Fort Riley, and the sister helped her mother bake all day long. Jacob insisted his wife keep fresh baked goods available. They were a popular item in his store. Dora Brown was a meek, submissive woman who never argued with her husband, and often suffered a blow from the man's fist for no good reason.

Growing up with Jacob Brown and his family had only hardened Zack even more. In his mind it was the fault of the Indians he'd known so much unhappiness. He often dreamed of how sweet and loving life would have been if he could have grown up with his own parents and sister. He never once considered Jacob and Dora his parents, had never even been able to bring himself to call them Mother and Father. To him they were Mrs. Brown and Jacob. He stayed with them only because he didn't know what else to do, where else to go. As soon as he was seventeen, he'd left without even a good-bye for Fort Riley to find Lieutenant-Colonel Shaver and tell him he was ready to join the army. The fact that Shaver had gotten him into West Point was nothing short of a miracle to Zack. He felt indebted to the man. Still, his own background made him feel a little out of place among the other commissioned officers.

For the first time since losing his family, he felt that he was where he belonged. This was all he had ever wanted, to be an officer in the army. Lieutenant-Colonel Shaver, the army, his troops, they were his family now. He had no desire to ever see Jacob Brown or Kansas again.

Zack stared out the window of his quarters to watch the construction of the gallows in the distance. He could not get over the feeling that the events of the past few weeks were an omen of some kind, not just for the Indians, but for himself.

Everyone at Fort Snelling, as well as most people throughout the country who knew about the terrible massacre of more than 450 innocent settlers, waited to hear President Lincoln's decision on the fate of the 307 Sioux men who had been tried and sentenced to hang. Zack himself quietly fumed, irritated with a clergyman named Bishop Whipple, who had gone to Washington to plead for clemency for the Sioux.

Whipple claimed that many of the accused were innocent of wrongdoing, that too often many Indians were blamed and punished for crimes only a few committed. The man even had the audacity to say that what had happened was partly the fault of the settlers, whites who encroached on land that had been promised to the Indians.

Maybe there was a bit of sense to that, but in his opinion there was no sense promising the Indians anything. The Indians that caused such slaughter didn't deserve to keep any of their land, didn't deserve trials, and certainly did not deserve clemency. He wished Whipple had not caused this delay. It wasn't fair to the families of those who had suffered and died. Tales of some of the atrocities only brought back ugly memories for him. He knew better than most just how awful it must have been for those who had died. He didn't want to hear what had been done to the women, or how many children were among the dead. Unfortunately, it was impossible to say exactly which Sioux had committed the atrocities. Around forty men had been proven murderers and rapists beyond a doubt, but an entire tribe had fled.

So be it. That made all of them guilty.

He turned to look at his jacket hanging on the wall, the chevron on the sleeves, a silver bar. First lieutenant. He breathed deeply with satisfaction. He had accomplished everything he'd dreamed of, except he hoped that one day that bar would be gold, maybe someday the winged eagle of a colonel.

The only thing that bothered him was that he still didn't feel the satisfaction he wanted to feel. Maybe it was just because he hadn't killed an Indian outright yet, or because he'd probably never find the Pawnee who'd killed his family twelve years before. How he would love to bury his sword in their hearts!

He walked over to a potbelly stove and took a kettle from it, then poured hot water into a washbowl under his shaving mirror. He studied his face in the mirror, rubbing at the stubble on his cheeks. He wondered if Lieutenant-Colonel Shaver was right in saying he was handsome. He supposed he was, but it had never seemed to matter much to him. Back in Junction City, where he'd lived with Jacob's family, many young girls had flirted with him, but he'd been too bashful to talk to them. Besides, girls were not his first concern. The army was the only thing he spent time thinking about.

There *had* been one woman . . . an older woman who was widowed. She was unlike the very proper young girls and older women he'd met in his life. She had asked him to personally deliver some supplies to her home, and while there, she had made him an offer no red-blooded, curious sixteen-year-old boy could refuse. He'd always felt a little guilty about what they did, had never told anyone. She'd been much older than he, but she certainly knew how to titillate a young man, and he had been curious for more reasons than most young men that age.

He had done it because he needed to know if he could be normal that way. After what had been done to his mother, he was never sure he could be with a woman without that vision preventing him from doing what should come naturally. After witnessing that ugly act, he was sure he could never take a woman for pure pleasure, but he had discovered he was as natural a man as any other, much to his relief. He hadn't planned to look for loose women and use them for his pleasure. What he really wanted was a wife, a good woman like his mother had been. But before he took one, he wanted to be sure he could be a proper husband to her.

He grinned at the memory, studying his teeth. They were white and even, and his hair was thick and dark. He supposed he was as much a man as any could be. He'd grown tall like his father, was well muscled, mostly from so much heavy lifting while working for Jacob. Older men teased him that his green eyes would melt girls' hearts. Perhaps they would, but he wanted to melt only one heart, that one special girl he might marry someday.

He had been with a few other women since that wild widow in Junction City, glad to know that was one part of his life the Pawnee had not destroyed. He shrugged off the thought and lathered his face. An army man didn't have much chance for meeting and courting pretty young girls, and pretty young girls were in short supply where he was. Most were laundresses, some of those the wives of enlisted men, the rest were the kind of women a man should stay away from, unless he didn't mind getting the clap. He avoided them completely. There were those maids Shaver had mentioned, but they didn't really interest him.

For now all that mattered was the decision about the Sioux. How many would hang? He hoped Lincoln would not decide to let all of them go. It was bad enough that three of the most notorious leaders of the massacre had escaped— Little Crow, who some believed had managed to get back to his people in North Dakota, and Shakopee and Medicine Bottle, who had supposedly fled to Canada. Soldiers had gone after them, but because Zack had been on the previous campaign with Colonel Sibley, he had been ordered to stay behind to rest up. He was very glad about that, since he wanted to stay and watch the hangings.

He finished shaving and dressed, making sure his uniform was completely in order. He put on his hat, and someone knocked at the door to his small room on officers' row. "Come in."

A young corporal entered, saluting him. "Word came, sir, about the hanging. You told me to let you know right away."

Zack nodded. "What did Lincoln decide?"

The corporal closed the door against the cold air outside. "He says we can't hang all of them. He wants only those who we know for sure raped or murdered somebody."

Zack scowled. "That's only about thirty or forty men."

Adams saw the disappointment in Zack's eyes. Everyone

at the fort knew why he hated the Indians. "President's order, sir."

Zack's hands closed into fists. "The president isn't out here! He didn't see what we saw! He didn't lose his family to those bas—" He stopped and took a deep breath. "I'm sorry, Corporal Adams."

"Yes, sir. If I may say so, sir, at least if we hang thirty or so, they've learned a good lesson. The Sioux won't forget this for a long time. We have to show some kind of fairness. That might be the best way to end the bloodshed."

Zack walked past him and opened the door. "The bloodshed won't end until all Indians are dead! Dismissed, Corporal."

Adams saluted him and left, and Zack stormed out after him.

Fort Snelling swarmed with outsiders—Minnesota citizens, newspaper reporters, some from as far away as Chicago. Cameras were ready, pens were ready, everyone there for the grand occasion. Thirty-eight Sioux men would be hanged.

Zack stood at attention with his platoon as the prisoners were led to the gallows. The Indians showed no resistance, no fear. In fact, their faces showed no emotion at all, except perhaps a resignation to their fate, a terrible look of defeat in their eyes. A few, mostly the young ones, did show hatred and bitterness, but the older ones simply lowered their heads and stood quietly as nooses were slipped around their necks. Zack had a good view from where he stood. He watched them carefully, wanted to shout that they were getting what they deserved, but that was a feeling he knew he had to keep to himself for the moment. His job was simply to stand and witness.

Nooses were all in place, and the crowd fell silent. Colonel Sibley read the order from President Lincoln that only those proven beyond doubt to have committed atrocities against whites be hanged. He named each Indian who would hang, stating that their names would be duly recorded. An army chaplain said a prayer for the "lost souls" about to die, asking God to forgive them for their ignorance of the Christian way. One of the Indians looked at Zack, who was surprised to feel a hint of pity at the look in his eyes. What was it he saw there? It wasn't defeat. It was more like a deep sorrow, but not for himself.

Their names were read off. "Red Eagle," Lieutenant-Colonel Shaver said when he reached the Indian man who had stared at Zack. Why had he done that? It was as though this Red Eagle knew him, knew about his past. It was said that Indians could be very spiritual, that they knew other men's dreams. Zack remembered hearing that Red Eagle's family was murdered by white men seeking gold. His wife had been raped, his children killed, while Red Eagle was off hunting. That had been his reason for joining in the massacre of whites.

Someone had told Zack once that hate and violence only breed more hate and violence. Maybe that was true, but right now he could not erase his own hatred. He didn't want to admit he could understand how Red Eagle felt. He told himself Red Eagle must have done something at one time or another to cause the prospectors to do what they had done. Besides, why turn around and murder other innocent people for it?

He looked away. Something in Red Eagle's eyes made him uncomfortable. The time had come for the multiple hanging. Zack waited, finally heard the thud of the lever that caused the huge platform to fall. Everyone gasped, followed by a round of cheers from all the soldiers. Already it had been reported that the two who had escaped to Canada had been caught. They would be returned soon and would also be hanged.

The deed was done, and Zack realized, after all the waiting for this special event, he had not even witnessed it. He had looked the other way. He glanced up then, and saw Red Eagle hung grotesquely, his eyes still staring at Zack. He quickly turned and dismissed his men.

He shivered. Something had been aroused in his soul, something he could not name. It was as though a kind of battle was taking place inside him, and it had begun when he and Red Eagle had looked at each other.

Something in those eyes had stabbed at his own hatred, as though trying to kill it. He glanced back once more to the gallows, where dead Indians were being cut down for burial. Red Eagle still hung there.

4

JUNE 1863

Strong Runner stood on a wooded hill, watching the white man's town below. They called it Lewiston, and it sat in the heart of Nez Perce country, a blatant slap in the face to his people and the treaty they had signed seven years before. He could not help the anger that boiled in his soul over the entire matter.

It had taken five years for the white man's government to ratify that treaty, five years before they even began providing the items promised. During that time the Nez Perces had kept their end of the bargain. Many of them, including himself, had even ridden as scouts for the U.S. Army, helping in campaigns against the Yakima and Rogue River Indians and any other tribes who remained warlike. His own people had been divided about whether or not they should adhere to the treaty, since during that time the white man's government did not keep one promise it had made.

Now this. Gold. For some reason white men thought it the most important thing on earth. They left their own homelands for it, sometimes risked their lives against the elements and other, more hostile Indians for it. When the gold seekers first came onto Nez Perce treaty land, they seemed to be concerned only with the back country. That did not seem so terrible to the peaceful Nez Perces, just so long as they were not there to settle. It was the permanent settlers who under treaty law were not to come and take their land. They had trusted the white man's government, kept the peace, and because they were sure the government, through the army, would protect their lands, they had allowed the gold seekers to use a piece of land between the Clearwater and Snake rivers to build a warehouse and proper landing sites for the steamboats that brought the prospectors.

It had been agreed that no other buildings would be constructed, and that no settlers would come; that Nez Perce farms and stock would not be violated. "What fools we are," he sneered. In only weeks the place he watched now, where there was to be only the warehouse, had become a white man's town. Nez Perce farms were overrun, fences torn down, their wood used by prospectors to make fires. Crops were destroyed, cattle and horses often stolen. Near every principal Indian village, inns were established, where white men sold whiskey to the Indians.

Strong Runner believed the firewater made a man weak and foolish, that it was only a tool the white man used to get what he wanted from the Indians. Whiskey often made it impossible for an Indian to think straight, and some once-proud warriors had become so dependent on it, they would sell their souls for another bottle.

It had all happened so quickly, and in spite of his Christian upbringing, Strong Runner felt only hatred and bitterness in his soul. Nothing had been done to stop this, and Strong Runner feared something had been started that they would now never be able to stop no matter how many treaties they signed. One treaty seemed always to lead to another, because the white man was never able to hold up his end of the bargain. It had taken them five years to legitimize the first treaty. It had been in effect only three years, and already it had been shattered in every way. Already the Great Father in the East wanted his people to sign yet another treaty, give up even more land. His people were again involved in treaty talk with white men from Washington, D.C.

They think us ignorant, he thought, *but many of us can read, white man.* He'd gotten hold of a copy of the white man's newspaper from Lewiston, *The Golden Age,* they called it. He'd read the article advising white settlers to "settle, occupy, plow up, and cultivate" treaty land, disregarding any Indian title to those lands. It was even rumored that the editor of another newspaper in the white man's town called Boise had suggested that if it were possible to infect blankets with smallpox, a shipment should be sent there and they would be handed out to the Indians.

Rumors had quickly spread through the tribe that farther east many Sioux men had been hanged for killing white settlers. Strong Runner did not doubt they had good reason. Now the Sioux were filtering farther west, causing problems for tribes already established there, including his own. That was the white man's most devious attempt at destroying the Indian race, pitting one tribe against another and letting them kill each other off. He could see it so clearly, but many of his friends could not. They went to war against other tribes because it seemed the right thing to do; and they continued to trust the white man's government.

Still, more and more Nez Perces were getting tired of broken promises, tired of being blamed for horse stealing when it was white men stealing horses from each other, not the Indians. A great majority of them, including himself, were to the point of making war against the whites. In spite of their Christian upbringing, the fact that many of them were educated and had settled into farming, making war still seemed their only alternative.

"What are you doing here, Strong Runner?"

The young man turned to see his father, Yellow Hand, approaching. They had come together on the hunt and were two days from the main village. "I am only wondering about the future," he answered.

Yellow Hand, still virile for his age, climbed the last of the steep hill to reach his son. He had himself been a superior runner when he was young, and now the Nez Perce said that the man's running spirit had been passed on to his son, who at twenty-four remained unbeaten in the foot races. "You are concerned because one day soon you will have children who will inherit this land." Yellow Hand smiled.

Strong Runner's scowl turned to a smile at the remark. In

two days he was to marry his beautiful Morning Star, now a woman. He was glad he had waited for her. "Yes, Father." His smile faded a little. "What are we to do?"

Yellow Hand sighed deeply, coming closer and putting a hand on his son's shoulder. "It is something we old men discuss every night. I remember when, through all this land, the rivers, mountains, lakes, valleys, there was not one white man. Those were good days."

Strong Runner turned and waved his arm, indicating the town below. "Now look what they have done! A whole town, settlers coming in, destroying all that we have worked so hard to build! To them we are no more important than insects. If they could, they would squash us like bugs and be rid of us! This is *our* land, Father! *Our* land! Not because *we* say so, but because *they* said so, in a valid treaty that they are supposed to obey! Where is the Great Father in all of this? Where are the soldiers who were supposed to keep these people out? We let them use our waters to bring men who were only supposed to go and look for gold, but instead many come, and they take *everything*! The gold is not enough for them. They want it *all*, and they want us *dead*!"

Yellow Hand nodded. "This is why I was against allowing the gold seekers to use this place to dock their boats, but many of the others continued to trust in the treaty."

Strong Runner closed his eyes for a moment, thinking about Morning Star. She would give him sons and daughters, but what did their future hold? "How much will be left for my children, and their children?" he said aloud.

"That is in God's hands, my son."

Strong Runner faced him. "*Whose* God? I am not so certain that our God and the white man's God are the same. If it is so, then He must be very angry with the whites for the way they disobey His commands. They tell us we must behave a certain way, be truthful, not steal, not kill. Then they turn around and do all those things against us! I have been going to the mountains alone to pray to *my* God, a God I am sure does not listen to the prayers of the lying white man!"

"It is not easy for a young warrior to sit still and let others take what belongs to him. I know this. I was a young warrior once myself. The only advice I can give you, son, is to remember that if you kill one white man, ten more will come.

If you kill them, they will send a hundred, a thousand, ten thousand. Their numbers in the land to the east are great. Right now they are involved in a war of their own, and that is why there are few soldiers to help us. When that war is over, more soldiers will come."

"And who will they come to protect? Us? Or *them*?"

Their eyes held in mutual understanding and fear. "We will not know until they come. For now you must not give so much thought to war and hatred, my son. You must give all of your thoughts and attention to Morning Star. You decided many years ago that you wanted her for a wife. Now she is eighteen summers, and she is ready to take a husband. Let this be a happy time for you, the happiest, as it was for me when I took your mother to my lodge."

Strong Runner nodded. "I only hope I do not lose Morning Star to white man's disease the way I lost my mother. That is something else I cannot forgive them for."

Yellow Hand's sorrow showed in his dark eyes. "Your mother's death is the real reason you hate the white man, is it not?"

"They killed her just the same as if they had shot her."

Yellow Hand blinked back tears. "I try not to think of it that way, but often I feel the same. Cholera is a terrible way to die." He patted his son's arm. "But for now you must think happy thoughts. Be glad for what you have now. I hope you will be as happy together as your mother and I were. Morning Star is beautiful, and she is getting a most honored warrior, one who owns many horses and runs as fast as the wind. He is a good hunter, will be a good provider. Morning Star will tend the fields while her husband brings home the meat."

Strong Runner smiled sadly. "If there is any game left after the white man takes his share." His hands moved into fists. "Sometimes I want to kill all of them, Father."

"I know the feeling, but you must not act on it. We will win by proving we are a people of honor, a people who keep their word, who can be trusted. Killing just one white man can start a war, my son, one that could destroy us once and for all. Listen to Chief Joseph and the other peace chiefs."

Strong Runner nodded. "I will try."

Yellow Hand grinned. "Come, then. We have had a good hunt, and you can add fresh meat to your gifts for Morning

Star's father. You will make me proud on your wedding day.
I want to give you my warbonnet of eagle feathers to wear. I
traded many horses to the Sioux many years ago for that fine
warbonnet. That was in the days when we roamed free,
hunted anyplace we chose, and often traded with the Sioux."

They walked down the steep hill together and mounted
their horses, sturdy Appaloosas. The Nez Perces were well
known for the spotted horses they bred and raised, some of
the finest in the Northwest.

In the town below, another steamboat prepared to dock,
bringing with it fifty more prospectors.

Iris Gray eyed Fort Snelling with wonder as the steamboat
that had carried her there to visit with her father prepared to
dock. The huge brick structure that sat high on a bluff at the
confluence of the Minnesota and Mississippi rivers was indeed intimidating. Her father had told her in a letter that the
original purpose of the fort was to keep the British in Canada
from using the rivers to encroach on U.S. territories, and she
could well understand why this was the perfect location for
such a guard. Now Fort Snelling was a training ground for
volunteers who had joined the Union Army.

Still, some of the soldiers had become involved with
fighting Indians, which seemed a strange situation this far
east. Most Indian trouble was much farther west, according to
newspapers she read, except for the Sioux uprising here in
Minnesota last year, which was the reason she had not come
last summer. It was safe to visit this year, except for a different danger, the awful war back home.

In spite of the oppressive heat, she felt a chill at the memory of the horrors of a civil war. At least sixteen hospitals had
been set up back in Washington, most in buildings meant for
other purposes, some in huge tents. Although her grandparents objected, she had volunteered her services at several of
them. The help was sorely needed, and her heart went out to
the soldiers. It still irritated her that she had been turned
down at first just because of a silly rule that nurses had to be
over thirty and "plain in the face," for fear of problems between lonely, wounded men and available young women. It
seemed ridiculous in her mind, since there was always a

shortage of help. Most women were too faint of heart for the job.

Over the past year hundreds of men showed up weekly, and about half of them died. She had seen things that had opened her eyes to the reality of just how awful war was, and she was glad her father was not directly involved. Thank goodness he had been chosen to train men rather than fight beside them on some bloody battlefield. It had been hard enough losing her mother four years earlier. Now John Gray was all she had left besides her maternal grandparents. She couldn't bear it if something happened to her father.

She had missed him so, and she intended to come and stay with him permanently as soon as she was finished with school the following year. That was why she had made it a point to keep herself informed on the Indian situation, since her father could be transferred to a post even farther west. In his letters her father had stressed that army life at western forts could be quite miserable. Iris knew he was trying to warn her to stay put. He knew his daughter well, knew she intended to join him, but he was afraid posts farther west would be too primitive for her.

Her father's warnings were no deterrent. She loved him too much, was convinced he needed her with him, no matter how much he protested her coming to dangerous, uncivilized places. He was sure that once the Civil War was over, the army would turn its attention to the Indian uprisings and the West would become the battleground for a different kind of war.

No matter. Nor did she care that her father thought it was too dangerous to travel because of the war. All the fighting was taking place farther south, now that the Union had defeated the rebels in the horrible bloody battle at Gettysburg. She and her grandfather had simply stayed to the north for the long journey. It had been tiring, from coach to train to a passenger ship across Lake Michigan and a steamboat up the Mississippi out of northern Illinois into Minnesota. Neither distance nor danger nor the hardships of the journey were going to keep her from seeing her father after nearly two years apart. She was convinced Colonel John Gray was very lonely and needed his daughter.

She had good memories of her childhood, when she and

her mother had followed her father from one army post to another. That life ended when her mother died, and it still hurt to think about it. Her father had not felt it was right keeping her with him without a mother when she was only fourteen years old, and she had been sent to live with her grandparents in Washington, which was where her parents had first met after her father graduated from West Point.

Excitement filled her soul. She had changed the past two years, grown taller, and at eighteen, was now a woman. Her father would surely be surprised. As the boat docked, she could see soldiers standing at attention, probably to greet her. John Gray was an important man, and that made his daughter important. How she missed this life!

For now she would only visit and go back to Washington, since her father was fairly certain he would himself be sent back east soon. He might end up in the war, which meant she could not join him anyway. She prayed that would not happen. After volunteering at the veterans' hospitals, it had taken several weeks for her to learn to manage her feelings and learn to be strong enough to care for men who had lost limbs or an eye, men who died right before her eyes from terrible infections. She had seen awful things, had forced herself to do what had to be done, always telling herself that any one of these men could be her own father. Oh, how she prayed he would not be sent into that war!

"Quite a fortress, isn't it?"

The words came from her grandfather, Carlton Harris, who had come along as her chaperon. Iris was sure she could have made the trip alone, but neither her father nor her grandfather would hear of it. "A young woman as beautiful as my granddaughter should never travel alone, especially when there is a war going on," her grandfather had scolded.

"Isn't it wonderful?" she asked him now. "I miss living at army posts."

"I can't imagine why," her grandfather answered. "It's hard on a woman to have to move constantly, never having a real home to call her own. Your mother put up with it because she loved your father so much, but I know she always longed to settle in one place."

Iris thought about her mother, Rebecca, a beautiful woman who had stoically followed her husband without complaint. As a child, Iris had thought the army life was very exciting; but now, as the woman in her began to awaken, she could understand how it would be difficult for someone who had been born and raised in one place, someone who had never known a life with no roots. But that was how Iris had grown up, and she actually longed to live that way again, missed the excitement and adventure.

Young men at the college she attended had begun showing an interest in her, although with a war going on they were in short supply. Still, none of them appealed to her. She preferred a man in uniform. Such men were lined up now on the dock. Her heart fluttered at the sight. Several of the soldiers looked close to her age, all of them standing at attention.

"Looks like you're getting quite a reception, child," her grandfather, an agile, healthy man for his age, teased. He easily picked up two of her bags. She could tell he had been quite good-looking in his youth, and her father had often mentioned that her mother had Grandfather's blue eyes but Grandmother's light hair and beautiful complexion. "And you look just like your mother," her grandmother told her often. Grandma was still pretty. Iris treasured both her grandparents.

The ramp was lowered, and Iris disembarked the steamboat ahead of forty new volunteers who had come for training. A soldier whose jacket sported a first lieutenant's silver bars stepped forward to greet her, and Iris could not help being struck by his looks. He was tall, with a fine build, his uniform clean and perfect, his green eyes quite exotic. "Miss Gray?"

"Yes."

He smiled, his teeth even and clean, his lips full. She would have been impressed enough by the uniform, but the man who wore it was strikingly handsome. The scar on his left cheek did little to deter from his good looks, and it made her curious.

"I am First Lieutenant Zack Myers. I've been sent to escort you to your father's quarters."

"Thank you, Lieutenant Myers. This is my grandfather, Mr. Carlton Harris," she added, turning to her grandpa. "He escorted me here." She pouted slightly when she turned to look at Zack again. "At his and my father's insistence, I must

add, not mine. I intended to make this trip alone. I wouldn't
have been the least bit afraid, and I hate being pampered, but
I didn't want to worry either of them, so I let Grandpa come
with me."

The old man just chuckled and shook his head. Zack put
out his arm and walked Iris to a waiting carriage, ordering another soldier to help her grandfather with their bags. He
helped her into the carriage and climbed in beside her to take
up the reins. "How long will you be here?" he asked.

"Oh, I don't know. A couple of weeks, I guess. I'd stay
forever if Father would let me. I grew up on army posts, you
know, and I miss it."

Zack was surprised with her answer. Most women hated
this kind of life, and most of the married men did not have
their wives with them. They preferred to stay in one place
and wait for their husbands to come to them. He had been
prepared to look upon Miss Iris Gray as just another visitor,
but she had turned out to be even prettier than rumor said
she was. Damn pretty . . . *gorgeous* better suited her. To top it
off, it was obvious she was an independent young woman
who was not afraid of coming to a place like this. She apparently didn't mind the inconvenience of life on an army post.

He liked that. He already liked everything about her, but
it didn't much matter what he thought of her. She was the
beautiful, educated daughter of a colonel. Women like that
didn't look twice at someone like him.

"Your father has a welcome party planned for you," he
told her, "food, cake, even a dance. I hope you'll be comfortable here, Miss Gray, that you enjoy your visit."

Iris glanced at him, and Zack met her gaze, studying her
beautiful blue eyes, not realizing that she in turn was thinking
how handsome his green eyes were, outlined with dark brows
and lashes. She wanted to ask about the scar, but was afraid
it might be too rude to do so this soon. "Thank you," Iris told
him, feeling an odd surge of desire deep inside that she had
never experienced before. "I am sure I'll enjoy my stay. And
you must promise to dance with me, Lieutenant Myers."

Zack looked away, but not before noticing Iris Gray was
round in all the right places, had full lips, a perfect complexion, a bosom that nicely filled the bodice of her dress. "I'm
not sure that would be proper."

"Oh, pooh! I'm not the kind of woman who cares about what is proper, Lieutenant. And why wouldn't it be? You are an officer in the United States Army, and you must already have my father's respect, or he would not have sent you here to fetch me."

He grinned inwardly at her spark. Yes, sir, he really, really liked this young woman. He felt a riffle of excitement at knowing she would dance with him if he asked. Still, he didn't want to get on the wrong side of her father or any other officers. After all, for him the army came first, above everything else. He had put in for transfer farther west, so he would have to be very careful, or his request would go unanswered. Besides, a Captain Jason Ward had arrived just a few days before, greeted with open arms by Iris's father. Every man at the fort knew Ward was favored by Colonel Gray because Ward's father was a wealthy lawyer from Vermont and Colonel Gray's best friend from his boyhood days.

Ward was quite struck with his own handsome looks and his "in" with Gray. That was obvious by his cocky attitude, and now Zack had to report to the man, who was only six years older than he. Zack already longed to be promoted to captain himself, just to get out from under Ward's control. He wasn't sure how long he could answer to the man without punching him in the mouth and landing himself in the guardhouse.

Ward had already been bragging about how well he knew Iris Gray, and that he intended to have every dance with her when she arrived. He would have greeted her himself that morning, but he'd been called into a meeting with Gray and some other officers. Gray did not expect his daughter until later, but Zack had been sent to the docks with a few men to be prepared for a welcome in case she arrived while Gray was in his meeting.

Considering Jason Ward's connection to Iris Gray and her father, Zack figured he had no choice but to stay away from the woman when she arrived, something he'd been sure would not be a problem . . . until now. He glanced at her once more and caught her watching him. She smiled slyly, but he forced himself to keep a straight face, clearing his throat and paying attention to the roadway ahead. Already he could see it would be difficult to turn away from a woman as pretty as Miss Iris Gray under any conditions, no matter how sensible it might be to do just that; but he had a feeling Iris herself would make it even more difficult to ignore her. It might be best if he didn't go to the dance at all.

5

*M*orning Star waited with great anticipation as Strong Runner rode to her father's tipi with five of his finest horses in tow. On the back of his own horse was tied a travois, loaded with more gifts.

This was the formal symbol that he wanted her for his wife. He looked so grand! Tall and muscled and handsome, today he wore a beautifully beaded shirt as well as the grand warbonnet his father had gifted him with as a wedding present. It was made of real eagle feathers, and it fell down each side of his horse, the deerskin base covered with hundreds of tiny, colorful beads.

Her heart pounded with love. She had loved him for so long, since she was ten years old! Eight more years she had waited, until they were both old enough. Finally she had come of age, but Strong Runner was not ready. He had first wanted to prove his manhood, to build his herd of horses, build a permanent lodge for her, gather and clean many skins that she could use to make clothing for them and their children. He'd hunted and killed three bears, wanting their skins for warm blankets for his babies. He had shared the meat with the whole village, and everyone honored him as a hunter and provider. He even had American money to buy other necessities, had gotten it by selling some of his prize horses to the army.

Now a lodge was ready, made of logs rather than skins. At times they would still have to travel to hunt, but this place near the junction of the Snake and Grand Ronde rivers would always be home, and they would keep a permanent lodge there . . . as long as the white man left them alone. She was happy to see him not just because today he would take her away as his wife, but also because she knew he had gone away to again spy on the whites at that town at Lewiston.

She was always afraid for him when he went away, whether to spy or hunt. Most of the white men who came for gold were smelly, bearded, rude people who treated the Nez Perce as less than animals, men who deserved no respect at all. They sometimes killed for no reason, stole supplies and stock, rode right over planted fields. They left dirty, littered camps, blew up mountainsides, contaminated water. They were loud and arrogant.

It had been one thing allowing the kind missionaries to come to this land, but this was different. These men did not come to teach, they came to take, not just gold, but everything else, and they came to destroy. It was something that angered Strong Runner greatly, and he often talked of open war against these new intruders.

Morning Star understood how he and the other young men felt, and she did not doubt that the Nez Perce men could wage a successful campaign for a while, until the white man's war east of the mountains was over. Then they would send more soldiers, more and more and more, until their own young warriors were defeated because of sheer numbers. She was afraid for Strong Runner, afraid of what the future might hold. Her mother had told her not to fear. She was marrying an honored warrior today. God would see to their future.

Her parents stood waiting with her, as well as her sister, White Bird, who had married Little Eagle, Strong Runner's best friend. Her brother, Two Owls, was also married, but today he was hunting. Others gathered around to witness the moment, and Morning Star hoped Strong Runner thought her pretty today. She wore a white tunic covered with blue beads in a sunburst pattern. She had been working on it for nearly two years, just for this special day. She had bathed in the nearby river, and her mother had shown her how to make herself more fetching by smearing the nectar of flowers under her breasts and at her throat. She wore wildflowers in her hair, and she had spread a scented lotion on her arms and legs. It was something white women used, but it smelled wonderful, a scent her mother was sure would please her daughter's new husband. Around her neck she wore her most treasured possession, the seashell necklace Strong Runner had given her when she was only ten years old.

Morning Star smiled proudly as Strong Runner dismounted, sure that many of the other young girls envied her. Strong Runner stepped up to her father boldly, holding out the ropes to the five horses, all gathered together in one hand. "I have come to ask for your daughter's hand. I have brought you five of my best horses, Sits-In-Sun, and on the travois I bring blankets, deerskins, and many beads, as well as a fresh-killed deer. The deer came to me yesterday as I rode home. It offered itself to me as one more gift for the father of my beloved. I thanked its spirit for giving up its body so that I might bring you many gifts."

Strong Runner looked at Morning Star then, and she felt a shiver. She had not forgotten that day at the creek . . . the way he had taken his pleasure with the Cayuse woman. This day he would do that same thing with her. What would it be like? Her mother and sister had both told her it was a pleasurable thing, except for the first time. The first time there was pain. She hoped Strong Runner understood that, sensed her fear and nervousness; yet she so wanted to please him.

"I give you my daughter," Sits-In-Sun answered. "You have brought fine gifts, showing the honor you feel in making her your wife." He took hold of his daughter's arm. "Is it your wish to be the wife of Strong Runner?"

Morning Star watched Strong Runner's eyes, saw the gentle love there. "It is my wish. It has been my wish for many summers." They were already good friends. They had been allowed to talk with each other, to walk together as long as they did not stray too far, where they could not be seen. There had been touches that sent fire through Morning Star's veins, and often Strong Runner had leaned close, rubbing his cheek against her own, whispering his desire to make her his wife, to be one with her.

Her father took her hand and put it in Strong Runner's hand. Strong Runner closed his fingers around her own, pressing lightly in reassurance that she should not be afraid. He led her to his horse, took hold of her by the waist, and hoisted her up. Those watching smiled, some making teasing remarks that made Morning Star's cheeks feel hot.

Strong Runner leapt onto the horse behind her, reached around her with his strong arms, and took up the reins. "At last we go to our lodge together," he told her. She scooted close, her back against him, then held on to the horse's mane as Strong Runner rode off with her, taking her to the one-room log house he had built for her. It was far enough from the main village that they could be alone without being out of sight of the others. It was the old Indian way to stay close to each other, in case of a raid by an enemy, and to help each other in hard times. They could not understand why some white settlers put their homes in the middle of nowhere, far from their own kind, too far apart to be able to come to one another's aid.

Morning Star felt elated. At last she was the wife of the re-spected warrior and hunter, Strong Runner! He halted in front of their lodge and reached around to embrace her from be-hind as he nuzzled her neck.

"I do not want you to be afraid, Morning Star." He licked her cheek. "Quickly you will learn the joy of being a woman, and you are the most beautiful woman in this land. Even as a child I knew you would be beautiful, and that you would belong to me."

He moved one hand to her firm breast, and Morning Star drew in her breath in surprise at the thrill the touch brought to her loins. "I want . . . to please you, my husband."

He untied the rawhide strings at one shoulder of her tu-nic. "It would be impossible for you not to please me. Just dreaming of you pleases me. Now it is real."

He let the tunic drop, exposing one breast to the daylight. Morning Star could barely breathe for the excitement of the moment. His fingers ever so gently toyed with her nipple.

"Your fruit is firm and ripe."

He massaged the breast, then untied the other shoulder

so that it, too, fell. He moved off the horse then, lifting her down with strong arms, and let her tunic slip to the ground so that she stood naked. Her mother had told her to wear nothing under the dress so that it would be easy for her husband to see and touch her. She stood before him, her breath coming in short gasps of excitement. "Do you like what you see, my husband?"

Strong Runner grinned. "I like it very much." He picked her up as though she weighed nothing, and he carried her inside, kicking the door shut and placing her on a bed of robes. He stood up then, folding his arms as she pulled a blanket over herself. "If you wish, I will wait. I wanted only to finally set my eyes on your beauty. Perhaps the rest is too soon for you."

Morning Star watched his eyes, knew he would be true to his word. "I have loved you since I was ten years old," she answered boldly. "After eight years, it is not too soon."

Strong Runner grinned and removed his warbonnet. He shook his black waist-length hair loose, kicked off his moccasins. He removed the beautifully beaded shirt, revealing a broad, muscled chest. He unlaced his leggings and stepped out of them, then untied his breechcloth and cast it aside. He stood naked before her. "Now *I* ask . . . do you like what *you* see?"

After years of watching him run like the wind, like a beautiful horse, now to see that secret part of him swollen for her reminded her of a stallion wanting a mare. He was as handsome a specimen of man as could be, and her fear was overcome by desire and passion. "Yes. I very much like what I see. You are a beautiful man, Strong Runner." She opened the blanket she had pulled over herself. "I long to lie close to you, to feel your skin touching mine."

He smiled softly, crawling in beside her. All his worries about the future left him for the moment. There was only this, the beautiful Morning Star lying naked beside him. He moved against her, relishing the feel of her velvety skin. He rubbed his chest against her breasts, pressed his hardness against her thigh. "The first time is not easy," he warned her, "but you will learn to enjoy taking my seed into your belly."

Morning Star felt him rubbing against her most secret place, awakening something beautiful inside her that made her want to open her legs wider. Strong Runner moved his magnificent body between them. He kept moving that mysterious part of himself against her, arousing a desire she never knew she was capable of feeling, one that brought with it wanton boldness. She loved what he was doing. It made her feel wild and alive. She felt great pleasure at being so intimate with this man, looking upon his nakedness, caressing his naked skin with her own, seeing the desire in his eyes.

Something ached deep in her loins, something both agonizing and wonderful. She gasped his name as a terribly beautiful sensation engulfed her, a throbbing, aching need that made her feel wild, on fire. "Strong Runner, what is this?" she moaned. "I want you, my husband. It feels good when you touch me this way. I have never known such pleasure."

His mouth came down on hers, something she'd never experienced before. She'd seen white people touch mouths a time or two. Apparently Strong Runner had wanted to try it, and it was a wonderful sensation. He licked and sucked at her lips, making her groan with the need of him. She felt him stroking her private place, and cried out his name again at the realization that this beautiful man she'd loved for so long could finally be joined with her.

Her heartbeat quickened when she realized he was positioning himself to enter her. She closed her eyes, and her hands clenched into fists. She felt a tearing, burning sensation then, and she could not help a cry of surprise and agony. She bit her lip as he rode her hard, rising up to his knees and grasping her hips. The initial stinging pain subsided slightly, just enough that Morning Star could sense how pleasurable this act must be. Strong Runner threw his head back, gritting his teeth, and Morning Star felt a pulsing deep inside. Was that the life coming out of him? Her mother had told her gently how this would be. She prayed that if he had just spilled his seed into her it would take hold, for she very much wanted to give this proud warrior many children.

Strong Runner relaxed but his breathing was harsh, his skin glistening with sweat. Morning Star was reminded of how he looked after a foot race, and it made her smile. Strong Runner frowned teasingly. "So, you took some pleasure after all."

Morning Star laughed lightly. "I was only thinking how you look as though you have just run a race."

He grinned in return, leaning down to brace his elbows on either side of her. "I have. I won, and now I have gotten the prize."

Her eyes teared with love and joy. "Was it worth the race?"

He lightly stroked her forehead with his fingers. "Oh, yes." He kissed her eyes. "But I fear I hurt you. I was told sometimes it is easier the first time with the woman lying on her back instead of on her knees."

Morning Star's smile faded. "Like that Cayuse woman?"

Strong Runner caught the hint of jealousy in the words. "She was nothing. You are everything. I will never again need to desire or touch another woman."

"Did I please you?"

"Can you not tell? My life is in your belly."

She reached up and traced her fingers over his beautiful mouth. "I hope it takes hold quickly. I want to give you many sons and daughters. It is through the children that our people go on and on. Nothing can stop us from carrying on the circle of life, Strong Runner." With both hands she pushed his hair away from his face. "Not even the white man."

Anger and sadness came into his dark eyes. "You think not?"

"Not as long as there is this, my husband, a man and a woman, loving, mating, creating more children to carry on the blood, the life of the Nez Perce."

He sighed deeply. "Sometimes I wonder if there is anything the white man cannot completely destroy if he so chooses. That seems to be what he is best at. Of all the Indian enemies our people have fought over the years, they at least fought with honor, were truthful to their word. The white man has no honor, and it is impossible for him to keep a promise or speak the truth. He does not even practice his own religion. He teaches it to others and expects them to follow it, but he does not live it himself. Sometimes I wonder if all we were taught about his God is even true. Perhaps it is just a way to convince us we must be peaceful and accepting so that he in turn can overrun us, cheat us, steal from us, and get away with it, because we have been taught it is wrong to fight back."

Morning Star smoothed her hands through his hair and let it fall back down to tickle her breasts. "Fighting back will only make things worse for us. I am afraid for you when you talk this way, Strong Runner."

He shook his head. "Never be afraid. Only remember that a man's pride can be thrown in his face only so long before he must stand up and do something about it. For now I am willing to continue at peace, but only because I have a beautiful new wife, and I do not want to leave her side." He leaned down and kissed Morning Star's mouth.

She smiled again, glanced around the room, noticing a stone fireplace, animal skins on the grass floor. Pots for cooking were stacked near the fireplace, one of the few good trade items they had gotten from the whites . . . besides guns. "This is a fine lodge you have built for us, Strong Runner."

He grinned proudly. "I have fresh-cured rabbit and deer meat for us."

"Then I will cook you a fine meal tonight."

"I do not care much about eating right now." He moved his lips and tongue over her mouth again, relishing the taste of her, the feel of her. He left her mouth to lick his way down her neck to her breasts.

This was yet another wonderful new sensation for Morning Star. It was strangely exhilarating to have this magnificent warrior lick and suck at her breast like a child, and it struck her suddenly that there were certain ways in which a woman could have great power over a man. Fiery desire burned in her loins again, and she grasped his hair, whispering his name as he moved from one breast to the other, making her nipples ache to be tasted. He trailed his tongue lightly in little circles around one nipple, teasing, making her beg him for more. He drew her breast deeply into his mouth then, groaning deep in his throat, making her gasp in sweet ecstasy.

He moved back to her mouth, keeping his lips against hers as he spoke. "I wish to be inside you again," he told her. "Perhaps it is too soon. I do not like bringing you pain."

Morning Star could not resist an urge to suck on his full lips, to touch his tongue with her own. "It is a pain that also brings pleasure," she answered. "It is better that we do this often, so that soon there will be no pain at all, only the plea-sure."

He smiled the handsome smile that had always made her feel weak. His hard shaft filled her again, and again she felt the pain, but this time not quite so badly. Yes, this could be a wonderful thing. She was sure of that. What woman would not enjoy being bedded by Strong Runner? How glad she was that he had chosen her and no other, that he had waited all these years just for her.

She arched up to meet her husband's rhythmic thrusts, a natural instinct telling her she could enjoy this more by mov-ing with him. She felt that wonderful thrill again as he rubbed against a magical spot as he took her. She felt a pul-sating explosion, and it made her cry out. She grasped his arms and pushed against him, and he plunged himself deep, groaning as he rammed harder, faster.

Morning Star suddenly noticed that the pain was nearly gone. She was beginning to fully enjoy this wonderful act of mating. The afternoon became long and dreamy in the arms of her handsome warrior. They washed, and she cooked for him . . . and they made love again . . . and again . . . and again.

Darkness fell, and the young lovers finally slept in each other's arms, unaware that in a meadow not far away, four white men, prospectors who had failed to find their dream of gold, were quietly making off with four of Strong Runner's finest Appaloosas. "We ought to get a good price for these at Lewiston," one commented. "Enough to get us up to the Da-kotas. Maybe we'll find gold there."

Another nodded. "These Indians sure know how to breed good horses, don't they?"

"That's all they're good for," a third man said, speaking softly. "Breedin' horses and breedin' with each other."

They all stifled their laughter. "I wouldn't mind doin' a lit-tle breedin' myself," the third man added. "Too bad we couldn't have stole ourselves a pretty little Nez Perce squaw."

"We're lucky to get this much," the first man answered. "Let's get the hell out of here."

6

$\mathcal{Z}$ack watched Miss Iris Gray turn gracefully on the dance
floor with Captain Ward, whose already-bloated ego was
about to explode. Zack figured if the man puffed his chest out
any farther, he'd pop his brass buttons.

This was the first officers' dance Zack had attended,
and just as he figured, he felt out of place. Most of the men
there came from families with money, earning their appoint-
ments to West Point because they or their fathers knew someone in Congress, or someone who had connections. Still, he
had every right to be there, even though part of him felt he
probably belonged outside, where a dance for the enlisted
men was being held.

He thought how Iris's hair was as golden as the yellow
grass outside the fort, her eyes blue as the sky. Her complexion was radiant, and a man didn't have to hold her to tell
how good she'd feel in his arms, not too heavy but not too
thin, with full, firm breasts.

What fascinated him most was that he was not just attracted to her physical attributes. She had a genuine sweet-
ness, a feisty spirit. She seemed unaffected by the fact that she

was the well-schooled daughter of a colonel, unaffected by her beauty. There was an honesty in her eyes that he liked, an honesty that told him her friendly nature and concern were genuine, not just a show.

She wore a rather simple velvet dress, as blue as her eyes, with a full skirt that accented her slender waist and fit nicely over her bosom. Unlike some of the officers' wives' gowns, hers wasn't a fancy, ruffled dress with a revealing neckline. It had pretty pearl buttons that paraded all the way to a dark blue velvet collar at her throat. The short sleeves were also trimmed in the darker velvet. The simple elegance of the dress fit the woman who wore it.

Zack tried not to stare at her. He mingled with the other officers, making small talk about what the future held for the western army and Indians; but most talk was about the Civil War. Every man there knew he could at any time be called back east and find himself in the middle of a bloody battle. The stories he had already heard from a couple of men who had been a part of it, and from news that filtered back to the fort, were enough to make any man uneasy.

The number of casualties was startling, enough to make a man wonder if the entire male population would eventually be wiped out. Trouble was, there were too many males at the dance tonight, and not enough females. Some of the unmarried officers danced with the only three single women present besides Iris. One was a new arrival, personal maid to Lieutenant-Colonel Shaver, whose wife had finally been able to join him after years of living back east while he served in Kansas. Because of the Indian problem, and then the bloody border wars between Kansas and Missouri, Shaver had requested his wife stay put. Now their children were both grown, a son at West Point and a daughter who was married, so Mrs. Shaver was free to join her husband, especially since he was in Minnesota, far from the Civil War.

Zack found himself wishing Iris could also stay permanently. He liked watching her, liked listening to her laughter, her voice. He'd overheard enough of her conversations with her father and his friends and with Jason Ward to know she was not just fluff. He could not help thinking what a perfect wife she would make for an officer.

He picked up a glass of punch, finding it incredible how army wives could manage to turn a mess hall into a ballroom that made the dance feel like an elegant affair in a palace back east. Women had a way of making do with what they had and bringing that feminine touch to places where living conditions were far from admirable. Punch was being served in china cups, and fancy cakes baked by the women had been set on platters. Men on fatigue duty had scrubbed the floors of the hall. Zack drank some of the punch, then turned at the sound of an already-familiar voice.

"We haven't had that dance yet, Lieutenant Myers. I'll be insulted if you don't come over and ask my father for a turn to the music."

Zack felt his heart beat a little faster at the words spoken by the very woman he had made up his mind to avoid. She stood near him, picking up her own cup of punch. He met her blue eyes, and they sparkled with mischief. "You wouldn't want to upset the colonel's daughter, would you?" She smiled, and dimples showed in her cheeks.

Before Zack could answer, Captain Ward approached. "Iris, I could have brought you some punch," he said with a confident smile. "Why didn't you tell me you were thirsty?"

"Don't be silly, Jason. I can fend for myself. I don't need to be doted on."

Jason laughed lightly, glancing at Zack. "Well, Lieutenant Myers, I believe you've already met Miss Gray. She tells me you picked her up from the boat yesterday."

"Yes, sir. It was my pleasure."

Jason's eyes narrowed slightly, and Zack could detect the instant jealousy there. "It's always a pleasure to be around Iris. I know her well, you know, knew her as a little girl. My father and Colonel Gray are great friends." He looked at Iris. "I am so glad I was sent here before Iris came to visit. It's been a couple of years since I saw her last, and even then I could see the child turning into a woman. Someday this young lady and I are going to be more than friends, I'm sure of that. I think we're destined to be together. You feel that way too, don't you, Iris?"

Iris pursed her lips thoughtfully. "I haven't planned that far ahead, Jason. But we certainly are good friends."

Jason laughed off her remark, and Zack knew he was only

trying to pretend she was joking herself, putting on a show to prove to Zack that he "owned" Iris Gray. "Isn't she beautiful?" he asked Zack, putting a hand to Iris's waist.

"Yes. Lovely," Zack answered, bowing slightly to Iris. Jason's cockiness irritated him just enough to cause him to make his move. "Excuse me," he said, leaving them to go and talk to Colonel Gray.

Iris smiled with satisfaction, hoping he was asking for a dance. She liked Zack Myers. He was the best-looking young man in the hall, and he was not a braggart like Jason, who to her memory had always been spoiled. There was nothing pretentious about Zack Myers. He was a gentleman in every way.

She watched Zack and her father, saw her father glance her way. She knew why, and apparently Jason did too.

"Finish your punch, love, and we'll dance again. Your father said I could dance with you all night without requesting his permission. You know why, of course. He hopes we'll end up more than friends eventually." He took hold of her arms and faced her. "I must say, Iris, you have turned into a ravishing young woman. My little Iris is all grown up, and nearly ready to live her life on army posts. You've always said you like living this way. I hope you know the reason I've never married is because I've been waiting for you."

Iris sipped more punch and set the cup aside. "You take an awful lot for granted, Jason. I have another year of school left, and all I want after that is to have some time with my father. I've seen little enough of him these past four years, and I know he's lonely. It's good to see you again, but I've given no thought to how and with whom I will spend my future. I do appreciate your feelings, though."

"And you'll think seriously about them, I hope." He flashed a handsome smile, his brown eyes glittering with pride. "You know you can marry only an army man, Iris." He whisked her back onto the dance floor to join a few other couples, but they danced only a few seconds before Zack Myers tapped Jason's shoulder.

"Pardon me, sir, but Colonel Gray has given me permission to dance with his daughter."

Jason stopped dancing, his smile fading. "Is that so? Well, you haven't asked *my* permission, and I am your commanding officer."

"Yes, sir, but in this situation, the only permission I need is from the young lady's father. If she wishes to dance with me, then I should be allowed the dance."

Iris could see the challenge in their eyes. "I do wish to dance with him, Jason. There are so few women here tonight for the officers to talk to and dance with. I don't mind obliging other requests. We really are being rather selfish, don't you think? Do be a gentleman about this."

Jason scowled at her, then smiled. "Certainly. I suppose I can share you for an evening, since it's only a dance." He offered her hand to Zack, and Zack did not miss the look in his eyes. The man would probably invent some miserable duty for him after this, send him into the heart of Indian country and hope he was killed.

Zack took Iris's hand and put his right hand to her waist, glad he'd been taught how to do this back east. Every gentleman officer should know how to waltz with a proper young lady. He turned her to the music. "Sorry to take you away from your intended," he teased.

"Captain Ward harbors a lot of fantasies about himself and his future," she answered, then laughed lightly. "He's always been full of himself."

Zack grinned. "I gathered that. I'm going to suffer for this dance, you know. It wasn't fair of you to make me feel guilty for not asking you."

"Oh, then you're doing this only out of duty and honor? You didn't really want to dance with me?"

Their gazes held, and Zack felt a sudden desire far beyond simple lust. "Yes, I really *did* want to dance with you. I'm just no Jason Ward."

"Thank goodness," she answered, laughing again.

"You know what I mean. I don't run in those circles."

"There is nothing wrong with that. Father tells me you graduated near the top of your class at West Point. I am quite impressed."

"Well, I'm just a farm boy at heart."

"A person's background doesn't matter. It's the kind of man or woman they become that is important. Honor, truth, devotion to duty, to loved ones. Father told me about your past, Lieutenant. I find it quite fascinating. If you would like to call on me for a visit, I would very much like that." Iris watched the change in his eyes, knew the mention of his past had brought him pain. "Oh, I'm sorry. I'm being much too personal much too soon. I just— Father told me how your parents died, why you joined the army. I found it interesting, that's all. I thought we could—"

"It's all right. I would very much like to call on you. I just have a feeling Captain Ward will find some way to get me off the post until you leave."

"Oh, dear, I'm sorry. If he does something terrible, I'll complain to Father. He'll fix it."

"I don't need anything fixed. I prefer to handle my own problems."

"Good. I am very impressed, Lieutenant. Thank you for the dance. I was getting a little bored dancing with the same man all evening. Now that you've asked me, perhaps some of the other single men will have the courage to do the same. Jason has them thinking I belong to him."

Zack felt more relieved. "So, you live with your grandparents?"

"In Washington. They're my mother's parents. She died when I was fourteen. It was very hard on my father. He left me in Washington to be raised because I was still so young, and being an army man—"

"No explanations are needed. Is it true you actually like army life?"

"Oh, yes! I find it challenging and adventurous."

Zack frowned. "From what I hear of living conditions on posts farther west, it could prove a little more of a challenge than you care to face, if you join your father next year like you say you will."

"Well, it can't hurt to try. But let's not talk about me. I want to talk about you. Is it true Lieutenant-Colonel Shaver is the one who found you in Kansas after your parents were—" She sighed. "There I go again, being too personal. I can tell you don't like talking about it."

"It's very hard for me. Yes, Shaver did find me. He's a good man. Got me appointed to West Point. If not for that, I probably would just have enlisted and never had the chance to move past sergeant. My first thought was to be in the army so I could fight Indians. I never dreamed I'd go to West Point."

Iris frowned, sympathy coming into her eyes. "And that's the only reason you joined? No man should do something out of pure hatred, Lieutenant. And being out just to kill Indians could get you in a lot of trouble. You need to think about that, and the fact that perhaps the Indians have a legitimate complaint." She felt him stiffen, knew she'd hit on a raw nerve.

"Complaint?" Zack struggled to remain calm. "A complaint is one thing, Miss Gray. Murdering innocent people is something else."

"What about when the soldiers kill Indian women and children? Don't you think that's unfair?"

Zack stopped dancing. "I prefer not to talk about any of this, Miss Gray. I don't mean to be rude, but thank you for the dance. I am afraid I have to leave."

"I'm sorry, Zack . . . I mean, Lieutenant. I let my curiosity get in the way of common sense sometimes. You will call on me while I'm here, won't you? I would like the chance to talk to you away from other people."

He studied her blue eyes. "I don't know. It might be better if I didn't." He nodded. "Good night, Miss Gray." He walked to a wall where hats hung on a hook and took his down. He glanced at her once more before leaving, hating himself for letting his past and his hatred get in the way of a pleasant conversation with a beautiful woman who was obviously interested in him.

"Well, our lieutenant left awfully suddenly."

Iris turned to see Jason standing behind her.

"What did you say to scare him away? Maybe he's just bashful around pretty young girls," Jason said snidely. "I don't think he's very experienced with women yet. Maybe he's going to the enlisted men's dance. That's where he belongs, you know."

Iris faced him. "You are rude and arrogant, Jason, and you are spoiling this dance for me. I'm sorry, but I would appreciate it if you did not dance with me the rest of the evening and gave the other men a turn. And please don't insult Lieutenant Myers. He's a good officer, a West Point graduate, and as worthy as the next man." She left him to join her father.

"Is he?" Jason muttered. "He's under my command, little lady, and I'll find something to occupy his time until you have to leave." *You don't know it yet, but you belong to me, Iris Gray.*

Seeing the woman you've become, knowing the perfect army wife you'd make, I'll not settle for anything less.

He'd have a good talk with the colonel. What Jason Ward wanted, Jason Ward got . . . and he wanted Iris Gray.

"It is done," Strong Runner told Morning Star. "There will be no more dealing with the white traitors! Chief Joseph has torn up the New Testament Bible that he has carried more than twenty years to show that we will never again listen to their lies, never again trust them, and never again sit in treaty council!"

He walked over to sit beside his wife near a fire that burned just outside their lodge. Morning Star stared at the flames, afraid for the future. She did not blame her husband for siding with Chief Joseph and Big Thunder, nor did she blame Strong Runner for feeling as Eagle From The Light felt, that all whites should be banished completely, and that those who refused to leave should be killed.

"It is a sad day," she answered. "In all the years I can remember, Chief Joseph has done all he could to do as the white leaders wished and remain at peace. He was the first Nez Perce convert, and he convinced many of us to take the white man's religion. He helped the mission work, adopted the ways of the white man. He aided the army as a scout against other Indians who tried to make war, yet he was never paid as promised. For all our efforts at cooperating the white man's way, we have been cheated out of our land."

"The land is still ours. The whites will find that out when we continue to hunt on it and live where we choose!"

Strong Runner poked angrily at the coals of the fire with a long stick. Morning Star understood his anger. White men had stolen his precious Appaloosas. When he reported it, nothing was done. When he found his horses, he was told he could not prove they were his, even though he had branded them as his own by cutting a tiny piece out of the right ear of every horse he owned. The army leader to whom Strong Runner had gone refused to help. He said that if Strong Runner tried to do something about it himself, if he hurt those white men or tried to take the horses back, he could be arrested, imprisoned, maybe even hanged.

It had been hard for Strong Runner to keep from getting those horses. It was not easy for a man like him to swallow his pride, but he had done so, mostly for Morning Star's sake. He did not want to make his new wife a widow after only two weeks of marriage. Now his pride had been hurt even more, his and that of the other Nez Perces who had discovered the white commissioners who represented the Great Father, Abraham Lincoln, had cruelly tricked them.

"We never should have divided ourselves," Strong Runner said aloud, as though to read her thoughts. "This is mostly Lawyer's fault. He was so willing to take anything he could get. He knew that by signing the treaty, most of the rewards from the white man's government would benefit only his village at Lapwai. They agreed to build the schools there, the blacksmith shop, a carpenter shop, the wagonmaker's, a church. Lapwai is the center for the rest of us. We all have to go there for government gifts. Lawyer is even paid white man's money for his cooperation, and they will build him a house that will cost him nothing."

The last words were sneered, and Strong Runner rose and paced. "Lawyer is a coward! He is no Nez Perce! He is a *white* man now, and he *shames* us!"

Morning Star sighed. "Your father and mine were against dividing ourselves under separate chiefs. They were afraid the white man would find a way to use that against us, and they did."

It had all been so devious. The Nez Perces could not agree as a group on what concessions to make in a new treaty, so they decided to go back to the old ways, when each clan had its own chief. Lawyer's clan wanted to go along with whatever the white man wanted. Joseph and Big Thunder, whom she and Strong Runner followed, wanted to be very careful before signing a new treaty. They had wanted to talk more, make sure the Nez Perces did not give up too much. Eagle From The Light simply wanted to kill all the whites and be done with them. They had decided to divide themselves and each leader would sign a treaty he felt was best for his clan.

Lawyer had quickly signed the original offer, gladly accepting a much smaller chunk of land in return for a house, his money, the schools, and all the rest of the promised gifts,

which Strong Runner and most opposing the treaty doubted
would ever be received. Lawyer had honestly believed that
just because he'd accepted a smaller piece of land, those who
refused to sign would continue to be free to hunt and live
anyplace they chose on the rest of the land promised in the
original treaty of 1855. Now they had learned that the commissioners had coerced other men from Lawyer's clan to sign
the treaty just to be able to show the government enough sig-
natures to make the treaty valid. They had been told that in
the eyes of the government, that meant the treaty applied to
all Nez Perces.

Again they had been tricked. Strong Runner had been
cheated out of his horses, and the entire tribe had been cheated
out of its land. Joseph, furious at the trickery, had turned his
back on the Christian religion. Those who taught it did not
practice what they preached, and in his eyes that meant the
religion must not be true. A man had to be true to his faith.
That was the Indian way. To the Indian, religion was as important as breathing, and a man must not disobey its teachings. If the white man could completely disobey his own
teachings, then perhaps he had only contrived those teachings
to trick and cheat the Nez Perces, forcing them into more
docile, submissive ways. He had made the mistake of destroying the Nez Perce pride, and he would surely regret it.

"What will happen now, Strong Runner?"

He shook his head. "I do not know. We will go on as we
always have, living our own way. The white man be damned.
His government be damned." He stopped pacing and looked
at her. "There could be war, Morning Star, but it is better to
die proud than to live to be an old man full of shame."

Morning Star nodded. "I know. I would not want it to be
any other way for my husband. But neither do I wish to have
to live without him."

He came and stood before her in all his manly glory, a
new pride shining in his eyes. "We are a strong people; we
hunt better than the white man, fight better than the white
man, ride better horses. There are no finer steeds in all this
land than our own Appaloosas. Now that we turn to our own
gods, we will be stronger. Our gods will smile on us again."

He reached out and she took his hand. Strong Runner
pulled her to her feet and held her close. "You will give me

many children, and they will grow old and have children of their own. Their children, our grandchildren, will live on all the land we now claim. We will lose none of it. It will still belong to the Nez Perces for generations to come, because we are strong and proud and we will make sure we never lose this land, from one generation to the next." He lifted her into his arms. "You will not lose me, Morning Star. This I promise."

She put her head on his shoulder as he carried her inside their lodge and laid her on the bed of robes. Her heart pounded harder when he pushed up her tunic. She wore nothing under it.

"I wish to try again to plant my seed inside of you. We will have a son, and I will teach him to hunt and to fight. I will school him in the white man's ways so the white man cannot trick him."

Morning Star smiled, opening herself to her husband. "We will keep trying, my husband, until a child grows in my belly."

He unlaced his leggings and knelt between her legs. Morning Star knew this was more than just trying to plant his seed in her. He was feeling angry, proud, determined. He was ready to show the white man the power of the Nez Perces. Part of that power was in regenerating their numbers, creating sons and daughters to carry on the way. This was also a way for him to show his prowess, to prove he was a man, a way of overcoming the shame they had suffered at being betrayed by men they thought they could trust.

He moved inside her, grasping her hips and pushing hard, building to a wild rhythm. Morning Star took him willingly, for just as her mother had promised, this act of love had become the most enjoyable thing a woman could ever experience. She loved pleasing this man, and took her own pleasure in return. She grasped his wrists, gasping in ecstasy until she felt that wonderful rolling feeling deep in her loins that made her groan his name and arch up to him in wild abandon.

Yes, he was a grand warrior! The Nez Perces were the best fighters in all this land. No other Indian tribe could overcome them, and neither would the white man! She was no longer afraid.

Zack pulled on his gloves and prepared to mount up, when he heard a woman call his name. He turned to see Iris Gray standing in a narrow opening between two stone buildings. He frowned, looking around to be sure no one else saw, then walked over to her. "You shouldn't stand there. There could be rats in there."

"You forget that I am army, Lieutenant. I know rats and mice often abound in places like this. I'm no fainting woman, I'll have you know!" She grabbed the front of his jacket and pulled him closer, then marched him between the walls to the back side of the buildings, where no one would see them. "Now, Lieutenant Myers," she said, letting go and facing him with arms folded. "What's your excuse?"

"My excuse?"

"For not calling on me. I've been here over two weeks, and I'm going home tomorrow, and you never called on me once! You've been busy or gone most of the time. Whether by your own choice or because that stupid Jason Ward made sure you were too busy to see me, you could have at least paid one short visit to explain."

Zack blinked, removing his hat and one glove so he could run a hand through his thick dark hair, never liking the way his hat flattened it. Iris had taken him completely by surprise, and a moment passed before he could think straight. "I . . . it was my own choice, ma'am. I just thought it best to stay away."

"Why? Because of Jason? I hope not, because he is deluding himself to think there is something between us. I am a free woman, Zack Myers."

Zack studied her eyes, wondering if she even realized how beautiful she was. "It had nothing to do with the captain. I just . . . well, you were here for only a little while anyway. God only knows where I'll be sent from here. I'll probably never see you again, especially if I go somewhere out of your father's command, so what is the sense of getting to know you better? I'd probably get to liking you and then have to be away from you, so why not just forget about it?"

A gentle, forgiving look came into her eyes. "Then you aren't mad at me?"

"Mad? About what?"

She turned away. "I thought you were angry with me for bringing up your parents and all, and for what I said about the Indian point of view the night of the dance."

"No, ma'am. I know you were just curious. Sometimes it's hard for me to talk about it, that's all. And I don't want anybody's sympathy. I don't want any preaching either. I hate Indians and I intend to get myself transferred west to fight them. I feel the way I feel and nothing can be done about it. I figured that upset you, so I just decided to leave it all alone, you go your way and I go mine."

She met his eyes again. "You must be so lonely, Zack Myers."

The remark was spoken with such compassion that Zack was caught off guard. A mist came to his eyes, and he blinked it back. "Sometimes," he answered.

She nodded. Zack couldn't hide his surprise when she stepped closer and took hold of his free hand. She leaned up and kissed him on the cheek, her lips soft, her scent intoxicating. "God is always with you, Zack. Remember that. And I intend to write to you. Do you mind?"

Zack could barely find his voice. "I guess not."

"Will you write back?"

"I don't know. Maybe."

She smiled softly. "All this wasted time. I'm leaving in the morning. Will you think about me?"

He couldn't believe how close she was to him . . . how tempting. He stepped back as though suddenly startled. "Sure. I, uh, I'd better go now. If someone saw us, it would go bad for you."

"And you, no doubt." She studied him almost lovingly. "Take care of yourself, Lieutenant Myers."

He nodded. "You too."

She raised her chin. "There is something special between us. I felt it the first time I met you. Do you feel it too?"

It would be real easy to love you, Iris Gray, he wanted to reply. "Out here it's easy for a man to take to a pretty woman, what with hardly any decent single women around to begin with. It's hard for me to be objective about it in this situation, if you understand what I'm saying. A man can't tell if he's feeling something real, or if it's just loneliness."

She nodded. "I understand. Would you think I was crazy if I said I'll miss you?"

He couldn't help a grin. "Yeah, that's a little crazy, but it's nice. Thank you."

She stepped closer again, touching his arm. "There's a loneliness inside you that goes deeper than just being out here and not having much of a social life. It goes back to a little boy who suddenly lost his whole world. He's still looking for whatever he lost then. When my mother died, I wanted to die too. It was so terrible. When I think of how it would have been if I had lost her the way you lost yours . . ." She blinked back tears. "Write me, Zack. Promise."

He put his hat back on. "I said maybe."

There it was again. He obviously hated talking about what had happened to his family. The minute she brought it up, he always started pulling away, his smile vanishing, his demeanor colder. "Maybe is good enough."

Before he could stop her, she leaned up and kissed him smack on the lips.

"God be with you, Zack Myers."

She darted away, running around the other side of one of the buildings. Zack stood staring after her, hardly able to believe what had just happened. He licked his lips, tasted some kind of cream. A fire moved through him at how soft and moist her lips had been, the thought that if they'd had time and more privacy, she might have been willing to let him kiss her, maybe several times, maybe let him crush her against him, feel the curves of her body. . . .

He shook away the thought. It was all ridiculous. The woman was surely addled. She hardly knew him . . . and yet she seemed to know him intimately. She had a keen insight for people's feelings. She had a wonderful sense of caring. He'd never known that in anyone, except in his own gentle mother.

She wanted to write him, expected him to write back. He wasn't so sure that was a good idea. What if her father found out . . . or Jason Ward? Men had a way of knowing who was getting mail from whom out here.

He pulled on his glove and headed back between the buildings to his horse. He'd been given the assignment of taking some men farther north to find some renegade Sioux who had supposedly stolen some horses from a settler. He was originally supposed to stay inside the fort and drill some new volunteers, and he had a gut feeling Jason Ward had arranged the switch so he would not be around when Iris left the next day. Jason wanted her all to himself for a grand good-bye. He would put on a good show of telling her how much he would miss her.

Zack couldn't help grinning at the look Captain Ward would have on his face if he knew he'd had his own private good-bye with Iris, that she'd kissed him on the mouth. He guessed she'd sure never kissed Ward that way.

7

Zack stepped inside Howard Shaver's office and stood at full attention, noticing Colonel Gray was also present. He saluted both men, wondering why he'd been asked to see them. Jason Ward had given him the order, but he had said it was not his place to explain the reason. He had only confused Zack by giving him a warning—if Zack expected to achieve any more promotions, he had better remember his place . . . and remember who Iris Gray belonged to.

Was he in trouble? Had someone seen Iris kiss him full on the lips the previous day? The one thing he feared most was a demotion. He could not bear the disgrace of it, not after working so hard to get this far. He had intended to make the army his life; but then, when he thought about that kiss, he couldn't help wondering if it might not be worth a demotion just to taste Iris Gray's lips again.

Army first, Zack Myers, he reminded himself. He could tell by Shaver's eyes something was amiss. Being called up before a colonel usually meant a change of duty, often even a promotion. If not for Jason's comment, he could hope this meeting meant he was finally being sent farther west to take part in some real Indian fighting, maybe even a promotion along with it. But this was nothing that good. Even more confusing, his orders had changed again. Someone else would go after the renegade Indian. Zack was to report to headquarters.

"At ease, Lieutenant," Shaver told him. "In fact, have a seat."

The look in the man's eyes was almost apologetic. Zack was more sure with every passing second that he was in trouble. If he was being sent west or getting a promotion, Shaver would be happy for him.

He removed his hat and took a chair across the desk from Shaver, who also sat down. Colonel Gray remained standing.

"Lieutenant, I am here only to tell you that Lieutenant-Colonel Shaver assures me you are trustworthy and honorable. I expect you to treat my daughter with the utmost respect. If I hear anything to the contrary, or get word that you have overstepped your bounds in any way, you won't be wearing that silver bar on your sleeve. Do you understand?"

Zack frowned. What the heck was the man talking about? *Had* someone seen the kiss? The man seemed to be talking about the future, not something that had already happened. "Yes, sir. Miss Gray is a very proper, very fine young lady." Why did it matter? Iris was leaving today. She wouldn't even be around.

"Lieutenant-Colonel Shaver also tells me he has no doubt you would risk your life for my daughter if it became necessary. I'm told you are quite skilled with a rifle and handgun, even earned merits at West Point for sharpshooting."

A little nudge of alarm crept into Zack's chest. "Yes, sir. Thank you, sir."

"Fine. I'll let Lieutenant-Colonel Shaver take over from here. I met you at the dance a couple of weeks ago but have not had much of an opportunity to speak with you, so I just wanted to get another good look at you. I am sure my daughter and her grandfather will be in good hands."

The man nodded and put on his hat. Zack started to rise to salute again.

"No need, Lieutenant," Gray told him in his usual blustery voice. He was a big man, with a rather overbearing and intimidating carriage. His white hair and a white mustache gave him an air of wisdom and authority, the traits a colonel should have—and traits that told a soldier of lesser rank he had better not cross the man. Zack nodded in reply, his thoughts reeling at Gray's words. What the hell did he mean? Iris was going back to Washington!

He turned his gaze to Shaver as Gray left. Shaver closed his eyes and rubbed them. "Yes, Zack, you're going east, not west. You're to accompany Iris Gray and her grandfather back to Washington. With this mess the country is in, the war back east, he isn't comfortable with her traveling so far. He didn't want her to come in the first place, but she's stubborn and loyal. Now she has a long journey home, and he wants her to have a little extra protection. Her grandfather is, after all, an old man who carries no weapons."

Zack blinked in disbelief. "But . . . Colonel Shaver, I've put in my request to be sent—"

"No one knows better than I do what you want, Zack. We can cut the formalities now that Gray is gone." He sighed deeply, leaning back in his chair and pulling at his red mustache. "Zack, there's more to this. I've had a request by wire from Washington for a good man of your rank, someone who can go into the field and train men on the spot. I get requests like that all the time, but I've managed to keep you here a whole year, knowing you don't want to go in any direction but west. I can't keep coming up with excuses, and I finally decided you need to go."

Surprise, hurt, and anger all joined forces in Zack's soul. "I don't understand. You promised me—"

"I said I'd send you west when I felt you were ready. You're *not* ready, Zack, because the only reason you want to go west is to kill Indians. I've told you time and again that as an officer you can't be in the army just for vengeance. I think you have a lot of hatred to work out from under your skin. You have to get your priorities straight, Zack. The fact is, you're in the army, and that means taking orders and going where you're needed. Maybe it will help you to get away from the sight of Indians for a while. Maybe getting involved in a different kind of war will help you gain some perspective, especially when you see firsthand the realities of hatred and prejudice, see the bloodshed. I'm doing this for your own good, Zack. I'm answering the request for someone of your caliber, and as long as you have to go east, I decided you might as well be the one to accompany Miss Gray back home. You'll have to report in Washington first anyway."

Zack gritted his teeth against an urge to shout at Shaver, reminding himself that it was Shaver who had helped him get this far. "For my own good? I thought you were more than just my superior officer, sir. I thought you were my friend."

Shaver scowled. "I am. That's why I'm doing this. Go and get a taste of war, Zack, before you go fighting Indians. The western tribes are more vicious than any Confederate soldier will be, and, by God, they're as formidable an enemy as our army will ever come up against. They're skilled horsemen, brave fighters, and damn clever. It will take good men to go up against them, and you aren't quite seasoned enough for it. You want to be a good soldier. I'm doing what I can to *make* you a good soldier. I'm sorry, Zack. This isn't what you'd hoped for, but there is too great a shortage of good men back east. When this is over and when I feel you're ready, you'll get that transfer west."

Zack rose and turned away, breathing deeply against the disappointment. "When it's over? We don't know how long that will be, and you know the statistics. I could be killed, or wounded badly enough to be discharged."

"You could. I don't want that to happen any more than you do, Zack. I'll be praying for you. I just feel you need to do this. You've got that deep hatred in your guts for Indians, and your view of the army is too narrow. You've got to learn you can't think the way you do if you intend to be a good officer. A good officer is rational. A good officer has to make decisions that sometimes benefit the enemy. A good officer has compassion, tries to see the enemy's viewpoint. That helps him *think* like the enemy, and when he can do that, he can sometimes outsmart them. A good officer sees the enemy as human beings, with reasons for what they do. A good officer is cautious. He doesn't let hatred make him do something irrational that could cost the lives of his men. I don't think you're quite capable yet of making decisions based on common sense, not when it comes to Indians."

Zack looked across the parade grounds, where a wagon was being loaded. He recognized Iris Gray's trunk. "Why not Jason Ward?" he asked. "I'm sure he'd just love to accompany

Miss Gray back east. The man is totally struck with her, thinks he's going to marry her someday."

Shaver rose with a sigh. "Captain Ward just arrived here a month ago, remember? Men don't get moved around that often, and you know it. He came here to train volunteers, just like what you do. Now that he's here, he'll have to stay awhile. Besides, he's one of Gray's pets. Gray is doing everything he can to keep his best friend's son *out* of the war."

Zack turned to face him. "Meaning I'm expendable."

Shaver studied him sadly. "In Gray's eyes, yes. But he also respects you, Zack, because of all the good things I've told him about you. He is trusting you with his daughter. Handle this right, and he'll probably see that you get a promotion."

Zack ran a hand through his hair, feeling a headache coming on. "Sir, do I need to remind you I have to answer to Captain Ward? I could tell when he sent me over here that he didn't like the idea of my taking the woman he thinks he's going to marry to Washington. He already gave me fair warning to keep my eyes and hands off her."

Shaver grinned. "He did, did he?" He folded his arms. "Well, he didn't have any business doing that. Let him worry and wonder. You have an assignment, and there is nothing he can do about it. Besides, by the time you get back, he'll probably be gone somewhere else. Your paths might never cross again. In the meantime, I don't imagine traveling for the next few weeks with someone as pretty as Iris Gray will be such a terrible thing, will it?"

The man was grinning, but Zack just scowled. *You don't know her,* he felt like answering. After that kiss yesterday, and knowing how forward and determined the girl could be, how was he supposed to keep his distance, especially when he looked into those blue eyes? He suspected accompanying Iris Gray to Washington would be one of the most difficult assignments he'd ever be given, even more difficult than going off to war. "I don't know, sir. You heard Colonel Gray's orders. One indiscretion, and my army career is over."

A twinkle came into Shaver's eyes. "Then you will have to use your good judgment, won't you, as well as learn some self-discipline. Traveling with a colonel's daughter will be your first lesson in both matters. My only worry is the much harder lesson you might face on the battlefield. Don't think I don't realize what could happen, Zack. It pains me to do this, and yet I feel I must. Sometimes a man has to do something that hurts when he knows it's what's best for those he . . . cares about."

Their eyes held. Zack knew the man almost said "those he loves," and he was touched. He knew deep inside that this assignment was probably for his own good, but not even Shaver understood what it had been like for him to witness his family's murders. No one could ever understand this hatred he carried.

"I understand you better than you think, Zack," Shaver told him. He put out his hand. "I will be praying for you. I hope to see you back here in just a few months. God knows this war has to end soon, or there won't be any men left to fight it."

Zack's emotions were mixed. He considered this man his best friend. He'd feel a little lost without him. He grasped Shaver's hand and squeezed. "I *will* be back, sir. You can bet on that. And when I get here, I hope I'll be on my way west."

Shaver nodded. "You just might be, Zack." He squeezed Zack's hand in return. "I hope you come to understand why I'm doing this."

Zack released his grip. "I'll try, sir."

"Go get yourself packed." Shaver turned and picked up a piece of paper from his desk. "Here are your orders and the name of the man you should report to in Washington. Twenty other men will also be going as newly trained recruits, some that you trained yourself, including Corporal Adams, so you aren't alone in this."

Zack took the paper and nodded. "Yes, sir." He put on his hat and stood at attention, saluting. "Good-bye, sir."

Shaver saluted in return. "Good-bye, son, and good luck. You'd better get going. You'll be leaving in an hour."

Zack nodded. "Yes, sir." Reluctantly, he turned and walked out, stopping to look across the way at the wagon that would carry Iris Gray's baggage down to a steamboat. "Dammit," he muttered. He didn't mind the thought of going off to war half as much as having to accompany Iris Gray to Washington. The latter assignment might prove the most dangerous of his career.

———————

"You're angry with me for that kiss, aren't you?"

Zack turned in surprise at the words. "What are you doing up here on deck? You're supposed to be in your cabin. How can I keep an eye on you if you go wandering around alone after dark on a steamboat full of lonely soldiers and the riffraff who work on this boat?"

Iris tossed her head. "None of those soldiers would dare offend the daughter of Colonel John Gray, and the other men leave me alone *because* of the soldiers. They know I'm being watched." She studied Zack's green eyes in the moonlight, ached to erase the cold elusiveness he showed her since they left Fort Snelling a week before. "Are you saying *you're* a lonely soldier?"

Zack frowned, wishing the silvery light on her hair didn't make her look so angelic. Why did she have to come and find him after dark? Something about the dark and the soft summer breeze set a romantic mood there on deck that he would rather not feel. "I don't understand you, Miss Gray. What is it you want of me? You've made things difficult for me since the first day you got off the boat at Fort Snelling."

She smiled, folding her arms. "And how is that? What have I done that's so terrible that you avoided me the whole time I was at the fort, and you've kept your distance so far on this trip, always watching me from afar, talking to my grandfather at times, but not to me? You're doing a good job of hurting my feelings, Zack Myers."

"Why should I care? I hardly know you, and I don't *want* to get to know you. You're the daughter of a colonel who, I might add, warned me to keep my distance and to treat you with respect. I also got a warning from Captain Ward, who thinks you belong to him. A man in my position, Miss Gray, doesn't stir the anger of men like that. I'm not about to do something that could end my army career just because you have some kind of whim. If anyone had seen you kiss me that last day before you left, I'd have been stripped of my bars and thrown in the guardhouse!"

She pursed her lips and turned away, bracing her hands on the deck railing. "I was right. You *are* angry." She pushed a strand of hair behind her ear. "I kissed you because I like you. I like you because . . . I'm not sure. I just could tell you were a very sincere, dedicated soldier, and I admire that. You aren't pretentious and cocky like Jason. When Father told me you joined the army because of what happened to your family, I was impressed." She faced him again. "You didn't join just to be all puffed up with your own importance and to strut around in a uniform."

"Miss Gray—"

"Please call me Iris."

"Miss Gray, I don't need you or anyone else feeling sorry for me. Nor do I need you getting me in trouble with a kiss, or by doing something like this. I have plans for my life, Iris Gray, and I don't need you upsetting them."

After a silent moment Iris stepped closer, holding her chin defiantly. "Was my kiss really so terrible, Zack? I enjoyed kissing you. Didn't you enjoy kissing me?"

Zack caught the smell of lilacs. In the moonlight her skin looked like velvet. He could not help thinking how utterly exotic it would be to lay her right down on the deck and make love to her under the soft moonlight. "What man wouldn't enjoy kissing you?" he replied. "I just have to wonder how many men *have* kissed you, since you're so free with such things."

She raised her hand to slap him, but he caught her wrist. "I'm sorry," he told her. He could see tears in her eyes, and he felt like a fool. "I'm just not very happy about being sent east," he told her. "Not because of the war. I'm not afraid of it. It's just that I wanted to go west to fight Indians, not east to fight other white men. I have no interest in this war, but a soldier goes where he's ordered to go." He let go of her wrist and she jerked it away.

"I do not give away kisses freely, Lieutenant Myers," she told him, her voice sounding shaky. "It just so happens I've *never* kissed another man on the mouth, but I kissed you because I couldn't help myself. I *did* feel sorry for you, whether you like that or not. I wanted to know you better. I thought I'd write to you after I left. I was so happy when Father told me you had been assigned to accompany the new soldiers to Washington. I thought we could get closer, become good friends if nothing more. You might judge others by how wealthy and important they are, Zack Myers, and think that you aren't good enough for certain people. *I* don't judge *anyone* by their wealth or social standing. I judge them by character and honor."

She wrapped her shawl closer around her shoulders as the breeze cooled. "I'm sorry you have to go to war." She looked away. "More sorry than you can know. I've seen what happens to men in war. I volunteer at a hospital in Washington. I've stood and watched doctors cut off men's arms, legs, feet . . ." She shuddered. "I've heard their screams, stood beside men who begged me to put them out of their misery, begged me to kill them. I've had blood on my hands, my dress . . ." She met his eyes again. "I will pray you don't end up like that, Zack. I would never want that. I also don't want you to think of me as some spoiled army brat who runs around flirting with soldiers and stealing kisses from them. I'm not like that at all, and I'm not some fainting beauty who won't get her hands dirty. I happen to be doing all I can to help in this war. I respect my father and the army, and I want to do my share for the Union cause, in which I believe. As for you . . . I have only been trying to strike up a friendship, give you someone to talk to about your family; but since being friends with me is such a terrible thing in your eyes, then fine. We won't be friends. I won't bother to give you the time of day from now through the rest of this trip!"

Zack sighed, still too angry about all that had happened to think straight. "Fine," he answered with a nod. "That might be best." He wanted to grab her and taste her mouth again. He wanted to kick himself for insulting her. "I *am* sorry for my rude remark. I had no idea you did hospital volunteer work." Damn, she was pretty when she was mad, and the woman was even stronger than he'd guessed. "I didn't really believe what I said about you giving out kisses. I just wanted to keep you from ever going out looking for me alone like this. Please don't do that, Miss Gray. And please don't feel sorry for me. I've made it on my own for thirteen years, and I am a well-trained army officer. I'll make it through this war."

Her gaze softened. "I hope so, Zack. And I hope you'll go with good feelings about me, and that you are able to go farther west. Please believe I had nothing to do with Father's decision to send you on this trip. I would never have done anything to get you noticed and sent into battle. Tell me we can at least be friends. We'll probably never see each other again once we reach Washington."

Zack sighed deeply, wondering at the feelings this beauty stirred in him, wishing he didn't admire her so. "I don't blame you for any of this. I never did. We can be friends as long as that's all we are."

I don't believe you, Zack Myers, she thought. *You're as attracted to me as I am to you.* "I understand. I simply like you as a person, and that kiss was . . . was just to let you know I care."

Zack drew in his breath and straightened, fighting an urge to yank her close and do the very thing he knew they should never do again. "I appreciate that. You're a very nice young lady, Miss Gray, but I still intend to keep my distance. I will, however, keep a good watch over you and see that you arrive safely."

"I have no doubt about that." She put a hand on his arm. "Good night, Zack."

Just get going before I go crazy with the wanting of you, he felt like saying. "Good night. I'll walk behind you and make sure you get to your cabin."

She nodded and turned, wishing she were not a colonel's daughter at all, wishing Jason Ward had not been sent to Fort Snelling. She'd be better off if she were one of those maids or a laundress. Maybe then someone like Zack would not be afraid to show an interest in her. She wished she could make him understand that his rank and education made him just as eligible as any other officer, but then, that wasn't the whole problem. The real problem was that Zack Myers was so bent on going west and getting his revenge that he would not let anything get in the way, not even love. If falling for a colonel's daughter meant giving up that revenge, he would not let it happen, and that was what she was sure was happening between them, no matter how much he protested, how cold he acted, how short a time they had known each other. She was falling in love with Zack Myers, and she was damn sure he was having the same feelings for her.

I'll break that barrier, Zack Myers. I am going to wait for you. I want to be a soldier's wife, and you need someone to love you. She marched to her cabin and turned to tell him good night, but he was already walking away, his back to her.

8

"You like him, don't you, child?"

Iris met her grandfather's eyes. She sat across from him on the train that carried them through Maryland south to Washington. So close. Within an hour they would be home and Zack Myers would leave, probably never to return. "Zack?"

"You know who I'm talking about." The old man's blue eyes sparkled.

Iris managed a smile, but she felt sad inside. "Yes. I like him very much."

Carlton Harris nodded. "So do I. He's joined us only a few times for meals at stops along the way, so I've never gotten to know him really well—seems like a man who's hard to get to know. Still, there is a sincerity about him, and he's certainly a man of honor, must be intelligent, since he graduated from West Point with honors. I admire a young man who is willing to go after what he wants." He leaned forward, patting her arm. "I just want you both to know that if Zack Myers is interested in you, honey, you certainly have my approval to see each other whenever the chance arises."

Iris studied the man's tired face, loving him for making this trip with her just to make sure she had a traveling companion. "I don't think he'll try, Grandpa. He kept his distance this whole trip, although he joined us for meals whenever we asked. I have tried getting closer to him, but he is determined there should be nothing more between us than a casual friendship. He won't do anything to risk his future as an officer in the army." She folded her arms and scowled. "That's Jason Ward's fault. Jason hung around me like a mother hen the whole time I visited at Fort Snelling, making sure no one else got the chance to even talk to me." *Except for the morning I kissed Zack,* she thought. She wished she'd never done that. She couldn't forget that kiss. "Jason warned Zack to stay clear of me or he might not get another promotion."

Carlton leaned back and sighed. "Well, Jason has to learn he does not own you, but that isn't to say you won't end up together after all. At least Jason is safe. Maybe it's best not to get too close to Zack, honey. After all, he's headed into war, and you know as well as anyone what can happen. He could be killed or badly wounded. Did you ever stop to think maybe that's part of the reason he has kept his distance? He knows what can happen. Why start something that could lead only to heartache?"

Iris looked out the window at the passing scenery. Maybe Zack's reasons for avoiding her were not entirely because he was worried about his career. She had given up thinking he might be falling in love with her, but now she realized that might be true after all. "Maybe you're right, Grandpa." She was lost in thought until the train rumbled into Washington. Outside on the platform, soldiers milled about, some leaving, some returning, many of those in bandages or on crutches. She watched an ambulance wagon hurry away . . . more wounded . . . more horror.

It was depressing to be back home amid all the chaos and agony, away from her lonely father, more depressing now, knowing Zack was going to join in the fighting, that he could come back in one of those ambulances . . . or in a coffin. She felt a panic growing inside, and she stood up before the train came to a full stop. "I have to find Zack, Grandpa, before he leaves with the other soldiers."

The man smiled and nodded. "I understand."

Iris hurried to the door, waiting eagerly for the conductor to open it when the train finally came to a halt. She descended the stairs to the platform, wishing she could pretty herself up a little more before bidding Zack Myers good-bye. It was terribly hot, and the long journey had left her weary. Her blue dress had soot stains on it from places where it had rubbed against the sides of seats or against a dirty railing.

Zack was in the next car with a platoon of men he'd been in charge of as well as escorting her. For the last part of their trip he had not ridden with her and her grandfather, sure that there was no longer any danger from Confederate bandits. She was afraid that now that they had arrived, he would simply leave without even a good-bye, but her fears vanished when she saw Zack coming from the car behind hers, looking her way.

Yes! He'd meant to come and find her first. There was something in his eyes she was sure was love, but the minute he caught her watching him, those eyes changed, showing indifference. *You don't fool me, Zack Myers.* She quelled an urge to run to him as he stepped down and walked in her direction.

"I, uh, I just thought I'd make sure you and your grandfather are all set. Can your grandfather see to your baggage and find a taxi buggy for you?"

"Yes, he can take care of all that." They looked only at each other for a moment, neither of them aware of the milling crowd around them. Iris took a deep breath and dared to say what she really felt. "You are just trying to spare my feelings, aren't you, Zack?"

"What?"

"This isn't all just because you don't care, or because you're worried about your army career. You just don't want to let yourself care too much, or allow *me* to care too much, because you know how much it would hurt me if you never came back."

She had caught him off guard. He'd been prepared to give her a quick good-bye, but he was finding that more difficult than he'd thought it would be. "I—" He closed his eyes and breathed deeply. "Iris, I know how it feels to lose someone close to you."

"Do you think I don't? I lost my own mother only four years ago."

He nodded. "It isn't just that. It's . . . it's just too hard for me to let myself care about anybody. To care that much and then lose them—"

"Zack, life goes on. Losing someone is a risk everyone takes. You can't let that stop you from ever having anyone special in your life. A person can't live like that. Everyone needs to be loved, and to love in return. You haven't had that since you were ten years old, and you blame the Indians for it. I understand, Zack. Please promise me you'll let yourself care again. Promise me you'll write, that when you return you'll come and find me. If it's a year from now, two years from now, I might be with my father, but he should be easy to find. Promise me, Zack!"

God, he loved her. He hadn't wanted this to happen. He had tried so hard to keep this from happening. "I can't decide anything until this war is over, Iris, and I know what's going to happen to me next, where I'm going."

She stepped closer. "I'll be praying for you . . . waiting for you." Without giving him a chance to stop her, she flung her arms around his neck and planted her mouth over Zack's.

Zack's first thought was to shove her away, but the minute her soft mouth met his, he lost all resolve. A desperate loneliness engulfed him, a fear of the unknown. Natural desires combined with the realization of his love for this woman left him no strength to deny her. She felt good in his arms, her breasts crushed against him. He moved his arms around her slender waist. He could kick himself for not taking advantage of all the chances they'd had to be alone on the journey. Now it was too late. He could take pleasure only in this quick moment of good-bye. He invaded her mouth hungrily, wishing he could invade other places, brand her as his woman. That might never happen now.

He heard catcalls and whistles behind him, and he realized his men were filing out of the car, catching him giving Colonel John Gray's daughter a passionate kiss. He quickly pulled away, grasping Iris's arms. "Dammit, now look at what you've done! They've seen us!"

"I don't care," she answered. "I love you, Zack Myers, and you can't deny that you love me, can you?"

Zack rubbed his lips with the back of his hand, wondering how she could still be so beautiful when she was tired from the long trip, her dress and her face dirty, her hair stringy. She was a mess, but she was still the prettiest woman he'd ever set eyes on. What made her more stunning was her fiery spirit, her refusal to give up on him. Any other woman would be so angry with him right now she'd probably hit him, not kiss him.

He couldn't answer her question. "Good-bye, Iris. I promise to write."

Tears welled in her eyes. "Good-bye, Zack. God be with you."

He looked into her eyes a moment longer before he finally turned away, determined not to turn back. He shouted angrily at his men to get their gear together and follow him. "I'll have no rumors spread about me and Miss Gray," he ordered. "The foolish woman is just a little overzealous with her good-byes, and she caught me off guard."

Several of the men snickered. "Can *I* go tell her good-bye, sir?" Corporal Adams asked.

Zack cast him a dark scowl that wiped the smile off his face. "You can follow orders," he answered curtly.

Iris smiled through her tears at the spectacle of Zack trying to pretend the kiss meant nothing. She knew better. The way he'd kissed in return . . . She'd never in her life felt the stirrings in her loins that kiss had awakened. For a brief moment she had imagined what it might be like to be held and kissed like that lying naked in bed with Zack, feeling him touch her in secret places, giving him pleasure in return, loving him the way he deserved to be loved. She watched him until he and his men disappeared into the crowd. She knew he would not come back for a second good-bye.

She turned away, her weariness and aching love for a man she might never see again overwhelming her so that she could not stop the tears. She felt a hand on her shoulder.

"It's all right, Iris," her grandfather told her. "Things will all work out. This war has to end soon. It can't go on much longer."

Iris nodded and took a handkerchief from a pocket of her dress. "I know, Grandpa. But then will come the problems with Indians. He's so full of hatred and bitterness because of his family I'm afraid there will always be a war in Zack's soul. That war is harder for him to face than the real war he's going away to fight."

———————

Dear Iris,

I hope this letter finds you safe and well. So far I am the same, but I have never seen such destruction as I have seen in Georgia.

Zack wrote quickly, never knowing when his troops might be called to action. General William Sherman was a taskmaster who often called for readiness by four o'clock in the morning. It was now nearly Christmas 1864, seventeen months since he'd left Iris at the train station in Washington, seventeen months of constant riding, on-the-spot training, marching through rain and cold nights, severing the South in half as Sherman wreaked havoc on Georgia. Now they rested in Savannah, and he and other officers suspected the next move would be up through the Carolinas. The weather was miserable, and he ached to the bone.

General Sherman shows no mercy, and although I do my duty as a soldier, it is upsetting to see whole cities burned and deserted. Sherman would, however, make a grand Indian fighter. I hope to someday serve under him again out west.

I understand now what you have seen in helping at the hospitals in Washington. When I was with Sheridan in Virginia, I witnessed an amputation, had to help hold the man down. I hope never to have to see such a thing again. Colonel Shaver was right in telling me this war would awaken me to what it really means to be a soldier. The fighting has been terrible, and the worst part is the fact that we are sometimes fighting old men, or young boys with no shoes. When I see the kind of men who are left to fight for the South, I know this war must end soon.

When this is over, I promise to come and visit before I go to my new command, which I hope will be in the

West. We learned about an Indian massacre in Colorado Territory and are now told the Cheyenne are committing raids and murders there.

Zack stopped a moment to shake off the memories such news made too vivid for him. He felt sorry for the innocent settlers who must be suffering greatly at the hands of the Cheyenne. Apparently an entire Cheyenne village had been wiped out by Colorado volunteers, and he supposed they deserved the punishment.

There is also trouble, we are told, in the Northwest with the Nez Perce, who have always been peaceful until the last year or so. Who knows what it is that turns peaceful hostiles into animals? It frustrates me that I can't be there to help, but at least by the time I go west again, I will be a seasoned fighter. I can hardly bear to think of what those people are suffering at the hands of the Indians, but someday I will be able to help put a stop to it.

I think of you often and hope this war will be over very soon. Say hello to your grandparents, and to your father for me the next time you write him. Please tell him to let Colonel Shaver know that so far I am alive and well.

Sincerely,

Zack

He studied the letter. Was it good enough? Should he tell her his true feelings, that he missed her terribly, thought about her all the time, fell asleep at night dreaming of lying in her arms? Should he admit he could remember every detail of her face? Should he tell her he loved her? No, that was too truthful. He didn't want to love, not Iris, not anyone. He had no room in his life for love.

He folded the letter and put it in an envelope, sealing and addressing it. He called a private into his tent, ordered the man to take the letter to be sent off with the other mail. He lay down on his cot, not bothering to remove his boots or uniform. A man had to be ready to jump up and fight in places like this. Snipers abounded, and he had discovered the

Confederates had a stubborn streak that would not let them give up against even the most formidable odds. The way some of them fought back, they truly seemed to think they could win this war, poor fools.

Strong Runner looked at the broken handle of the ax the government had sent in his last annuities. He had tried to use it to chop up some firewood, and not only had the handle broken, but the blade had chipped. He looked down at the broken blade and picked it up, throwing it and the handle aside angrily.

"Useless!" he fumed. "It is all useless! The blankets they gave us fall apart in the rain! What kind of fools does the white man's government take us for! They let the settlers come here and steal all our land, put up fences, build their homes, let their livestock graze on land we need for our horses! They do nothing about it! *Nothing!* We sign *treaties* that mean nothing."

Morning Star sat on a log nearby, breastfeeding her eight-month-old son, Wolf Boy. "I do not know what to say, Strong Runner. How can we go to war against forces so strong? Already we are surrounded by whites. We trade with them, yet for the slightest wrong they shoot us or hang us. We try to complain to the agent, but he is never there."

Strong Runner's hands clenched into fists. "I would like to kill all of them! The farmers, the miners, those who plant whole towns on our land, the government agents, the whiskey traders! Nothing they promised has come to be!"

Morning Star closed her eyes against tears. In her arms was her most prized possession, the fruit of the love between her and Strong Runner, the son of a proud, respected warrior. What lay in her precious child's future? And it hurt to see her husband always so angry and frustrated. "Come and sit beside me, Strong Runner. Watch your son feed from his mother's breast, and feel the peace. Somehow if we just continue doing what is right, we should win peacefully. All these years we have not made war against the white man."

Strong Runner sighed deeply, walking over to sit down beside her. "They say the Sioux chief, Red Cloud, is winning his war against soldiers and settlers in Montana."

"Perhaps, but they also say an entire Cheyenne village to the south was destroyed, many women and children murdered during the time of the frost. And when the white man's war is ended in the East, more soldiers will come . . . many more. It was soldiers who captured and hanged all those Sioux men in the land far away near the great waters." She blinked back tears. "I do not want to watch my husband die that awful way. Promise me you will remain at peace. We have this little bit of land here, our dwelling. You have many horses again."

Strong Runner shook his head. "That is no longer enough. It is not so much the loss of freedom and the useless supplies. It is the broken promises, the lies! The insults! Some thought it was funny that we were sent forty *dozen* pair of white women's elastic garters! White women's *garters*! How can they think us to be such fools! They actually thought we would laugh off such a mistake, that we would be happy to get such a silly trinket!"

Morning Star looked at him, capturing his dark eyes. She could not suppress a smile, but choked back a need to laugh aloud. "It is quite funny, my husband. I remember a time when our people laughed much. That is the gift the garters brought . . . laughter. It is a long time since I heard laughter from you, or even saw you smile; and you have such a handsome smile."

Strong Runner wanted to continue his scowl, but as always, his beautiful wife found a way to calm the storm in his soul. He studied her raven hair, and his gaze fell to her full breast, and to his strong, healthy new son who suckled there. The sight was calming, and helped soothe his growing hatred for those who seemed bent on destroying the Nez Perces. The sight of Wolf Boy's fierce feeding brought a soft smile to his lips. The boy always seemed to be hungry, and poor Morning Star hardly had time for her chores between feedings. They had been married only a year and a half, and already this woman of his had given him a son.

"I do not know what I would do without you in these times, Morning Star," he told her. "You are my refuge, the water that cools the fires of war in my heart. You take the lance out of my hand, and for you I will try to keep the peace, but it is so hard."

She nodded. "I know, Strong Runner. Your heart is proud, and that is as it should be. But we can take only one day at a time, and be glad for the peace we have that day, for our lives, our son's health. Old Chief Joseph says we should sign no more treaties, but that we also should not make war."

Strong Runner leaned closer, bending down to kiss her breasts and kiss his son's cheek. "Here is another warrior in the making." He met her eyes. "Who is to say for certain we could not win a war for our land? I am not so sure that's true, Morning Star."

"And who is to say we would not all be killed? I do not want my son to die like those Cheyenne at Sand Creek. If he must live the white man's way, then so be it. Perhaps we have no choice. We have already lived among them for many years."

"And always we were treated with respect, until now. The white traders and mountain men understood us. Some even married our women. But these new whites who come, they think us no more important than a bug. It is not the same, Morning Star. We ask for help against these new ones who come here and steal from us, and I know what the answer will be. When the white man's war is over, he will send his blue-coated soldiers to Indian country, not to protect the Indians, but to protect their own kind. They are coming, Morning Star, and I do not like the feel of it."

She reached up with her free hand and touched his cheek. "We can only wait and see . . . and stand as one people. We can only hope that when the Great Father in Washington no longer has to worry about his war, he will be able to give more time to our problem and find a way to see we are treated fairly. I have to believe this in order to sleep at night, and I have to believe my husband will not have to go to war."

Strong Runner could not bring himself to dash her hopes. He forced a smile. "Then maybe it will be so." He turned and straddled the log, pulling his wife and son into his arms. "Maybe it will be so."

9

Zack huddled into his slicker, shivering in spite of the woolen army coat he wore under the rain guard. Being wet was bad enough, but cold and wet was worse. He and his troops forged ahead, through mud and cold wind, obeying Sherman's orders to continue north toward Columbia, South Carolina. He and his men were guinea pigs of sorts, the advance guard for Sherman and his army of over fifty thousand men. Ahead of them lay Columbia, and after they took that, they would head into North Carolina and then Virginia—Richmond, the capital of the Confederacy. The only thing that gave him and the others the strength to go on through the miserable, muddy, bumpy roads and drippy, wet forests was the knowledge that an end to the war was surely at hand.

How could the South possibly go on? Lee's troops continued to retreat, a pitifully small number of men who were starving, many of them marching over frozen ground with bare feet. This was one of the coldest winters this part of the country had ever known, and the weather seemed to be taking as much a toll on the beleaguered rebels as was the oncoming Union Army.

He felt sick at some of the sights he had seen, homeless, penniless families, their rickety wagons packed with all the belongings they had left in the world, leaving homes where they had lived all their lives, many of them already headed west to start anew. Besides the thousands of displaced southern whites, the roads along the way were also filled with Negroes, many of them also fleeing, fearful of guerrilla attacks from angry, defeated southern slave owners. Sometimes Negroes could be seen standing on the front porches of grand homes that had once belonged to a wealthy southerner. He could not help feeling sorry for those Negroes who strung along with the Union troops, begging for food and help. They were a poor, uneducated lot who had suddenly been emancipated but didn't quite know what to do with their newfound freedom.

He felt a little guilty for being a part of so much destruction since first leaving for that swath through Georgia. Now there would be even more atrocities, but this was war, and a soldier obeyed his orders. His own orders were to send men ahead to make sure General Sherman did not stumble across a land mine. There were many planted sporadically along some of these back roads, and several men had already been wounded. There was also always the danger of sniper fire and occasional attacks from lingering hate-filled citizens who rallied themselves for one last stab at their Union invaders.

He was weary of the fighting, the tension of always being on his guard, the fear of death. Still, they all forged ahead, eager to finish this war. It would surely end when they reached Richmond. Once that city was taken, the rebels would have to surrender. Lee was on the run.

Never had he been so miserable. He had always thought it was supposed to be warm year-round in places like this. As far as he was concerned, the cold of Minnesota in winter was better than this. The cold, damp air seemed to penetrate all his clothing and work its way right into his bones. No matter how hard he tried, he couldn't seem to get warm, and these last few months had taught him the not-so-glamorous side of being a soldier, as well as how it feels to be at war, to wonder where the next bullet will come from, what it's like to sit in a saddle from sunup to sundown, to sleep on wet ground.

Sometimes they even slept in trees just to stay off the cold ground at night.

Corporal Adams rode beside him, carrying the cavalry guidon, the forked flag hanging limp and wet. "How long do you think before we make Columbia, sir?"

"Just a couple more days, probably sooner if we had decent weather. We—"

Zack was unable to finish the sentence. A shot rang out, and a bullet slammed through Adams's head, coming out of his left temple and whizzing past Zack so closely that he felt a rush of air. His horse reared as Corporal Adams fell from his horse, the guidon still in his hand. "Adams!" Zack shouted. He started to dismount, then heard another gunshot from somewhere in the thick forest to his right. A bullet tore into his right shoulder, but he managed to stay on his horse. "In the grass! In the grass!" he shouted to the men ahead of him. Pain engulfed him, and he was only vaguely aware of more gunfire, men shouting, rebel yells from somewhere in the trees, bugle calls behind him as the long line of thousands of Union soldiers prepared for yet another battle. All the sounds seemed muffled as Zack pulled his carbine from its boot. He raised it as he saw a few men emerge from the trees. He fired at one of them, and the man went down. Then he thought he heard an explosion, followed by a man's terrible screaming.

"My leg! My leg!" someone shouted.

More rebels came from the trees, some with guns, some with bayonets, some armed only with rocks. Zack dismounted to fight hand-to-hand, but was surprised to discover he couldn't quite keep his balance. He fell to the ground, shouting orders for his men to fire at will. Already he could hear more soldiers coming from the rear, and he wondered at the daring and near stupidity of the Confederates who had attacked them. There couldn't be many of them, and they would momentarily be surrounded by hundreds and eventually thousands of Yankee soldiers.

He spotted another, pulled his Colt .44 from its holster, and fired again, not even sure what had happened to his carbine. Against sickening pain he managed to crawl to the man who was screaming, thinking to do something to help him, knowing somewhere in the back of his mind the man had probably stepped on a buried mine.

He managed to get to his feet, stumbling toward the sound while gunfire raged all around him. Visions of the Pawnee attacking his family flashed into his mind so that suddenly he was back there, trying to reach his mother and sister, help them. He fell again, crawled through cold, slippery mud to the screaming soldier. The calf of his leg seemed to be cut nearly in half, the bottom portion lying at an odd angle and a piece of bone protruding from the stump just below his knee. Blood poured from the wound, mixing into the water and mud as it began raining even harder.

"Oh, God, help me! Help me, Lieutenant!" the man sobbed.

Zack quickly untied a scarf from around the private's neck and wrapped it around the injured leg, just above the knee, to tie off the bleeding. He got to his knees and pulled his sword from the scabbard he wore. Since the man's leg remained attached only by muscle and a little skin, he knew what he had to do. In spite of the pain worsening in his arm and chest, he managed to bring the sword down and hack off what was left of the leg.

Just then he heard a rebel yell, and he turned in time to face a man charging them, carrying only a hunting knife. Quickly he rammed his sword hard through the rebel's chest, and let the man fall with the sword still in him. Before he could yank it out he felt another jolt, this time in his right hip. He wasn't sure what had hit him, a bullet or perhaps another rebel's sword. He knew only that the pain was horrible.

He looked at the private he'd tried to help. He was just a boy, perhaps seventeen, and he lay there, crying. Suddenly he saw little Emily's face. He crawled over and put his arms around the private, unaware of the considerable fighting going on around him. Rain poured down in a sudden torrent, and he remained huddled over the private, trying to keep him from getting wetter.

Zack felt his mother put a cool cloth on his forehead. She always did that when he had a fever. He'd been sick this way once when he was younger, feverish, a cough that brought terrible pain to his chest. The trouble was, this time when he coughed it brought other pain, through his arms and shoulders, and in his right hip and leg. He wanted to ask his mother why, but he couldn't seem to find his voice, and she was such a blur, even though she leaned close to him.

"Mother," he whispered.

She leaned even closer, but it was not his mother's voice. "What did you say, Zack?"

"Hurts . . . everywhere," he groaned.

"I know. I just thank God they sent you here to Washington." She put cool hands to either side of his face. "Can you see me, Zack? Do you know who I am? Please don't die, Zack, please. I couldn't bear it. Father's dead, Zack. Do you hear me? Father's dead, and I just want to die too."

He heard tears. The woman leaned down to put her head on his shoulder. He struggled to think who it might be. It wasn't his mother. His mother was dead. . . . He blinked, his vision clearing a little more.

He remembered now, riding with Sherman, all the destruction. This was not why he'd put on a uniform, gone to West Point, become a sharpshooter. This wasn't the kind of war he'd wanted. Vaguely, slowly, it all came back to him.

He focused on the top of the room, realizing after a moment it was not a regular room at all. It was a tent. He could hear others now, groans all around him, someone screaming farther away, maybe in another tent. It smelled, bad smells, the smell of the sick and dying. He tried to move, but couldn't without terrible pain. It hurt so bad to breathe, he grunted and broke out in more sweat.

His movement and groan caused the woman who'd been crying on his shoulder to straighten. Maybe he was dying. She had golden hair, like an angel's, and such a pretty face in spite of the fact that it was covered with tears. Her hair coming loose of the bun at the top of her head fell in little strings around her face. Finally his senses cleared. "Iris!" he said softly in surprise. "How . . . did you . . . get here?"

"Oh, Zack!" She shivered in another sob. "You know me! That has to be a good sign!" She took a handkerchief from her pocket and blew her nose and wiped at her eyes. "You're in Washington, Zack. They brought you up the coast by ship with some other wounded men. The army surgeon said you were unconscious or delirious most of the time. You lost so

much blood, and you nearly lost an arm, but they saved it."
She applied the cool rag to his forehead again.

Zack struggled to concentrate on what she was telling
him. Washington? He was in Washington? So much information all at once, and she seemed so distraught. Iris! His beautiful Iris! She was right there beside him, wearing a plain gray,
bloodstained dress. It didn't seem possible. How many times
had he thought about her while in that damned war? Every
day. Every night. He had tried so hard not to care, but it
didn't work.

"Every day I checked the rosters of the dead and
wounded," she was saying. "And every day I went through
every single hospital building and tent, praying I wouldn't
find you, because that would mean you were so badly
wounded you couldn't be left in the field to recover. But if
you *did* have to come here, I wanted to be the one to tend to
you. I so wanted you to return to me whole and healthy,
Zack, but I know you're going to get better now. You'll get
over this pneumonia, and you'll recover from your wounds, I
just know it. God sent you to me. It's a good sign, Zack, and
I so much need some hope. Did you hear me tell you? Father's dead, Zack. He's dead! I still can't believe it."

Dead? Colonel Gray? How? He was having trouble sorting
all this in his confused mind. And he had been badly
wounded. He managed to move his hands into fists just to
make sure someone hadn't cut off an arm. He wiggled his
toes. Yes, he could feel them. He tried to talk again, but a
horrible racking cough engulfed him, the agony of it enhanced by the pain in his limbs and hip. He spit up phlegm,
and quickly Iris cleaned it away. She helped him drink some
water, and he leaned back against a stack of pillows.

"We have you in an inclined position," Iris told him. "The
doctor says you must not lie flat. You could drown from a
buildup of fluid in your lungs."

Zack found it astounding that this young woman who
was so well bred, the daughter of a colonel, would be working in a stinking hospital tent, surrounded by blood and gore.
She was surprisingly strong. "How bad . . . wounds?" he managed to groan.

Iris dabbed at her eyes again. "You took a bullet through
your right arm and into your chest, Zack. Another in your

right hip. They weren't sure you'd live at first, but after a few days it wasn't so much the danger of the wounds, according to the ship doctor. It was the pneumonia they were concerned about. The doctor here said that if you could lick the pneumonia, you'd probably heal completely, but it will take a long, long time. I'll help you, Zack. I'll be here every step of the way. I'm even going to see if they will allow me to take you home, to my grandparents' house, once you're a little better. I can't bear for you to have to lie here in this horrible place, all alone. I know you'd heal faster at my grandparents' home, and I could be with you all the time, give you all my attention."

He studied her blue eyes, still wondering if he had died or lost his mind. It just didn't seem possible he could be in South Carolina one minute, and then wake up in Washington, D.C., with Iris Gray sitting beside his bed. He must have been completely delirious for at least a week, maybe longer.

He noticed then how worn Iris looked, still beautiful in her own natural way, but so much thinner, dark circles under her blue eyes. Had he heard her right? Her father was dead? "Your . . . father?"

New tears came. She shook her head. "He was sent to Virginia. It was a rather sudden decision. He was a good friend of General Grant's. Grant, President Lincoln, and other leaders think Lee will be forced to surrender soon, and Grant thought Father would like to be a part of the momentous event. Father was in command of troops headed through Virginia into North Carolina to join Sherman when he arrived there. He was to ride into Virginia with the victorious Union march to be a part of the last campaign, but he was killed. . . . " The words caught in her throat. "By sniper fire before he ever reached Sherman. I still can't believe it. It happened about a month ago. I still expect him to come home, put his arms around me and tell me it was all a mistake."

She jerked in a sob and wiped her eyes again. "I was never able to picture my father gone that way. He was such a big, robust man, so healthy for his age. I was going to go and live with him next summer . . . so we could be together more. I always imagined taking care of him, even after he retired. He was so lonely after my mother died. Now I have no one. No one . . . except you, Zack. Thank God you're not dead too. I wouldn't have wanted to go on living."

His heart ached for her, but he felt that little touch of alarm at the words *I have no one except you*. Did she take it for granted he would always be there for her? Take it for granted he loved her? He closed his eyes. Hell, yes, he loved her; and with her father dead, he sure as heck couldn't keep denying it. If he got well, he couldn't go away and leave her all alone. She had her grandparents, but they were getting old. He hadn't wanted to care about her like this, but right now he felt his heart going out to her, making it impossible to turn away from her. If only he could move, he'd embrace her. She needed his strength, and he had none to give her.

He reached out his left hand. Iris saw the gesture, and she gratefully took his hand with her own. Zack closed his fingers around her hand. "It's going to be all right, Iris. I'll be all right and things will get better." Should he say it? Was it just his need of her, or perhaps the long months away from her? Was it because she looked like an angel sitting there? Or maybe it was because he felt sorry for her in her loss. "I love you, Iris."

Her eyes widened, and more tears came. "Oh, Zack," she whispered. She leaned down and kissed his hand. "I love you too."

"What are you doing here!" Strong Runner sat proudly on his Appaloosa gelding, glaring at the three men who were erecting a wooden fence only a mile from his dwelling. All three had stood watching him carefully as he approached, and he in turn kept a steady eye on them, making sure they did not reach for a rifle or handgun. As he came closer, he realized they were unarmed.

"We, uh, we're building a fence, as you can see," one of them told him. "There's been an early thaw this year, enough that we can dig holes for posts at least. We've decided to take up residence here—pretty country. Came out for gold, didn't find any, but we don't want to leave. We've already sent for our wives." The man who spoke was tall and thin, wore a dark suit, and sported a beard nearly to his waist.

Strong Runner felt nauseated at the sight of the beard. He could not understand how white men could stand to have so much hair on their faces, let alone that they would let it grow so long. "What is your name?"

The man swallowed and looked at the others. "Bates. Lewis Bates. This here is my brother, Jonathan, and my brother-in-law, Charlie Moser. What's it to you, Indian?"

Strong Runner studied the other two. Jonathan was skinny like his brother, but shorter, his beard close cropped. Charlie was a hefty man, rather unkempt, his hair greasy where it stuck out from under his cap. All of them looked rather cocky, like most whites who came west to mine or settle. "I want to know because I will report your presence to the soldiers and the agency. This is Nez Perce land. You have no right putting up a fence here. My own dwelling is only a mile away."

They all looked at one another again before Lewis Bates answered. "And what might *your* name be, so that we can report you as a troublemaker?"

Strong Runner's horse skittered slightly, and all three men jumped back, as though they expected violence. If not for his own anger, Strong Runner thought how their reaction would be humorous. And if times were different, there *would* be violence. These three would be dead. "When one man tries to take another man's land, the one who tries to take it is the troublemaker. Get off this land. Go and settle somewhere off the reservation!"

Charlie snickered, glancing at his brother-in-law as though this were all a big joke. Lewis stood a little straighter, looking confident. "You know whites are settling all around here. It can't be stopped, Indian. Besides, the Nez Perces have been cohabiting with whites for a generation now. Why are you so upset? You *are* a Nez Perce, aren't you? All you Indians look alike, you know."

Strong Runner shook his head. "If you whites had any intelligence, you would see that all tribes are different. Your ignorance shows, but apparently you are not embarrassed by it. And just because others settle here does not make it right. They are stealing Nez Perce land, and we will see that they leave . . . one way or another."

"And what's that supposed to mean?" Charlie said, putting his hands on his hips. "If you're thinkin' on makin' war, Indian, you'd better think twice. Our own civil war is likely to end soon, and then you'll see plenty more soldiers out here, *plenty* more. They won't be here to protect your lands. They'll be here to protect *us*. It's a plain and simple fact that we're here to stay, Indian, so get used to it. Nothing is going to change. And just because you Nez Perces got yourselves educated and Christianized, that don't change a thing. An Indian is an Indian, and Indians have no rights."

Strong Runner nudged his horse forward, then gave it a silent order using only his feet and legs. Wind Rider was his best mount. He'd worked with the animal many hours, and he felt they shared the same spirit. The horse seemed to understand his anger, and the Appaloosa made a quick turn so that its rump bumped into Charlie, knocking the man to the ground.

"Hey! What do you think you're doing!" Lewis shouted.

"Goddamn Indian!" Jonathan grumbled. He turned to help Charlie to his feet.

Strong Runner whirled Wind Rider in a full circle to face all three men. "That is just a little warning. You are on Nez Perce land! Stay, and you will find out just what rights we have. Your fence cuts through land I use for grazing my horses in the spring. However much you build each day, I will take it down at night. Send your soldiers! It will do no good. Already the soldiers have given up their forts on the road the white man uses to reach his precious gold in Dakota Territory. They have failed there, and they will fail here!" He yanked a tomahawk from his gear, wanting to laugh at the terrified looks on the white men's faces. "You think the Nez Perces will never make war! Do not be so sure! Leave your women where they are and go home to them, where you belong!"

They backed away more, and Jonathan pointed his finger at Strong Runner. "We're going to report this, you savage! You people had better be careful, or you'll lose what little land you have left. And the only reason the soldiers up in Montana are having trouble is that there aren't enough of them. You just wait till our civil war is over, redskin! You just wait. They'll come, more than you could ever count! Someday you'll see our fences all over your damn land, if you're even still alive to see it!"

They turned and ran for their horses, and Strong Runner

watched them, remaining ready to defend himself. They mounted up, and Charlie pulled out his rifle. Lewis ordered him not to bother. "There could be more of them hiding somewhere," he warned. "You know how sneaky Indians can be. Maybe he tried to start something on purpose!" He looked back at Strong Runner, then at the other two. "He won't get away with this."

Charlie shoved his rifle back into its boot, turning to glare at Strong Runner. "Dirty Indian!" he shouted. "Your days are numbered!"

The three of them turned their horses and rode off. Strong Runner watched until they were out of sight, his emotions burning. Hatchet in hand, he dismounted, walked up to the fence, and hacked away at it for nearly an hour out of pure rage. With every ounce of energy and strength he kicked down freshly buried posts, split rails into pieces, until finally exhaustion took over and he stood there panting, sweating in spite of the cold weather.

With tears in his eyes he dropped to his knees and bent over to catch his breath. He gripped his hatchet and threw back his head, sighing deeply. "Send your soldiers," he groaned. "I am ready!"

10

MAY 1865

*I*ris was relieved when after six weeks Zack was taken to a more pleasant hospital, set up for patients who needed long-term care. For eight weeks now she had visited him there daily, had watched him go from hardly being able to walk at all to walking with only a slight limp. He was sure to be released soon.

Her original request to bring him home to her grandparents' had been denied. Those in charge declared that an army man with no family of his own belonged in an army hospital. Some of the other nurses, all older and married, had frowned on her even suggesting it. They said it was shameful and wrong, and as soon as they realized Iris was in love with Zack Myers, she had not been permitted to nurse him. She was allowed only short daily visits. She couldn't even help with the physical therapy needed for rebuilding his muscles and strength.

"Fiddle," she murmured. "He'll be out of here soon, and then no one can stop us from doing whatever we want." She adjusted her hat, a straw bonnet decorated with silk flowers. She had decided that today she would do no nursing. Today was a day for celebrating. She would look as pretty as she could for Zack. He was well enough that they should start thinking about the future, and she was determined that meant marriage. Zack had not mentioned it, and she knew he was afraid of such a total commitment, afraid to care that deeply. Once on the mend, he had not said that he loved her again in spite of the fact that every day before she left him she said she loved him and kissed him on the cheek. She could see him slowly withdrawing from her in spite of their warm conversations and his friendly, gentle attitude. The scared little boy was often there in his eyes, and took over more and more the stronger he got. That little boy had had loved ones torn from his life, and he never wanted to feel that loss again.

She entered the large, airy room where Zack stayed, only to find it empty. Several of the other men greeted her warmly. They all knew she came every day to see Zack, and Zack had often mentioned the ribbing they gave him after she left.

"Your sweetheart is waiting in the gardens out back," one of the men told her teasingly.

"You sure look pretty today, Miss Gray, but then, you always do," said another. "Just *extra* pretty today."

"Thank you, Tom." Iris was pleased at the remark. She *wanted* to look good for Zack today. She'd worn a yellow, ruffled dress to match the pretty spring day. It was warm and beautiful, and with Zack better, and the news she'd heard . . .

"You ready to celebrate?" Tom asked her.

She smiled. "Yes. Isn't it wonderful? The war is finally over."

Sadness filled Tom's eyes for a brief moment as he rubbed his thigh, now just a stump. "Yeah, I'm sure glad of that."

"Oh, I'm sorry, Tom. I only meant—"

"Sure, I know. We're all happy about it. It's just too bad there's so many wounded men like me, and so many men like your father."

Iris nodded, the aching pain returning to her chest. *Daddy*, she thought. It still did not seem possible that she would never see her father again. How he would have loved to celebrate today.

She hurried out to find Zack, descending cement steps and walking behind the building. She loved D.C. in the spring. Home gardens already sported daisies and crocus. The magnolia trees were opening, the grass a soft green color. In spite of her losses, her heart was full of hope, love, joy. Zack was almost completely mended. Lee had surrendered to Grant. Zack could return to the army life he loved, and she would go with him. She was not going to allow him out of her life again.

She rounded a corner at the back of the building to see a man standing near a huge rosebush, and her heart took a leap. She had not seen Zack in uniform since he'd left her at the train station nine months earlier. "Zack?"

He turned, and she drew in her breath at the sight of him. He, too, must have heard the news and had the same idea that they should celebrate. He was wearing his dress blues, a yellow stripe down the sides of his pants. Gold braid adorned the front of the hip-length jacket in the form of five crossbars with a cloverleaf design on each end of the bars. More gold braiding in a figure-eight and cloverleaf design decorated the cuffs of the jacket, and he wore his black felt wide-brimmed hat turned up at one side, signifying that he was an officer. The silver bars of a lieutenant adorned the shoulders of his jacket. He wore no weapons, but Iris knew that he was eager to put them on again . . . for a different kind of fighting.

She didn't want to think about that now. He looked splendid, tall, so handsome! He'd put on weight, although he was still a little thin. To think of the condition he was in when he was first brought there, it seemed a miracle to see him standing like that. He smiled, the handsome smile that had first smitten her when she met him at Fort Snelling. "You heard," she said.

He nodded. "It's over. But that isn't the best of it."

Iris watched him carefully. His green eyes sparkled with eagerness. This had to have something to do with the army. "Where did you get that uniform?"

He walked closer, still showing the slight limp. He had been exercising the hip and leg every day, determined that someday there would be no limp at all. "A corporal brought it to me a couple of weeks ago. I was saving it for something special. When I got the news this morning—not about the war being over—something else—I wanted to look my best for you."

"And what news is that?"

Their gazes held lovingly. Zack was on fire for her. It was good to feel healthy again, to be free of pain except for the lingering ache in his hip. She looked especially beautiful today, like a yellow daisy. How could he not love her, much as he'd wanted to fight it? She'd been so dedicated and strong, coming to see him every day while also helping nurse other men. She had been faithful, dependable, loving, had all the qualities an army officer needed in a wife.

Did he dare think he could marry the daughter of Colonel John Gray, even though the man was dead? He'd met her grandparents, knew they would not object. The only thing left was to get permission from Howard Shaver, now a colonel, according to the letter he'd received this morning. "Do you remember Lieutenant-Colonel Howard Shaver?"

Iris nodded. "He's the one who found you after your family was killed." There it was, deep in those green eyes of his. Whenever his family's death was mentioned, there was a little change in him, a fleeting look of bitterness, hatred, anger, even when he was happy.

"Yes," he replied. "I got a letter from him this morning. He's been promoted to colonel, and he has asked that I come back under his command; but that isn't the best of it. Remember when I told you about that private I tried to help after I'd been shot?"

Iris folded her arms and smiled at his excitement. "I remember."

"I never have been able to even find out who it was. But he apparently remembered me. He was sent to a different hospital. He told the army doctor I saved his life, and the doctor went to his commander and told him, who in turn found out who I was, who my superiors were and so forth. Word got back to Shaver, who decided I should be rewarded. He has connections here in Washington. His letter this morning was to inform me that I have been recommended for promotion to captain! And he has requested I be sent out west under his command. He's being transferred to Fort Connor in Nebraska Territory. The area is being called Wyoming now, looks like it might become another state. The post is the base for Brigadier General Patrick Connor's Indian campaign. They're trying to get the Sioux to settle down, and they need reinforcements. With the Civil War over, I can finally go back out west!"

Iris wanted to be happy for him, but she knew by the things her father had told her that Indians, especially the Sioux and Cheyenne, could be a much more formidable enemy than the Confederate Army. They were very skilled at warfare, cunning, clever, and prone to committing life-threatening acts of bravery just to "touch" their enemy. She grasped Zack's hands. "Oh, Zack, I'm happy for your promotion. Just please don't let your hatred of the Indians get in the way of making the right decisions."

His smile faded. "This is what I've always wanted, Iris. Nothing is going to spoil it for me. I just—it's pretty remote out there. I doubt there are many comforts, and God only knows how much I'll get moved around over the next few years. With all the Indian trouble, we've got to concentrate on the West now. New posts are being built all the time, and it seems the government is in almost constant talks with different tribes. Shaver says the problem in the Northwest with the Nez Perces is growing. A lot of them are educated, even Christianized, yet there is still trouble brewing. That just goes to show that even educating the Indians doesn't take the violence out of them."

Iris sighed, squeezing his hands. "Zack, I know you don't want to hear it, but you must give it some balance, and allow yourself to understand how they must feel. You won't be able to make rational decisions until you can put yourself in their position once in a while. If you can understand them, that could lead to instances where you can *avoid* a battle, solve a problem peacefully."

He let go of her hands. "Indians don't understand peace. They only understand killing anyone they consider the enemy."

Iris closed her eyes and sighed. "It's always this way. Colonel Shaver thought sending you here for a taste of war, getting you involved in something besides the Indian matter, would help ease some of the intensity of your feelings against the Indians. He probably thinks giving you this promotion will also help. The higher you move in rank, the more intelligent decisions you will have to make, Zack."

He removed his hat, running a hand through his dark

hair, and searched her eyes pleadingly. "How can I make you understand, Iris?"

She watched him sympathetically. "I wish you *would* try to make me understand. I have asked you so many times to explain it, Zack, but you always refuse to talk about it. I *love* you, and you've said you love me. When you were saying how remote Fort Connor is, you were hinting at something, weren't you? Were you trying to tell me you'd like me to go with you?"

God, she was beautiful. Did he dare take such a treasure to a dangerous, remote place like Wyoming? Still, she'd proven her strength over and over, and he damn well knew she wanted to be an officer's wife, had originally planned to be with her father, no matter where he was stationed. "You know I would, Iris. I haven't said much over these months about . . . about how much I love you. I kept hoping that once I was better, I'd come to my senses. But I know I'll always need you, Iris; sick or healthy, I need you with me."

She wanted to shout with joy. It was as much as a marriage proposal, although she knew he'd have to get permission from Colonel Shaver first. The man cared about Zack almost like a son. He'd never refuse the request. For the moment, though, this man with whom she wanted to share her life had to learn to share *everything* with her, not just outer pain, but the inner pain.

"Then open up to me, Zack. A man and woman who love each other to the point of being husband and wife"—she felt a quick rush of passion and desire at the meaning of those words—"should be able to share all things, Zack, not just . . ." She felt her cheeks getting hotter. "Not just bodies, but what's inside. You know me pretty well that way. I'm an open book, but you, Zack Myers, keep a lot of things inside, including what happened when you were ten years old, and it continues to fester inside. Tell me about it, Zack. Please."

She watched him turn away, prayed he would not react with anger, the way he usually did.

"Zack Myers, I will not marry you until you tell me. Help me understand, and maybe then I can help you deal with it."

He stood with his back to her, gripping the back of a wooden lawn chair so tightly his knuckles were getting white. She waited, knew he was struggling on the inside, wanting to hide his pain. If he truly loved and wanted her, he had to prove it by sharing that one part of him he had refused to share with anyone before.

"I was milking our cow, Jessie," he said, his voice strained. "She was being stubborn. She'd lost a calf and after that she just wouldn't give any milk. My pa—" He hesitated. Oh, how it hurt to think of his father and the way he'd died. "Pa told me to try to milk her again before I went to the fields to help with picking corn. It was fall in Kansas."

He took a deep breath, still refused to face her. "They came so fast. They must have been hiding in the cornfield. My baby sister, Emily . . . she came to the barn to talk to me. She started teasing me and I chased her out of the barn. That's when we saw her . . . our mother . . . lying on the porch at the house, an arrow in her chest. I'll never know if she died right then or later, after they—"

He stopped to clear his throat, and Iris could see he was struggling with the words.

"After they raped and scalped her."

Iris closed her eyes, putting a hand to her stomach.

"Emily ran to her before I could stop her. I could hear my pa screaming somewhere in the cornfield. The soldiers who found him said he was tortured. I ran to try to help my mother and sister, tried to push them off my mother, but one of them grabbed me, slashed my face with his knife. That's where my scar came from." He shook his head. "It was all so quick and I was so young. There was nothing I could do. They slit my little sister's throat so deeply, they nearly cut off her head and they . . . they scalped her too. I ran into the house to get Pa's gun and locked the door. I couldn't figure out why they left me alive, until I realized they thought it was all a game. They were waiting for me to come back out. When I didn't, they set the house on fire."

He took another deep breath, quickly wiping his eyes and sniffling before continuing. Iris listened in total sorrow, wishing she could erase the memory for him.

"What they didn't know was my pa and I had dug an escape tunnel, out from a root cellar." He shook his head. "If only we had known they were out there. We could have all escaped. I'll always remember that morning, climbing out of a warm bed up in the cabin loft, hearing my pa giving orders, my mother making breakfast. We had pancakes. I'll always remember that, remember my mother's face, remember her telling me to eat plenty so I'd have energy for my chores. She was a good woman, gave us reading and writing lessons herself because we didn't have a school to go to. We were a happy family." He finally turned and looked at her. "Until that black day!"

His green eyes narrowed in hatred, and his lips curled slightly as he spoke. "The Pawnee destroyed that happiness, destroyed my family! I crawled through that dark tunnel, dirt falling in my hair and eyes. I was terrified! I made it out, several yards behind the house, hid in a little dugout covered with boards and brush. When I peeked out, I saw our house burned nearly to the ground, same with the outbuildings. I was afraid to come out, until I saw soldiers come. I learned later that the same bunch of troublemakers had attacked some other settlements. The soldiers were on their trail. Too bad they didn't get there sooner." He blinked back tears. "When I got back to the house, I noticed my sister's—" His voice choked, and he stopped to clear his throat again. "My sister had a doll she carried with her everywhere. She treated it like it was a real person. She called the doll Miss Nancy." He rubbed his lips when they began to tremble. "Miss Nancy was, uh, she was lying next to Emily. I told the soldiers to bury the doll with her. She would have wanted that."

"Oh, Zack, I'm so sorry. What can I say? What can I do?" Iris stepped closer, tears in her eyes.

Zack quickly wiped his eyes again, struggling to keep his composure. "Nothing, of course. It sounds silly, but what made it all cave in on me was when one of the soldiers said there was a dead cow in the burned-out barn." He was unable to speak for the next few seconds. "Poor old Jessie. I have no idea why their killing that dumb cow made it all worse."

Iris touched his arm. "Zack, there is nothing wrong with a man crying over a memory like that. Maybe you need to—"

"The only thing I need to do is stop the Indians from killing anyone else!" he said, facing her again. His eyes glittered with fire, and his face darkened in anger. "No settler out west will be safe until they're all either dead or pushed onto reservation land to stay! Look what happened in Minnesota with the Sioux! Sure, we put a stop to it, but they all just retreated into the Dakotas and they're still making trouble! Red Cloud and his renegades have even managed to close some of the forts out there. The Sioux and Cheyenne both have been on a rampage, but that will stop once more soldiers are sent west, now that the war is over. They've had their heyday, and it's going to stop!"

Iris faced him squarely. "Then let it stop through fair treatment and through treaties, not because men like you ride out and slaughter them like dogs! Don't be another John Chivington, Zack! You know what happened at Sand Creek. After all the celebrating over a military victory, the truth came out that Sand Creek was nothing but the slaughter of women and little children. That was no brave battle. It was *murder*! Why *shouldn't* the Cheyenne be on the warpath after what happened at Sand Creek! And what about the Indians who attacked your family? Did you ever discover who they were, why they did it?"

Zack stiffened defensively. "They know the leader was called Three Feathers. His wife had been raped by white hunters, so they say."

"There! It was an eye for an eye, exactly the same as *you* are thinking! What if we were married, Zack, and Indians came and raped and murdered me? You would want to go out and kill every Indian in sight, wouldn't you? You would want *them* to hurt the way *you* hurt. What makes you think it isn't the same for an Indian man? Perhaps it's worse, because Indians can't get any kind of justice through our legal system. They have no defense, nor do they have the power to bring charges against any white man, no matter what terrible things white men might do to them. Don't you see? Revenge just breeds more hatred. It's a vicious circle that can end only when one party or the other decides to *let* it end. You could kill every Indian you see, and it wouldn't bring back your family. *I* can give you a *new* family, and as an army officer stationed in the West, you can do your share of keeping the peace. Maybe you'll have peace inside at last, just from knowing you're loved again."

He studied her eyes. "I don't think I can ever stop hating them, Iris. And I don't understand why you defend them, especially after what I have just told you."

Iris grasped his hands. "Think about it, Zack. Is their hatred going to be any less after Sand Creek? Where does it all end, Zack? When they're *all* dead? Is *that* how you want it?" He did not reply, but she read the bitterness in his eyes, eyes that could be so gentle and full of love one minute, so full of hatred the next. She shook her head. "No, Zack. It can't be that way. Remember one thing. They *were* here first. They think they are defending what is theirs, the same as any man would do. And when they do awful things to women and children, it's usually because awful things were done to their women and children. And if you want me to marry you, I have to know one thing first. I have to know if you are capable of shooting down Indian women, or putting your sword through the heart of a little Indian child. Is that the way you would fight them? Would you kill little children, Zack? I need to know, because I won't marry a man who could do a thing like that, not even if he were a five-star general!"

She let go of his hands and stepped back. His eyes were still red and watery. She watched his jaw muscles flex as he stood there, reeling with emotions and memories, but his gaze did not leave her own for one moment.

Zack thought about Emily, how free of hatred she'd been at her age, how ignorant of bigotry. It had been no different for him at ten years of age. He swallowed before speaking, still finding it difficult not to break down over reopening old wounds.

"All children are innocent," he answered.

Iris nodded. "That's right." She closed her eyes and took a deep breath of relief. "I'm so glad you answered that way. You're a good man, Zack Myers, an honorable man, too honorable to be as brutal and unrelenting as part of you thinks you want to be." She reached up and touched his shoulders. "Someday all that hatred will be gone, Zack. And I intend to help chase it away. You'll be a better soldier for it. And probably a better husband."

He suddenly put his arms around her and pressed her close, kissing her hair. "You'll marry me, then?"

She reached around his neck and breathed deeply of the scent of him. It felt good to have his strong arms around her. She kissed the scar on his cheek, rested her head on his shoulder. "You know I will."

He grasped the back of her neck with one hand, massaging gently. "It feels so good to hold you, so good to be loved. I'll have to get Colonel Shaver's permission, but I have no doubt he'll give it. We'll probably have to wait until I get my orders, and can go out there to see what it's like."

"It doesn't matter, Zack, as long as I'm with you." She kissed his cheek again. "But for now I have to stay behind anyway. Grandmother has taken ill, and I owe her and my grandfather so much. I must stay here and help him take care of her. The doctor thinks she's dying. I can't leave them now."

Zack studied the blue eyes that had begun to haunt his nights. "I'm sorry. I guess we have no choice but to wait, then." He met her mouth again, searching deeply, suddenly on fire for her. How could he wait to be inside this woman? That was all he had wanted since he'd first met her, to see her naked, touch her secret places, taste her breasts, claim her for himself. She returned his kiss hungrily, and he felt an aching need that told him he was more healed than he thought. His hip hurt him, but he suspected he could easily forget the pain if he were inside Iris Gray. He left her mouth, kissed her eyes, her forehead, her cheeks.

Iris leaned her head back and let him kiss her throat. "Zack, I don't want to wait for you to go out and come back. I want to be your wife," she said, feeling a wonderful desire rush through her blood. "Wire Colonel Shaver right away. Find out where he is and get an answer."

He found her mouth again. Iris savored the kiss, the way his full lips parted her own suggestively. How could she wait weeks or perhaps months to share her body with this man?

He kissed her throat again. "I just thought—" Another kiss. "You'd want a waiting period after the proposal." Another kiss. "But I don't really want to wait either."

They stopped kissing long enough to look into each other's eyes, and both felt the fire growing. "I am not going to let you leave before I know the full pleasure of being a woman," Iris told him. "And no one but you can give me that pleasure. Marry me before you leave, Zack. I don't want to wait even another day, but if you wire Colonel Shaver right away, we should have an answer in just a few more days."

"And what if he says no? Would that really stop us?"

She smiled through tears. She loved him so, wanted so much to bring out the love in his soul, do everything she could to erase the hatred there. "It could cost you your promotion. I thought that was the most important thing to you."

He grinned. "Not anymore. Some soldier told me once that a woman can make a man do some pretty strange things. Now I know what he was talking about." He met her mouth again in a fiery kiss. God, how he needed her, wanted her, worshipped her. He opened his eyes just long enough to notice an older woman, a nurse, looking from the window of the hospital building. He released her lips, gently pushed her away. "We're being watched."

They laughed at the sight of each other, their faces warm from passion, both of them breathing heavily, hardly able to think straight for want of the other. Iris pushed a piece of fallen hair behind her ear, smoothed her dress. "There is a shed behind my grandparents' house," she told him. "Grandfather keeps it spotless, and Grandma has some old quilts stored in there. My grandfather went to visit a sick brother in Maryland for the day. I have to get back and see to Grandma. She's suddenly having trouble getting around."

Zack wasn't sure what she was getting at. "I'm sorry about your grandmother. When they brought the carriage to take me for a visit a couple of weeks ago, she seemed fine."

Iris's eyes teared. "It has all come on rather suddenly. The doctor says her heart is failing her. I can hardly stand so much loss, Zack. My mother, my father, now perhaps Grandma. She's been so sweet to me." She sniffed back her tears. "Zack, I love you and need you so much. Pretty soon all we'll have is each other, don't you see? Through each other we'll find the love we've lost." She took his hand. "Come home with me to visit Grandma. As soon as I know she's resting, I'll tell her we're going for a walk. We can go around back, sneak into the shed . . ."

Zack frowned in surprise. Was she saying what he thought she was saying? Desire surged through him almost painfully. "If we do that, we'll have to get married no matter what Shaver's answer is."

She smiled through tears. "Didn't we already agree on that?"

Zack squeezed her hand. "Are you sure you want to do this?"

She nodded. "I'm sure. Come home with me now, Zack.

I want to make love. I don't want to wait. My buggy is out front, and right now you don't really have to answer to any-body."

He leaned down to kiss her mouth. "I don't want to wait either."

Iris thought she might faint with desire. She watched his eyes, suddenly unsure of herself. "Do you know how—I mean, I don't know much about this. Have you been with . . . you know . . . other women?"

Zack could not help a quick laugh. "I know what to do."

She pouted. "I don't like the way you said that. How many? Who were they?"

Zack just grinned, pulling her close again. "Does it matter now? The point is, none of them were important, and I have never been in love like this, Iris Gray, never gave a thought to marriage. For nearly four months we've talked about love, talked about everything else, been good friends. I guess that's the best way to start, as good friends. Today you got some-thing out of me nobody else ever has, and that's part of what I love about you. You like to know a person from the inside out. I love you. It feels good to say it."

She touched his lips. "And I love you."

He kissed her once more, then took her hand and led her around to the front of the building. He winced with pain as he climbed into the buggy, but he was determined to ignore that pain once he got Iris Gray into that old shed.

*I*ris nervously tucked a blanket around her grandmother's lap. "Are you sure you'll be all right this way for a little while?"

"Yes, child, you go take a walk with your young man." She glanced at Zack. "You two are very much in love, aren't you?"

Zack smiled. "Yes, ma'am,."

"Do you intend to marry her?"

Zack nodded. "Yes, I do, if your husband will approve."

The old woman waved her hand as though it were a silly remark. "Of course he'll approve. He likes you very much, Zack, and anyone Iris loves we love too. I'm just happy Iris has found someone, especially an army man. She so worshipped her father, you know. His death has been hard on her."

"Yes, Mrs. Harris. We all know what it's like to lose loved ones. When her mother died, you lost a daughter. I lost my whole family when I was only ten."

"Iris told us about that." She sighed. "There is a time to mourn, Zack, and a time to look to the future. Now you and

Iris must look to the future. I hope that you get clearance to marry soon. I fear I don't have long left in this life. I would like to see her married before I die."

"Grandma, don't talk that way." Iris leaned over and hugged her, and her grandmother patted her shoulder.

"I am only saying that I'd feel better knowing my baby will have a good man to take care of her."

Iris straightened. "I don't need taking care of. You know that. I'm marrying Zack only because I love him and I want to be with him." She placed a hand on Zack's arm. "Besides, maybe it's Zack who needs taking care of."

Her grandmother laughed. "That's what most men don't realize. They think they're taking care of the woman, but most of the time the man could never get by without her."

Zack laughed lightly. He could see where Iris got her spirit, and he wondered if her mother had been the same way. She must have been, to have followed her husband so faithfully from one fort to another. Zoe Harris held a lingering beauty, and he could tell she must have once been as pretty as Iris, for she greatly resembled the picture of Iris's mother that sat on a mantel nearby. It was obvious by the picture that Iris's mother had also been a handsome woman. He knew it hurt Iris to see her grandmother suddenly growing so thin and pale and weak. Such things shouldn't happen to a strong, spirited woman.

"You two get along now. I'm fine," Zoe told Iris.

Iris looked up at Zack, and he felt excitement begin to move through his blood.

"All right, Grandma," she said. "We'll be back in . . ." She looked up at Zack again, feeling her fevered desire begin to heighten. "An hour or two." She looked back at her grandmother. "Zack could be called back to duty anytime, now that he's so much better."

"I'm glad you're up for a promotion, Zack," the old woman told him. "At least as an officer you will have decent accommodations. Even so, army life can be hard. You take good care of my Iris."

"You can be sure of that, ma'am." Zack turned and picked up Iris's hand-knitted yellow shawl, made for her by her grandmother. He put it around her shoulders and followed her out the door. Neither of them said a word for the first few minutes, until Iris stopped walking and nodded toward a dirt pathway several yards south of her grandparents' little frame house.

"That leads to the shed around back. There are a lot of trees, so no one will see us go there."

"You're really sure about this?" Zack asked her again.

She studied him soberly, love and longing in her eyes. In reply, she took his hand and led him down the pathway, through a wall of lilac bushes and to the shed. She lifted a board that served as a latch and moved inside. Zack followed, and she latched the door from the inside. One window on the rear wall let in enough light for Zack to see that this had once been a horse shed, but it was clean and neat inside, the floor cement, the stables long ago scrubbed out and painted.

"Grandpa built a bigger shed for his two horses and the buggy. He decided to use this one for storage." Iris walked to a shelf and took down a feather mattress. Zack quickly helped her, laying the featherbed on the floor of the stall. Already Iris was taking down some blankets. She spread them over the mattress, then turned and met his eyes, hoping he understood her fear, not so much of the pain, but a fear she would not please him. What if they did this and he found he didn't like her? Would he still marry her? "You do love me, don't you, Zack? I hope you don't think I'm terribly bad wanting to do this."

He smiled softly, touching her cheek. "I could never think bad of you in any way, and yes, I do love you. I just want you to be sure. There's no going back after this, Iris. I just don't want you doing it out of fear and loneliness because of the loss of your father and now your grandmother's illness. You've had no mother to . . . you know . . . talk to about things like this."

She grasped his wrist and turned her face to kiss his palm. "I have you. You can teach me everything I need to know."

Aching need surged through his loins at the offer. Maybe she *was* doing this out of loneliness and need, but so was he, and what was so wrong with that? It didn't change the fact that they loved each other, and love made it right. "I'll gladly teach you," he said softly. "Not everything at once. This afternoon we'll just . . ." He leaned closer. "Be one."

The moment their lips met, each knew there was no turning back. Oh, how she wanted him! He desperately needed to be loved, and she would be the one to do it. She shivered when he broke off the soft, delicious kiss and grasped her arms, pushing her back slightly, his eyes moving over her.

"Wear yellow more often, Iris. It's beautiful on you. The way you look today, how could I have said no to anything you asked?"

He began unbuttoning the front of the dress, and Iris stood frozen, waiting, her heart pounding. He pulled the dress open, down over her shoulders, his eyes glittering with desire.

"God, you're so beautiful, Iris."

Her breasts swelled above the ruffles of her camisole, and he touched the firm mounds with the backs of his fingers. Iris felt faint at the thought of his seeing her this way, and her nipples began to ache. He pulled the straps of her camisole off her shoulders.

"What if your grandfather comes back?"

"He seldom comes in here, and he won't know we're here. The door is latched from the inside. Besides, he won't be back until tomorrow." Iris wondered where she found her voice. As she talked, he unlaced and unhooked her camisole. Her heart pounded as he pulled it open and stared at her breasts. "Zack," she said in a near whisper. "I'm scared."

He met her eyes. "Do you want to stop?"

She shook her head. "No. I just want to please you."

He gently cupped one breast in his hand. "You can't help but please me."

He moved one arm around her, pressing her hips close to him while he held her breast more fully in his hand, his thumb moving over her nipple, arousing something so deep inside her that she felt lost in him. His mouth covered hers again in a deep, wet, hungry kiss that made her feel more confident and less afraid.

From then on young passions knew no bounds. Iris felt her clothes coming off, and it thrilled her to allow this man to look upon her nakedness. Girls at school had giggled about things like this, some swearing they would never let a man do something like this to them; one said her mother had warned her that this was a humiliating thing, something a woman simply had to put up with as part of being a wife, and only for the purpose of giving a man children. If the man wanted her to enjoy it, she must swallow her pride and pretend to like it. To actually enjoy it was sinful. Only whores enjoyed having sex with a man.

Iris decided the woman had probably just chosen the wrong man. How could it be sinful to enjoy this with the man you love? Wasn't that how it was supposed to be? How could she truly please him if he didn't see she took her own pleasure in return? She wasn't sure of all the answers. She knew only that she did not have to pretend to enjoy the delight of Zack Myers's strong arms that lifted her and laid her down on the feather mattress. She did not have to pretend to like the feel of his naked body lying next to her own, the taste of his hot kisses, the feel of his full lips caressing her throat, his strong hand cupping a breast, the exotic sensation of his warm tongue pressed against a nipple, his lips closing around it.

It all felt wonderful, and she didn't care if it was sinful. In her eyes it was right. She loved this man with every bone of her body, yearned to be touched by him. They had been friends long enough. It was time to be lovers. His lips moved back to her own in a heated kiss of passion while he moved his hand down over her belly and between her thighs. Her heart pounded wildly when he moved his fingers into her most private place.

She returned his kiss with a wanton desire that surprised her. Zack was caressing her intimately, touching a part of her that made her want to be wild and bold. She wanted to open herself to him, and it made her so ache for him that her breath came in gasps and she pushed against his hand. He left her mouth to lick her neck, and she whimpered in ecstasy, then cried out when a pulsating feeling deep inside consumed her, making her scream his name in utter rapture.

Zack smothered her cries with another kiss. He groaned as he moved on top of her, and Iris was filled with a mixture of anxious desire and trepidation. She could feel his hardness against her belly, knew what a man looked like down there from her work as a nurse. She had even deliberately peeked at Zack once when dressing his hip wound.

Still, what she had seen was not the same as what she felt now. She'd never seen a man like this and wasn't sure how long it would take or how it would feel. She was prepared for pain, but was sure it must eventually feel good.

"I love you so, Iris," Zack whispered, kissing her throat, her breasts, moving himself between her legs. He kissed her mouth, sliding his tongue inside. There was no time for hesitation, doubt, objection. She gasped with pain when she suddenly felt his deep thrust. "It will be all right," Zack groaned. "I promise."

Iris dug her nails into his arms, gasping with each surge of his hot hardness. In spite of the pain, she could already sense how incredibly wonderful this could be.

Zack in turn wondered if any other man had ever known this kind of ecstasy. The pain in his hip caused him to favor his good leg in propelling his thrusts, but the erotic pleasure of being the first man inside Iris Gray, the only man she would ever know, helped ease the pain of his wound. Pleasing this beautiful woman was more important, getting the initial pain over with so that the next time she could enjoy it more. She had offered herself to him so sweetly, and he was not going to fail her. He was her man and she was his woman, there was no doubt of that after this. All that mattered was seeing desire and surprise on Iris's face as he explored her. He'd thrilled at feeling her hot moistness, knowing he was pleasing her, knowing by her sweet climax she was ready to take him.

He never thought he could love this much. He muffled his own groans of delight and Iris's cries of pain and pleasure by smothering her with kisses. His seed spilled into her then, much too quickly. He wanted to enjoy this feeling for hours, but it was probably best for her sake that it was done with.

They lay panting and sweating in each other's arms, overcome with joy and love, delighting in each other's bodies. Zack pulled a blanket over them, and they lay there for a few minutes, saying nothing. Iris snuggled against him and kissed his chest. "Did you like it?"

Zack grinned, holding her close and stroking her hair. "You couldn't tell? It usually lasts longer than that, but it felt so good, and being the first time and all, it happened a little too fast. I couldn't help it. It felt *too* good." He rubbed her bare bottom. "Are you okay?"

"I think so. It hurt, but I can tell it will get better." She kissed his chest. "Oh, Zack, I love you so. I'm glad we didn't wait. I have no regrets." She leaned back and looked into his eyes. "How is your hip? It must have hurt."

"I'm all right. It was worth the pain."

Only a few moments later each could feel the fire growing again. Iris put a hand to his chest as though to ward him off.

"I could lie here with you forever, but if we're gone too long, Grandma will wonder. Besides, I should get back to her."

Zack reached out and toyed with a strand of her hair. "We'd better find a preacher. I could get orders anytime now, and I intend to do this quite a few more times before I have to leave. We can't keep sneaking around like this, so we'd better get married as fast as we can. Soon as we get dressed and leave, I'll wire Colonel Shaver."

"I wish I could go west with you right away, but Grandma—"

"I understand."

"I love you, Zack. I'll be so glad when you're settled somewhere and I can join you and we can do this all we want. Do you think it's wrong for me to enjoy it so much?"

Zack broke into a grin, shaking his head. "Why on earth should it be wrong? We love each other. A woman should take pleasure in it same as a man." He got up, knowing if he didn't dress quickly he wouldn't be able to leave her. For some reason he suddenly remembered his sister talking about Mr. Brady's bull hooking up with Jessie. It made him laugh.

"What are you laughing about?" Iris studied the scar on his hip. He had such a beautiful body, tall, broad, strong; narrow hips and firm thighs. She felt sorry for what he had suffered, remembered how easily she could have lost him when he was first brought back so sick and wounded. She could not imagine being without him now.

"My sister," he answered. He turned and reached down to pick up his longjohns. He pulled them on. "I told my pa once that maybe old Jessie wouldn't be so ornery and refuse to give milk if she had another calf. I said all we had to do was hook her up with a neighbor's bull. He pulled on a cotton undershirt. "Later Emily asked me what I meant about hooking them up. I told her to quit asking so many questions and I chased her out of—" His smile faded, and he picked up his pants, pulled them on, and began buttoning them. "You'd better get dressed. Take a bath when you get back to the house. We'll have to put everything back the way it was."

"Zack."

He met her eyes.

"Don't pull inside yourself again. I've worked too hard to get you to talk to me. It's good that you were able to talk about a good memory instead of a bad one. I'd like to know more about your family, about the good times, what life was like in Kansas. I never lived in one place more than a year or two, and my parents were seldom together for very long at any one time. I never knew the kind of family life you had. You can use your good memories to tell me what it was like."

Zack turned away again, picking up the fancy uniform jacket he'd worn for her. The whole day had been strange, spilling his story about the Indian attack, now actually making love to Iris Gray. The woman weaved a strange spell that made him reveal his emotions in a way he'd never thought possible. She even had him doubting his own convictions about Indians, but the memories always brought back the hatred, the need to kill. "Yeah, maybe," he answered. "We'd better get going."

Iris rose, keeping a blanket around herself, wondering how she could allow him to be so intimate with her, yet now feel reluctant to let him see her naked, watch her dress. "Turn around," she said.

Zack finally grinned again. "I'll fold blankets and put them back while you dress. I promise not to peek."

She cast him a look of doubt, but when he turned around to pick up a blanket she quickly pulled on her drawers. She glanced back, noticed he'd turned around and was looking at her bare breasts. "You promised. How can I trust you as a husband if you're going to break your word like that?" She grabbed her camisole.

Zack folded his arms, already aroused again, wondering how he was going to manage to keep his hands off her for the next day or two until he got a reply from Shaver. "I'll keep every promise I ever make to you," he told her as she pulled on her stockings, then her petticoats. "Except when it comes to not looking when your clothes are off. You had better realize that kind of promise is impossible to keep with a woman as beautiful as you."

Iris could not help a smile. She walked up and hugged him, her camisole still unlaced. "It's just us now, Zack, forever. I'll go wherever you go. No matter what happens, I'll always love you."

Zack moved his hands inside the camisole, rubbing her bare back. "And I'll always love you. Thank you for giving yourself this way, Iris, trusting me like this. I'll get a wire off to Shaver as soon as I leave you at the house. Right now you'd better finish dressing, or I'll have to get those blankets back down."

She stepped back to look him over. "My handsome soldier, soon to be a captain. I'm so glad you're alive and well. I pray you'll never suffer another wound." Again she saw the change in his eyes. She knew he was thinking the same as she, that he was on his way west to fight Indians. He most certainly could be wounded again. More than that, there would always be this struggle inside him, this need for revenge.

Iris was determined to change that. She was going to erase all that hatred he'd lived with for so long.

"It won't go away overnight, Iris. It might never go away."

Iris turned away and finished dressing. Zack Myers might not be easy to live with once he went west and became involved in Indian fighting, but that didn't matter. He would need her then more than ever, and she would follow him, no matter how remote and dangerous the location.

Zack opened the door to the hotel room, and Iris laughed when he picked her up in his arms. He carried her inside and kicked the door shut. Both of them were a little light-headed from drinking wine with her grandparents and a few men with whom Zack had been hospitalized. The ceremony had been simple, held in the hospital ward where Zack had spent the last two months mending. They were married by an army chaplain after Zack received the wire from Colonel Shaver approving the marriage with his own congratulations. Between the time of Shaver's letter and Zack's wire, his promotion had been approved, and Shaver had so informed him, along with orders to report at Fort Connor by May 20. That left them only two nights together, after which Zack had no choice but to leave her and head west.

Zack felt heady with all of it. The prettiest girl in Washington had married him, and he never dreamed he could be this much in love. He hated the thought of being apart, but at least she would be with him as soon as she could.

He set her on her feet and looked her over. She wore a simple gown of white satin, the only one she'd found in town that fit her. There had been no time to have one made. It was only three days since their tryst in the shed, three days of hellish waiting for both of them. He felt on fire for her, enjoyed the way her gown fit her body, the white of her full, firm breasts exposed just enough to tantalize him. The dress hugged her slender waist, and the skirt was straight in front, outlining slender hips and legs. Her golden hair was done up in a mass of curls beneath a wreath of flowers that decorated the veil she'd worn. He took the pins from it now, removing the wreath of flowers, thinking how angelic she looked in white.

"I love you so much, Iris. For years I never thought I could feel this way, never thought I'd be loved the way you love me."

Iris took his hands. He'd told her during his hospital stay about what life had been like with Jacob Brown and his family, the terror and loneliness of being so unloved and unwanted after being torn from the security he'd had with his real family. "I'll love you just as much as any of your family did, Zack, and I'll give you a new family. You'll *belong* again. We'll belong to each other."

He leaned down and covered her mouth with his, picked her up and carried her to the bed. There was no need for preliminaries. Both wanted to feel the satisfaction of being one just as fast as they could. In the midst of hot kisses her skirt and slips were pushed up and her drawers were pulled off. Then he was suddenly inside her, groaning her name, pushing deep in a furious need to have her then and there. Iris took him with great pleasure, thrilled to realize it didn't hurt as it had that first time. She arched against him, crying out his name in return, their young love eager, lustful, insatiable. She felt his life spill into her, and the next moment he lay down beside her, pulling her slips and skirt back down over her thighs.

"I didn't mean it to be this way," he told her. "I was going to let you change first, maybe put on a pretty nightgown."

Iris turned and met his lips in a slow, still-hungry kiss. "So you could take it off me?" she teased.

He laughed. "Do you have a fancy gown in that carpetbag?"

"Silk and feathers. I used money from my inheritance. It wasn't much. I hope you don't mind that I spent some of it on a nightgown I didn't even get to use."

He moved on top of her, resting his elbows on either side of her. "I still want you to use it As far as whatever money you have, I never even thought about it. I'll be able to provide for you pretty well on an officer's pay with army housing. We'll save anything you have in a bank here in Washington for a rainy day."

Her smile faded when she realized what could cause that rainy day. "Please promise me you won't do something irrational and get yourself killed, Zack. You know what they say about what clever fighters Indians can be. Father used to tell me about it in his letters. They can be hiding nearby without a man even knowing it, and—"

"I know exactly how clever and skilled and sneaky they can be, remember?"

Iris saw the bitterness return to his gaze. "I'm sorry, Zack. I didn't mean to bring up bad memories at such a special time. I was only thinking about how awful it would be to lose you." Her eyes teared. "I just don't ever want to have to be without you, Zack. I've lost nearly everyone I love, and by the time I come out to you, my grandma will be dead too. I'll hate leaving my grandfather, but he'll go live with his brother. At least he'll still have someone. He'll want me to be with my husband." She reached up and tangled her fingers in his thick hair. "It feels good to call you that—my husband. I am Mrs. Zachary Myers, the wife of a captain." A tear slipped down the side of her face. "Oh, how I hate to see you go without me."

"You're doing the right thing."

"And I love you for understanding." She traced her fingers over the scar on his cheek, praying no other Indians would give him new scars. "I love you, Zack," she whispered.

He suspected what she must be thinking, and he pulled her into his arms. "It will all work out," he told her.

He began unbuttoning the several covered buttons that ran up the front of her dress. Iris watched him, thinking about the newspaper article she had read the day before. She had said nothing about it because she had not wanted to bring up the subject just before their wedding. Maybe Zack already knew about it. She wasn't sure. The article was about a Sioux Indian leader called Red Cloud, and how successful he had been at raiding along the Bozeman Trail, the major route to gold country in northern Nebraska Territory, the place some were calling Montana. The government was desperately trying to work out a new treaty with the Sioux. Red Cloud's raids had nearly closed the trail to the public, and soldiers at forts all along the Powder River were in great danger. That was exactly where Zack was going, and she would go there too, no matter what the danger.

"We have all night tonight, all day tomorrow, and tomorrow night," Zack told her. "Let's make the best of it, Mrs. Myers."

She smiled through tears. "Yes, we really must, Captain Myers."

He finished unbuttoning the dress and pushed it open, unlacing her camisole. They must think only about the moment now, enjoy it to the fullest. She prayed she might already be with child, so she could give him the family he had needed for so long.

Part Two

12

SEPTEMBER 1865

Strong Runner lay awake, listening to wolves howling in the mountains. Something did not feel right, but he could not quite determine what it was. He knew only that he felt uneasy. It seemed most nights were like this for him now, his mind so full of turmoil that sleep was never an easy thing.

The men who had tried to build a fence on his grazing land had not come back, nor had he heard anything from the agent about the matter; but he could not help feeling the issue was still not settled. More than that, he could not help wondering how long it would be before whites took over all Nez Perce land. Already the white man's quest for the yellow metal had forced the reduction of Nez Perce land to one-tenth the size it once was. In Strong Runner's thinking, it all still belonged to his people, at least to those who had opposed the treaty that had taken away so much.

The Thief Treaty. That was what he and others called it, and that was exactly what it was. Land had literally been stolen from them, nearly seven million acres for eight cents an acre. The promised payments had taken years to come, and now the white man's government wanted them to give up even more! What land was left to them was being overrun by the white settlers who had brought in their gamblers and prostitutes, saloons, whiskey peddlers, merchants. All had come to gold country to get rich—and none of them respected the Indians or had any concern for what belonged to the Nez Perce.

He turned to Morning Star, rubbing his hand over her belly, which was still flat, but inside another child was growing. His seed had taken hold again, and he hoped for another son. Their first son, Wolf Boy, was seventeen months, already walking. He was strong and healthy, and Strong Runner was proud of him. Someday he would make a fine warrior . . . if indeed the Nez Perce still existed.

"You are again thinking about the whites and what will happen to us, my husband." Morning Star spoke the words more as a statement than a question.

Strong Runner sighed and took his hand away, lying down beside her on his back. "I did not mean to wake you."

"You did not wake me. When you cannot sleep, I cannot sleep, and that is not good for the life that grows inside of me. He needs me to rest so that he can grow strong."

"You need not lie awake just because I cannot sleep myself."

Morning Star turned and kissed his shoulder. "We are like one spirit. When you are restless, I am restless." She lay her head on his shoulder. "When are you going to learn that lying awake thinking about it will get nothing done? When you are in council with old Chief Joseph, young Joseph, Eagle From The Light, and the others, then something can be done. But in the night nothing will be accomplished, except that you lose sleep, and you need sleep to be strong."

"I wish you were right when you say something can be done when we sit in council, but it does no good for us to continue to oppose yet another treaty. What difference does it make? The whites go ahead and take what they want, treaty or no treaty. Their promises mean nothing. They have no honor."

"This is true, but that does not mean we must give up our own honor. We must remain a people of our word and show the white man's Great Father that we are not the ones doing wrong. It is his own people."

Strong Runner got up from the buffalo robes on which they slept. "They do not care about right and wrong, and whatever they want, their Great Father gives them."

Morning Star could see his silhouette in the shaft of moonlight that came through a window. He wore only a loin-cloth, but in spite of the cold September weather, his near na-kedness did not seem to bother him. She snuggled under a bearskin blanket and studied his magnificent build, the hard thighs and buttocks, the flat belly, the way his slender waist led to broad shoulders and strong arms. She still worshiped this man she had married, was still as stirred sexually by him as she had been when she first began to feel that way about men. She was proud of his looks, his strength, his skills. He was a good provider. They never lacked for meat, except that now he had to travel farther and put himself in danger to get that meat. Sometimes he was shot at by white men just for riding onto what they considered their property, even though Strong Runner and other Nez Perces had never truly given up any of that land.

"No matter what happens, Strong Runner, we will raise our children to respect what belongs to others, to honor their Nez Perce blood. We—"

Strong Runner held out his hand and walked to the window. "Wait," he said quietly.

Morning Star listened curiously. Her husband had the ears and nose of a wolf. Suddenly he bolted outside, and Morning Star heard a grunt. She jumped up and ran to the window, and in the moonlight she could see Strong Runner wrestling on the ground with someone. "Get him!" someone else shouted. Two more men appeared from behind a woodpile. It was then she smelled smoke.

She turned to see a bright orange glow outside the win-dow under which Wolf Boy slept. She ran over and grabbed him from his bed, looking around frantically in the dark. She had no doubt the men outside were white. Should she find Strong Runner's rifle and shoot them? Her heart rushed in a panic while outside she could hear the horrible sound of the blows of fists, men laughing, cheering.

Strong Runner! Were they beating him? If she shot any of them, the whole Nez Perce tribe could suffer for it. It would be just one more excuse to say it was the Indians who were the aggressors, the violent ones. But this ... how could any white man's court say it was not their own kind who started this?

She realized then that the roof was also aflame. She ran to get Strong Runner's rifle in the corner of the room, and screamed when a piece of roofing fell. She held Wolf Boy close and ran outside, and before she could put the boy down to aim the rifle, someone grabbed it out of her hand.

"You figure on shootin' somebody with this?" a man asked. "A pretty little thing like you? I guess all you Indians are the same, huh? Man, woman, kid, it don't make much difference."

Morning Star screamed when Wolf Boy was ripped out of her arms and another man grabbed her from behind. Wolf Boy was thrown down to the ground, and he began crying for his mother, but she could not come to him. Morning Star fought viciously as the men groped at her, ripped away her flannel gown. She wore nothing underneath. She felt her back hit the ground as she struggled wildly, and through her terror she saw the orange flames eat away at the little log house she had shared with her husband since that first night he brought her there. Shadows of men leaned over her, blocking the view of the flames. Strong hands and fingers pried at her, bruising her. A fist landed in her face, and she smelled the odor of whiskey and the sour smell of unwashed men. She screamed for Strong Runner, but in the back of her mind she knew he would not come.

Strong Runner was engaged in his own battle. The first man he attacked was no longer standing, and he had also managed to punch two white men who came at him at the same time. Still, there were simply too many of them. At first he thought there were only two or three, and when he had seen the first one crawling right under his window, he had acted in rage. Now he wished he had gone for his gun first. Wrong as these men were, he would probably have hanged for killing them, but it would have been worth it.

Now it took four of them to wrestle him back to the ground. He felt blows, kicks, spittle. For the present he ignored the blood and the pain and kept rearing back at them, desperate to protect his wife and son. He heard Morning Star screaming his name. What was happening to her? Were there even more than this?

"Look out, boys, we've got a wild Indian on our hands!" someone shouted. Strong Runner grabbed one of them around the neck and squeezed, refusing to let go. The others pulled at him, kicked him repeatedly while the man he held made ugly choking sounds. In the moonlight Strong Runner could see his eyes beginning to bulge—familiar eyes. It was the heavyset man who'd been with those building the fence the day he'd chased them away. Moser. Charlie Moser.

"He's killin' him, Lewis! Do something!"

Lewis. Lewis Bates? Those men had come back to repay him for tearing down their fence, a fence being built on land that did not even belong to them! So this was white man's justice! He squeezed harder, and then he heard the gunshot, felt the hot pain in his lower left side. He tried to hang on, but it was impossible. He let go, fell to his knees. He struggled to get up, but in the next moment he felt grass against his face.

"Come on. They've got the woman over there. Why should they have all the fun while we stand around here gettin' beat up?"

They've got the woman. Again Strong Runner tried to rise. He could hear someone choking, gasping for breath, and he could also hear his son crying for his mother, and Morning Star screaming his name. He could not go to her. He could not help her. He rolled onto his back, the pain in his left side excruciating. Through fading consciousness he could see the glow of flames. The little home he'd built for his wife was engulfed in them.

"There's no time for all of us to have at her," someone said. "More of them could come. Let's get the horses and get out of here."

The horses? He'd managed to build another herd of valuable Appaloosas, horses for which he could get a lot of money from the foolish miners. They were taking it all! His home, his horses, his wife . . . his honor. The sound of his son's crying came closer. In the bright light of the flames he could see the boy toddling over to him. The child plunked down beside him and laid his head across Strong Runner's chest. Strong Runner put a hand to the boy's dark hair.

"This will never . . . happen to you, my son," he groaned. "I will make sure of it . . . if I have to kill every white man . . . I see."

Colonel Shaver stood up and waited anxiously. His aide had announced Zack Myers had arrived, and Shaver had told him to have Zack come straight in to see him. It was November of '65. He could hardly believe it had been over two years since he'd sent Zack off to war, the hardest thing he'd done since being in the army. Thank God he hadn't been killed. Now here he was married to Iris Gray! It warmed his heart to think of it.

Zack walked through the door, limping slightly but looking healthy and strong. "Zack!" He put out his hand, ignoring Zack's salute. "Thank God you're all right. When Iris first wrote me about your injuries, I wasn't sure what to expect."

Zack removed his gloves and walked closer to grasp his hand. "Good to see you again, Colonel Shaver."

"Well, it's damn good to see you too, Zack! I could never have forgiven myself for getting you involved in that war if it had turned out any differently for you. I feel bad enough that you were injured." He released Zack's hand and motioned for him to sit down. "Take off your hat and coat. It's plenty warm in here."

Zack obeyed. "You did the right thing, Colonel, sending me back east. I learned a lot in the war, saw a lot and experienced things that helped me understand what the army is all about." He hung his hat on a chair post and removed his woolen overcoat before sitting down.

"And you saved a man's life, even after you were wounded," Shaver answered. "When I got that report I knew you were due for a promotion."

Zack's smile broadened. "Thank you, sir. I was very happy and proud to get the promotion, and I need the better pay now that I'm a married man."

Shaver chuckled. "Yes, I suppose you do, considering you married a colonel's daughter. Quite the beauty, Iris is."

She certainly is, sir. I wish she could have come with me, but her grandmother is dying, and she felt she should stay with her."

"Yes, I can understand that. It's probably just as well. I'm sure you discovered on your way out here how bad the Indian situation is." Shaver watched Zack's eyes, knew what it meant to him to be there.

Zack nodded. "We had no problems, but it was obvious the men who rode here with me as well as the stage driver who took me to Fort Laramie were nervous." Zack removed his gloves. "I have to tell you, I'm eager to head a patrol assigned to help keep travelers on the Bozeman from being attacked by the Sioux."

Shaver rubbed at his red mustache, which was beginning to show a lot of gray. "What you really mean is you're eager to start killing Indians."

Zack frowned. "Not exactly. Iris has set me to thinking about that." He studied the gloves as he talked. "I meant only that I want to keep others from suffering what my family and I suffered. If I can do that, it will be a small way of avenging what happened to my father and mother and sister. I'll never get over the hatred, sir, and if the opportunity arises . . ."

"Oh, the opportunity will most certainly arise, Zack. Rest assured there isn't a garrison at any fort out here that is safe from attack by the Sioux. Red Cloud is on a rampage. We've got settlers and miners trooping right through their hunting grounds, and they're damn mad. I can't say as I blame them, but at the same time we can't condone their attacks. The thing is, we're here to protect the *Indians'* rights as well. Remember that." Shaver rose and turned to a map behind his desk. "As far as the Bozeman, gold prospectors continue to pour through there into Montana, and we can't seem to stop them, so the government has decided to bring in more soldiers to try to keep the peace." He pointed at the map. "Here's where we are now, on the east side of the Powder River. We'll soon be moving to better ground on the other side of the river, and Fort Connor will become Fort Reno, I'm told, named after Major Jesse Reno, killed back in 'sixty-two. At any rate, it's from this base that Brigadier General Patrick Connor has been leading campaigns against the Sioux. Now it has become necessary to build forts even farther north, increase our garrisons all along the Powder." He moved the pointer farther up. "A couple more forts are planned. One right about here, northwest of where we are now, and one even farther north in the Montana Territory. That's where the gold is. That and this whole Powder River area are in the heart of Sioux hunting grounds."

He turned to face Zack. "You'll be helping establish the first new fort next spring. Colonel Henry Carrington will head the expedition, last I knew. You'll be under his command, when the time comes, but I'll be going also. We'll be taking along Company C of the Twenty-seventh Infantry. I'm giving you command of those troops." He sat down on the corner of his desk. "You ready to take on your new duties? How are you physically?"

Zack shifted in the chair. "Still some pain in the hip, but it gets better every day, sir."

Shaver grinned. "Zack, when we're alone like this, feel free to call me Howard. You're still obliged to obey every command I give you, mind you, and will be reprimanded for disobeying; but you're a good soldier, and I don't expect that to happen. Outside of that, you're not just any other soldier to me. We both know that."

Zack was touched by the remark. "Yes, sir . . . Howard. It feels a little awkward to call you that."

"I suppose it does." Shaver rose and walked behind his desk. "As far as that new wife of yours goes, bringing her out here is going to be pretty damn dangerous. I'd like to have my own wife here, but it's a rough life for a woman— unpleasant, dirty, uncomfortable. It's not even easy for the men, most of whom are poorly trained. You'll spend a lot of time the next few months getting them into shape. Many of them have already been through the Civil War and are tired of army life, others are new and don't know a damn thing about what they're doing. There are even a few foreigners among them. For enlisted men, the housing is poor and sometimes the food is worse, and the days can be pretty monotonous for those assigned fatigue duty, building new forts, roads, telegraph lines, cutting wood, doing carpentry work, or something as menial as peeling potatoes. The heat out here can be unbearable, and so can the cold in winter. It isn't always easy to stay in control of these men, so you have your work cut out for you."

Zack rose. "I can handle it, sir. I had a lot of experience up at Fort Snelling."

Shaver nodded. "That's why I figured you'd do all right out here. Teach those malcontents how to shoot straight, will you?" He laughed lightly. "At least some of them have new breech-loading rifles. Believe me, that means a lot when you're fighting Indians. When they come at you, they just keep coming, no time for muzzle-loading. And they're as good with a bow and arrow as we are with our rifles, better, in many cases. They can shoot an arrow while hanging off the side of a horse. They'll ride right into rifle fire, risk their lives just to touch the enemy—count coup, as they call it. That seems to be important, more important than killing a man from a distance. The way they fight and their reasons for fighting are much different from ours, and we have a lot to learn before we can fight them effectively." He sat down in his chair. "Our only advantage is that they don't always follow through. Fighting soldiers is like a game to them. They hit fast and hard, kill, maybe take a couple of prisoners, and God help those poor prisoners. The bastards do have a talent for torture."

Zack felt the quick, bitter hatred at the memory of his father's screams.

"They seem to believe they can get some kind of strength and honor from an especially brave captive," Howard went on. "At any rate, they'll often ride off and give up the fight, even when they're winning. To them it was just a chance to show off their numbers, their skills, prove their warrior abilities, their bravery. They go back to camp, brag to their women, torture their captives, if they have taken any, and return to fight another day. I guess their theory is if they constantly pull these surprise attacks, keep all of us scared and anxious, we'll eventually give up and leave."

Zack paced a moment, more aware than ever of the work that lay ahead of him. Not only learning how to fight Indians without losing control of his own hatred and doing something that could cost lives, but training men who either didn't want to be there or were so green they hardly knew the right way to button their jackets. He'd seen some who were dressed so slovenly they deserved to be thrown in the guardhouse. He faced Shaver.

"There is something that bothers me more than fighting Indians or getting these men in shape, Howard."

Shaver leaned back in his chair, folding his hands across his belly. "What's that?"

Zack drew in his breath, hardly able to control the searing anger he felt whenever he addressed the subject. "Our scouts. Since arriving here I've seen them, and I know what a Pawnee Indian looks like, how he wears his hair."

Shaver studied him closely, noticing the fire in Zack's eyes that had flared up like setting a match to an oil lamp. He slowly rose. "I knew you'd have a problem with that."

"Pardon me, sir, but what the hell are Pawnee Indians doing here?"

Shaver walked around the desk and came closer. "They're here because they hate the Sioux. The main reason the Indians will never win any war with us, Zack, is because they don't stick together. Before we came along, different tribes warred with each other over hunting grounds, and old hatreds have remained. The Pawnee have resigned themselves to the fact that we're here to stay, but they still have that need to be warriors, and they still hate the Sioux; so now they scout for the army and fight the Sioux and Cheyenne side by side with soldiers. They have scouting skills few white men can boast. If you're going to be stationed out here, then you'll have to accept that. I know it's damned ironic that our own scouts happen to be Pawnee. I'm sorry about that, but it's a fact and it's one you'll have to live with. In fact, there's someone I want you to meet."

He walked to the door, felt the air thicken with Zack's inner rage and turmoil. He knew how hard this was on him. He called to a private in the outer office. "Go get Thomas, will you?"

"Yes, sir."

Shaver came back inside, standing near Zack. "Zack, you've got to learn that what happened to your family can't be changed, not by your hatred for the Pawnee, not by killing every Indian who walks the face of the earth. It happened. Similar atrocities have been visited upon the Indians by whites. It is a clash of cultures that is going to take years to straighten out. White settlement can't be stopped, and *that's* a fact of life the *Indians* have to learn to live with. It's as difficult for them as it is for you to face your own memories."

"I didn't mean to turn this meeting into an argument or

to seem uncooperative, sir . . . I mean, Howard." He looked at Shaver, who was almost shocked by the look in his watery eyes, suddenly bloodshot from sheer anger. "But Pawnee? *Anything* but Pawnee!"

Someone knocked at the door then, and Shaver glanced in that direction. "Come in, Thomas."

The door opened, and Zack turned to face an Indian man who bore a scar on his right cheek that ran from under his eye, across his nose, and over his lips. He stood tall, handsome if not for the scar, his skin very dark, making the scar show up even whiter. His black eyes held Zack's gaze proudly, almost defensively, as if he could immediately sense Zack's hatred.

"Captain Myers, this is Thomas Red Hand. He's a Pawnee and one of our best scouts. Thomas, this is Captain Zack Myers. Captain Myers is more than an officer to me. He's a close friend. He's a good man, a good officer, an excellent shot. He'll be training a lot of the men here until we are ready to move up the Powder. You should know that I met him when he was only ten years old, back in Kansas. His family had been massacred by Pawnee Indians."

Thomas stiffened, glanced at Shaver and back to Zack. "That so?"

"That's so," Zack answered, his voice gruff. "Their leader was called Three Feathers. You're old enough to have known him. *Did* you know him?"

Thomas studied him quietly. "I knew him. He was a distant cousin, in fact. Got himself killed by the Sioux." A hint of humor passed over his face. "So, you hate the Pawnee because they killed your folks; I hate the Sioux because they killed many of my own people, even my own father." The corner of his mouth twitched. "Funny, ain't it?"

Zack blinked, not quite sure how to react. "Not to me."

Thomas shrugged. "You got a lot to learn, I think, about Indians. If the colonel says you're a good man, then I guess you must be. Either way, you and I, we'll end up havin' to work together, so I guess we gotta get along."

Zack watched his dark eyes. What made him most angry was the realization that he could sink a knife into this man's heart and he still wouldn't feel any better about his family than he did now. Nothing could satisfy the need he'd felt to kill that day the Pawnee attacked. Nothing could ease his frustration over the fact that he'd been too small to do anything about it. "I guess we do," he answered, his chest aching from his confusion and hatred.

"I am assigning Thomas to your command, Captain Myers," Shaver said. "It's either him or another Pawnee, and Thomas speaks the best English and is our best scout. He's a good man. I think working with him will help you get over the feelings you have about the Pawnee in general. In a man's lifetime, Captain, enemies can become friends and friends can become enemies. We fought our own kind in the Civil War, which proves you can't pin the word *enemy* on any one people. Right now the enemy, so to speak, are the Sioux, not the Pawnee. I'd like you to shake hands with Thomas and get to the job of training your troops. I'll show you around the fort."

Zack continued to glare at Thomas. He'd been given an order, and he had no choice but to obey. With all the effort he could muster, he grudgingly put out his hand. Thomas took hold of it and both men squeezed tightly. "I hope you can be trusted, Thomas Red Hand." Zack grimaced.

Thomas grinned. "And I hope *you* can be trusted, Captain Myers. Perhaps if we find ourselves in battle with the Sioux, I should not present my back to you. Sometimes a man gets shot by accident in such battles . . . by one of his own men."

Zack gladly let go of the man's hand. "I am not a back shooter, Red Hand, or a murderer, unlike some men I've known."

Thomas nodded. "Nor am I." He looked Zack over. "I see the hatred in your eyes, and I understand it. It would be funny, would it not, if you and I ended up being friends?"

Zack struggled against an urge to hit the man. "Get this straight, Red Hand. I will work with you because that's what I am ordered to do. I'll do my job the best I can, as I am sure you will also. That doesn't mean we have to be friends. That will never happen."

Thomas glanced at Shaver, eyebrows raised. "You sure I should be working with this man?"

"I'm sure. Go on back about your business, Thomas."

The Indian looked at Zack once more. "Glad to meet you, Captain Myers." His eyes still glittered with a hint of humor that Zack did not appreciate, mainly because it confused him. There was something about the man he almost liked, and that only made him more angry. He ignored Thomas's last remark.

Thomas turned and left, and Zack faced Colonel Shaver. "Is this some kind of test?"

Shaver smiled. "In a sense. It's also a necessity. You can't help but work with scouts out here, Zack, and most of them are Pawnee. I've seen them stand and fight right beside our men, risk their lives the same as the soldiers do. Their reasons might be different, but at least we can depend on them. I know it seems a cruel twist of fate, but that's how it is."

Zack took his coat from the chair and pulled it on. "Then I guess I'll just have to live with it." He picked up his gloves and hat.

Shaver folded his arms. "This Indian problem isn't going to go away soon, Zack. Be aware of that. You're going to be fighting side by side with some, and fighting against others. We're in a mess out here, and I don't see an early end to it. Even as we speak, the Nez Perces farther west are stirring up more trouble. And there is still trouble down in Texas and the Southwest with the Comanche and Apache. With the war over, more whites are going to come west, especially the ones in the South who have lost everything. You might as well dig in for the long run, and face the fact that you're going to have to learn the Indian ways, their culture, how they think, how they fight. Men like Thomas Red Hand can help you. If you want to be a good soldier and move up in rank, you're going to have to bury the hatred and take a different outlook on the Indian."

Zack felt almost sick from standing face-to-face with a Pawnee Indian and having to shake his hand. "Yes, sir," he answered.

Shaver sighed. "Come with me. I'll show you where your quarters are."

The man walked past Zack and out the door. Zack followed him out, stopping for a moment when they walked out onto the boardwalk in front of Shaver's office quarters. Thomas Red Hand was leaning against a hitching post, whittling a piece of wood with his hunting knife. Zack glanced at the knife, remembering. . . . He met Thomas's eyes then, and the man was watching him.

"I use it only for hunting and carving," he told Zack, "and sometimes for killin' a Sioux warrior." He held up the knife. "Never killed a white with it, man, woman, or child." He pointed to Zack's cheek. "I got my scar from a Sioux warrior. Where'd you get yours?"

Every muscle in Zack's back and neck hurt with tension. "Pawnee," he answered. He turned to follow Shaver.

13

*I*ris answered the door of her grandparents' home, and her eyes widened in surprise. "Jason!"

Jason Ward smiled. "Hello, Iris."

She stepped back. "Come in. How long have you been in Washington? What brings you here?"

He stepped inside and removed his hat. "Well, I got a month's leave. Now that the war is over, there is some reorganizing going on at Fort Snelling. I'm not sure where I'll be sent next, so I decided I'd go see the folks and then come see you. I'm so sorry about your father, Iris."

She blinked back tears. "Thank you, Jason. I'm afraid my grandmother is also dying now. I've been staying here taking care of her since she's bedridden."

Jason frowned. "I'm really sorry about that too. My parents didn't say anything about it."

Iris led him into the parlor. "That's partly my fault. I've been so busy taking care of Grandma, I haven't done any visiting. I haven't seen your parents since Father's burial at Arlington. They probably don't even know—" She hesitated.

Jason was going to be upset when he heard she was married, especially when he heard who her husband was.

"Know what?" he asked.

Iris sat down in her grandmother's favorite love seat. It was a deep maroon color and made of velvet. She motioned for Jason to sit down beside her. "I'm glad you never had to go to war. That you're fit and . . ." She looked him over. He was in uniform, a major's uniform. Jason, too, had apparently received a promotion, which meant he was still one rank above Zack. He could use that to give Zack problems. "And I see you've been promoted!" she finished.

Jason grinned proudly, that pompous look coming into his eyes. "Yes. I am a major now." He touched one of the bars that adorned each shoulder, indicating the gold, seven-pointed leaf insignia at both ends of each bar.

"I see. Your father must be proud. I know mine would be if he were here."

Jason turned sideways, facing her as he put an arm on the back of the love seat. "I'll be a colonel someday, maybe even a general. How would you like to be a general's wife, Iris?"

Iris could hardly find her voice. "What?"

Jason laughed. "I sprang it on you pretty quick, didn't I? With the war going on and all, I was just too busy to write, and I knew you were busy here working with the wounded and all, so it's been impossible to keep up with everything, but now that the war is over . . . heck, Iris, not a day has gone by that I haven't thought about you. And I know ever since that visit to Fort Snelling you've been thinking about me."

Iris struggled not to show her anger. The gall of the man! He actually thought she had been pining away for him just because of who he was, that he could walk in there after months and months of separation and no letters and ask her to marry him! She'd always known he had a tremendous ego, but this was too much.

"I figured with your father dead, you needing a husband . . ." he rattled on. The way he said "needing a husband" made her cringe. Did he really see her as a helpless female who needed a man to take care of her? Zack had never looked at her that way. To Zack she was an equal. He needed her just as much as she needed him. She liked being strong, liked being needed by him, not just to keep him happy in bed. Zack needed her in other ways. She missed him so! She couldn't wait to go to Fort Connor and be with him, no matter what the dangers.

Jason grasped her hand. "Please say you'll consider it, Iris. I'd like to see you often while I'm on leave. Besides, you know we belong together. We always have."

Iris pulled her hand away. "Jason, stop."

His smile faded a little, and he sighed. "I'm sorry. I really rushed it, didn't I? It's just that—"

"Jason, what in the world made you think you could go for months without seeing me or even writing and then just walk in here and as much as tell me we should marry!"

He puffed his chest out a little, looking confident. "Because we've known each other since we were kids. We've always been friends, and after your visit to Fort Snelling, our dances together . . ." He grabbed her hand again. "I saw how you looked at me, Iris. We both felt it."

Iris shook her head. "Maybe *you* felt something, but I have always thought of us as just friends, an acquaintance that couldn't be helped because of the friendship of our parents." She put her left hand over their joined hands. "Jason, I'm sorry for the misunderstanding. I am already married."

He stared at her a moment, stunned. He looked down, only then noticing the ring on her finger. Someone had stolen Iris Gray from him! Someone else had claimed her, the perfect wife for an army man! Everything was so perfect. He was moving up in rank, and he had planned on going to his new assignment with a beautiful new wife on his arm, or at least a promise of marriage. It was not so much that he loved her. Love was really a rather silly emotion. He'd wanted her because she was so beautiful and would make him the envy of all the other men. "Who?" he managed to choke out. He pulled his hand away. "Someone here? I don't believe it, Iris. I always thought you wanted to marry an army man."

Iris rose. "I *did* marry an army man. He was badly wounded in the war and was sent here for recovery."

"What!" Jason rose. "You married some *stranger*? What the hell was it, Iris? Pity? You know the regulations! It's natural to have feelings for a wounded man, and natural for a wounded man to have feelings for the woman who nurses him, especially when she looks like you! For God's sake, Iris—"

"I knew him before he came here," she interrupted.

Jason blinked in confusion. "Before? Was it someone who'd been stationed right here? You never mentioned another man when you visited me at Fort Snelling, Iris."

Iris folded her arms. "Jason, I did not go to Fort Snelling to visit you. I went there to visit my *father*. You have let yourself believe certain things simply because that's the way *you* wanted them. You never bothered to ask me how I felt about anything. You can't go through life thinking you should have everything you want just because you want it. And marriage is more than just having the perfect army wife on your arm when you go to an officers' ball. Be that as it may, there was no other man in my life when I visited there. I *met* him there. His name is Zack Myers, and he's a captain now. He's stationed at Fort Connor, and as soon as my poor grandmother has passed on and my grandpa is settled, I am going there to be with him."

She watched Jason's face pale, saw the anger in his brown eyes. "*Myers!*" He turned away, his hands tightening into fists. "Zack Myers!" he repeated. "I *knew* they never should have let him accompany you home!" He whirled. "How could you! Myers is nothing but a damn farm boy! He never would have made West Point if not for Lieutenant-Colonel Shaver. The idiot has a soft spot for Myers just because he found him after Myers's family was killed by Indians! So what! So he lost his family! Why does that make him so special?"

Iris checked an urge to hit him. "How dare you treat something like that so trivially! What have you ever known about that kind of loss, Jason? And what do you know about needing someone, *loving* someone? You don't love me. You love only *yourself*, and you love what I can do to help further your career. You love the idea of showing me off!"

He gritted his teeth in rage, and Iris thought how handsome he was when he was in a good mood but how ugly he could be when crossed. He was a spoiled brat as a child, and now he was no different. "I can't believe my ears," he said.

"Believe it, Jason. Zack was badly wounded saving a man's life. He nearly died from pneumonia and infection. It took him a long time just to walk again. I saw him nearly every day, and we had a lot of time to talk, to become friends, to learn about each other, understand each other. He is a very troubled man because of the memories and nightmares of what happened to his family. But he is also sensitive and kind, a man who cares more about others than himself, a man who knows how to love in the truest sense. He got word he was being sent to Fort Connor, and we decided to marry before he had to go. He got permission from Colonel Shaver—"

"Of course he did!" Jason nearly shouted. "He's Shaver's *pet*! If your father were alive—"

"If my father were alive, he would have given his permission, because he loved me and would have wanted me to be happy!"

"He *never* would have permitted you to marry anyone but *me*!"

"What is going on?" The words came from Iris's grandfather. "You two are shouting. It's upsetting Zoe."

Jason turned to him. "I'm sorry, Carl. I've just found out about Iris's marriage to a man not worthy of her."

Carlton frowned. "Hello to you too, Jason. It's been a long time."

Jason sighed, walking over and putting out his hand. "Hello, Carl. I didn't mean to be rude. I came here to visit all of you, but Iris has told me about this marriage of hers and—"

"It's a good marriage, Jason. They love each other very much, and Zack Myers is a fine young man on his way up. I'm sure he'll take good care of our Iris. They're good for each other. I'm sorry this visit hasn't turned out as you expected, but I wish you would quit the shouting. You have a fine career ahead of you, so I'm sure you will find yourself a worthy wife. There are plenty of women who would be proud to be married to a handsome officer like yourself."

Iris could see some of Jason's anger fading at her grandfather's clever words. Their eyes met, and her grandfather smiled and winked. His wisdom was part of what she loved about him, and she hated the thought of leaving him behind alone after her grandmother passed away.

"Maybe so," Jason replied, turning and looking down his nose at Iris. "I still feel you have sold yourself short, Iris. And I am still one rank above Zack Myers. He had better hope I'm not sent to Fort Connor or wherever else he might go. I'll watch every damn move he makes. One wrong move and he loses those gold leaves on his shoulders, maybe even the bars!"

Iris stepped closer. "Zack Myers deserves every single rank he earns. He had to work harder than most to get where he is. Don't you dare ruin it for him because of your own petty jealousy! We've always been friends, Jason Ward, but that will end if you deliberately try to destroy my husband's career!"

Jason sneered at her. "I won't have to do that. He'll do it himself when he gets involved in the Indian wars. Everybody knows how he hates Indians. He'll let that hatred make him do something stupid and he'll lose everything because of it. I'll just sit back and watch it happen."

Iris folded her arms defensively. "I would love Zack if he weren't in the army at all. The love we share is something you would never understand. I'm sorry if you're hurt, Jason, but I am *not* sorry for marrying Zack Myers! I love him and I am proud of him; and contrary to what you think, I believe in him. Someday he will become one of the best officers the army can boast. He has what it takes to get there— determination, bravery, desire, and, most of all, compassion. Being a good officer takes more than just attending West Point and having a rich father."

Jason flinched. "You've sold yourself short, Iris Gray. Your father must be turning over in his grave." He turned and nodded to Carlton. "I'm sorry about your wife, Carl. I'll let my parents know. Maybe there is some way they can help. I'd stay and visit longer, but you can understand why I have to go."

Carlton nodded. "God be with you, Jason. And God help you understand what has happened here. I care about Zack Myers, so don't let your anger make you hurt someone who does not deserve it."

Jason looked back at Iris. "We'll see." He stormed out but had enough courtesy not to slam the door.

Iris looked at her grandfather with tears in her eyes. "I just hope he never ends up in the same command with Zack."

Her grandfather walked up and put his arms around her. "Zack can hold his own, child. He'll be all right, especially once he has you with him."

Iris rested her head on his shoulder. "He needs me, Grandpa, and I need him." She had been reading about more Indian trouble since Zack's last letter. She could not help wondering how involved he was, worrying that he might charge after some warrior out of pure hatred and get himself killed. Most of all she worried what fighting Indians might do to his soul. Zack was going to have a hard enough time dealing with the Indian problem. He didn't need someone like Jason Ward hounding him.

Strong Runner awoke to a man with a mustache and beard and wearing spectacles bending over him. A white man. In that first moment of consciousness he remembered only what he had been doing before he'd felt the awful pain in his side. Fighting white men, trying to stop them from burning his home and hurting his wife and child. His arm flew out in rage, catching the man in the chest and sending him flying. He stumbled backward and landed on his rump.

"My God!" someone shouted. A pair of hands grabbed Strong Runner's arms as he tried to fight more. "Take it easy, Strong Runner! It's all right. That man over there saved your life. He's an army doctor!"

"I want no white man touching me!" Strong Runner replied bitterly. He forced himself to a sitting position while the doctor picked himself up from the floor.

"You shouldn't move around, Strong Runner," the soldier holding him said. "You'll reopen that wound."

Strong Runner shivered with pain but refused to lie back down. "Where are my wife and son?"

The doctor and soldier glanced at each other, and the doctor rubbed his eyes as though very weary. "Morning Star and your son are with her mother. They're going to be all right."

Strong Runner recognized the soldier as Lieutenant Steven Lynch, one of the many officers from Fort Lapwai who were supposed to defend the Nez Perces against white encroachment. "What happened to them? Are they hurt?" He held Lynch's gaze, and he knew the answer. "They raped Morning Star," he growled. "How many? How *many*?"

Lynch sighed deeply. "Someone will be punished for this, Strong Runner."

Strong Runner's lips curled into a sneer. "Do not lie to try to calm me, Bluecoat! We both know——" Pain seared through his side, forcing him to stop and grit his teeth before finishing. "We both know no one will be punished!" He studied Lynch's blond hair and blue eyes, thinking how he hated these soldiers, hated all whites now with a deep passion.

"Do you know who did it?"

Strong Runner grabbed the arm of a chair and used it to help himself stand up. "I know. But what good would it do to tell you? They would deny it, and that would be the end of it." He felt light-headed. "Where are my clothes?" He looked down at himself, realizing he wore only a breechcloth. Gauze was wrapped heavily around his middle. "I must go and see Morning Star . . . and my son. What did they do to my son?"

"Your son is fine," the doctor replied. "He's a solid, healthy boy. He has some scrapes and bruises, but nothing that won't heal quickly. It's the same for Morning Star. Physically she's fine. Her mother says she wanted very much to be here with you, but right now she's afraid to be around white men. We promised her mother we would let them know as soon as you were better. I do wish you'd lie back down, Strong Runner. This is the first time you've been fully conscious since your father brought you in the night before last."

Strong Runner moved his hand to the back of the chair so he could remain standing. "It has been that long?"

The doctor nodded.

Strong Runner breathed deeply against pain. "What day is this? What time is it?"

"It's Tuesday morning, about ten o'clock," Lynch answered.

Strong Runner rubbed his eyes. He prayed Morning Star would forgive him for failing to protect her. He didn't know all of those involved, but he knew who their leaders were, and someone had to die for this! It was the only way to save his own pride. "I must go to Morning Star."

"You really shouldn't——" the doctor objected.

"I must go to her!" Strong Runner growled, trembling with rage.

Lynch shook his head and handed him a doorskin shirt. "Your father brought some clothes for you. You weren't dressed when this happened, and I'm afraid all of your things were burned when they set fire to your cabin." He watched Strong Runner struggle into the shirt. "One thing I admire about you people is the way you take care of each other and share everything you have. I'm afraid not many of my own people are willing to do that."

Strong Runner managed to get his arms into the shirt and he pulled it down over his bare belly; his dark eyes drilled into Lynch's blue ones. "You do not need to tell me how unwilling your people are to share. They share *nothing*! And they want *everything*!"

Lynch handed him a pair of buckskin leggings. "There is a coat here too, and winter moccasins. It's pretty cold out today, Strong Runner. Will you at least rest and keep yourself warm once you get to your wife?"

Strong Runner sat down and pulled the leggings over his feet. He had trouble getting up again, and Lynch and the doctor helped him. Strong Runner yanked his arms away and laced the front of the leggings.

"I wish you would tell me who attacked your place, Strong Runner."

Strong Runner met Lynch's eyes. "Did Morning Star say anything about who it was?"

The lieutenant ran a hand through his hair. "She won't talk to any of us."

"Nor am *I* talking. If I told you, you would question them, and then nothing would be done, because we both know—" He shivered in another wave of pain. "We both know there is no justice for my people here. No white man's court will punish their own for bringing harm to an Indian! And if you know the names of these men, and then something bad happens to them, you will know I was the one who hurt them."

Lynch shook his head. "Don't do it, Strong Runner. You will only make more trouble for the Nez Perces."

Strong Runner could feel perspiration beginning to bathe his face. He knew he must lie down again soon, but it would not be here. "And so it will always be the same. Being at peace with the white man means letting him come and take our land, our horses, our women, and never doing anything about it. It means giving up everything, little by little. *I do not intend to give up anything more!*" He breathed deeply for strength and sat down in a chair. "I need . . . the moccasins."

The doctor walked over and helped slip them onto his feet, then stepped back as Strong Runner rose again. "Tell the lieutenant, Strong Runner," the doctor pleaded. "Let the *soldiers* do something about this." The man shivered when he saw the look in Strong Runner's eyes.

Strong Runner turned and picked up the wolfskin coat his father had left for him, glanced at Lynch once more. "Start doing your job, Lieutenant, or your stay here may not be so pleasant and peaceful."

He staggered to the door, praying he would not pass out before he could reach Morning Star. When he opened the door, he saw that his father was waiting outside, sitting on a wooden bench. Strong Runner suspected the man had been there since he was first brought in.

"Son!" The old man rose and came over to help him. "Should you be up like this? I did not even know you were conscious."

Strong Runner trembled, as much with the awakening horror of what had happened to his home and family as with pain. "I have to get away from this fort . . . these soldiers. I must see Morning Star."

"Come. Get on my horse if you can, and I will lead it to our lodge." Yellow Hand helped his son ease up onto his Appaloosa.

Strong Runner forced himself to hang on to the horse's mane for the half hour it took to walk to the main village at Lapwai, where Morning Star's parents lived. On the way, others welcomed him, told him they were glad to see him getting better. Some began offering clothing and blankets. Morning Star's sister, White Bird, said they would share whatever food they had, and her husband, Little Eagle, came to walk along beside the horse, telling Strong Runner he would help him build a new lodge and would cut his firewood and hunt game for him until Strong Runner was well enough to do those things himself.

They reached the dwelling of Sits-In-Sun and Little Bear, and Little Eagle helped Strong Runner get down from the horse. Strong Runner faced him. "There might be a better way you can help me," he told Little Eagle. "I know who did this . . . and I am going to kill them."

Little Eagle looked taken aback. "Those are dangerous words, Strong Runner. It is a bad thing, going after white men."

A cunning look came into Strong Runner's dark eyes. "I will find a way. They touched my woman, hurt my son, tried to kill me! They stole my horses, and they want to steal my land! They left me helpless. Now I am *ashamed*! Ashamed that I was not able to help Morning Star." He turned away, his legs feeling weaker. He opened the door to the log house, and the first thing he saw was Morning Star, who looked up at him in surprise from where she sat on a stack of robes.

Their eyes held as she slowly rose, and hers filled with tears. "My husband," she said in a near whisper. "I wanted to come to you but I was afraid of . . . the soldiers."

He slowly shook his head, his own eyes tearing at the sight of her. Her face was badly bruised, her bottom lip swollen, her eyes blackened, her arms covered with bruises and scratches. He glanced at the bed of robes, where his son lay sleeping, and he thanked his god that the boy was all right. He moved closer to Morning Star, and her mother quickly and quietly left them alone.

Morning Star hung her head. "If you no longer want me—"

He grasped her arms. "Never say that. *Never!*"

She jerked in a sob. "There were . . . many . . ."

"Do not hang your head, Morning Star! You are still my beautiful wife, the mother of my son. Please tell me you still carry our baby in your belly!"

Morning Star nodded. She slowly raised her eyes, and with tears running down her cheeks, she reached up to touch his face. "I was so afraid you would die. I could not come to you right away. They hit me so hard I could not think or see. When I awoke, I was here, and they told me you had been shot. When they said you would live I was afraid you would no longer want me, because . . ."

He squeezed her arms, struggling to find the strength to say what needed saying. "I will always want you . . . as much as the first day I took you for my wife. It is I who am

ashamed, Morning Star." He shook his head. "I failed to protect you. I ask your forgiveness."

She shivered, put her arms around him, and wept against
his chest. "You are my husband, my warrior. You did all that
you could do. There were too many of them." She broke into
bitter sobbing, and Strong Runner clung to her, one arm
around her shoulders while he wrapped his other hand into
her thick coal-black hair.

"It will not be that way the next time," he told her. "I *will*
be your warrior. I will avenge this and win back my honor."

She wept harder. "No, Strong Runner. They will only kill
you."

"I will find a way." He rested his face against her hair. "I
will find a way."

14

Jᴜʟʏ 1866

I ris thought how much more she would enjoy this beautiful country if not for the constant Indian scare. She had never been any farther west than Fort Snelling, had never seen such mountains, such spectacular scenery. Zack had written her about how magnificent this land was, but how difficult the terrain made his job. The problem was that the Indians knew it better than anyone, had learned to brave the elements, how to survive its harsh winters, how to move among the rocks and rolling foothills with the stealth and cunning of wild animals.

That made this a land of treacherous beauty. Zack had begged her not to come yet, telling her no one was safe traveling these parts; but when she considered the Indian problem could continue for several years, she had decided to go anyway. They had been apart long enough. She ached for him, needed to feel his arms around her, wanted to be there for him in case he should get hurt. They had been married a whole year already, and all she had had with him were those two wonderful nights after their wedding.

In honor of her father and because she was now Captain

Zack Myers's wife, she was given full army escort from Fort Laramie. She had been able to take a train most of the way through Nebraska. It had seemed incredible to her that a railroad could stretch all the way across the continent, but once she saw how far it had already progressed, she believed a transcontinental railroad would come to be after all, especially with the war over and the country ready to go on to better things.

Of course, the building of the railroad was just one more thing that riled the Indians. "The railroad chases away the game," the sergeant who led the troops accompanying her wagon had told her. "And the Sioux know it will only bring more white settlers into what they consider their hunting grounds. We have our work cut out for us the next few years, that's for sure."

In spite of the danger to her own husband and to other white settlers, she could understand to some extent why the Indians were angry. Zack had been transferred farther north, to a new post called Fort Phil Kearny, newly built for the sole purpose of protecting settlers and prospectors headed straight through Indian land to the gold fields of Montana. That land was part of what had been promised to the Sioux and Northern Cheyenne by treaty, another of many treaties now being broken. The Indians had been told that no white man would step foot in that country.

Now a group of sympathetic whites back east called Friends of the Indians were making the soldiers' job more difficult. They raised a fuss over every campaign against the Indians, yet most of the members had never stepped foot out west, had never experienced an Indian attack, and had no idea what it was like to live in constant fear of being captured and tortured.

Iris opened the top buttons of her dress, aching from the jolting ride in the front seat of the covered wagon. The heat was oppressive, and she wore a slat bonnet to protect her face against the relentless sun. The private driving the team of horses reeked of body odor, but she couldn't blame the poor man for the way he smelled. She was grateful to the twenty men who accompanied her, led by a Captain George Denver and Sergeant Henry Sievers. Ten to fifteen more men were to meet them somewhere near the point where the Sweetwater and the Powder rivers met. Over thirty men to protect one woman! That alone told her just how dangerous this area was, and she prayed for the safety of the men riding with her and those coming to meet them. They would be led by Captain Zack Myers himself, coming to greet his wife and stay with her for protection until they reached Fort Phil Kearny.

Her heart beat faster every time she thought of it. Finally they would be together again. He had warned her life would not be easy, and she had already seen just how desolate and lonely posts like Laramie and Fort Caspar could be. She was prepared for any discomfort she might have to face as long as she could be with Zack, but she knew there would often be long stretches of loneliness when he would be sent out on patrol. There were few other women at these dangerous, desolate forts, but she would just have to make the best of it. She was an army wife now, and she was prepared for that kind of life.

She had turned her face into a northern breeze that helped rid her nostrils of the smell of the man beside her, when she saw them—Indians! "Private Randall—"

"Already saw them, ma'am. I'm sure Captain Denver has too. Sometimes it's best to just mosey along and pretend you're not afraid. We'll try to make that area up ahead where there's lots of rock formations for protection. If we break into a run, it will only tempt them to give chase. Could be they're just curious and don't intend to try anything, but you'd better get into the back of the wagon."

Iris obeyed, visions forming in her mind of how awful it must be for a white woman captive among the angry, warring Sioux. She had heard stories, could not help thinking about what had happened to Zack's mother and sister. This must all be so difficult for him. It would be so much worse if his wife were killed or taken captive before they even got the chance to see each other again.

She hated being inside the canvas-covered wagon, even though she was at least out of the sun. It was stuffy inside, and she felt as though she were suffocating. Captain Denver ordered the men to move a little faster, and her heart pounded with dread. For the next several minutes it seemed there would be no trouble, but then she heard the thunder of many horses pounding across the open sod, the shouts and war whoops of attacking Indians. The wagon lurched forward when Private Randall whistled and whipped the horses into a dead run. She watched out the back, unable to see clearly because of rolling dust that partially hid the soldiers who covered the rear of the wagon. She gasped when she saw one man fall from his horse, an arrow in his back.

Now she could see the painted Indians in the distance, riding hard toward the troops, some with tomahawks raised, all ready for a good fight. "Keep your head down, ma'am!" Private Randall shouted. Iris obeyed, but she felt sick at the thought of men dying just to protect her. Zack! Would she ever see him again? The wagon hit a rut, bouncing so hard that her body flew up in the air and came back down with a hard jolt that caused her to hit her head on one of her trunks. She rolled sideways, putting a hand to her head to feel the spot. She felt something warm and wet, saw blood on her fingers.

Suddenly the wagon halted, and Private Randall ordered her to stay inside and lay low. He jumped down, and Iris lifted a piece of canvas and peeked out to see they were now surrounded by rocks. The sound of yelping Indians came much closer, and she jumped when a rifle was fired from underneath the wagon. The air rang with gunfire then, and the battle was on. In all the years Iris had moved from post to post with her mother and father, living among soldiers, she had never been involved in an actual battle, seeing soldiers in action. During the Civil War, she had seen only the awful aftermath of fighting.

She covered her ears. It was indeed frightening to hear the thunder of rifle fire and the threatening yells of hostiles bent on driving whites out of the West. To think that Zack was exposed to this kind of danger almost daily made her realize just how difficult it was going to be living with the daily worry that he would ride away and never come back.

Something hit the wagon with a thud, and she peeked over the back gate to see an arrow stuck in it. Just then a bullet pinged against one of the iron canvas supports, and she ducked back down again. There came another thump, and an instant later the canvas was on fire from a flaming arrow. Quickly she grabbed a blanket and beat at the flames, praying she would live to see Zack again. Sweat began to pour down her face, stinging her eyes and soaking her dress. She untied her hat and tore it off, unbuttoned the dress a little farther in front, and then lifted her skirt to wiggle out of her slips.

Outside the battle raged. She heard a soldier cry out. The air rang with rifle fire, reeked of dust and gunsmoke. She dared to peek out of the back of the wagon again, and her eyes widened at the sight of what seemed like at least a hundred Indians. She looked around the wagon, realizing there were two boxes of extra rifles and ammunition that the soldiers had picked up at Fort Laramie. She raised the lid on one box, took out a rifle, stared at it.

She had never shot a weapon in her life, but she decided perhaps she'd better learn. The sergeant had mentioned these were Springfield rifles. It was a new kind of gun that didn't take long to reload like the old muzzle-loaders did. The problem was, she wasn't sure how to use one of them. She grabbed a box of shells and took one out, studied the gun, and pulled open the chamber. She stuck the bullet in and carefully closed the chamber. With shaking, sweaty hands she turned to the back of the wagon, sticking out the barrel of the rifle, raising it, and aiming.

It was impossible to pick a target. The Indians were riding in circles around the cluster of rocks behind which the soldiers had taken cover. Sometimes they slid down to the sides of their horses as they rode. Now she understood what Zack meant in his letters about what skilled horsemen these Sioux were.

She fired the rifle, but saw no one fall. The explosion rang in her ears and caused her to lurch backward with a stinging blow to her shoulder. With tear-filled eyes she scrambled to put another bullet in the chamber of the gun, determined to help, but before she finished she heard the blessed sound of a bugler playing the sound to attack. She knew the meaning of every army bugle call, and this one meant more men were on their way.

Her heart raced with hope, and she set the rifle aside, looking out the back of the wagon again. The Indians had gathered, shouting among themselves, pointing to the north. Iris scrambled to the front of the wagon, and she saw them, a new company of soldiers coming out of the north! They charged at a hard gallop, and when Iris turned to look out the back of the wagon, she could see the Indians riding off to the south, apparently unprepared to stand against more soldiers.

Men around the wagon began cheering, some standing up and waving their rifles at the retreating Indians.

"It must be Captain Myers, sir!" Sergeant Sievers shouted to Captain Denver.

Iris's heart leapt with joy. Zack! It was only then she realized what a mess she was, sweaty, her hair falling out of the bun on her head, her dress dirty from dust and sweat. She must even smell bad! This was awful, seeing her husband for the first time after all these months and looking like this! Still, at least she was alive! She scrambled out of the wagon, watching the oncoming troops, her eyes on the man who led them. As he came closer she saw his captain's uniform, saw he was more handsome than she remembered, tanned by the western sun, the dark skin of his face making his eyes look even greener.

He jumped off his horse before the animal even came to a halt, hurried over to her, and swept her into his arms, and she knew it didn't matter how she looked or smelled. It mattered only that she was there. Oh, how good it felt to have his arms around her again. He had come to her rescue like a knight on his horse, sword and all.

"Are you all right?" Zack grasped Iris's arms and pushed her away so he could check her over. "You have a cut on your forehead!"

"I'm fine! I'm fine!" She put a hand to his scarred cheek. "Oh, Zack, let me look at you. I can't believe you're really standing here." Her eyes teared. "And I must look so terrible!" She put a hand to her face, tried to smooth back fallen strands of hair. She must even have blood on her face.

"My God, you look beautiful. Just the fact that you're alive and unharmed makes you beautiful. If you had been killed—"

She saw the agony in his eyes.

"We best go quickly, Captain. Them damn Sioux might go get s'more and come back."

Iris looked at the man who had spoken the words, her eyes widening at the sight of a dark, rather mean-looking Indian with a scar across his face. Both sides of his head were shaved so that there was hair only down the middle. He wore white man's pants and boots, and a calico shirt, but he had a bone necklace at his throat and a beaded earring in one pierced ear. She looked back at Zack. "Who is that?"

Zack frowned, turning to his Pawnee scout. "This is Thomas Red Hand, one of our scouts." He looked at Iris, and she saw the glint of hatred in his eyes. "He's Pawnee."

"Pawnee!" She glanced at Thomas again, her mind racing in confusion. "Aren't they the ones who—"

"Yes. How's that for stuffing it down my throat? I joined the army to fight Indians, hating the Pawnee most of all. Out here the Pawnee are the best scouts the army has against the Sioux—old enemies."

Thomas stepped closer, and Iris was surprised to see a hint of a grin on his otherwise intimidating face. "So he is stuck with me," he told her. "Your husband has much to learn about us Indians, but I am a good teacher." He turned to his horse. "Better get your woman in that wagon and get moving." He mounted his horse in one leap.

"Sergeant Sievers!" Zack shouted, still watching Iris.

"Yes, sir!"

"Get the men organized. Put the dead over their horses and the wounded inside the wagon."

"Yes, sir!"

Iris and Zack just watched each other, so much to say and not knowing where to start, longing to kiss, to share bodies again. "This is a hell of a way to see each other again," he told her.

"Let's hurry and get to the fort," she answered. "Do you . . . do we have a place to stay . . . I mean—"

"Someplace private?" Zack finally smiled. "Yes, I have private quarters. And Shaver promised me a couple of days off once you arrive."

"Oh, Zack, I'm so glad to finally be here, Indians and all. By the time Grandma died it was already winter, and when you told me to wait till spring because of Indians . . . I just couldn't wait any longer to be with you."

He looked around to be sure the men were obeying his order, scanned the hills then for Indians before meeting her eyes again. "I wanted you to come. I was just afraid of losing you the way—" He closed his eyes and sighed. "We'd better get going." He leaned down and kissed her cheek. "God, it's good to see you, Iris. There aren't many comforts at the fort, I'm afraid."

"You know I don't care as long as we're together." He looked wonderful, and he seemed different, more manly than when he'd left her, if that was possible. His new authority had seasoned him, made him even more attractive; and the fact that he had accepted working with Thomas Red Hand showed he was learning to live with the memories. How ironic that he had to ride with Pawnee scouts! How was that affecting him? They had so much to talk about.

He helped her into the wagon, and the private who'd been driving it this far climbed back up on the seat. Iris twitched her nose at his smell, but she was glad he was unhurt. "Did you fire a rifle out the back of the wagon?" he asked her with a grin.

Iris glanced at Zack. "Yes, I did. I thought I could help, but I don't think I hit anything."

Zack grinned. "Sounds like something you'd do." He glanced at the private. "Be good to her, mister."

The private nodded. "Yes, sir. If you don't mind my saying so, sir, she's one pretty woman, prettiest I've ever seen."

Iris saw desire flare in Zack's green eyes. "I have to agree with you there." He turned and mounted a roan gelding, urging the horse into a trot to the front of the troops, where he joined Captain Denver. The two men talked for a moment, then each shouted orders for their men to move out. Thomas Red Hand rode ahead of all of them.

Iris noticed two men were draped over their horses. Someone groaned, and she turned to see two more in the back of the wagon, both sitting up while a third man tried to bandage them. It upset her to think they were suffering and two had died just so she could get safely to her husband. Her old nursing instincts took over, and she climbed into the back of the wagon to help, suspecting she would often be needed for things like this at Fort Phil Kearny. She didn't mind. It would give her something to do when her husband was out on assignment. She just hoped Zack would never come back draped over a horse.

———

Lewis Bates slipped a split rail into the hole he'd drilled in the post. Only a mile away, just beyond the woods near where he built the fence, lay the blackened ruins of what had been the home of the Nez Perce Strong Runner. He figured Strong Runner to be dead by now. If not, he had either not recognized his attackers or chosen not to tell who they were for fear they would come back. Then again, maybe he *had* told but no one believed him. After all, he, his brother Jonathan, brother-in-law Charlie and their friends were all good Christian men.

The fact remained, no soldiers or lawmen had come to question him. Besides that, he was confident that since he was white, nothing would be done about it anyway, which was why he had gone there alone. What did he have to fear? Strong Runner was probably damned scared. It had worried him some when he learned the big Indian was still alive, but he figured if nothing had happened by now, there would be no more trouble from that one.

This was prime grazing land. Someday, when all the Indians were gone, land like this would be very valuable. He intended to be the owner. It was time to go ahead and begin fencing it off again.

He laid down another post and picked up his hand drill, positioning it near what would be the top end of the post. He pushed and began cranking the drill, sweat soaking his clothes as he worked. He was oblivious to an approaching figure behind him, the Indian's moccasined feet making no sound against the soft grass. He had no idea the Indian had hidden in nearby trees for hours, sure Bates would return to continue work on the fence. Now the Indian slithered through the tall grass, preparing for just the right moment, knife in hand. Not until a strong arm came around his throat did Bates realize he'd been stalked. He saw the glint of sunshine on the big blade of a knife, watched in horror as it was plunged into his chest. Then there was nothing to remember. . . .

Strong Runner yanked the knife from Lewis Bates's chest and let him slip to the ground. He wiped off the knife, looked around. No one was about. The agent and bluecoats at Fort Lapwai thought he was still recovering at his mother-in-law's lodge. If any of them asked to talk to him, Sits-In-Sun, Little

Bear, Morning Star, and the others would say he was not well, that he was resting and did not wish to see anyone. After all, his recovery had taken months, thanks to these men. He had come down with an infection that nearly killed him, and it had taken all this time to regain his full strength. No one would know he had been here.

"Two more," he muttered, sliding the knife back into its sheath. "If I can kill your brother, and the fat one called Charlie, my honor will be satisfied." He pulled the dead body into tall grass, where it would not be seen, then hurried back to the underbrush and laid low. He'd been watching these men, knew their work habits. Bates's brother, or perhaps the one called Charlie, should be coming along soon.

15

"Captain Denver commands infantry and I command only cavalry," Zack told Iris. He could feel her sudden nervousness after so many months apart, and he hoped a little small talk would relax her. He bolted the door to the tiny area assigned to them, one main room with a cookstove and heating stove, as well as a few overstuffed chairs and a rocker he had ordered for her through the supply post. "The head man here is Colonel Henry Carrington. He's the one who directed the construction of this fort. We've been here only a month. Most of the men like Carrington all right, but he seems a little wishy-washy at times. Colonel Shaver says there are rumors higher up that not everyone is pleased with Carrington's handling of the situation out here. Some civilians want him to lead all-out attacks against the Sioux, but he doesn't think we have enough men to conduct that kind of campaign, and he's probably right."

Zack felt a little nervous himself. He glanced toward the back of the room, where a narrow doorway led to a small bedroom. Finally he wouldn't have to sleep alone anymore. He turned to Iris, drinking in the sight of his weary wife, beautiful in spite of her dirty face and dusty hair. "I can't tell you what it means to me to have you here, Iris."

Iris shivered with a mixture of anticipation and, to her surprise, bashfulness. This man was her husband, but they had been apart so long that it felt a little strange suddenly being alone with him. "I've dreamed of this moment for so long," she answered. "I just . . ." She looked down at herself. "I'm such a mess, Zack, and I'm still a little shaken by that Indian attack. I feel so responsible for the fort losing two men and others being injured—"

Zack raised his hand to quiet her. "Believe me, Red Cloud and his Sioux make that kind of trouble for us all the time. Whether men are out on an escort or just on woodcutting duty, there's bound to be trouble. We have to send a full force with the men who cut wood or do the haying, just to protect them." He came closer, studying her blue eyes. "Put it out of your mind for now." He grasped her arms. "Just think about us." He smiled softly. "And the fact that you're here." He looked around the room. "It isn't much, but for a western fort, this is luxury. Actually, this is as fancy as it gets."

Iris glanced at the cookstove, the furnishings. She met his eyes again and smiled through tears. "I've lived in cramped quarters off and on all my life, Captain Myers. This will do just fine. All it needs is a woman's touch."

Both of them felt the pull of desire, the awakening of needs long buried. "*I* need a woman's touch too," he told her.

Iris studied his face. "And I need to feel a man's strong arms around me. Just be a little patient, Zack."

He crushed her close, kissing her hair. "I ordered Sergeant Sievers to have some men bring over a bathing tub and some hot water for you. I'll have to go report to Colonel Shaver about the Indian attack and write a report. That will give you time to clean up. I'll get a change of clothes and use the bathhouse. By the time I get back, you'll feel a lot better." He kissed her hair again. "Thank God you got here safely. If I had lost you . . . especially to Indians . . ."

"You won't lose me, Zack. I'm here now, and I'm never leaving." She turned her face up to his, felt his mouth claim her own, and both felt the fire of being too long apart. Even when they were together those few days, they had not had enough time to satisfy fully the needs of newlyweds just learning all the secret intimacies about each other. Now that they had this quiet moment together, Iris felt torn. She loved this man, had ached to be with him again, yet she'd hardly had time to grieve over her grandmother before leaving.

He broke off the kiss, and she rested her head on his shoulder, the terror of the Indian attack and the fear she could have lost Zack before ever getting to hold him again falling in on her grief. The crash of emotions welled up in a sudden burst of tears as she realized this man was her whole world now.

"Zack, my Zack," she wept. "Just hold me. We're all each other has now."

Zack knew well what she was feeling, the loneliness, the desperate yearning to be loved, to know she still belonged to someone and that someone belonged to her. "I'm right here," he said softly. He let her cry, led her over to the rocker when the tears finally began to subside. "I'll have that tub and hot water sent over and go make my report. We have a lot to talk about, honey, but you need to rest up first. You take that bath and get into bed. I'll be back later." He knelt in front of her, capturing her gaze. "I love you, Iris. I know you've been through a lot, but we'll have each other, and I'll take good care of you."

Iris wiped her tears, angry with herself for behaving this way on her first day back with her husband. "I'm sorry, Zack. I'm usually stronger than this. It's just . . . so much has happened in such a short period of time."

"Don't apologize. It isn't necessary."

Iris grasped his hands. "I love you, Zack. Thank you for being so understanding. You go ahead, I'll be all right."

Zack leaned up and kissed her cheek. "I still can hardly believe you're really here."

She touched his hair. "Oh, Zack, I can't imagine my life without you. I hope God allows us to grow old together."

"We'll watch each other grow old and fat and gray," Zack answered. "I promise."

He kissed her once more before leaving. Iris followed him to the door. Now that she was with him again, she didn't want him out of her sight for even a few minutes. She studied the pointed logs that formed a wall around the fort, a wall that spelled danger, its pointed top designed to make it more difficult for an Indian to crawl over it. She shivered at the thought of how easily she could lose her husband.

She took a deep breath, telling herself she simply had to be brave now, not just about the Indian danger, but also about the discomfort she was going to have to put up with living so far from civilization. She closed the door and took another look around the small main room of Zack's quarters. Somehow she would have to make this little place home, a rug there, better curtains at the windows, the smell of bread baking. Yes, she would bake Zack some fresh bread. He would like that.

Minutes later men showed up with a tin bathing tub and filled it with buckets of water. "Lukewarm, ma'am, not hot," Sergeant Sievers told her. "With the heat outside and the air so hot in here, you'll cool off better if the water's not too warm." He handed her some towels. "Your husband said to bring some extras."

Iris felt a little embarrassed at the way the two men with Sievers were looking at her, and she realized that in these remote locations she would probably have to get used to being stared at. "Thank you, Sergeant," she replied, taking the towels from him. "Are there many other women here? I met one when we came in, a Mrs. Dewey."

"Yes, ma'am. That's Major Dewey's wife. Besides her and a servant girl she brought along, there's my own wife, Janet, and three other women, all wives of enlisted men. You won't be able to associate with any of them much, of course, you being an officer's wife."

Iris longed for the company of women. She had spent so much time caring for her grandmother, and before that, nursing wounded men from the war, that she'd had little time for socializing. She'd lost touch with the friends she had made in school, some of whom had married and scattered to other parts of the country, now that the war was over. "With such a scarcity of female companionship here, Sergeant Sievers, I hardly think it will matter if a woman is the wife of an officer or an enlisted man. I never have believed much in the separation of the two, even though I grew up being taught army protocol."

Sievers grinned. He liked Captain Myers's wife, had already heard about her father, and how beautiful she was. That had been no exaggeration. The fact that she would consider socializing with the enlisted men's wives impressed him. The woman apparently was one who did as she damn well pleased, once she made up her mind. Already the men were talking about how she'd picked up a rifle and shot at the Sioux who'd attacked the soldiers bringing her there, how she'd nursed men in the Civil War and even nursed the wounded men from the attack that afternoon. She was some fine woman, he figured.

Iris thanked the men again and hinted that they could leave. The other two who had been staring at her seemed to awaken from a kind of stupor, and the look on their faces was so humorous that it helped ease Iris's earlier grief. They nearly tripped over themselves going out the door, and she felt good about the kind look in Sergeant Sievers's eyes. He was a rather homely man, big and awkward, perhaps in his mid-thirties, with brown eyes and sandy hair. He seemed a good-natured man, the kind who would do anything for anyone whenever they asked.

She bolted the door and disrobed, then sank into the tub of water. Now she had time to gather her thoughts, but her ears still rang from the explosion of rifle fire. The journey there had been a rude awakening to the realities of life in Indian country, but she would have it no other way if it meant she could not be with Zack.

She emerged from her bath feeling happier just to be clean. She wrapped her wet hair in a towel and searched through her bags for a cotton nightgown, her shock and grief over the past few hours slowly being replaced by much more pleasant feelings. Zack would be back soon, her man, her husband. She powdered herself and slipped on her gown, deciding not to wear any drawers under it. She unbolted the door so Zack could get in, then went into the tiny bedroom to find a chest of drawers and a hand-made bed.

She walked to a corner of the room and pushed aside a curtain that hung there covering a small cutout in the wall just big enough for a chamber pot. She turned back to the bed and sat down, rubbing her hair with the towel to get out most of the moisture. Her wet hair helped keep her cool. A washstand was right beside the bed, and she looked to see there was water in the pitcher.

She lay back and closed her eyes. She could hear voices in the quarters next door, and she realized she and Zack would have to be quiet in their lovemaking, since these two small rooms were one of six officers' quarters, all located side by side in one log building. The walls of the hastily built rooms were thin.

That was her last thought before dozing off, her body exhausted from the struggle earlier in the day. She dreamed of Zack, so handsome, his lips so soft and full and sweet, his touch so gentle. It was easy to imagine him touching her, whispering words of love. . . .

Gradually she realized it was not a dream. "Zack," she whispered as a hand reached inside her unbuttoned gown to fondle her breast.

"God, Iris, I've ached for you for so long."

Iris opened her eyes and looked into his soft green eyes and the dark hair that tumbled around his tanned face. There was nothing more to say. No matter what they had been through these past months, no matter how much there was to talk about, this had to be done first.

She leaned up and met his mouth, melding his tongue with hers, letting his kiss sink deep as he pressed her into the feather mattress. From then on they could not get enough of each other . . . so long apart . . . too long. She felt him slipping the gown over her shoulders, her breasts, her belly, her thighs, all the way off. She felt him kissing her ankles, her knees, her thighs. She grasped his thick hair and cried out his name when he kissed her private places. His lips moved over her belly, back up to her breasts, taking them into his mouth hungrily while his fingers explored the heat between her thighs in circular motions that brought on an almost agonizing sensation. Now that her need for this man had been so quickly reawakened, it took only moments for the magical, erotic pulsations to move through her. She was ready for what she needed most . . . Zack inside of her.

Zack took her mouth in another heated kiss, and she wanted to cry out with the glory of sharing bodies again, but Zack's smothering kisses kept her from doing so. She opened her legs, urging the now-naked Zack to come inside her. He pressed his hardness against her belly teasingly. "You've got to be still, he said softly, grinning. He pulled a pillow to her chest and rose up. "Use this."

Iris smiled, feeling wanton and wicked and terribly in love. She pulled the pillow to her face and pressed it there when he grasped her hips and entered her, pushing deep, leaving her breathless. At last she was with her Zack again, reveling in being united in body as well as spirit.

This was more wondrous than any time yet, for separation had made them desperate with a need to become one. She answered his every thrust with her own rhythmic movements, her cries of ecstasy smothered by the pillow. She felt his life surge into her then, and the next thing she knew he was dragging the pillow away and meeting her mouth in hard, hungry kisses. His lips moved to her throat, her breasts, where he lingered, tasting her nipples as though starved.

"Just stay right here," he groaned. He never even pulled away from her. Already she could feel his shaft growing hot and hard again, and he plunged deep inside, satisfying her every need, reminding her why she was willing to bear anything to be with this man, her friend, her lover, her husband. She grasped his forearms, moved her hands up the hard muscle of his upper arms, trailed her fingers over his strong shoulders, and dug her nails into his back when he began moving even faster again, reclaiming her. She suspected his passion and near aggressiveness was due in part to the realization that he could have lost her today to an enemy that tore at his soul.

Again his life spilled into her, and finally he relaxed, settling down beside her. "I meant just to lie beside you, hold you," he told her. "I'm sorry, Iris. Maybe you weren't ready. My God, you weren't even fully awake. I saw you lying here, looking so beautiful—"

Iris turned and put her fingers to his lips. "It's all right. It's what we both needed. We'll have plenty of time to talk and get settled in. We had to do this first." She met his eyes and smiled. "Hello, Captain Myers. It's nice to be here."

Zack laughed lightly and moved on top of her. "Hello, Mrs. Myers. Welcome to Fort Kearny." He kissed her mouth again, and for the moment they gave no thought to the dangers there, the difficult life of living on a remote army post. They were just Zack and Iris, and this was all they had . . . each other.

Morning Star walked beside Strong Runner as they approached headquarters at Fort Lapwai. She thought how ironic it was that Lapwai was the Nez Perces' word for "place of the butterflies." If only it still were a quiet, beautiful place in the mountains where butterflies gathered in the spring. Now the beauty was scarred by the cutting of trees for heating stoves, to keep bluecoat soldiers warm in winter. White man's buildings were scattered over several acres, and soldiers marched in routine drills, many of them now staring at her and Strong Runner.

Strong Runner had not wanted her to come. He suspected he might be arrested, and he did not want her to see that. He felt she had been through enough these past months since her rape. He had not even made love to her since then, afraid of stirring up ugly memories for her, and too full of hatred and vengeance himself to be able to relax enough to mate with her. In spite of what she had suffered ten months before, giving birth to another child had helped ease her lingering horror. Three-month-old Jumping Bear, Strong Runner's second son, rode in a papoose on her back, and Strong Runner carried two-year-old Wolf Boy in his arms, thinking perhaps this would be the last day he saw either of his sons for a long time.

The soldiers had come for him that morning, ordering them out of the dugout in the side of a hill where they lived now, a house that could not be burned. They had remained near her parents' village, but Strong Runner had talked of moving farther west again, near the Blue Mountains, where Chief Joseph had taken his people to the Walla Walla Valley, land that supposedly still belonged to the Nez Perces and was not quite so crowded with whites as this area. The only reason they had not gone there yet was that Strong Runner did not want to look as though he was running away.

Perhaps staying there had been the right decision . . . but Morning Star could not help being afraid for her husband. Never had any Nez Perce man been called to appear at the fort. Strong Runner had never said he'd killed those white men, and she had never asked. She had begged him not to do it, yet she understood it was something he *must* do. There were times he had disappeared, and after one of those disap pearances, the three white men had been found dead, their throats slit. Morning Star had only to look into her husband's eyes since then to know the truth.

Now she followed quietly along as her husband was taken to fort headquarters for questioning. She was afraid of the sol diers, had heard about atrocities committed by them against other Indian tribes, how many Cheyenne had been murdered two years before at a place called Sand Creek . . . women, lit tle babies . . .

She had swallowed her fear and called on her reserve bravery to come with her husband. If he was to be arrested, this could be her last chance to be with her beloved. She blinked back tears at the thought of losing this man she loved beyond her own life. She must not do or say one thing that could make him look guilty.

Did they find some kind of proof? Her heart pounded with fear and dread as they climbed the steps that led into the big white building. The fort commander sat at a desk in side with several other soldiers around him. She recognized the man behind the desk as Colonel Clayton Porter. He had lost part of his left arm in the white man's war back east, but he remained in the army. He was not always very fair in judg ing problems between the Nez Perces and white settlers, and Morning Star felt even more alarm, especially at the fact that there were many other soldiers in the room.

Strong Runner turned and handed Wolf Boy to her. Their eyes held in mutual love and dread. "I love you," she told her husband in the Nez Perce tongue. She backed away, keeping hold of Wolf Boy's hand. Strong Runner faced Colonel Porter.

"Why am I here?" he asked.

Porter rose, folding his arms. "You don't know?"

Strong Runner raised his chin proudly. "If you want to question me about the deaths of white men, it is useless. I have no information that will help you. If I were their killer, would I have stayed so close to this place where there are so many soldiers? Would I be that foolish?"

Porter's dark eyes drilled into Strong Runner's as though to threaten him, but Strong Runner did not flinch or cower. "Not foolish, by God. Not you, Strong Runner! Staying here was very clever." He leaned over his desk. "You came in here last year complaining about white men settling on your grazing land, telling me they tried to put up a fence and you tore it down. You gave me names at that time—Lewis Bates, Jonathan Bates, Charlie Moser. Later your home was burned, your wife abused, you yourself beaten and shot. You have always refused to tell me who did that, and now all three of those men are dead, each one killed trying to put up another fence, their throats slit. Do you really expect me to believe there isn't a connection?"

Strong Runner folded his arms, his dark skin glistening from sweat. "I expect nothing from you," he answered. "I only tell you there is nothing I can say that will help you. Why do you not talk to other whites who knew them? Perhaps these men had enemies among their own kind. I have heard that among the miners and the scum of the earth who come here to get rich, there are many fights, some murders. White men love their whiskey, love to gamble. Perhaps some other white man to whom they owed money decided to kill them. Or perhaps they found gold. White men seem to find it easy to kill each other over gold. Their reasons for killing are much different from the reasons a warrior kills."

Porter watched him closely, and Morning Star thought she saw a quick glint of humor in his eyes. "And why does a warrior kill, Strong Runner?"

Strong Runner took a moment to answer. "For his hunting grounds, or to protect his people, his children."

"His woman?"

Strong Runner showed no emotion. "Sometimes."

Porter sighed deeply. "I brought you here for a last warning, Strong Runner. You know damn well that this fort is being closed temporarily, until more troops can be sent here to beef it up. We have been unable to stop the flow of whites because of the gold discoveries. I wish for your sake I could change all that, but what's done is done. Those settlers are here to stay, and you're going to have to accept that. Personally, I believe you killed the Bates brothers and Charlie Moser, but since our troops are being withdrawn for the time being, I'm not going to do something that could stir up more trouble than already exists around here. I can't pull out of here in the middle of an all-out war with the Nez Perces, and I'm afraid that's just what might happen if I have you arrested. Besides that, I have no real proof, and you know it." He came around his desk. "You're a clever man, Strong Runner, but I'm giving you fair warning. If one more white man dies that way, and if he's someone closely connected with those other three, I *will* arrest you, because I know you're guilty. I'll come up with false evidence, if that's what it takes. The settlers are up in arms over what's already happened. They want justice, and I can't give it to them. But, by God, I'll hand over a Nez Perce warrior to be hanged if this happens again!"

Strong Runner scowled. "And why is it there must be justice for the white settlers, but when the Nez Perce demand the same justice for themselves, they are ignored?"

"Because, I'm sorry to say, most of my people don't think you're important enough to deserve justice." Porter put his hands on his hips. "Most of them would prefer all of you got the hell out of here and let them claim all of this land. That's not my personal opinion, mind you, just an explanation of the overall picture."

Strong Runner's eyes narrowed to slits of hatred. "All my life my people cooperated with yours, traded with them, even took their religion, and this is how we are being repaid." He leaned closer to Porter. "It will not last forever. A man can swallow his pride for only so long." He drew in his breath to quell his growing anger. "I am leaving this area, my friend, going to the Blue Mountains to join Chief Joseph. He refuses to sign any more treaties or to agree that *any* of this land belongs to whites! I also refuse to sign any more treaties. After tomorrow I will be gone. If any more white men die, you will have to find someone else to blame." He turned, picking up Wolf Boy.

"Strong Runner."

Strong Runner kept the boy in his arms and looked back at Porter.

"You might as well face the fact that more settlers are going to come here. It can't be stopped. If I were you, I would advise Chief Joseph to accept it and come to Lapwai. The government will see that your people are cared for."

"Cared for?" Strong Runner's lips curled in disgust. "We have never needed to be cared for like weak children. Since the Nez Perces were created, we have taken care of ourselves, fed our children, protected our people against enemy tribes, survived the bitter winters. If we cannot take care of ourselves now, it is because the white man has killed off the game that once fed and clothed us; it is because the white man has put his filth and trash into our mountain streams and made the water undrinkable; it is because the white man has cut down so many trees that the rains wash away the hillsides, and because he has taken all the dead wood we once used for the fires that keep us warm in winter. He has stolen our prize horses, and he claims so much land that there is little left for us to grow enough food to sustain ourselves. One day, my friend, your people will have nowhere left to turn. They will use up the trees and the water and the animals and ruin the land, and they will all die. I wish that I could be here to see it happen, but my own people will die first."

Morning Star could see that Colonel Porter understood the truth in Strong Runner's words, but he stuck his chin out defensively, pretending to be unimpressed. "Maybe someday your people will see the benefits of our way of life," he answered. "In the meantime, take your own advice and leave Lapwai for now. I have no doubt you will be forced to return someday."

Strong Runner hoisted Wolf Boy to his other arm. "I will do whatever it takes to protect this son I hold in my arms, and the son who sits in the cradle on his mother's back, and all my future children. If it means my own death, then so be it, but many bluecoats and many white settlers will also die!"

He turned and left.

"Damn savages!" a lieutenant swore, starting out after him.

"Let him go!" Porter told the man.

"He killed those men! You *know* he killed them!"

"And I will remind you you're talking to a superior officer!" Porter answered. "I've done all I can do about this, and I don't intend to start a war over it!"

The lieutenant scowled, stepping back into place. "Sorry, sir. I just hate to see a guilty man go free like that."

Porter rubbed his eyes. "God knows plenty of our own kind are getting away with murder." He dismissed the men and sat down wearily, knowing the situation with the Nez Perce was far from over.

Outside, Strong Runner held Wolf Boy in one arm while

he put the other around Morning Star. "I am free," he told her. "We will go now to Chief Joseph's village."

Morning Star stopped walking. She looked up at him with tear-filled eyes, then moved her arms around her husband and son and wept. "I thought for certain they would arrest you today," she sobbed. "I have never known what the truth is, not from your own lips. But in my heart . . . I know you have avenged the wrong that was done to us."

Strong Runner touched her hair, tears filling his own eyes. "I will never forgive myself for being unable to help you."

"Surely you know that I have never held you to blame. You are my warrior, my beloved. I know that you would die for me, and for our sons."

Strong Runner wiped the tears from her cheeks. "And do you know that the reason I have not mated with you is because of my own guilt? My feelings have not changed because of what happened. You still belong only to me, my wife. Those men did not touch your heart, your soul, as I have. I know the shame that you felt, but there is nothing to be ashamed of. You were wronged. Now I have done what I can to right the wrong. That is all I will say about it. We will go to Chief Joseph's village, and you will be my wife again, if you are willing."

Morning Star felt all the old desire for her husband sweep through her. "I am willing," she answered. "I wish to be one with my husband again. You said you would do whatever it takes to protect your sons and your future children. I knew then that you would be a husband to me again. We can erase the bad memories, Strong Runner, if we hold only to each other and let our love bring us more sons and daughters."

He touched her cheek. "And perhaps we will not wait until we get to Chief Joseph's village. Perhaps we will go back to our dwelling right now and begin wiping away the bad memories."

She sniffed, reaching up to touch his face. "That would make me so happy, Strong Runner."

Strong Runner looked back to see Colonel Porter watching them. In spite of the tender moment he had just shared with his wife, he could not help grinning at the bluecoat who was so frustrated over being unable to arrest him. He had been very careful, and his plan had worked. He turned and walked away with Morning Star, on fire to be one with his woman again. All around them soldiers were packing gear and cleaning out furnishings and paperwork, preparing to leave Fort Lapwai. Strong Runner hoped it would be forever, but he knew that was too good to be true. The soldiers' retreat was only temporary. When they returned, many more would come.

16

DECEMBER 1866

Zack pulled on his boots after stoking up the heating stove. He hated the thought of going out into another cold day, but he had no choice. He thought how lonely and even colder he'd be if Iris weren't there. It was so nice to come home to her after spending the days fighting bitter winds, sleet, and snow, let alone the Sioux. In these two little rooms that had become home, he was always welcomed by the warmth of the heating stove, and the warmth of his wife's arms. He hated leaving it all again, often for several days at a time.

"Breakfast is almost ready," Iris told him, "such as it is. Come sit down to the table, Zack. We have a little time to talk before you go out on duty." She was glad that at least today Zack's duty was merely to be on standby in case of trouble. She hated it when it was his turn to ride out to supervise the wood trains, when she had to sit alone for days at a time, wondering if he would come back.

Fort Kearny needed a constant supply of wood for heating, cooking, bathwater, and such—so much wood that it was impossible to cut and stack enough to last the winter. That meant cutting wood constantly with crews taking turns at the cutting sites, camping there for a week at a time and bringing in wagon loads of wood with each crew rotation. Traveling to the woodcutting site was a dangerous journey of at least two hours each way in good weather. Zack and his cavalry troops shared patrol duty with two other captains, their mission being to guard the wood trains and loggers. Red Cloud's Sioux attacked the wood wagons nearly every time they ventured forth, and already many lives had been lost. "I wish the command at Fort Snelling would just order the evacuation of this place," Iris told Zack, studying him as he sat down to the table. He'd slept restlessly, and there were tired lines about his eyes.

"That's just what Red Cloud is hoping for—badger and hit at us until we give up."

She turned to take biscuits out of the oven, and Zack glanced at the flickering flames in the heating stove through the partly-open air vent. *Wood,* he thought. *This whole mess is over wood.* If things had been planned correctly, a supply would have been built up while the fort itself was being built. By the time the fort was completed, it was already autumn, the nights getting cold. Red Cloud damn well knew that to survive, they needed wood, and to get wood, they had to travel over three miles through the Sullivant Hills, hills just the right size for a war party to swoop down on the wood wagons so fast there was little time to take cover. Colonel Carrington's idea of posting a large cavalry escort for the wood trains, with a lookout post on higher ground overlooking the utility road, had helped save lives. The lookout personnel could alert the cavalry guarding the train whenever they spotted a war party approaching.

Zack rubbed his eyes, weary more from the constant exposure of him and his men to Sioux attack than from actual physical weariness. And he worried about Iris. He glanced at her, feeling uneasy at the vulnerability of the entire garrison at Fort Kearny. Their only saving grace was that so far Red Cloud's warriors seemed more interested in playing teasing games with the soldiers than in all-out war. He suspected that if they rallied themselves full force, they could take this fort. Maybe they knew that and simply enjoyed keeping everyone nervous. If it was just himself, he wouldn't be so worried, but there was Iris and the other women. Lieutenant Grummond's new young wife was here now, another daring female arrival.

Iris worried him most of all. His precious wife was three months pregnant, although she hardly showed yet. "How do you feel?"

Iris turned with the pan of biscuits in her gloved hand, looking pretty in a simple blue calico dress, a dusting of flour on her cheek.

"I'm fine, Zack. Don't be worrying about me. You have enough on your mind."

Zack sighed and rose, going to sit at the crude pine table he'd had some men build for them. "I wish Captain Denver hadn't been transferred to Laramie. Captain Fetterman is nothing like Denver. He's a hotheaded idiot, and he's undermining Colonel Carrington's authority, making some of the men think Carrington is a coward for not riding out and attacking every Sioux village he can find." His hands moved into fists. Fetterman had had the gall to say he could take eighty men and wipe out the whole Sioux nation. The man knew nothing about what clever strategists the Sioux were, nor did he understand just how many of them there were and how understaffed the forts were. Fetterman and Captain Brown, the regimental quartermaster, had recently had a virtual showdown with Colonel Carrington, bragging that they should be allowed to ride out along the Tongue River and attack every Sioux village they could find. Zack figured Carrington must know Fetterman was trying to show him up for a coward and earn himself some kind of fame. "I'd laugh at Fetterman's harebrained ideas if they weren't so dangerous," he told Iris. "I'm worried he's going to disobey one of Carrington's commands one day and get his whole company slaughtered."

Iris set the biscuits on the table, wondering what kind of Christmas they would have. Zack might not even be around Christmas day. He might be out there in the Sullivant Hills again, some warrior's arrow or rifle pointed at his back. The thought made her shiver. "I just hope you never have to ride with Fetterman. I don't like the man one whit." She turned to pick up one of the china bowls that had survived her trip west, and she dished some stew into it from a black kettle on the stove. "He's arrogant and too cocksure of himself. He's got people grumbling about Colonel Carrington. Janet Sievers called him a coward." She turned and set the bowl in front of Zack. "I think he's just being cautious. The army's mission here is not to go out and make war. It is to guard the Bozeman Trail and the whites who travel it. I hope you remember that, Zack."

"No one knows better than I do what Indians are capable of. I'd like to do exactly what Fetterman *thinks* he can do, but I know it isn't that easy, and I know our purpose for being here." He glanced at the spindly wreath hung near the bedroom door that Iris had made from a few needled branches. "I'm sorry this won't be much of a Christmas," he told her. "Next time I'm on wood patrol I'll cut you some thicker pine branches. Maybe we can even have a small tree, but we'll have to cut it up for wood right after Christmas. I can't even get you a decent present. The Sioux have practically cut off our supplies, and what does come are just the basic necessities for survival." He sighed, looking down at his bowl of stew. "This is all probably more primitive and lonely than you even figured."

Iris placed her hands on his shoulders from behind. "Zack, I could be back east attending parties, surrounded by crowds of people, and I'd be more lonely than I am here, because you wouldn't be with me." She leaned down and kissed his cheek. "I am just fine, and I'm happy just to be here with you, so quit worrying over our circumstances."

He grasped her forearms lightly. "It's just—Christmas, the baby—I worry about you having a child out here. If the Sioux ever decided to attack the fort full force, I'm not sure we could hold them off, and we lose another man almost every day. Now with Fetterman causing all this unrest among the men . . ."

Iris touched his thick dark hair. "Eat your stew, my darling husband. It's not much of a breakfast food, but it's all we have today. They're cutting down on the rations of ham, and the chickens aren't laying enough eggs to supply the whole fort. Thank goodness the Indians haven't run off all the cattle yet. We'll have beef for at least part of the winter."

"Let's hope more supply wagons manage to get here past Red Cloud before the winter is out. If they don't, we'll all starve."

Iris tried not to face the reality of the remark. She sat down across from him, picking up a biscuit to put a tiny bit of honey on it. "What does Colonel Shaver have to say about Fetterman?"

Zack swallowed some stew. "He doesn't like him any more than I do. The man has a way of making caution look like cowardliness. Shaver says he'd rather be a live coward than a dead idiot." Iris laughed lightly, and Zack grinned. "Fetterman's mistake is thinking the Indians are ignorant fools, when all the while they laugh at men like him, realizing he's the ignorant fool. I'm half tempted to send you back east. I don't like the location of this place. We're too open to attack and have too few men to defend with."

"Do you really think you could get me to go?"

He smiled grimly. "Even if I could, it would be too dangerous now to let you go through those gates out there."

Iris watched him bite into a biscuit. She took a deep breath before her next remark. "Much as I'm horrified at the thought of what happened to your family, I still can't bring myself to hate all Indians. Red Cloud and the Sioux have every reason to fight back. The Bozeman cuts right through their hunting grounds, land that we promised no white man would step foot on, and now they pour through like a waterfall. How can any of us expect the Sioux to act any differently?"

Zack swallowed, a hardness coming into his eyes. "Don't defend them to me, Iris. I can hardly see them as human beings."

"Thomas Red Hand seems very human to me. He has a marvelous sense of humor."

He waved her off. "That's no sense of humor. He's just plain cocky. You can't tell me part of him doesn't take pleasure in seeing the Sioux bait us like they do, and he sees nothing wrong with what his people did to my family."

"He sees the other side of it, Zack. I think he's trying in his own way to make you see the other side of it."

Zack straightened, glaring at her. "Why are you bringing this up now? You know how I feel. I'm trying, Iris, not to let it come between us or affect my decisions. That's the best I can do. Down inside, my feelings will never change."

She blinked back tears. "I'm bringing it up because I don't

want you to let Fetterman make you do something rash because of your own hatred for Indians. I want you to be happy, Zack, and until you come to terms with what's eating at your insides, no matter how much you love me and our children, there will be something missing for you. You will never know total peace."

He sighed and rose, not finishing his breakfast. "I don't have time to talk about this now." He walked over to take his wool coat and cape from a hook. "I'm more worried about you being pregnant and what's happening around here." He put on his hat. "The woodcutters will be heading out soon. My men and I are assigned backup duty, and I have to get things prepared." He opened the door, and a rush of cold air and snowflakes swooped in. "On top of everything else, it's so damn cold out there that half the men who go out with the wood trains end up suffering frostbite."

"Zack."

He closed the door again and turned to her.

"Don't leave angry. If something happened—" She grasped his hand. "I try to get you to talk only because I think it's important that we *do* talk about it."

His green eyes warmed. "What's important is getting this whole Indian situation settled once and for all. I'm just worried that's going to take a lot longer than anyone figured. I hate the thought of you having to live this way for years." He leaned down and kissed her cheek. "Stay inside. We'll talk about it when I get back tonight."

He hurried out, and Iris went to a window to watch him walk across the parade grounds toward the commander's quarters. *When I get back,* he'd said. She prayed the same prayer she'd prayed nearly every day since coming there— that he would indeed return . . . unharmed. "But you *won't* talk about it, Zack. You'll find an excuse not to."

Iris heard the bugle call to alarm. She knew the sound, always dreaded it. The wood train had left that morning at ten o'clock, an hour after Zack had left. She glanced at the clock . . . one o'clock. She grabbed her wool cape, tied it around her neck, then hurried out, her concern making her oblivious of the cold and snow. Men were scurrying everywhere, and she felt an ache in her heart knowing that part of the reason for the trip had been to gather Yule logs and pine branches for Christmas decorating.

She spotted both Zack and Fetterman heading for command quarters. She hurried across the parade grounds, knowing she wouldn't be allowed inside, but if Zack was going to ride out to rescue the wood train, she wanted one last goodbye. Sergeant Sievers's wife was also running toward headquarters, as was the young Mrs. Grummond and Mrs. Carver, a corporal's wife. The four of them gathered on the boardwalk in front. Iris walked over and put an arm around Mrs. Sievers's shoulders, not caring what the others thought of her friendship with an enlisted man's wife. "I'm sure everything will be all right," she told the woman, ignoring Mrs. Carver's frown.

"Thank you, Mrs. Myers," Mrs. Sievers said.

All four women could hear arguing now, the loudest voice being that of Captain Fetterman. "Let *me* go, Colonel Carrington! I'll wipe out every one of those savages!"

"You will do nothing but go to the wood train and do whatever is necessary to protect those men!" Carrington answered. "If the Sioux run off, make sure they keep going past Lodge Trail Ridge, but under no circumstances are you to pursue the enemy beyond that point! You'll be followed by Lieutenant Grummond and Captain Powell and their cavalry. Captain Myers will be on standby if you need further help."

"I won't need help," Fetterman replied boldly.

Iris's heart pounded harder. She did not like the idea of Zack riding into a bad situation created by William Fetterman. Just then the regimental quartermaster, Captain Brown, charged up to headquarters on horseback. He was the man who had plotted and schemed with Fetterman to get Colonel Carrington's permission to wipe out the Sioux village by village. Brown dashed inside, leaving the door open. Iris heard him ask Carrington to be allowed to go with Fetterman also.

"I'm leaving Fort Kearny soon, sir. I'd like a chance at killing a few more hostiles before I do," Brown announced.

Carrington repeated his orders. "Help the wood train, but pursue the enemy no farther than Lodge Trail Ridge. Beyond that point you'll be too far away for any help to reach you if you should need it. We don't have enough breech-loaders, thanks to headquarters being so slow with provisions. Most of the men will have only muskets, so be extra careful. And remember that at close range an Indian with bow and arrow is as deadly as a man with a rifle."

"I want command of the troops, Colonel," Fetterman demanded. "I've got seniority over Captains Brown, Powell, and Myers."

There came a moment of silence. "All right," Carrington answered, resignation in his voice. "You're in charge, but remember that *I* am your superior, and I expect my orders to be obeyed. Now, get your men together and get out there!"

Iris and the women stepped back as the men came trooping out.

Zack glanced at Iris, then hurried over to her. "What are you doing here? You aren't even dressed warm enough for this weather!"

"Zack, be careful! Remember Colonel Carrington's orders."

She could tell by his eyes that he wanted to hold her for a moment, but not in front of the men. "I'll be careful," he assured her. He turned and ran to a private who was bringing up his horse. Suddenly everything was chaos on the parade grounds as men mounted horses and got themselves in order. Mrs. Carver had already left to find her husband. Janet Sievers watched the maneuvers with a hint of panic in her eyes.

"I don't feel good about this," she told Iris.

The words brought a tight pain to Iris's chest. "Do you see your husband?"

"There! He's talking to Captain Fetterman. I hope he'll ride with your husband and not with him."

"I'm so afraid," Mrs. Grummond said, tears in her eyes as she watched her husband amid all the preparations. "I hate it here, all the danger. George and I have been married only a little while. I don't know what I would do if something happened to him."

Iris could understand what fort life must be like for a new young wife who had never lived this way before. It was her own saving grace that she had been prepared for what army life would be like. "Just be proud of your husband. I'm sure they'll be all right," she tried to assure her, actually trying to assure herself at the same time. "Your husband will be back by tonight, and before long you'll be transferred someplace else, maybe somewhere more civilized and less lonely."

Mrs. Grummond only shook her head and wiped her eyes. She hurried away, and Iris was tempted to get back to the warmth of her living quarters, but she could not make herself go. She felt too restless. She noticed an extra man from another regiment as well as two civilian volunteers approach Fetterman, apparently asking permission to go along.

Iris quickly tried to count the men, guessing there to be at least seventy present. More arrived. She thought about Fetterman's remark that he could wipe out the entire Sioux nation with eighty men.

Too soon the men were prepared to depart. Iris noticed that Sergeant Sievers was riding under Captain Fetterman's command, and her heart fell. She liked Sievers, felt sorry for his wife, who had also noticed he was with Fetterman. Fetterman's infantry marched away at a near run. Carrington shouted to Fetterman, again warning him about his boundaries. It angered Iris to think that Carrington could be so intelligent in building and running a fort, and in his strategy for handling the Indians, yet he allowed Captain Fetterman to run him over.

She noticed Thomas Red Hand ride up to Zack. They spoke for a moment, then Thomas rode out ahead of the cavalry troops. Although Zack had never quite accepted the man, Iris felt better when Thomas accompanied Zack on these expeditions. He was always making little remarks that showed great humor and intelligence, and she suspected Zack saw it too. He just didn't want to admit an Indian, especially a Pawnee, could have any good qualities. She saw Colonel Shaver standing not far away, and she hurried over to him. "Do you think this is something worse than the other attacks?" she asked him.

"Could be," Shaver answered, watching the tail end of the troops pass through the gates. "Thomas Red Hand is the scout who rode in with news that the wood train was under attack again." He looked down at her. "Don't worry about Zack. He knows better than to go against orders and risk the lives of his men."

"It's Fetterman who worries me. He could inadvertently lead Zack right into a mess. I don't understand why Colonel

Carrington would allow so many men to be at the mercy of Fetterman's orders."

"I just hope Fetterman has sense enough to stay close to the wood train and get those men back here safely," Shaver said.

Iris longed to tell Zack she loved him, to hold him just for a moment, but he was too busy. She could see he was edgy but eager to join the fighting, yet Carrington ordered Grummond to ride out next, asking Zack to hold back. Zack argued that Thomas Red Hand suspected this time there was a much bigger war party than usual, but Carrington waved him off.

"Red Cloud is just trying to unnerve us with his usual pretense at a big attack. He thinks to kill a few men and run again, like he always does. Maybe Captains Fetterman and Grummond can teach him a lesson. We'll surprise Red Cloud by coming on with more and more forces. By the time you arrive, I'm sure Fetterman and Grummond will have things in hand."

A disgruntled Zack rode up to Iris, who couldn't help but think how handsome he looked mounted up in uniform, so skilled and sure. A sergeant waited at the head of his troops, holding the cavalry guidon, a forked flag signifying that branch of the army.

"Stay inside," Zack told her. "I don't like the feel of this one, and I don't think we should be riding in scattered forces like this." He glanced at Shaver. "Take care of her, sir. By the time I ride out of here we'll have only a skeleton force left at the fort. For all we know, that's how Red Cloud has it planned." Iris could see the worry in his eyes when he looked back at her. "Take care of that baby."

She put a hand to her stomach. "Just do as Colonel Carrington says and don't go past Lodge Trail Ridge," she reminded him. "I want this baby to have a father."

"Fetterman has his eighty men," Shaver put in. "If he thinks he can defeat all the Sioux with them, let him do it on his own. It's what he wants. Sometimes glory comes at a high price. Remember that, Zack."

The words brought a sinking feeling to Iris's stomach.

"Please get back inside, Iris," Zack told her. "You shouldn't be out in this cold."

She reached out and touched his leg. "Be extra careful, Zack." With tears in her eyes she walked back to their quarters and watched out the window. Nearly another hour passed with Zack waiting for further orders. Suddenly she heard gunfire in the distance, and the fort came alive. Howitzers were moved into place, and Iris realized there now must be Indians outside the fort. She jumped when a couple of the howitzers were fired. Then a man came riding in at a hard gallop, and she recognized the fort medic, Dr. Hines. He was very upset as he spoke with Carrington, and Carrington immediately ordered Zack and his men to leave. Zack said something to Colonel Shaver, then glanced toward their quarters before leaving. Iris's heart ached for him.

Iris's only consolation was that Thomas had also ridden back to the fort and was now with Zack and his men. Thomas was a good scout. He would know if Zack was headed into something he should stay away from. She watched Shaver hurrying to her quarters, and she opened the door for him.

"Hines says the Indians retreated from the wood train, but there is no sign now of Fetterman and his men," Shaver said. "Zack is riding out to find him. Even Grummond is nowhere around. A few Indians forayed around the fort a while ago, but they have already ridden off again."

Iris breathed deeply against panic. "What do you think happened to Fetterman?"

"Hard to say. I think this whole thing has been some kind of setup by Red Cloud. Zack will have to be mighty careful."

Iris fought an urge to scream. "Thank you, Colonel Shaver. I'm sure you have a lot to do. I'll be all right."

Shaver squeezed her shoulder. "We might have to order the women together into one place, just a safety precaution until we're sure Red Cloud doesn't intend to attack the fort. In the meantime, you'd better do some praying, Iris."

She nodded, closing the door as he left. "Yes, I'll do that," she said to herself. She struggled against an urge to weep. She had to be strong now, and she had to have faith.

17

$\mathcal{Z}$ack headed north, keeping to the east of the wood train. He already knew the Indians had retreated from their attack on the wood wagons. The problem now was to find Grummond and Fetterman, and he did not like the thought of what might have happened to them. Carrington had insisted he bring along three box wagons, in spite of how they slowed him down. Carrington said the wagons were necessary in case there had been high casualties.

Those words stung. Obviously the man suspected the worst. He knew these hills must be swarming with Sioux, probably more than Fetterman had figured, but he was more concerned about the fort being left with not nearly enough men to defend it. The hardest order he'd ever obeyed was to ride out of there while more Indians were making threatening moves against the fort. He'd wanted to stay there and defend the post—and Iris—not go riding after that damned fool Fetterman. His only consolation was that Lieutenant-Colonel Shaver was at the fort. He would keep an eye on Iris, and at least at the fort they had howitzers. The big guns should keep the Sioux at bay.

Do not worry about your wife at the fort," Thomas said as though reading his thoughts. "Those Sioux will not attack the fort. They were only trying to keep Carrington from sending more men into the field." The words were nearly shouted as the men rode fast enough to catch up to Fetterman, but not so hard as to wear out the horses. For all Zack knew, the animals might be needed for a chase, maybe even a quick retreat, although he had no plans to run from any damn Indians.

"How many do you think there are out here?" Zack shouted back.

They crested another hill, and Zack raised his hand to call a temporary halt. He and Thomas scanned the horizon—no sign of the soldiers who had gone out ahead of them. "Many," Thomas finally answered. "Many more than have ever been sent against us up to now."

Zack sighed with frustration. "Dr. Hines said the wood train was safe, but he saw no sign of Fetterman, even when he rode as far as Lodge Trail Ridge. You know what that means."

Thomas nodded. "The fool went beyond the ridge, against Colonel Carrington's orders. He would not listen when I tried to warn him that Red Cloud will send decoys. It is an old, old trick, and you white men keep falling for it. The attack on the wood train was only the bait to get more soldiers out there. Red Cloud has probably heard about Captain Fetterman's boasting that he could wipe out the whole Sioux nation with eighty men. He must have gotten a good laugh out of that." He looked at Zack. "Now you also will be going beyond the point where Colonel Carrington said we must not go, thanks to that fool Fetterman."

"We have no choice now. We'll stay well to the east of where I figure Fetterman rode, ride a little farther north, cross the Bozeman Trail before heading west. I hope to close in on whatever has happened, maybe trap the Sioux between Fetterman and Grummond's men and us."

"I know the Sioux," Thomas sneered. "We will be too late. We must be very careful, or our own scalps will decorate some Sioux warrior's belt."

The word *scalps* always brought a sick feeling to Zack's insides. For another hour he and his men made a sweep of the hills far beyond Lodge Trail Ridge. Zack could sense the jittery nerves of his men, and all senses came even more alert when they heard gunfire beyond a ridge to the west.

Zack turned and headed his men in that direction. Thomas Red Hand charged ahead of him, cresting a rise, then rode back to Zack. "You cannot go beyond the ridge!" he told him. "Many Sioux, perhaps two thousand! The shooting has stopped, but I cannot tell what was happening."

"No sign of Fetterman?"

"There are so many Indians, it is hard to tell. Perhaps we should not even show ourselves."

Zack glanced up the hill. He could hear a distant din of war whoops and shouts that sounded like men celebrating. He had learned that in these rolling hills there could sometimes be hundreds of Indians just on the other side of a ridge, but unless they were screaming at the top of their lungs or shooting guns, one would never know they were there. The hills acted as a sound barrier.

"I'm not going back to the fort until I find out what happened to Fetterman and Grummond. If they're out there amid those Indians and any of them are still alive, we have to see if we can help!" He ordered his sergeant to spread the men out as a show of force, then had them ride to the crest of the ridge in one long line, rifles ready. "My God," he muttered when he saw what waited in the distant valley below. "There are thousands of them."

The soldiers were spotted quickly, and some of the Sioux mounted horses and rode partway up the hill, taunting the soldiers, making warlike gestures, yipping and shouting, motioning for the soldiers to come down and join them. One shouted something to them in the Sioux tongue. "What did he say?" Zack asked Thomas, gripping the reins of his horse tightly as he struggled with the urge to pull up his rifle and shoot those beckoning them.

Thomas shook his head. "He said that they have killed the rest of the bluecoats. Come on down and get their bodies."

Zack drew a deep breath. "Do you think he's telling the truth? You're talking about at least eighty men, Thomas!"

"I do not know if it is true. I know only that you must not go down there. Fetterman and his men might be there . . .

and they might not. Either way, you would be riding into a trap. Fetterman did not care that he put the lives of so many men in danger. Do you want to kill Indians more than you want to save the lives of fifty-four men who would have no chance down there? Do you want your woman to become a widow so soon?"

Zack closed his eyes, sorely tempted to position his men and start killing Indians. If he could send for reinforcements, he would, but there were hardly any men left at the fort. As long as they stayed there on the ridge, he could at least see where the Indians were and which way they went. He would know they were at least not attacking Fort Kearny.

"If Fetterman is down there, there is nothing we can do for them," Thomas told him. "They are surely already dead. He made a bad choice, and Red Cloud was ready for one so foolish. Do not follow in his shoes."

Zack met his eyes. "Why in hell do you care?"

Thomas shrugged. "Because I am Pawnee, and the Sioux hate me as much as they hate bluecoats. I might as well have blue eyes . . . or green ones. I sure as hell don't wanna go down there."

"And if those were Pawnee down there, you'd be with them, killing and scalping just like those Sioux."

Thomas frowned. "Perhaps. A man does what he must to survive, Captain. That's what those Sioux are doing. That is what *you* are doing. Survival of the fittest."

Zack thought how he had used that very term that morning when talking to Iris, referring to the Indians as animals; yet in these primitive battles, he and the other soldiers had to think the same way. He studied the scene below, the celebrating Sioux reminding him of a pack of wolves parading around their kill. "Maybe so," he answered. "Then again, maybe it has become survival of the smartest." He looked at Thomas and saw a quick flicker of anger in the man's eyes, followed by a glint of humor.

"That is where you white men have the final victory. We Indians, we're pretty smart ourselves, but we never look too far into the future or plan big battles weeks away like you do. Those Sioux down there have captured the moment, taken their prey. They could come up here and kill all of us, perhaps go to the fort and kill everyone there, but they won't.

They have fought enough for today, counted many coup. They tricked Captain Fetterman into following them into the hills, where I am guessing thousands lay waiting in the tall grass until Fetterman and his men were in the valley. Then they swooped down upon them. If their trick had not worked, they would have gone their own way and tried another day, rather than come and attack the fort. Once he saw that the wood train was safe, Fetterman should have gone back to the fort."

The Indians began to leave, heading west. "I can't believe they aren't coming up here after us," Zack commented.

"They are done for the day. They would rather you rode down there and saw what is left of your fellow soldiers. They think it will teach you a good lesson not to come after them, that maybe it will frighten you so that you will leave their hunting grounds. If Fetterman is down there, be prepared for a terrible sight. They want to make sure you see what could happen to you if you do not leave this land."

Zack straightened, squinting to see better. "Look there." He pointed to the ground.

The day had warmed just enough to cause the snow to melt, but it was still close to freezing, and the damp air seemed to penetrate Zack's bones. He wondered if it was more than that, a sickening cold that came from realizing what he must be seeing in the distance. White men's bodies, probably stripped. The waiting became almost unbearable, but he knew he was doing the right thing. Why add fifty-four more men to the possible eighty bodies below? If he thought there was even a glimmer of a chance of winning such a battle, he would gladly ride down there and kill until he couldn't see straight. But he was not going to be responsible for the death of fifty-four others. If Fetterman had led his eighty men to slaughter, it would be a terrible legacy. This would ultimately be blamed on Colonel Carrington, even though the man had warned Fetterman not to go beyond Lodge Trail Ridge.

Even worse than that was the fact that this left the fort seriously understaffed in the middle of winter. He worried about Iris, wondered how they were going to manage to bring in enough wood. A victory like this would make Red Cloud and his Sioux even more confident. They would continue to lit them hard, harass the wood trains, perhaps prevent more supplies from reaching the fort. Never had the fort's location seemed so remote.

They waited all afternoon, most of the men watching silently, all lost in their own horror at what they saw as the Indians continued to ride away. Zack was glad they at least seemed to be heading away from the fort. They could see more bodies now, strung out along the trail the Indians took. The last of the warriors finally disappeared over a distant ridge.

"Ride out and see if they keep going," Zack told Thomas. "Make sure they haven't turned around to wait for us to ride down there and pick up our men."

"You want *me* to go over there and see?"

Zack glanced at the man. "That's your job, isn't it?"

Thomas rubbed the scar on his cheek. "Guess so. Maybe I should go back to my people and quit this scoutin' stuff before I get myself scalped."

"Maybe."

Their gazes held in mutual challenge, yet Zack sensed an odd friendship with the man, something he could hardly bear to admit to. "I will wave my blanket if all is clear," Thomas said with a faint grin. He rode off, and Zack watched and waited. It took over a half hour for Thomas to ride through the valley and up the next hill. He crested that rise and disappeared over the side. Zack waited with alarm until the man reappeared and waved his blanket over his head.

"Let's move in," Zack told the sergeant next to him. "Bring the wagons. We'll probably need them."

The next couple of hours were filled with horror. It was obvious by their wounds that Fetterman and Brown had shot themselves before the Indians could get to them. The bodies of nearly all eighty men were strung out over a half-mile— stripped, mutilated, scalped. The body of Isaac Fisher, one of the civilian volunteers, was riddled with so many arrows, it was difficult to count them, but Zack figured it had to be at least a hundred. Frozen pools of blood dotted the landscape, and the bodies were stiffened into grotesque forms, some with arms reached out as though to defend themselves, many with eyes wide open and staring, some with arrows shot into their eyes.

Zack ordered the bodies to be picked up and piled in the wagons, a horrifying job that caused some of the men to vomit. He didn't doubt more than a few might try to desert after seeing this. His own horror did nothing to deter him from remaining in the army to kill Indians. What he saw only enhanced that desire, and he looked forward to the next battle. What he saw brought back all the ugly memories. With every dead body he saw his mother and Emily. He never had been allowed to see his dead father's body, but he could well imagine what the man must have suffered, and he was reminded why he was there in a uniform. He had already killed his share of Indians in other skirmishes, but now he knew that wasn't enough. What hurt the most was that he had arrived too late with too few men. It brought back the terrible powerless feeling he'd known as a child, not being able to help his family. Once again it was Indians who made him feel this way.

He walked among the bodies as they were picked up, recognizing most of the men, except those whose faces were too mutilated. His gut ached when he found Lieutenant Grummond. The man's young wife would be devastated by this. He drew in his breath in agony when he recognized another familiar face, a man to whom he had grown close. He had been stripped and scalped, his chest split open.

"Sergeant Sievers!" Zack groaned. He turned away, blinking back tears.

"I told you how it would be," Thomas told him. "They think maybe now you will leave."

Zack turned to look at him, seeing only a Pawnee. "Get the hell out of my sight before I pull my pistol and kill you!" he warned.

Thomas frowned. "I am on *your* side, remember?"

"I mean it, Thomas!"

Thomas nodded thoughtfully. "You are not to blame, nor am I or Colonel Carrington, or even Red Cloud. It is Captain Fetterman's fault, and his alone."

Zack's jaw flexed in anger, and he couldn't hide his hatred.

"One day, Captain, you will see me only as a man."

Thomas turned and walked away. Zack stared after him, fighting the urges of a young boy to run up and kill a

Pawnee. He looked around at the sight of eighty men massacred on the battlefield. All these years since his family was murdered, and nothing had changed. He wondered if it ever would.

The warrior rode toward the small boy, and the boy shivered at the sight of a face decorated grotesquely with war paint. The Indian's eyes were bloodred, his teeth gleaming white as he smiled with vicious glee, hatchet raised. As he came closer, he got bigger and bigger, like a monster. The little boy tried to run, but his feet were so heavy. Why was it so hard to move?

The warrior was coming closer! The boy could not even turn around. He stood in transfixed terror as he watched the hatchet come down to slice across his neck. Somehow he could still see. He watched his head roll away, tried to run and pick it up. Blood ran out of it, and what was left of his neck ached fiercely . . . so fiercely . . .

Zack bolted upright, rubbing his aching neck, his whole body drenched in sweat. He shook his head to clear his thoughts, felt his face to make sure his head was still attached. His breath was coming in pants, and with great relief he realized he was in the tiny bedroom with Iris.

"Zack?" Iris touched his shoulder. "Are you all right?"

He ran his hands through his hair. "Just another bad dream."

Iris sat up. "You were tossing and groaning. I was about to wake you."

"I'm sorry." He sat on the edge of the bed in his long-johns, resting his elbows on his knees, his head in his hands. "It was like all the other ones I've had over the years. They went away for a while, but after what I saw two days ago . . ."

Iris sighed, aching for him. "It's too bad you had to be the one to find them, but better that than to have been with Captain Fetterman."

Zack threw back his head and took a deep breath. "I would have tried to stop him. Powell and Brown and most of the men with him believed in him. He led all of them to their deaths. I hope to never be responsible for such a thing." He rose and walked to the back window, looking out into the darkness. The wind had picked up.

"Winter is setting in harder. I feel a blizzard coming on. I doubt Red Cloud will be much bother again before next spring. Indians seldom do much warring in the dead of winter. They're too busy keeping warm and keeping food in their bellies."

"Then we should be safe for a while," Iris answered.

Zack turned. "Maybe, but they know we have to keep bringing in wood all winter, and they know we need our supply line kept open." He looked at her apologetically. "I didn't want it to be this way for you, Iris, these tiny rooms we live in, this constant threat, you being pregnant out in this godforsaken place. With the money you inherited from your father, you could be living damn good back east."

"Zack, I knew what to expect. Have you heard me complain?"

"No, and I love you for it. I just hope the Sioux won't take any more drastic measures before spring. Maybe reinforcements will arrive by then. I'm just not sure you should have come back in here tonight. Carrington thinks all the women should stay in the powder magazine for another day or so, until we're more sure the Sioux aren't going to come after the fort."

She scooted back against a pillow. "I am not in the army, Zack Myers, and I don't need to follow Carrington's orders. I know what cleaning up after the Fetterman massacre did to you, and that nightmare proved it. I wanted to be with you. Now, come back to bed. It's so cold."

He studied her lovingly, thinking how beautiful she looked by the dim light of a lantern. Her flannel gown made her seem soft all over. He liked lying next to her in that gown, feeling her breasts through the velvety material. It made him feel warm and loved, and fiercely protective. He sat down on the edge of the bed beside her. "I have to tell someone, Iris."

"Tell me what?"

He rubbed his neck again. "Thomas Red Hand. The other day after we found the bodies . . . I wanted to kill him. Not just because he was Pawnee, but because he was Indian, *any* Indian. Seeing that horrible mutilation reawakened memories

I'd rather leave buried, and when I found Sergeant Sievers's body and looked up to see Thomas standing there, it just poured in on me. I told him to get out of my sight before I shot him. It frightens me to think I really could have done it."

Iris hurt for him. "At least you controlled the urge. You should apologize to him."

He looked incredulous. "To a Pawnee?"

"No. To a *man,* just a man. Thomas is just as much a part of the army as you and the other soldiers."

Zack shook his head. "I don't know. I can never quite bring myself to trust him."

Iris shivered and scooted under the pile of quilts that covered the bed. "What you felt only shows what that hatred you carry can do to you. That's why you need to stick it out in the army and keep fighting Indians until you come to terms with your past. And I *do* think you should apologize to Thomas. He's a good, dependable scout."

Zack wondered how he had gotten by in life before he'd met her. "And you're a good, dependable wife." He moved under the covers with her. "And beautiful." He put his hand on her belly. "I worry about you having this baby out here."

"Indian women do it, and so have a lot of white women." She thought of Janet Sievers, and wondered where she would go if anything happened to Zack. All her family items had been sold, Grandma was gone, Grandpa had sold the house and moved in with his brother. She had saved the profits from the sale of her father's estate. Someday Zack would retire and they could live comfortably on the money, but without him, no amount of money in the world could comfort her.

"Make love to me, Zack. I want you to make love to me as often as we can when you're here. I'm always afraid—"

"Don't say it. I won't end up like Sergeant Sievers. I promise."

Iris didn't doubt that Sievers had made the same promise to his own wife. She snuggled in close to Zack, enjoying the feel of hard muscle beneath his woolen longjohns. He nuzzled her neck as he pushed up her flannel gown, and she wiggled out of her drawers. It was too cold to completely undress, and this was enough, his fingers working magic, exploring, caressing, bringing forth sweet urges from inside her. He unbuttoned his longjohns and moved on top of her, and she gasped when his hot shaft moved into her sweetly, teasingly, slowly.

She breathed deeply with the ecstasy of taking her man, giving him pleasure in return. The constant danger of losing him made this act even more intense, a celebration that he was alive and right there by her side.

He pushed harder, and she arched up to him in abandon. "I need you so, Iris," he groaned. "You are my peace." Moments later his life spilled into her in sweet release. He settled in beside her, pulling her into his arms. "Maybe if I hold you the dream won't come back." He knew he needed to stoke the heating stove, but the orders were to conserve as much as possible and he didn't want to leave Iris's side.

Christmas was only two days away, and for the families of eighty men it was going to be a very sad one. At least reinforcements were on their way, but that news was dampened by the knowledge that Colonel Carrington was being blamed for the Fetterman massacre and was being relieved of duty. Colonel Shaver would be in charge until someone else was appointed. He didn't know yet who that would be, but one thing he *did* know, something he had not told Iris yet, was that one of the men coming to Fort Kearny was Major Jason Ward. Iris had told him about Jason's reaction to their marriage when he visited her back in Washington. The man's presence was going to make their life there even more miserable.

He held Iris tightly, kissed her hair. "I'll talk to Thomas."

Iris smiled to herself, glad to know her husband felt some little bit of remorse for his threat to Thomas.

18

Zack pulled up the fur collar of his wool army coat, protecting his neck against a cold wind. He stared at the site where eighty frozen bodies had been buried, and he could not quell the feeling that this was some kind of omen of more disasters. The thought made the cold air seem even colder. He couldn't make himself move as others began leaving the mass graves. The memorial service was over, and those women present were weeping openly, as were some of the soldiers. Poor Mrs. Sievers had to be practically dragged away. Her cries of sorrow pierced Zack's heart, stirring up his rage again. He could not forget how brutally her husband had been killed.

As though sensing his thoughts, Iris touched his hand. "Thomas is still here," she told him.

He knew what she was really saying. He looked down at her watery eyes. "The hell with it!" he said, blinking back his own tears.

"You promised me, Zack Myers."

He studied this woman he had married, this woman who refused to give up on him. "What is it about you that makes it so damn hard to win an argument with you, or to deny you anything?"

She smiled through her tears. "It's called love, Zack, and you are capable of much more of it than you know."

She turned and left him. Zack stared after her, suddenly feeling ridiculously helpless. He scowled. He did not want to talk to Thomas, certainly not today of all days; but if he didn't, Iris would give him that strange, silent treatment that told him she was not happy with his decision. The worst thing was, part of him actually *wanted* to apologize. He'd been wrong, and he damn well knew it. When he saw Thomas walking away from the grave site, he called out to him.

Thomas waited as he approached, and Zack was sure he saw a smirk on the man's face. He'd probably been waiting for an apology. Zack swallowed his pride and pushed down his hatred, pretending it wasn't there for the moment. As he drew closer, he saw beyond the smugness in Thomas's look. There was something more in his eyes, a little spark of concern, even hurt.

"I, uh, I want to apologize for how I reacted the other day," Zack said. "I wouldn't really have shot you. I was just—"

"Yes, you *would* have shot me, Captain. I know the look. And you do not want to apologize. I suspect it is your *wife* who thinks you should apologize, and she is a woman with whom it is difficult to argue."

Zack hunkered deeper into his collar. "I have memories that became too vivid when I saw what had happened," he told Thomas. "It made me so angry, I couldn't think straight."

"It is called hatred, my friend."

Zack bristled at the word *friend*. He held Thomas's eyes boldly. "Yes, that's exactly what it's called. I've lived with that hatred for sixteen years."

Thomas himself shivered against the wind. "Follow me," he told Zack. He walked soundlessly through fresh snow to the side of a storage building, where they could stand out of the wind. Zack followed him around the corner, and Thomas pulled a thin cigar out of an inside pocket in his wolfskin jacket. "Want one?"

"No," Zack answered. "I've apologized, so nothing more needs to be done."

Thomas's black eyes bored into him. "It does if I have to

worry about you shooting me in the back next time we get in an Indian fight. You could do it and say the Sioux shot me. Don't say you ain't thought of it, 'cuz I know you have."

Zack stared at him a moment, then slowly nodded. "I have, but the fact remains I didn't do it. I don't kill a man senselessly, with absolutely no reason, like your Pawnee killed my family."

Thomas lit his cigar and took a puff. "Like a white man shot my wife? Just because she was Indian?"

Zack felt a wave of guilt and concern rush through him. "What?"

"My wife. I had a wife. I felt the same about her as you feel about the woman you married." He leaned a little closer. "It's called love. I guess you know what that is. A white man shot my wife, Captain, for no good reason, just like your family was killed. You white men have a word for it. It's called *prejudice*. Me, I figure there's no sense hating a whole race for what a few people do."

Zack leaned against the wall of the storage shed. "I'm sorry about your wife, Thomas. I really am."

The Indian kept the cigar between his teeth. "Now, there's a real apology. I can see in your eyes you mean it." He drew on the cigar again and took it from his mouth. "There's somethin' you have to understand about Indians, Captain, about yourself, about this whole mess. You got to understand that the white man and the Indian fight for different reasons. There's even a difference in your reasons for fighting and them other soldiers' reason."

Zack folded his arms in an effort to stay warm. "I'm listening, but only because Iris would want me to. Have your say."

Thomas leaned against the wall beside him. "The white man wants to own everything. It is not enough to take the gold from Indian land and leave. He wants everything—the land, the game, the trees, the gold. He would own pieces of the sun and the moon if he could. And what for? Only for power. Only for one man to brag that he is richer and owns more land than the next. The Indians own nothing, and they don't *want* to own anything, except maybe horses. All they want is their hunting grounds preserved so that they can feed their women and children. Nearly all fighting between Indian tribes has been over hunting grounds, nothing more. They try to keep whites away because they dirty the water, cut down the trees, kill all the game, and make it so that the Indian cannot survive. That is all they are fighting for—survival. When they kill whites it is to frighten them into staying away. The whites think the only way to make them stop is to turn around and kill all Indians. Good, bad, they don't care. Indians are no more to them than a deer or a rabbit. You soldiers are supposed to be here to protect Indian lands from the whites, but because most soldiers feel the same about Indians as the white settlers do, they are not protecting the Indians at all. They think only to protect the settlers, and in doing so the Indians feel betrayed. The forts the soldiers build are only a sign to them that more whites will come. So the Indians turn around and kill soldiers. They make no long-term battle plans. They live only in the moment. They see soldiers, they go after them, scare them a little, kill a few . . . or maybe many. Then they disappear again, hoping maybe this time the soldiers will leave. They think if the soldiers leave, the rest of the whites will leave."

Zack stared out at the fresh graves. "What's your point, Thomas?"

Thomas puffed on the cigar again, took it from his mouth, and stared at it absently. "My point is that as long as the reasons for the fighting remain so different, and as long as the whites continue to break the treaties, this kind of thing will continue, for many years to come. Until the white man sees the Indians as human beings, nothing will change. Even most soldiers do not see them as human, but *you* do. That is why there is such a rage in you."

Zack glanced sidelong at him. "You think so, do you?"

"I know so. When other soldiers fight the Indian, they see the Indian as no different than wolves or bears, something inhuman. Therefore most other soldiers fight with no more concern than killing a wild animal. But you . . . you hate. You truly hate. And no man can hate an animal that much, only another human being. Somewhere deep inside you know it is *wrong* to hate."

Zack turned away, finding Thomas's insight unnerving.

"It is good that you see us as human," Thomas continued. "It will make you a better officer. But you have to see us as individuals, not as a whole nation. I could have been your friend, Zack Myers, but when a man says he would not mind shooting me in the back, I think twice about calling him friend."

Zack turned to face him again. "I said I was sorry—"

"Get rid of your hatred, Captain," Thomas interrupted, "and maybe you will begin to see the Indian for what he really is, a human being afraid his wife and children will starve, afraid his entire race will die out. How would you feel if you saw that happening to your own people?" He stuck the cigar back in his mouth. "You think about your own feelings. If you see me as a man, I will continue riding for you as scout. If you can see me only as Pawnee, a man you want to kill whenever that rage in you rises, I will ask to be assigned to someone else."

The man turned and left abruptly without another word. Zack watched him, thinking how lonely life must be for a man like Thomas Red Hand, an Indian living in a white man's world, belonging nowhere. Damned if he wasn't trying to tell Zack he wanted to be his friend.

He'd have to give what Thomas said a lot of thought, but not just then. The next day was Christmas. He wanted to spend it with Iris, talk about the baby. He didn't want to talk or think about the Indian situation, this awful massacre, or how lonely Christmas was going to be for Sergeant Sievers's and Lieutenant Grummond's wives.

Iris shivered and pulled her shawl closer around her shoulders. She thought of Christmases back east with her grandparents, how warm they had been with the cookstove fully loaded to bake sweet potatoes and turkey, the heating stove as well as a fireplace lit in the parlor, a beautifully decorated pine tree sitting in a corner. Before that there had been happy Christmases with her parents.

She was thrilled to be spending her first Christmas with Zack, but they had to continue to use their wood supply sparingly. She'd decided to use as little as possible during the night so that there would be enough to build up the cookstove in the morning in order to cook a ham for Christmas dinner. She felt a little guilty having a ham. Only officers had been allowed the treat, considered an extravagance out here. The enlisted men would all eat beef stew together in a cold mess hall, but she'd been told they would at least be treated to pumpkin pie, and someone had managed to bring back a scraggly pine tree that now sat in the mess hall, decorated with popcorn and candles. Later that night a Christmas dance would be held there, but the atmosphere would be far from gay. Even if they could have all the food and wood and gifts they'd like to have, nothing could quite overcome the pall that hung over the entire fort because of the Fetterman massacre.

Outside a blizzard raged, the wind packing temperatures of thirty below zero. She felt sorry for the men who had been assigned the duty of constantly digging snow away from the north fort walls. It drifted so high that if left there, the Sioux could walk right over the walls if they decided to attack. She didn't want to think about that danger, not on Christmas.

She placed two split logs into the cookstove, being careful to pick some that were good and dry. She stuck a poker into the coals and stirred them, and they burst into flames again. She closed the heavy iron door at the front of the stove and latched it, then opened the draft just enough to keep the flames alive. She felt strong hands come around her shoulders as she straightened, felt a warm blanket envelop her.

"I'm so worried you'll get pneumonia under these conditions," Zack told her. "I hope this cold doesn't affect the baby."

Iris smiled and leaned back against him. "Zack, our baby is all warm and snuggly inside my belly. He or she is more comfortable right now than anybody at this fort." She grasped the blanket and pulled it even closer, enjoying the feel of her husband's strong arms, the pleasure of the moment, the safety she felt right there in those two little rooms. "Someday we'll be stationed someplace where we can have a real house, and I'll be able to decorate properly and fix you a real turkey. We'll have presents, and a big tree for our children to play under with their new toys."

Zack hugged her tightly. "Just this much is more than I've had in sixteen years. I haven't celebrated Christmas since I lost my family. It feels good to have someone to share the holidays with again. I can't wait to smell that ham cooking." He kissed her hair. "I'm just sorry we can't have a tree and that we couldn't wake up to a nice hot fire this morning."

Iris turned, opening the blanket to wrap it around both of them as she put her arms around him. "It doesn't matter. I'm happy enough having you here." She leaned up and kissed the scar on his cheek. "We have each other, Zack, and our baby. There will be better Christmases. It won't always be like this."

Zack enveloped her in his arms as she reached the blanket up around his shoulders. Their lips met in a kiss that spoke more of gratitude than passion. The kiss lingered, grew deeper as both realized how close they had come to losing each other.

Zack's hands massaged her bottom, and he moved his lips to her neck. "I like the way you feel under a flannel gown," he said softly, "your hair tumbling down like it is now." Their lips met again, warm, delicious. Iris had been wanting to ask him how his talk with Thomas went, but she'd decided to wait until after Christmas. He'd said nothing when he came home, and she didn't want to spoil the day, knowing how talk of Indians and Thomas could often throw him into an angry mood.

Neither of them paid heed to the sound of horses and shuffling footsteps outside until someone knocked on their door. Iris quickly pulled away, keeping the blanket wrapped around herself as she darted to the bedroom, embarrassed she wasn't dressed yet. Zack wore only pants, socks, and his woolen undershirt. Iris watched through the curtained bedroom doorway as he quickly ran his hands through his hair, and she laughed lightly when he pushed at his pants and walked around for a couple of seconds to shake out his heated desire. He glanced at the bedroom door in mock anger.

"You're a vixen, Iris Myers."

There came another knock, and Zack grabbed a shirt that was hanging over the post of Iris's rocker. "Coming!" he shouted as he pulled it on. Leaving it unbuttoned, he went to the door and opened it.

Iris watched as he stood there a moment, saying nothing. "Thomas!" he finally spoke up. "What is it?"

Iris's heart fell. Had Thomas come with more bad news?

Would Zack have to leave on some dangerous maneuver today of all days?

"I brought you a tree and extra wood," she heard Thomas
tell him.

"What?" Iris caught the note of surprise in Zack's voice.

"Your woman is carrying. And white women make a big
thing of your Christian holiday. I brought you a tree. Here."
Before Zack could say a word, Thomas shoved a small pine
tree into the doorway. "I will pile the wood outside your
door," he said.

Surprise overcame Iris's modesty, and she came out of the
bedroom as Zack turned with the tree. It was not the prettiest
Iris had ever seen, but under these conditions it was beautiful. Thomas had already nailed boards to the stump so that it
could be set on the floor without falling over.

"Zack!" Iris came closer to look at the tree where Zack set
it in a corner of the crowded little room. "He brought us a
tree!" She met her husband's eyes. "What on earth did you
talk about yesterday? After what you said to him the day of
the massacre, why would he do this?"

Zack well knew the answer. The Pawnee scout was trying
to prove again that he could be a friend. A fury of emotions
churned his gut. He didn't answer Iris. He only looked toward the door as he heard the sound of wood being piled
against the wall outside. He realized that to get the tree and
that wood this early in the morning, Thomas would have had
to leave yesterday after their talk, go out alone into dangerous
country, and risk being murdered by the Sioux. He must have
loaded it all the previous night, spent the night out in the bitter cold, gotten up at sunrise, and hauled the wood back to
the fort through blizzard winds. He looked at Iris again, realizing she was thinking the same thing.

"He must be so cold," she told him.

They just looked at each other for several seconds.

"There is enough ham for more than just us, Zack," she
told him then. "Lieutenant-Colonel Shaver is joining us, but
there's plenty for one more."

The thought wrenched in Zack's belly. Invite a Pawnee Indian to share Christmas dinner with them? He'd looked forward to him and Iris and Howard Shaver celebrating together.

How could he add a Pawnee to the guest list? It seemed ludicrous.

Iris knew the hell he was going through, knew the last thing he wanted was to spend this first Christmas he'd celebrated since his family was murdered with a Pawnee Indian! She studied the confusion in those green eyes she loved so. "Zack, this is the best Christmas gift you could give me, to show you are finally beginning to rid yourself of all that hatred."

He turned away. "It's Christmas, a day for good memories, not ugly ones. I planned on sharing today with my wife and my best friend." Friends. Was that what Thomas was really trying to be?

"And what is Christmas all about?" Iris answered. "It's a celebration of the birth of a man who taught love and forgiveness. It's a day to be shared with others, not just friends, but enemies too. It's a day to celebrate life. If not for Thomas, you might have gone riding right into a trap the day of the massacre. I don't know what you talked about yesterday, but I think he wants you to see him as a man, maybe even a friend, not just as a Pawnee Indian."

There came another thud as more wood was piled outside.

"I can't believe he did this," Zack muttered. He walked to the door, opened it, waited for Thomas to straighten from setting down another stack of wood. "Come inside, Thomas."

"It is not necessary. I will leave the wood and go."

"Come inside, dammit!"

There was a moment's hesitation. Zack stepped aside then and Thomas walked in. Zack closed the door, and Iris huddled against the cold air that had rushed through the open door. She moved closer to the stove, studying Thomas, who only glanced in her direction.

"Did Shaver put you up to this?" Zack asked him.

Thomas grinned a little. "Is that what you think?"

"It would be like him. He's always after me about my opinion of Indians, thinks I joined the army only to be able to go out and kill Indians."

"Well, that *is* why you joined, isn't it?"

Zack scowled. "You didn't answer my first question."

Thomas folded his arms. "No. Lieutenant-Colonel Shaver

did not ask me to do this. I did it on my own. Why can't you just accept the gift, Captain Myers? Is it not the practice of you Christians to give gifts on this day? This is my gift to you."

Iris felt tears sting her eyes. "Thank you, Thomas. We accept your gift in the friendship it was intended, but you shouldn't have done this. You could have been killed going out there."

He shrugged. "I took the chance they would not care about one man alone."

"But you could have gotten stuck in the snow," Iris told him.

"I took one of the wagons that is rigged as a sleigh."

Iris's eyebrows arched in pleasant surprise. She glanced at Zack. "Just like a Santa Claus," she said teasingly.

Zack gave her a look of irritation. "Hardly a likely comparison," he told her.

Iris ignored the remark. "There must be some way to thank Thomas for what he's done," she told him.

Zack shook his head in resignation, then turned to Thomas. "We're cooking a ham, and there's more than just the two of us can eat. Would you like to share Christmas dinner with us, Thomas?"

Thomas looked at Iris as though to get her okay, then back at Zack. "I would not want to spoil the day for you. I did not bring the wood just to get a piece of ham. I brought it because my people killed your family, and because a white man killed my Pawnee wife. I brought it as a symbol that there is wrong on both sides, but there is also good on both sides. I will take my meal with the enlisted men at the mess hall. It is good enough that you accept this gift from me."

Zack closed his eyes and sighed deeply. "I'm the one who should be giving you something. Colonel Shaver is joining us for dinner. It will be a tight fit in this little room, but I do wish you would come too. It's all we can do right now."

Thomas glanced at Iris again, to be sure that she truly did want him to eat with them. "I will come," he said, looking uncertainly at Zack. "When?"

"About three o'clock," Iris answered.

Thomas nodded to Zack. "I will be here."

He turned and left, and Zack stood staring at the door. "I'll be damned," he muttered.

Iris only smiled. She walked up to him, wrapping the blanket around both of them again. "Merry Christmas," she said softly.

19

JUNE 1867

Zack sat down beside the bed, leaning over to study his new son. "I had Howard Shaver prepare a birth certificate," he told Iris with a grin. "Jacob Carlton Myers."

"I wonder where we'll be when the next one is born," Iris answered, her voice still weak. Why was it still such an effort merely to talk?

Zack touched the sleeping baby's tiny hand. "I don't know how you can think about another child after what you've been through." He closed his eyes and sighed. "God, I thought for a while there I'd lose both of you."

Iris remembered swearing to herself during labor that she would never have another child. Mrs. Sievers, who had stayed on at the fort doing laundry simply because she wanted to be near her husband's grave, had told her that the pain of childbirth was a pain soon forgotten. That was hard to believe then, but she was beginning to understand.

"Mrs. Sievers says the second one comes easier," she answered Zack.

He took hold of her hand. "I hope she's right. I'm just sorry for the misery this winter." He sighed. "Thank goodness you had the baby now and not in the middle of winter. The poor little guy could never have survived the cold."

Iris squeezed his hand. "He's strong like his father. He would have survived."

Zack shook his head. "Maybe. I guess all we can do is take a day at a time and be glad for the peaceful ones," he added. "Since Jacob's birth yesterday morning, the weather has been glorious, warm, no wind, birds singing, spring wild-flowers covering the foothills. I have a healthy new son, and my wife is going to be all right." He studied her blue eyes, wondering how he could ever live without this woman. "You *are* all right, aren't you?"

Iris managed a smile. "I'm just still so weak."

"I'll set up a cot in the other room so I don't disturb you at night. You can sleep in here with the baby until you're stronger. I've asked Private Jameson to build a cradle for us." The baby's little fists jerked upward and he wiggled his legs, letting out a little squeak. Zack leaned closer. "Who do you think he'll look like? It's hard to tell right now, he's still so red and squished."

"Squished?" Iris's smile widened. "He's beautiful, and he's going to look just like his father. I especially hope he'll have your eyes."

Zack managed a smile in return. He had circles under his eyes, and his face looked too thin. The winter had been hard and cruel, cold and hungry. Several men had died. The fort's remote location, combined with deep snows, had left them cut off from the outside world for months. Iris caught a note of sadness and apprehension about Zack's attitude today, as though some new problem had arisen that he didn't want to tell her about.

"Zack, when you came in here this morning after getting your orders from Shaver, I could see by your eyes something was wrong. You don't need to spare me. What's happened?"

Zack shrugged. "I might as well tell you. I've known it was coming. I just never said anything to you because I was hoping the orders would get changed."

Iris cuddled her baby closer. "What orders? Are we being transferred?"

Zack grunted. "Right now I wish we were." He rested his elbows on his knees, toying with his hat in his hands. "I wanted some time to enjoy my new son, but that might not happen. I have a feeling I'll be given every kind of miserable duty I can be given. I'll probably be sent out on wood-train guard more often than the others, in the hopes I'll get an arrow in my back. My only hope is that Shaver can intervene and keep things fair."

Iris felt a surge of alarm. "Zack, what on earth are you talking about?"

He sighed, meeting her eyes. "Major Jason Ward. He's with the reinforcements I'm riding out to meet in a few minutes. You might say I'll have a new boss now."

Iris closed her eyes in despair. "Jason. I haven't talked to him since—" She looked at Zack. "Since he came to see me in Washington."

Zack rose from the chair, obviously irritated. "You said he left there pretty damn mad."

"Very."

"It wouldn't surprise me if he deliberately asked for this post, knowing we'd be here."

"Maybe it's just coincidence, Zack. Maybe he's already married or engaged. Even if he isn't, once he sees how happy we are, that we have a child now, he'll see everything is for the best. Surely by now he's over that silly jealousy of his. And he's enough of an army man to know he can't let things like that affect the decisions he makes."

She could see that Zack didn't believe any of it. "We'll find out soon enough," he answered. He leaned over the bed, kissing his son's soft cheek.

"It will all work out, Zack." Their eyes held, and both knew the months ahead would not be easy. With the warming weather would come more Indian trouble, and now there would be Jason Ward to contend with. Iris wondered which might be worse. "Zack, remember he's your superior officer. He'll try to goad you, if I know Jason, make you do something he can call you on charges for, demote you, or send you to the guardhouse. Don't let him get to you. Show him and everyone else the kind of soldier you are, the kind of man you are. Let *him* look the fool."

He braced a hand against the pine post that formed a headboard for the bed, then leaned down to kiss her gently on the lips. "I'll handle Jason Ward. You just get your rest and get stronger, and take good care of our son." He used his free hand to smooth her hair back from the side of her face. "Have I told you I'm the happiest man alive right now, in spite of the dangers around this place, in spite of Jason Ward? My beautiful wife has given me a son. I have my own family again. I'll never let anything happen to you." He kissed her once more and straightened. "I'll send Mrs. Sievers back over to help you out while I'm gone."

Iris sighed. "I think helping me with the baby has been good for her. She had such a lonely winter. I hope there are more women coming with the reinforcements."

"I've heard there are a couple, but we'll be losing Grummond's wife. She's leaving as soon as we have enough men that we can spare some for an escort. She's always hated it here, even before her husband was killed." He studied her lovingly. "I hope you don't hate it too much, Iris. It worries me, you living this way. You're accustomed to better than this."

"I have a new baby, and I'm with the man I love. Location doesn't matter. You know that, Zack. I knew what I was getting into." She smiled. "Now maybe if we're lucky, one of those new women arriving will be Jason's wife."

He shook his head. "I don't think we'll be that lucky." He put on his hat. "How do I look? I don't want one thing wrong with my attire."

"You look wonderful, Captain Myers. You still make my heart beat a little faster."

He laughed lightly. "Calm it down. After what you've been through, I'm not about to get you pregnant again too soon."

"We'll just have to take our chances," she replied. "Unless you intend to sleep on a cot in another room for the rest of our marriage."

Zack thought she had never looked more beautiful. He loved her more every day for all the sacrifices she was willing to make for him. "I, uh, don't think that's possible, much as it would probably be best for you." He adjusted his hat. "Got to go. Thomas already rode out ahead to see if the pathway is clear. Give Jacob a hug for me when he wakes up."

He turned and left, and Iris shifted in bed, leaning down to kiss her baby's forehead. "Sleep tight, my precious." She could hear Zack shouting orders somewhere outside.

"Damn you, Jason," she murmured, settling back into her pillow again. She had no doubt he had asked to be sent there.

Jason held up his hand and ordered his regiment to draw a halt. From his vantage point he saw a large troop of cavalry headed his way. "That must be our greeters from Fort Kearny, Lieutenant Cooper," he told his first lieutenant. "Maybe they can explain the constant presence of that lone Indian who's been sneaking along beside us to the west. I'm of a mind to have him shot down, but I suppose I'd better wait and see how things have been out here since the Fetterman incident. I wouldn't want to invite an attack until we're close enough to the fort to get help." He looked back at the one hundred fifty men with him. "Although I doubt any war party would be foolish enough to attack this many soldiers. Maybe now that we're here there won't be any more trouble."

"Yes, sir," Lieutenant Cooper answered. Jason did not catch the smirk on the man's face, too pompous even to consider that anyone would dislike him or have no respect for him.

"We'll move forward," he told Cooper. "Slowly. Lieutenant-Colonel Shaver should be thrilled to see so much help coming." He headed his horse forward at a light trot, and Cooper signaled the others to follow.

"I hear they've had quite a time of it at Kearny, sir, near-starvation, frostbite, scurvy."

"Yes, they have, and after losing Fetterman and those eighty men, they've had a mere skeleton crew at the fort. I'm surprised Red Cloud didn't take advantage of that. He could easily have taken the fort. He is apparently not very intelligent. Nor was Fetterman, although he surely could have been saved if those who had been sent after him had done their job."

Like Zack Myers, he thought. He'd been assigned to some dangerous duty, but being in charge of Zack would make it all worth it. "We'll straighten out Red Cloud and his savages," he added.

"I'm sure we will, sir."

For the next few minutes nothing was said as the two men scanned the hillsides. Lieutenant Cooper felt uneasy.

They had all heard the story of Fetterman's massacre last December, the lurid details of what had been done to most of the men. The Indian riding alongside them to their left made him nervous, and he suspected he made Major Ward nervous also, although Ward wasn't the type to ever let on he was afraid of anything.

"Well, well, well," Jason said, more to himself than anyone else. He reined his horse to a halt again. "Look who's come to greet me."

Cooper called to a sergeant to halt the troops, then looked at Ward again, who said nothing as he waited for the men from the fort to draw closer. The captain who led them stopped the big roan gelding he was riding and saluted Major Ward. "Welcome to Fort Phil Kearny, sir," he said.

Ward saluted in return, neither of them smiling. The animosity between the two men was palpable.

"Captain Myers, I see," Ward said. He turned to Cooper. "This is my First Lieutenant, James Cooper. Cooper, this is Captain Zack Myers, an old acquaintance."

Cooper saluted Zack. "Glad to come help out, Captain," he said.

Zack turned his gaze back to Jason. "Glad to have you. We need all the help we can get out here."

"So we've heard," Jason answered. "I have enough men with me to put an end to Red Cloud's barbarism and make the Bozeman Trail safe once and for all. I just hope you can be of more use to me than you were to Fetterman, Captain Myers."

Zack could see the shock on the soldiers' faces at the remark, but he did not flinch at the insult.

"Captain Fetterman disobeyed orders," he answered. "He rode right into a trap. I might add, Major Ward, that he also thought he had enough men to wipe out the Sioux. Don't underestimate their numbers or their skill, Major, and don't fall for their tricks."

Jason straightened higher in his saddle. "I don't need a man of lesser rank telling me how to handle Indians. I am surprised you've even been given a hand in fighting them. I would have thought that you, of all men, would make a wrong decision like Fetterman did, considering how much you hate Indians. I don't doubt, Captain, that your inability to control your hatred will cause you to lead your men to their deaths. When that happens, I will be right there to see those silver bars ripped off your shoulders."

Some of Zack's men shifted uncomfortably in their saddles, embarrassed for him. Zack sensed the anger some of them were feeling at the remark.

"Captain Myers is one hell of a good officer," his new sergeant, Mendel Bailey, blurted out in Zack's defense.

Zack glanced sidelong at the man. "Watch your mouth, Sergeant Bailey. Major Ward wasn't talking to you."

"But, sir—"

"It's all right, Bailey." Zack looked back at Jason as Thomas Red Hand rode down the hill to join him. "Major Ward and I go back a ways."

Jason turned his attention to Thomas, noticed the gun he wore strapped to his hip was army issue. "You must be a scout," he told Thomas.

Thomas already did not like the look of contempt in the new major's eyes. "Thomas Red Hand," he answered. "Pawnee."

Jason adjusted his hat, leaning one arm on the pommel of his saddle. "Pawnee?" He grinned at Zack. "Well, that must really stick in your craw, Captain." He looked back at Thomas. "You should have made yourself known, Thomas. I had a mind to have one of my men shoot you. We weren't sure why you were riding beside us all this time."

Thomas glanced up the hill. "I was making sure there were no Sioux on the other side waitin' to swoop down on you. I'd have signaled if that was the case, then ridden to Captain Myers to help you out."

Jason's smile looked more like a sneer. "Considering the kind of help Fetterman got, I'm not so sure I'd *want* Myers riding to my rescue. Besides that, I have enough men here to take care of any Sioux war party."

"That so?" Thomas glanced at Zack and grinned, then looked back to Jason. "You gotta get a couple things straight if you're gonna be stationed out here, Major. First off, Captain Myers here is pretty damn good at what he does. Far as Fetterman goes, the captain was only sent out to see what had happened to the fool. By the time we got there, it was too late to help him, but if he could have, the captain would have done what needed to be done, no matter the danger. Fetterman thought *he* had enough men to take care of things too. But when you're up against two, three thousand warriors, even if all they've got is arrows and tomahawks, you ain't got a chance. You'd best remember that."

Jason's face darkened with anger. "I don't need an uneducated savage telling me how to operate! General Sherman's orders since the Fetterman massacre are extermination! If Red Cloud continues to make trouble, we will act without mercy! And *you,* Thomas Red Hand, had better remember your place. You're a scout, not an officer!" He glanced from Thomas to Zack. "And I'd be mighty careful when you and the captain are involved in any kind of fighting." He looked back at Thomas. "Chances are you could be shot. Considering the captain's background, I wouldn't turn my back on him if I were you."

"That remark is uncalled-for!" Sergeant Bailey sputtered.

"Leave it be, Sergeant," Zack told him, his eyes on Jason. "The major is new out here. He has a lot to learn." He spoke the words with a confidence he knew would infuriate Jason Ward. "One more thing you should know, Major Ward," he said boldly. "Accusing me of possibly shooting one of my own men in the back runs close to insubordination. You might be my superior, but Colonel Shaver would be very disturbed to hear you say such a thing. The men out here are half starved, their nerves shattered. Some have lost parts of fingers and toes to frostbite. They live with the constant danger of ending up like Fetterman and his men. They don't need the idea planted in their heads that one of their officers might make a decision that could cost them their lives, or the suggestion that they could lose one of their best scouts just because an officer might not like the fact that he's Pawnee."

Jason's jaw flexed in suppressed anger. "So, you admit you *don't* like the fact that he's Pawnee."

Zack glanced at Thomas, who only grinned. Zack looked back at Jason. "Of course I don't. But I've worked with Thomas long enough not to see him as Pawnee anymore. He's just a man, and a damn good scout. Out here good scouts can save a lot of lives, so I'd treat him with respect. What's important is doing what we're here to do, and the last I knew, we were supposed to be protecting the Indians' rights just as much as the settlers and miners."

"Well, that has changed, Captain Myers," Jason answered pompously. "Red Cloud has defied us on all counts. He simply will not face the fact that the white man is here to stay. The time has come for Red Cloud to stop murdering innocent people."

Zack nodded. "My wife has always said it's best to look at both sides of the picture. Thomas here has taught me more of the same. It might not hurt to sit down with Red Cloud and have another talk."

"Talking's done. It's time for more action, and since you're such an *experienced* Indian fighter now, I'm sure you won't mind being on the front lines, will you?"

You bastard, Zack wanted to shout. "I obey orders, sir," he answered. "If that's the order, that's what I'll do."

Jason shifted. "Well, if you have your superbly skilled scout at your side, I'm sure you'll be safe." He looked Zack over. "By the way, how is your wife? Did she survive the winter all right?"

Their eyes held in challenge. "She did," Zack answered. "All the men sacrificed food and warmth to be sure the women were comfortable. She's even given me a new son. He's only a few days old. Mother and baby are doing fine."

Zack took great pleasure in the look of surprise and jealousy in Jason's eyes.

"Well, congratulations." The word almost stuck in Jason's throat. He'd hoped by now Iris would be sick of life out west, sick of Zack Myers. Better yet, he wished Zack had been killed with Fetterman, that he'd find Iris was a poor, lonely widow wanting to marry someone more important than a captain.

"Well, we aren't here to talk about women and babies. We're here to rid this area of its problems with the Sioux and to reinforce this post. We'd better get to the safety of the fort. I want to talk to Colonel Shaver and get acquainted with the daily routine around here and get my men settled."

Zack nodded. "The fort is only a mile from here, just around that hill behind me. You have to be careful of these hills, Major Ward. A thousand Indians can hide behind one of them, and you wouldn't even know it. He looked over at Thomas. "Better get back up where you came from, Thomas."

"Sure thing, Captain."

Zack scowled at the man, who looked ready to laugh.

"Say hello to the missus for me," Thomas added with a wink. He and his Appaloosa rode off, and Zack turned his horse to lead Jason and his men to the fort. Sergeant Bailey and some of Zack's men glowered a little at Major Ward, quickly detecting his arrogance and disgruntled that he had insulted Zack.

Zack felt Jason Ward's eyes drilling into him from behind. *I'm the one who'd better watch his back,* he thought. He'd have to be extra careful in every decision he made. Jason Ward would be after his bars and his very hide. He wasn't going to get either one.

20

"You just got back from wood-train duty a week ago, Zack. It isn't fair. There are two other captains at this fort besides the one Jason is sending you to relieve. One of them should go instead." Iris sat in her rocker feeding four-week-old Jacob, keeping a blanket over her breast. "Can't Shaver arrange for someone else to go? Jason is being unfair and Shaver knows it."

"He also knows that the last thing I want is special treatment where Jason Ward is involved. Jason thinks he can tire me out and break my nerves so I'll make a mistake. Better yet, he figures maybe I'll get killed. Then he can move in on my poor, lonesome widow."

Iris pouted. "I would never allow that man anywhere near me or our son. And as soon as I am up to going out, I intend to have a word with Jason!"

Zack sat down in a chair across from her, lighting a pipe. "You'll do no such thing. That would be worse than Shaver saying something. I don't need my wife speaking for me." He puffed on the pipe. "I'll handle this my way. The best way to get Jason Ward's goat is for me to simply obey orders and do my job and not complain."

"Well, he's doing nothing for the morale of the men, not even the ones he brought here. They've heard the stories, know the dangers out there. Surely they can see how unfair he's being to you."

Zack leaned closer, pulling the blanket away to watch his son feed at his mother's breast. "Let the man make an ass of himself. He's costing his own career, not mine."

"He could also cost you your life."

Zack set the pipe aside for a moment, leaving his chair to bend down and kiss her breast, then little Jacob's forehead. "Better to die proud and respected than be thought of as a coward. Jason knows that if I complain, I'll look like a coward. I'm not about to satisfy his purpose."

"It frightens me, Zack. After Fetterman—"

He met her eyes, his hands braced on the arms of the rocker. "Thomas is a good scout, and now we have plenty of reinforcements. Things will work out. Right now Captain Henderson is pretty sick and needs to be replaced in the field, so I guess I'm the man to do it. Personally, I think Henderson has a bad case of nerves himself."

"It just frustrates me so, Zack, wondering if you'll be killed before—"

He cut off her words with a gentle kiss. "Everything will be fine."

There came a knock at the door. "Oh, dear!" Iris pulled little Jacob away from her breast and grabbed the front of her dress together. She laid a blanket over the front of her and propped Jacob against her shoulder, patting his back as Zack opened the door to see Jason standing there. He frowned in surprise.

"Major Ward. What are you doing here?"

"Well, your wife is an old friend, you know, and she's had a baby. I thought I'd say hello and have a look at the boy."

"That's up to Iris."

"Come in, Jason," Iris called. She laid Jacob down in her lap. "Come and see the baby."

Zack grudgingly stepped aside, hating the idea of Jason Ward even entering his living quarters. Jason grinned, as though he actually thought Iris might be glad to see him. He marched inside, removing his hat. He was dressed in full uniform, and Zack suspected the man had probably shown up that way just to try to impress Iris.

"Well, it's been a long time, Iris. Are you recovering well from the birth?"

"I'm doing fine. This is our son, Jacob Carlton."

Zack closed the door, remaining there and folding his arms while Jason knelt down to study the baby. "Looks like he'll have his father's hair and your eyes."

"Perhaps, but some of the other women tell me a baby's hair and eyes can both change from what they are at birth. He does seem to be quite healthy. Considering the conditions here this past winter, it's a miracle there were no significant problems."

Jason rose. "Personally, I wouldn't even let you be out here. You're too good for this kind of life, Iris. Zack shouldn't expect—"

"I am out here of my own accord," she interrupted. "Zack warned me not to come, but I wanted to be with my husband. I am perfectly happy here, in spite of the loneliness and danger. I have to say that for all your supposed concern, you certainly aren't doing anything to ease my fear and anxiety, sending Zack out on dangerous duty again so soon!"

"Iris, don't get involved," Zack told her.

Jason smirked. "I'm only picking the best man for the job," he told her, rising.

"We all know what you're doing, Jason. You were too angry the last time we spoke for me to believe you're concerned about seeing me again or that you care about seeing my son. What is your real reason for being here? Did you think you could make me believe everything is fine now, or that I wouldn't see that you're trying to get my husband killed?"

Jason gave Zack a scathing look. Zack stood there in uniform pants and an undershirt. Jason had caught him off guard, and he damn well knew it. Now he looked at him as though it were terrible to find him out of uniform in his own home. Jason looked back at Iris. "Your husband will do a good job getting himself killed all by himself, I expect," he said. "I had hoped that by now you would have realized your folly in marrying beneath yourself. But since you keep insisting you love this farm boy here, and since he'll probably never achieve a rank that will allow you to live in the style you were accustomed to, I guess you'll have to accept the problems that go along with that."

Iris picked up Jacob and stood. "I would like you to leave now, Jason," she told him. "Outside of these quarters you have full control over Zack, and you have obviously chosen to use that power to try to destroy him out of your ridiculous jealousy." She faced him boldly. "Ridiculous because I never loved you. We were never promised to each other. We were never more than friends, and that only because our parents were close and we were thrown together because of them. You obviously don't care one whit about my health now, or my baby, so please leave. You have no right coming in here and trying to wield your rank."

Jason held his chin in a cocky pose. "I am afraid I have every right, Mrs. Myers, since these quarters no longer belong to you and the captain here. They belong to me. I want both of you out of here in the morning."

"What!" Zack's hands moved into fists. "What the hell are you talking about?"

"Watch your tongue, Captain. You're talking to a superior officer." He looked around the rooms. "You've made it quite cozy in here, Iris. These two little rooms aren't exactly the kind of quarters I was used to back at Laramie, but out here they're considered better than anything else available. Since I outrank your husband, I have the choice of what quarters I want for myself, and this is what I want."

Iris held the baby closer and gritted her teeth against an urge to scream at the man.

"You know the only space left is one small room at the end of this building," Zack said in a near growl. "You're one man. We're two people with a baby! We need the extra room."

Jason shrugged. "Too bad. It's the price you pay for bringing a family to a remote post like this one. Be out by ten in the morning. I'll even give you an extra day before going out to relieve Captain Henderson. That will give you time to help get your family resettled." He put on his hat, nodding to Iris. "Nice seeing you again, Iris." He looked at Zack, giving him a sociable grin. "Be ready to move out with some extra men tomorrow, Captain." He turned and opened the door. "You two have a nice evening."

He walked out, and Zack stared at the door, his fists still clenched. "*Damn* him!" He looked at Iris with fire in his eyes. "You'll be miserable in that one little room! There's no space in it for anything but a bed and a trunk and a heating stove. Not even a cookstove! It's fine for a single man, but not a family, and he damn well knows it!"

"Of course he knows it. We'll move there and we'll make do, Zack. It's that simple. We have no choice. We won't be stationed here forever, and someday, somehow, Jason Ward will get his due."

Zack took a deep breath to try to calm himself. "Well, I'm not sure how much longer *I'll* last before I have to land a fist into that man's smug face!"

"That's just what he wants. He can have you demoted, thrown in jail. He wants you to look bad in front of me. You told me yourself he's baiting you."

Zack grabbed a jacket. "Well, he's doing a damn good job of it!" He pulled on the jacket. "I need some air. I'll be back in a while to help you pack. I'll have Sergeant Bailey bring a wagon over in the morning."

He walked out, and Iris carried the baby into the tiny bedroom and laid him on the bed. "I hope there is room for your cradle where we're going," she said. Her eyes teared at the thought of leaving these two small rooms that had become her first home with Zack.

She had promised she could accept whatever army life brought her, and she would do just that. "Just like Mama," she said softly. She missed her mother. As a new mother herself, she had so many questions, many that only a mother could answer. But there was no mother . . . no grandma. She wiped her tears angrily, opened the trunk at the foot of the bed, and began throwing things into it. "You'll get yours for this, Jason Ward," she fumed. "I just hope you don't take my husband down with you!"

Zack finished shaving, wishing he could jump back into the cool waters where he had just bathed. The refreshment had lasted only minutes, and even though it was only seven A.M.,

It was already hot and sultry. It was going to be a miserable day.

All seemed quiet this morning, maybe too quiet. Howard Shaver had come up with the idea of establishing a strong point out near the Sullivant Hills, a vantage point about four miles from Fort Kearny, where a soldier guard could watch the woodcutting at what they'd come to call the "upper pinery" and the "lower pinery." Both cutting camps were in constant danger from Red Cloud's continued attacks, and were too far from the fort for help to reach them quickly; thus, Shaver had decided this observation camp was necessary and should be manned night and day, guard troops and loggers serving a week at a time rather than a month, and then relieved by new men. Knowing they didn't have to stay out in dangerous territory for so long at one time helped keep wood-train duty from being so frightening and ominous.

Observation this morning had established that all was well at both logging camps, mule teams being hitched, a couple of trees already felled. Zack had decided to bathe and shave in Little Piney Creek, about four hundred yards across open ground from the main camp, to which he had been assigned this week. It consisted of a corral of wagon boxes, something that could be used for protection in case of attack. It was a rather crude kind of fort, but wood was too precious and hard to come by to be used to build a more secure wall for the observation camp. The wagon boxes would have to do. The wheels had been removed from the several huge freight wagons so that there was no space under them where Indians could crawl through.

Zack gathered together his bar of soap, towels, razor and lathering brush, mirror and dirty clothes, putting them into a canvas bag. He headed back to the main camp, feeling very uneasy over the fact that he had not seen Thomas that morning. The man had ridden out before sunrise to scout the surrounding hills but had not reported yet. Company C, 27th Infantry, was on duty this week, and there had been no trouble; but that morning the air seemed especially heavy. Zack wondered if it just seemed that way because of his uneasiness. He reached the main camp, noticed Privates Sam Gibson, Nolan Deming, and John Garrett were all on picket duty as assigned. A Lieutenant Jennes was also with the small company of men.

He scanned the Sullivant Hills, seven hundred yards to the east. Along their barren crests ran a wagon road, which then descended the hills and headed north, past the main camp and on for another mile to the upper pinery. To the south was the lower pinery. He walked over to Private Gibson and used the man's binoculars to scan the hills and the broad, open prairie to the west.

"Have you noticed anything unusual?" he asked Gibson.

"No, sir. I just wish Thomas Red Hand would come back."

Zack handed back the binoculars. "So do I. Keep your eyes peeled." He walked to his tent, one of several erected outside the circle of wagon boxes. He set his bag of personals in the tent, thinking how glad he'd be when this day was over. Then he could go back to the fort, back to Iris. He felt sorry for her having to cope with a baby in the small room in which they now had to live. The place was miserable in this August heat, and two-month-old Jacob had a heat rash that made him irritable. The constant danger of attack, and there had been several already this summer, made everyone even more edgy. Having to put up with additional harassment from Jason Ward made matters worse for him and Iris. He didn't mind for himself, but it infuriated him that Iris should also have to suffer. If the man really had loved her enough to want to marry her, how could he deliberately make her life so miserable now? Thank God she *hadn't* married the sonofabitch, he thought. The arrogant bastard would have made a lousy husband.

Food was again scarce. The Sioux made it difficult to hunt, and they had attacked and turned back the last two wagon trains of supplies from Laramie. No matter how well guarded, horses and mules were stolen almost nightly. The government still did not seem to understand the gravity of the situation, was still not supplying enough men to truly do a good job of guarding the area. More men were lost every week. Morale continued to be low. Zack did not doubt that some of these men would desert if not for the fact that they were too afraid of being caught by the Sioux. All were well aware of how horribly the savages could torture a man before he died.

Zack tried not to think about that. Thomas had tried to explain that torture of the enemy was part of Indian culture, part of their religious belief that they could draw strength from torture. The braver the victim was, the more strength they could steal from him. Besides that, the more they tortured their victims, the more they would frighten the remaining soldiers and settlers into leaving.

He wondered if he would ever understand the Indians' way of thinking. If not for his own memories and hatred, perhaps he could. Thomas had come closer to helping him understand than anyone had so far. He was still surprised at himself for thinking of the man as a friend. He had never said it outright, or even admitted to himself that he could be friends with a Pawnee. Thomas had said nothing about it, but he damn well knew how Zack felt now, and he had seen that I-told-you-so twinkle in the Indian's eyes a few times.

Pawnee. A damned Pawnee . . . and here he was worried about the man. Where in hell was he? He studied the activity around the main camp. The wagons were arranged in an oblong circle, the final gap filled by two large barrels. The area was only about one hundred feet long and perhaps sixty feet wide—spare mules kept inside the circle. Men were posted at both cutting sites, and at the main camp he had only thirty-one soldiers. He wished there were more, but having to guard this camp, the cutting sites, and also the fort itself forced them to keep skeleton troops at each place. There just were not enough men to go around, and any extras had to be garrisoned at the fort, ready to ride out and help wherever trouble might show up. For Iris's sake he was glad that the bulk of their men were at the fort, even though Jason Ward was there also. The man could strut like a rooster all he wanted. He could not impress a woman like Iris.

Iris. She had put up with so much. Motherhood seemed to cast a special glow on Iris, making her even more beautiful in spite of the fact that the heat and weariness had made her lose more weight than she should have. Now she was almost too thin, and he was worried about her.

"Captain Myers! My God!"

Zack spun around at the words, shouted by Private

Garrett. A lone rider galloped at a mad pace over the foothills toward the camp. On his heels was a swarm of Indians, too many to guess their numbers, painted savages screaming war whoops. They disappeared into a gully, and a sudden quiet ripped the air. They reappeared, still screaming their war cries, coming over the next hill, still chasing the lone rider, headed right for their camp.

"There must be thousands of them!" Lieutenant Jennes yelled as he ran toward Zack.

"Take your places!" Zack ordered. "Thank God we at least got in that shipment of more Springfields a couple months ago!"

"They're attacking the woodcutters, sir!" Private Gibson hollered. He was watching the camps again with his binoculars. "It's like they just came out of nowhere! I swear I can see Red Cloud himself over there!"

Men scrambled, and shots could already be heard coming from the northern woodcutting site. "Damn!" Zack muttered. Never had an attack come so suddenly, mostly because Thomas usually gave good warning. "Thomas!" He grabbed Private Gibson's binoculars, focusing them on the lone rider, wearing a red shirt, head shaved on both sides. He recognized the black gelding the man rode. "No wonder he couldn't give us warning. They must have caught Thomas by surprise too, and that's not an easy thing." He watched a moment longer. "Good God, he's got an arrow in his side!" He lowered the binoculars when he saw Thomas's horse stumble. Thomas rolled off the animal and lay still.

Zack felt sick inside as he handed the binoculars back to Gibson. Thomas had risked his life trying to get back there and give them warning before it was too late, but Indians, perhaps a thousand of them, were already surrounding the wagon box corral, just far enough away to be out of rifle range. They rode back and forth, goading their enemy, taunting, chanting, showing off, brandishing spears and rifles. There would not even be a chance to send for help or ride out and help the men at the cutting sites. Zack could only hope that once the shooting started, it would be heard back at the fort. These foothills had a way of buffering sound, sometimes totally insulating it from places close by. A battle could rage only a mile away and not be heard, and they were a good four miles from Fort Kearny.

"Spread out, men!" he shouted. "Make every shot count!"

He took his own position, grabbing up his Springfield-Allin .50-caliber rifle. The new guns were their only hope. The Sioux were probably banking on being able to charge in after the first shots were fired, giving the men no time to re-load. They would get a big surprise.

Suddenly the attack was on, a thousand Indians against thirty-two men. There could be even more Indians beyond the hills. "I love you, Iris," he said quietly, drawing a bead on a painted warrior. "Remember me."

Iris unbuttoned her dress against the sweltering heat. She glanced at her mantel clock, something she had brought with her, given her by her grandma. There was no mantel to set it on, but she treasured the clock and refused to give it up. It sat on top of her trunk and had to be moved every time she opened the trunk to get out clothes.

Nine o'clock. It was only nine o'clock, and already hot. She dreaded the day ahead. Little Jacob lay sleeping, finally. He had fussed all night, and she had bathed him and soothed his heat rash with baking soda again that morning. She prayed his heat rash would clear up, and she felt so sorry for him.

She walked to the door, which she'd left open to get some air. Across the parade grounds she could see Jason talking to Howard Shaver. How she hated Jason for pushing her and Zack into this small room to live. She knew Colonel Shaver did not like the arrangement either. If it wouldn't make Zack look favored, he would probably have given up his more comfortable quarters for them; but even if he did, Zack would have none of it. No special favors.

Zack. She missed him, was worried to death about him, and something didn't feel right. She stepped outside, scanned the distant hills, saw nothing, heard nothing, yet she could not quell the anxious feeling that made her chest hurt. She waved to Howard Shaver, motioned for him to come over. To her disappointment he brought Jason with him. She had done up her hair quickly that morning, and strands of it still hung about her face. It was too hot to try to put any color on her cheeks, too hot to wear a nicer dress. It wasn't that she cared what she looked like to Jason. She simply hated him seeing her bedraggled and worn. It would only make him happy. He would think she was getting what she deserved.

"What is it, Mrs. Myers?" Howard asked, always strictly business around her and Zack when in the presence of others.

"I don't know. I just have this terrible feeling of dread. Something is wrong, Colonel Shaver."

"A woman's intuition, I suppose?" Jason grinned. "I think you're just hot and tired, Iris. I heard the baby crying last night. Is he sick?"

"Heat rash," she answered. "He's sleeping right now, but I'll have you know that this feeling I have is not just that of a silly woman who is tired." She turned her attention to Shaver. "Colonel Shaver, I assure you this is nothing silly. Zack and I are so close, and I feel . . . I feel as though he's calling to me, that he needs me. I wish you would send someone out to make sure everything is all right at the guard camp."

"You're just missing your husband," Jason spoke up.

"I am accustomed to my husband having to be in the field," she snapped. "I've never had this feeling that something terrible has happened."

"Calm down, Mrs. Myers," Shaver said. He looked at Jason. "Go and assemble some of the troops, Major. No action yet. Just have some men ready in case they're needed."

"Yes, sir." Jason gave Iris a look of disgust before he left. "You really should think about going back east first chance you get," he told her. "You don't look well at all, and this is no place for a new baby to have to grow up. You don't belong here, Iris."

"I belong with my husband, and so does our little boy. And I believe Colonel Shaver just gave you an order, Major Ward."

Jason sniffed and turned away. Iris looked up at Howard Shaver. "I hate him, Howard."

Shaver folded his arms. "I'm not too fond of him myself,

but I had no control over who was sent here to relieve us. I'm sorry about the problem over living quarters, Iris, but Zack wouldn't let me intervene in that. If it makes you feel any better, I suspect this fort as well as Reno and Fort C. F. Smith will be closed within a year. If my guess is right, you and Zack will be heading someplace new, and just about anyplace would be better than this." He patted her arm. "Try to get some rest while the baby is sleeping."

"Howard, don't treat me like a fragile ninny! You know me better than that. I am telling you something is very wrong. Please send someone out to see."

Shaver grinned. He liked this plucky woman Zack married, wished his own wife had her gumption. As soon as he was sent farther west, his wife had headed back east, refusing the danger and discomfort of the western forts. "Tell you what I'll do. Thomas usually rides in here right about now to report. If he doesn't show up within an hour, I'll send someone to find out why. Will that do?"

Iris rubbed her arms, feeling an odd chill in spite of the heat. "I suppose."

"Iris, Thomas is one of our best scouts. You know that. If something is wrong, he'll show up here any minute to let us know."

"Yes, I suppose he will." She stared past him in the direction of the base camp, but it was too far away to see or hear anything.

"Don't worry," Shaver reassured her. "You know I have special feelings for Zack."

"Thank you, Howard."

"You're a good woman, Iris, a perfect wife for Zack. He has changed a lot since he married you. He's proving himself one hell of a good officer."

"He's a better man than Jason Ward. He doesn't deserve what Jason is dishing out."

"I am well aware of that." He tipped his hat. "Sit tight. I'll keep you posted."

Shaver left. Iris watched men begin to scramble, saddling horses, checking rifles. She hoped this feeling she had *was* just from being tired and missing Zack. The stories she'd heard about how Fetterman's men had been found still haunted her. How horrible it would be for Zack to die that way, the same way his family had died . . . and just when he was beginning to rid himself of all that hatred.

"Thomas, where are you?" she murmured. He was already late.

21

"Don't waste bullets, men!" Zack shouted. "Private Harrison, Lieutenant Jennes is a better shot than you. You keep a fresh rifle loaded for him at all times!"

"Yes, sir!"

"Lieutenant—same goes for the rest of the men. Assign the poorer shots for reloading!"

"Yes, sir!"

Orders were shouted, men scrambled, some diving into the wagon boxes for cover rather than ducking outside of them. Hearts beat furiously with terror as even more Indians appeared on the hillsides.

"Jesus God, we're all gonna die today!" one private groaned.

Zack kept his rifle ready, taking aim as another several hundred Sioux made yet another approach. The first wave of Indians had swooped down upon them with surprising speed, their faces painted in black, green, and yellow. He knew the Sioux's main strategy was to send in a war party to draw the soldiers' fire, then more would charge in for the kill while the soldiers paused to reload their rifles. He and his men had surprised the warriors by firing repeatedly, spilling Indians and ponies with a constant volley that had left them confused.

The Indians had paused to reconsider their strategy, and now they were coming again. The air was already filled with blue smoke from constant rifle fire, and it stunk from burning manure inside the wagon corral. The Sioux had shot arrows tipped with burning pitch into the corral, and they caused several manure piles to burn. Never in his army service had Zack had such an opportunity or reason to kill Indians. There was no time to think what might be right or wrong about it, or to reason why Red Cloud and the Sioux were so angry. There was only time to defend himself and the other thirty-one men fighting for their lives inside the circle of wagon boxes.

A herd of mules outside the circle had already been whisked away by the Indians, and the men guarding the herd had barely made it into the safety of the corral before the bulk of the warriors attacked. Their situation still seemed hopeless. Thank God the wagon boxes contained additional stores of extra rifles and ammunition.

"The logging camp is on fire, sir!"

Zack glanced southward toward Piney Island to see the flames. "Maybe some of the civilians and soldiers there escaped," he answered. "If they can get to Fort Kearny, Colonel Shaver will send help!"

There was no time for further conversation. The storming Sioux were upon them again, and again rifles burst repeatedly. Horses plunged to the ground, warriors spilled from them into clouds of dust. Some of the Indians charged forward and ducked over the side of their mounts, firing arrows from under the horses' necks. Zack and the others fired a furious barrage of bullets, so constant that the barrels of some of the rifles began to overheat.

Zack forced himself to remain calm, but he could not help wondering if today he would die. He tried not to think about Iris . . . little Jacob. He could only pray the fort itself was not also being attacked.

"The tents! They're in the way!" someone yelled.

Even more Sioux came at them from the northwest, headed for the area where tents were erected outside the cor-

ral. Several soldiers scrambled to tear them down, and managed to collapse all but one of them. They dove back inside
the wagon boxes just as the Indians got close enough to be
fired upon. Arrows rained down all around them, more savage rifle fire. Gun barrels overheated to the point where they
began to warp and were of no use, and new rifles had to be
kept loaded to replace them.

Another onslaught was miraculously turned back, and
Zack knew their only hope was that the Sioux would keep
this a game, as they often did in times like this, hitting, retreating, hitting, retreating. They might even just leave once
they'd had their fun.

"Look up there, Captain," Lieutenant Jennes shouted,
pointing to a hill to the west. "Women and children!"

Zack studied the several hundred Indian women and children perched on the hill, watching. He knew what that
meant, and so did the rest of the men. It was very unusual for
women to be with a war party. They were allowed to come
and watch only when the warriors intended there would be
a big kill. The Sioux meant to wipe them out to the last man.
"Sweet Jesus," he muttered. He noticed some of the men were
preparing for suicide in case the Indians got inside the corral.
They frantically removed their shoes and shoelaces, then
looped one end over their right foot, tying a loop into the
other end that could be used to hook around the trigger of
their rifles.

Zack knew what they planned, had heard the story often
enough but had never seen a man actually do such a thing.
If the Indians got too close, they intended to stand up and
place the end of their rifle barrels under their chins, then pull
the trigger with the string around their feet. He remembered
in the Fetterman aftermath it had been obvious Fetterman
had killed himself with his own handgun. He closed his eyes,
thinking about Iris, not sure what he'd do if it became obvious they would lose this battle. His father's cries of torture
still sometimes woke him up in the night.

"My God, there's more yet!"

A private spoke the words nearby, sounding ready to cry.
An eerie silence overtook the men, all of whom were afraid to
even stand up. They crawled around to get more ammunition. Zack could hear one man weeping. Nerves were already

frayed to the breaking point, and the day was still young. The heat was sweltering, and there was no shade inside the wagon box corral. Everyone was bathed in sweat, which trickled down over smoke-blackened faces, making them almost unrecognizable.

"There must be two, three thousand of them!" Lieutenant Jennes lamented.

"Stay calm, men," Zack warned. "You know how the Sioux fight. They'll keep sending a few hundred at a time, and as long as we have these repeaters we can ward them off. We've already proven that. Just hang on until help arrives."

"Help *won't* arrive," a private sobbed. "Thomas is the one who'd . . . go for help . . . and he's layin' out there dead! We're gonna end up like Fetterman and his men!"

"Keep your head, Private, or I'll have you punished when this is over!" Zack snapped. "We need everybody to stay alert, and we can't give up!" Deep inside he felt sorry for the terrified young man, but the mention of Thomas made him sick. He never thought he could feel this despondent over the death of an Indian, a Pawnee, no less. All this time he had tried to deny his feelings for the man, and now it was too late to call him friend to his face. Thomas had taught him a great deal about life out west, how to fight Indians, how to try to understand them . . . how a man was just a man, Indian or not.

Again the Sioux attacked, and again gunfire raged to the point that Zack could hardly hear. The sound grew fainter as his ears reacted to the constant noise, but he did hear a man cry out, and he turned to see Lieutenant Jennes fall, a hole in his head. "Damn you! Damn you all!" Zack growled as he aimed and fired, one, two, three . . . aim and fire . . . four, five, six. It was kill or die. Dust and smoke rose together, making it difficult to see his targets. The stench of burning manure stung his nostrils. Gunfire and war cries mingled in one great, frightening voice. Over and over he fired, until again his rifle overheated. He set it aside and grabbed up a replacement, shooting at Indians and their ponies. The private who had wept that help would not come fell dead not far away. To his left another man sprawled, shot in the head.

Again the Sioux backed off under the heavy fire. They simply did not have the weapons to answer such a volley, but

Zack knew that if help did not arrive by late afternoon, they would be defeated by sheer numbers. Besides, they would run out of ammunition by nightfall. He wiped his sweaty face with his shirtsleeve. The midday sun was relentless.

Men crawled around reloading, checking the dead men, helping the wounded. Zack found it incredible that more had not been killed, that he was still alive.

"Water. We need water," Sergeant Bailey reminded him.

Zack nodded. "We can't get to the creek. All we have here are a couple of canteens." He looked around, spotted two large kettles near the dead embers of a fire the cook had made earlier, several yards beyond the corral. He remembered the cook had poured fresh water into the kettles just that morning. "Those things are full of water." He nodded in the direction of the kettles. "There are coffee grounds in the bottom, but right now who cares? Water is water."

Bailey nodded, then turned away. "We need a couple of volunteers to go bring in those kettles. They've got water in them."

Private Gibson and Private Grady scrambled beyond the wagon boxes and made a mad dash, then fell to their bellies and grabbed the kettles, dragging them along as they scooted back toward the corral. The Indians fired a few shots from a distance, and the bullets pinged against the kettles, but the two men made it back unhurt.

Some of the men cheered, but Zack's attention had been taken with something else while watching the two men pull the kettles in. A movement. Thomas. He was still alive! He needed help. If the Sioux saw him move, realized he was not dead yet, they might grab him up and make off with him . . . a Pawnee . . . a hated enemy. They would take great pleasure in making him suffer. Suddenly it didn't matter that Thomas was Pawnee, or that Zack had always thought he'd enjoy watching a Pawnee suffer. This one was Thomas.

"I'm going after him."

"Sir?" Bailey asked, confused.

"Thomas. He's still alive. I just saw him move. If the Sioux realize he's alive, he's in for a bad time of it."

"Sir, you can't go out there."

"I have to."

"Let me send somebody else. You're needed here to stay

in charge. The Sioux could attack again any second, and you heard their rifle bullets hit those water kettles. They'll shoot at you."

"I have to go."

"Sir, you can't—"

"It has to be me. I can't explain it, Sergeant." He handed the man his rifle. "Lieutenant Jennes is dead. You're in charge if I don't make it back."

"Sir, your wife and baby—"

"My wife will understand. Believe me, she'll understand." Zack ducked between two wagons and made a mad dash toward Thomas, dropping, rolling, crawling on his belly while bullets whizzed around him and spat at the dirt near him. He finally reached Thomas. The man lay facedown, and he was trying to crawl. "Thomas!" Zack put a hand on his shoulder. "Try to get up! I'll help you back to the corral!"

Thomas looked at him, his eyes full of pain, then frowning in surprise. "What're you . . . doin' out here?"

"I came to help you! Come on! If the Sioux see you're still alive, they'll take you off, and you'll wish you were dead, by God!"

"Then shoot me and get the hell back to safety. I'm dyin' anyway. . . . You've got a wife . . . kid . . ."

"I'm not going back without you! Now, get up! You can do it! We've got to run!" Zack ducked lower when a bullet whizzed just above his head. He looked back to see the Indians were coming at them again. "Goddammit, Thomas, run! Do you want them to get me too? I don't intend to die like my father did! Come on!" He grabbed Thomas under the arms and pulled. The man managed to get to his feet. He hung on to Zack, and both men half ran, half stumbled toward the corral while bullets flew past them in both directions. The soldiers were shooting back at the oncoming Indians in an effort to keep them from reaching Zack and Thomas before they could get to safety.

Zack cried out when he felt something smash into the back of his right arm. He stumbled forward, and both men fell. They were not far from the corral by then, and the Indians were gaining. "Come on! Come on!" Zack screamed at Thomas. He pulled at him with his left hand. Thomas, an arrow still sticking out of his side, managed to get to his feet again, and both men made it to the corral, literally falling between two wagons, where soldiers pulled them inside the rest of the way.

"Help him!" Zack ordered one of the men. "Give him some water, but leave the arrow in him until the medic can look at him. Sometimes pulling an arrow out does more damage than leaving it where it is!"

"Sir, your arm!"

"Just wrap it, sleeve and all, for now! There's no time for anything else! Use my neck scarf!"

Zack had no idea if a bullet still rested in his arm or if it had gone all the way through. The pain made him feel sick to his stomach, but he knew he had to ignore it. There was too much to be done. A private untied his neck scarf for him and quickly wrapped it around the wound and tied it. Zack knelt over Thomas, who now lay on his back. "Don't you die on me, you goddamn Pawnee!"

Thomas opened his eyes and gave him the half grin that always irritated him. "You gonna feel bad if I do?"

It was then that Zack realized what he had just done. He'd risked his life to save a Pawnee Indian! "Hell no," he answered. "I'll just be pissed. I couldn't let the army lose one of its best scouts."

Thomas kept grinning. "I think . . . I'll live just so's I can keep gettin' under your skin. Or maybe . . . I should let myself die . . . just to piss you off. Which would make you madder?"

Zack's eyes teared at the realization he actually cared about the man. "The way things are going, it might not matter. We'll all be dead." He squeezed Thomas's shoulder, then left him to help in the renewed fighting.

The battle raged on, the air reeking with smoke and stench, bodies of Indians and horses scattered everywhere outside the wagons. In brave action and with remarkably skilled horsemanship, warriors charged in over and over again to grab up the bodies of the dead and wounded, sometimes two riding together, both reaching down and taking an arm, carrying a fellow warrior out of rifle range. On the hillside to the west the women were singing and chanting, urging their men on.

Everything suddenly became clear for Zack. All they

wanted was for the white man to stay out of their hunting grounds, quit killing their game. It was so simple, yet had become so complicated. He was developing a new respect for the very savages bent on murdering all of them. Their bravery and horsemanship was astounding. He had no choice right now but to kill as many as he could just to stay alive for Iris and Jacob, but something was changing inside him. It had started when he saw Thomas was still alive.

The noise of gunfire and war cries and chanting began to fade as the assault on his ears began to deafen him. Zack realized his arm was numb, but he kept firing, reloading, firing. Sometimes the Indians got so close he could see the whites of their eyes, and then it hit him what he saw there.

Red Eagle! The tragedy he had seen in that Indian's eyes the day of the hanging in Minnesota was in the eyes of some of these warriors. The Sioux rampage and the ensuing hanging had been five years before, and still nothing had changed. The Sioux had merely been pushed even farther west.

All around him gunfire roared, yet things had become nearly silent. He continued to aim and shoot along with the rest of them, and his eyes and nostrils stung. Sweat dripped from his forehead, nose, and chin. Another rifle overheated, and he threw it aside, picked up yet another.

How long would this kind of thing go on? What was the answer? Most likely he would die today and never understand that look in Red Eagle's eyes, never fully comprehend why his parents and sister had to die . . . why he alone had been left alive. If he was killed today, would the hatred live on through his own son? He didn't want Jacob feeling this when he was older, but there seemed no answer. Some Indians had given up the fight and submitted themselves to reservation life, but they remained bitter. Even Thomas often showed an underlying bitterness. It was in his eyes, like Red Eagle, like the painted, screaming warriors who threatened to murder everyone in this corral today. The hating and fighting would not end until the Indian and the white man understood each other, which might never happen, not until the Indians could have their hunting grounds returned to them in their original pristine state, which most certainly would never happen, maybe not until all Indians were dead . . . or maybe all white men. That wasn't going to happen either, and so they were left to this.

The Sioux began circling. He could hear another man crying. He wondered what time it was, remembered he'd looked at his pocket watch not long ago and saw that it was twelve-thirty. How long ago had that been? One hour? Two hours?

"They're pulling back again!" someone shouted.

Zack remained in position, discovering every muscle was so taut that he literally could not move. His neck ached from constantly arching it sideways to aim. His left hand was frozen to the stock of his rifle, his right hand curled achingly behind the trigger. His shoulder was sore and probably bruised. His head pounded and his ears rang.

"Look at them up there, riding back and forth," another man yelled. "Some are huddled. They look confused."

They all heard it then, the boom of a howitzer. Earth and rocks exploded in a cloud of dust not far from the main body of warriors.

"My God, was that real?" Sergeant Bailey asked.

Then came another boom, another explosion. The Indians began to scatter.

"Yee-haa!" a private yelled. "Help's coming! I'll bet it's Lieutenant-Colonel Shaver!"

Some of the men began to stand up in their battle-scarred wagon boxes. Another boom of a howitzer shook Zack out of his frozen position. He relaxed his hands, his shoulders. Men began cheering, hugging each other, some crying with relief. He looked around, saw Lieutenant Jennes and two privates lying dead. A couple more men besides himself had been wounded.

He stood up and watched a large battalion of men in blue uniforms approaching along the roadway, led by Howard Shaver and the flag representing the man's command. Jason Ward was with him, but that would be standard procedure. Right then he'd be happy to see even Jason, though the bastard would probably try to say he'd saved the day. These men around him were the brave ones, the ones who deserved the glory.

He walked over and shook Sergeant Bailey's hand. "Good job, Bailey," he said. Their eyes held in mutual respect.

"You all right, sir? You really shouldn't have gone out there like you did. We could have lost you."

Zack nodded. "I know, but it was something I had to do."

"I understand. Thomas is your friend."

The words struck deep. Zack looked over at Thomas, and left the sergeant to go kneel beside him. "Help's coming," he told him. "Hang on, Thomas."

"Just to . . . piss you off," Thomas answered.

Zack grinned. "I'll be damned," he muttered, realizing Howard Shaver was again coming to his rescue. It had been seventeen years since he was that ten-year-old boy who hated the Pawnee with such passion it made him sick to his stomach. Now here he was, praying a Pawnee Indian wouldn't die. He noticed the post surgeon's flag. "The doc is with them," he told Thomas. "You'll be all right."

"Good thing . . . I didn't have my back to you . . . durin' all that shootin', huh?"

Zack felt a tightness in his chest. He leaned closer. "It's a *damn* good thing. The hell of it is, all these Indians I got to kill, and I've never had the opportunity to shoot a Pawnee. Life sure isn't very fair, is it?"

Thomas grinned. "It sure ain't."

22

*M*en cheered, some cried. The post surgeon passed a bottle of whiskey among the weary, smoke-blackened, sweat-stained soldiers. Each man took a long swallow while the surgeon checked the bodies of the dead men to make sure there was no pulse.

Howard Shaver rode up to Zack and dismounted. "Zack! You're wounded!"

"I'll be all right." Zack winced with pain as he spoke, glad the bullet wound to his arm was all he'd suffered.

"Iris has been worried sick. When Thomas didn't ride in, we knew we'd better get some men together."

"Thomas is hurt bad," Zack told Shaver. "I want the surgeon to look at him right away. He took an arrow." He saw the surprise in Shaver's eyes, knew what the man was thinking. "We don't want the army losing one of its best scouts, do we?"

Shaver grinned slyly. "Of course not."

"There are two wounded men over there, sir." The words came from Jason Ward as he approached Zack and Colonel Shaver. Zack noticed the man was strutting authoritatively, as though he were in charge. "I've got the surgeon—" He noticed the bloody neck scarf wrapped around Zack's arm then. "Captain Myers, you're hurt too. I'll have the surgeon tend your wound right away. The other two men—"

"It can wait," Zack interrupted him. "So can the other two. None of our injuries are life-threatening, but Thomas Red Hand could be dying. I want the surgeon to take care of him first."

"What?"

Zack could see the anger in Jason's eyes at practically being given an order by a lesser-ranking officer. "I want Dr. Redding to tend to Thomas first. My men laid him on a blanket over there in the shade of one of the wagons. He's got an arrow in his side. It's been there for hours. He's not going to last much longer without help . . . *sir!*"

"I will give the orders on how to clean up this mess, Captain," Jason answered, "and I will remind you that officers come first, then the lower-ranking men. Thomas Red Hand is a volunteer scout. Besides that, he's an *Indian*. You of all people shouldn't care less how quickly the surgeon gets to him. I'll have Dr. Redding look at your wound right away." He turned and started to walk away.

Zack reached out with his left hand and grabbed hold of Jason's arm in a viselike grip. "Redding is going to tend to *Thomas* first!"

Their eyes held in challenge, and some of the other soldiers noticed the confrontation. One man nudged another, and in seconds the celebrating quieted. Jason jerked his arm away. "You're looking to lose your bars, Captain!" His brown eyes narrowed in rage.

"I don't give a damn! I want Thomas tended to right away! You ask the two wounded men over there. They'll agree."

Jason took a deep breath. "And why are you concerned about a Pawnee Indian, Captain Myers, you of all people? I wouldn't have been surprised to find a bullet in his *back* rather than an arrow in his side!"

The man barely got the words out before Zack landed a big fist into his face and sent him sprawling. The rest of the men stared in shock as Jason lay prone, stunned. Moments later he rolled to his side, blood dripping from his nose. He put a hand to it, got to his knees, then noticed blood was running through his fingers and dripping to the ground.

"You broke my nose, you sonofabitch!" he growled.

Zack stood ready, and Howard Shaver said nothing. He kept his eyes on Zack, taking great pleasure in the turn the man had taken, sticking up for Thomas. He also knew the rivalry between Zack and Jason was something the two of them had to settle between themselves.

Jason got to his feet and stumbled toward Zack, his face a bloody mess. "I'll have you wearing a private's uniform and shoveling manure for this!" he roared. He ripped off his own neck scarf and held it to his nose.

"I don't give a damn if you *hang* me!" Zack answered. "Dr. Redding!" he called out. "Tend to Thomas Red Hand first! He's badly wounded. The others can wait!"

The surgeon turned from where he'd been wrapping another soldier's head in gauze. The man had suffered a splinter wound. Redding asked another soldier to finish wrapping the wound. He picked up his bag and walked to where Zack and Jason stood facing each other. He looked at Colonel Shaver. "What exactly are my orders, sir? Major Ward told me—"

"Go see what you can do for Thomas, Dr. Redding," Shaver told him.

"Yes, sir."

"This is the most blatant act of insubordination I have ever seen!" Jason told Zack. "You have just made the worst mistake of your life!"

Zack kept his fists clenched. "Maybe *you* have, Major! None of these men here would want Thomas Red Hand insulted, nor would they want him to die while the doctor sews up a simple cut on someone else! I'd say that shows pretty poor judgment on your part!"

A furious Jason hurtled headlong into Zack, and a stunned troop of soldiers watched as captain and major rolled in the dirt. Shaver stepped back and did nothing to intervene. Zack, bigger and stronger, but also weary and wounded, managed to heave Jason off him. Jason fell backward, and Zack reached down and grabbed him by the front of his uniform. He jerked him to his feet, holding him at bay in spite of the awful pain in his arm.

"I don't intend to fight like a child while a good friend lies over there possibly dying!" he shouted.

Jason landed a fist in his stomach, then his jaw. Zack stumbled backward against a wagon. He grimaced with pain in his arm, but when Jason came at him again, Zack landed his left fist across Jason's right cheek. Jason went down again, and this time he stayed down. Zack touched his throbbing jawbone and came away with blood on his fingers from split skin. He looked at Howard Shaver, panting.

"I don't care how you handle this, sir," he told Shaver. "I don't regret it!"

Jason got to his feet again and started for Zack, but Shaver put out his arm and stopped him. "No more! Morale is low enough without these men watching two officers fight! You will both report to me tomorrow morning at seven!"

"Fine," Jason seethed. "We know who is in the wrong here! Captain Zack Myers hit a superior officer!" he panted, blood still streaming from his nose as well as from a new cut on his right cheek. He kept his eyes steady on Zack. "Not only that, but he deliberately disobeyed my orders and tried to override them!"

Zack stepped closer. "Well, you can add *this* to my charges, Major Ward! I went out myself and saved Thomas Red Hand! That's how I got this arm wound!"

Jason looked over at one of his men. "Bring me something to hold under my damn nose!" he ordered. The man went scrambling through his gear, and Jason turned his attention back to Zack. "*You* went after him? Explain yourself, Captain!"

Zack turned to Howard Shaver. "Thomas came riding in full speed, an arrow in his side."

Sergeant Bailey handed a bottle of whiskey to Zack, and Zack gulped some down before he continued. "I don't know how it happened, but this time the Sioux must have surprised even Thomas. Just before he could reach us, his horse fell, and Thomas was thrown. He lay still, looked dead. The Indians were on us then, and there was no chance to see how he was. Later I saw him move." He handed the bottle back to Bailey. "I knew if the Sioux realized he was still alive, they would grab him up on their next attack and take him off with them. Nobody knows better than I do what he would have suffered. I know the rules, sir. Don't risk a soldier's life for a scout. I wasn't about to be responsible for one of my men getting killed for doing something he wasn't supposed to do in the first place, but I also was not going to let a friend die that way! Somehow I—" He sighed in resignation, realizing the enormity of what he had just done. He truly could lose his bars. Iris would live in near squalor if he were knocked down to a private. "Somehow I guess I thought I could make up for not being able to help my father." He wiped at his face with his shirtsleeve, mixing sweat, soot, and blood.

Shaver studied Zack's bloodshot eyes, filled with joy at what Zack had done. Considering how he had felt about Indians all these years, it was a remarkable gesture. Assigning Thomas to Zack's command had worked out even better than he'd planned. "Go on over there and see if you can help with Thomas," he told Zack. "I know you'd like to be with him."

Zack winced with pain, realizing he'd probably hurt his arm more by fighting. "Thank you, sir." He glanced at Jason, feeling very satisfied at the sight of the man's bloody face. No matter what happened over this, it felt damn good to vent his frustrations on the egotistical bastard. He might pay dearly for this, but he had licked Major Jason Ward in front of a hundred men. He left them to go to Thomas's side.

Shaver turned his attention to Jason. "I'll have the doctor look at you as soon as he's done with Thomas."

"Sir, with all due respect, I am a *major*! Officers are to come first! Much as I hate Captain Myers, he, too, should be tended to!"

"Thomas is a valuable man also, Major. I know the rules, but this is my decision now, not Captain Myers's. And I will remind you that your own wounds are not from any fight with the Sioux! It was wrong of Captain Myers to hit you, but as his superior officer it was even more wrong of you to continue the fight after Captain Myers specifically said he did not want to do so at this crucial time. You showed poor judgment for a major and you allowed your emotions to get the better of you. *Both* of you did! I will give this a lot of thought tonight, and we will discuss it in the morning! Right now let's get the hell back to the fort. Those Sioux out there could decide at any time to swarm over us like ants on a cookie. Have some of your men start loading what's left of the extra Springfields and ammunition into the wagon we brought. We're going to abandon this camp for a few days, and I don't intend to let Red Cloud come here and arm his men with brand-new rifles!"

Jason drew in his breath and straightened in an attempt to retain a picture of authority. "Yes, sir." He saluted, then turned to direct the loading of the rifles, taking a wad of gauze from one of his men and holding it to his nose again, cursing Zack under his breath.

Iris lay wide awake, listening to crickets, waiting for any unfamiliar night sounds. Any coyote call or hoot of an owl could actually be the Sioux calling to one another. Knowing that out there, somewhere not far away, could be two or three thousand warriors still eager for blood made sleep impossible. She looked over at the mantel clock that still sat on the trunk. An oil lamp shed light on the clock. The lamp was kept constantly burning so that Zack could get up and find his gun quickly in case of Indian attack.

Four-thirty A.M. Iris was sure she could not have slept more than two hours all night. After what she had heard and seen yesterday afternoon—Zack, his face black and bloody, a dirty neck scarf tied around his injured arm—she could not stop thinking about it, nor would she forget the terror she'd felt before he was rescued. She'd been so afraid he would return in the back of a wagon, thrown in with other dead bodies.

She turned to watch him sleeping. Tears came to her eyes again at the realization of how close she had come to losing him. Never had she been more aware of how much she loved him and needed him. She was not sure how much longer she could bear this constant terror, and now, after all he had been through, Zack might lose everything he had worked so hard to earn. That was another reason she could not sleep. As far as she was concerned, it was all Jason Ward's fault. She was glad Zack had humiliated the man in front of all the others. He deserved it, and Zack certainly deserved to vent his frustrations on the man who had caused both of them so much distress, let alone the fact that Jason had acted as though Thomas's life meant nothing.

She rested on one elbow, studying her husband by the

soft lamplight, still marveling at what Zack had done yesterday—fighting over Thomas Red Hand, risking his entire career because he was afraid Thomas would die, risking his own life to get the man to safety. He had been too weary to explain all his reasons, but he didn't need to. What mattered was that he was free, free of all the hatred, a whole man. He hadn't said so himself, but it was there, in his eyes, in his actions. It was especially obvious when he had gone to be with Thomas while the doctor took out the arrow. He'd helped hold the man down, had sat with him for a long time afterward, even after his own wound had been dressed. Iris had sat with him, and she had never loved him more. It was as though the bruise on his face and his wounded arm were symbols of his liberation from hatred and from years of suffering a guilty conscience over not being able to help his parents.

She glanced over at Jacob. The baby rested peacefully for once. He lay in a little bed Zack had the post carpenter build. It had slats on the sides to keep the baby from falling out, and the wooden bottom was softened by feather-stuffed pillows covered with blankets. There was so little room in their tiny one-room quarters that the baby's bed had to be shoved up beside their bigger bed, but right now she didn't care. They were all close, and after the sick dread she'd gone through the previous day, it was wonderful having husband and baby near. The main worry now was that Zack could lose his rank. She could not believe Howard Shaver would let that happen, considering how he felt about Zack, but army protocol was army protocol, and Jason Ward was not a man to let this go.

Zack was lying on his left side because of his injured right arm. Thank God the injury was only a flesh wound. The bullet had gone right through, and although the arm would be mighty sore for weeks, the doctor was sure Zack would retain full use of it. The only danger now was infection, and after what she'd seen at the army hospital back in D.C. . . .

She decided not to think about that. God surely had not brought her husband through that awful battle yesterday just to let him die of infection from a wound that otherwise was not threatening.

Zack stirred against her, seemed distressed. Iris did not doubt that in his sleep, memories of yesterday's battle invaded his dreams. He grew more restless, and she pulled away, knowing that sometimes memories could make him thrash wildly. His mumbles grew louder until he suddenly sat up, breathing heavily.

"Zack?" She cautiously touched his shoulder. "It's all right. The battle is over. You're here with me."

Zack took several deep breaths before turning to look at her. He glanced around the tiny room, his eyes resting on Jacob for a moment before meeting hers again. "I can't believe we survived yesterday," he told her. "Thousands, at least two thousand . . ." He shook his head, reached out and touched her face. "I'm sorry I woke you."

"You didn't. I couldn't sleep anyway. I haven't quite gotten over the feeling that you were never coming back to me. I've just been lying here watching you. And I'm worried about tomorrow."

"Don't be." He lay back down with a deep sigh, moving his left arm around her as she snuggled against him again. Sometime during the night it had rained, and the weather had cooled. It felt good to be able to lie close without being too hot to touch.

"I've resigned myself to the fact that I could lose my rank," he continued, "but it doesn't matter, not compared to how it felt to save Thomas, and how it felt to hit Jason Ward. My saving grace is Jason's behavior. He could get himself in a lot of trouble by trying to get *me* in trouble. Howard will use that to help me, I'm sure of it."

"You know I will support you and be with you no matter what happens."

Zack turned and kissed her hair. "I know. That's the only thing I'm worried about. I couldn't bear to have you and Jacob living in worse conditions than this, and that could happen. If it does, I'm sending you back east. With the money from your father's estate, you could get a place with your grandfather and—"

"I won't leave you, Zack! You know better than to even suggest such a thing!" Iris rose up on one elbow to face him. "We'll use my money when you're ready to retire from the army, and you aren't ready yet. You've just been through something that could make you an even better officer, and I'm betting Howard Shaver already sees that. Even so, I wouldn't care if they reduced you to a private. I've never been more proud of you." She leaned down and kissed him, being careful not to bump against the stitched cut on his lower left jaw. The kiss lingered, turning from love and gratefulness to something more.

It had been two months since they'd made love. This was the coolest night they'd had in the past three weeks, and gratefulness over the fact that Zack was alive and well, that they were together, brought on all the buried needs and aching desires. Iris needed her husband completely again, felt desperate to prove to herself he really was alive and there beside her.

She shivered with desire when Zack felt her breasts through the light cotton gown she wore. "Take it off, Iris," he whispered when she kissed his neck. "I want to touch you, to know this is real and not a dream."

She sat up and pulled off her gown. Zack studied her, thinking how much more beautiful she seemed now that she had given him a son, although she still needed to put on a little more weight. The harsh winter and a constantly active, hungry baby kept her too thin.

"It's been a long time," he told her, his eyes raking her nakedness. "I'm so tired, Iris, but I want you so."

She leaned down, offering her breasts. He drew a full nipple between his lips, moved his tongue against it and pulled more of the breast into his mouth, groaning as he tasted her. He had gone to bed naked because of the heat, and although Iris had never dared such a thing before or even thought about it, the aching woman inside of her knew instinctively what she had to do, no matter how brazen it might seem.

"My arm, Iris . . . I can't—"

"I know," she whispered. She moved on top of him. Her hair tumbled around his face as she leaned down to let her breasts tickle his chest while she met his mouth. Tonight she would be the aggressor. Her man needed her, they needed each other. For a little while they would forget the trouble Zack could be in, forget the horror of the battle, forget the danger that lay just beyond the fort. She reached down and guided him into her, letting him fill her to ecstasy. She thrilled at the realization that the baby had not left her unable to enjoy this, and by the glazed delight in Zack's green eyes, she knew she was pleasing him also.

She began moving her hips rhythmically, feeling some pain at first, but soon the intense sensations overwhelmed her, reminding her of all the wonderful reasons for being Zack Myers's wife. She leaned closer, and Zack licked her breasts. He reached up and grasped her behind the neck with his left hand, pulling her down to meet his mouth in a deep sensual kiss. He rolled up on his left side then, forcing Iris onto her back and supporting himself with only his left arm. "I'll take charge now. To hell with the arm." He pushed hard, needing her, wanting her. It seemed so incredible that he was really alive and there with her.

Concern about his arm and the awful weariness from the grueling battle suddenly meant nothing. This was something he had to do. He felt victorious, the conquering hero, a man who had mastered his worst enemy, his inner demons. He had won more than one battle the day before, and now the victor would enjoy the spoils. He moved in quick thrusts, both of them struggling not to make too much noise because of the baby and the thin wall that separated them from the quarters next door. Zack rose to his knees and Iris arched up to meet him, grasping his arms and enjoying his full manhood, that surged into her in throbs of ecstasy. He drew in his breath and gritted his teeth when the long-needed release came. He remained inside her for several seconds before finally pulling away and collapsing beside her. Iris pulled a blanket over her nakedness, surprised at her brazenness, yet feeling exhilarated. "I've never loved you this much," she told him, resting her head on the pillow beside him.

He moved his right arm enough to put a big hand on the side of her face. "And I don't think I've ever loved *you* more, or appreciated you and Jacob more. I don't know what will happen later today, Iris, but I know you're a woman who can overcome just about any obstacle. You're strong and beautiful and brave." He grinned. "And now I know how daring you really can be."

Iris felt herself blushing. "Do you still respect me, Captain Myers?"

He kissed her hair. "You can be as wild as you want, Mrs. Myers, as long as it's right here in this bed."

Their eyes held in joy, but their smiles faded when both of them realized what could happen later. "It will all work out, Zack. God will make it work out."

He leaned over and kissed her softly. "I'm glad you have so much faith. While you're at it, pray for Thomas. I'm really worried about him. Doc Redding says it looks pretty bad."

"I've already been praying for him. We'll go see him later this morning, after the meeting with Howard Shaver. I hope he rested well last night."

"Yeah. So do I." Zack sighed deeply. "You didn't hear what—" He stopped talking for a moment, swallowed.

"Zack?" Iris leaned up, noticed tears in his eyes. "What didn't I hear?"

He seemed to be having trouble saying the words. "You went out to feed Jacob after the doc finished wrapping Thomas's wound. The doc went to tend to the other wounded soldiers then, and Thomas looked at me so strangely." He swallowed again, rubbed at his eyes. " 'You finally callin' me your friend?' he asked. He had that damn sly grin he always gets when he knows he's getting my goat." He took another deep breath. "Something happened in that one quick moment we looked at each other before he passed out again. I, uh . . . I took hold of his hand and told him yes, I was calling him friend. I felt something kind of wash over me, a wonderful feeling of freedom. The trouble is, I don't think he heard me."

Iris lay down and moved an arm under his neck, letting his head rest on her shoulder. She felt him shiver, felt his tears on her skin.

*I*ris finished tucking her hair neatly into a bun on top of her head, using yet another hairpin. She picked up a straw bonnet and placed it over the bun, then tied its blue ribbons under her chin to hold it in place. She studied herself in the small mirror she'd managed to procure from supplies. It was not big enough to see her entire dress, but she could at least see herself from the shoulders up. She decided she looked as good as could be expected after what she'd been through the past couple of days, and with such poor facilities for bathing and dressing.

It was already getting hotter again, the air turning muggy from the rain of the previous night, and she decided not to wear any powder or color on her face. It would only streak later if she perspired. She looked down at her dress, realizing she would not seem very elegant today, with no crinoline petticoats under her skirt. She wore a simple blue calico dress with only one cotton slip, and even that was too warm in spite of short sleeves and a scooped neckline. She looked back into the mirror, taking a deep breath to calm her nerves.

"You don't need to go with me," Zack told her.

She turned to face him as he buttoned his shirt. "Whatever happens, I intend to be there to show my support, and my firm belief that you did the right thing."

She studied the stitches on the cut along his bruised jawline. She still could not quite get over the joy and relief at seeing Zack ride through the fort gates yesterday, after the awful, sick dread that he and his men had been massacred. Watching Colonel Shaver ride out with all those men after Thomas did not report had been the most frightening experience of her life.

"Jason Ward and this whole fort are going to know I stand behind my husband. If Jason thinks that stripping you of your rank is going to make me love you less or make me leave you, he has a mighty lesson to learn. Personally, I don't think Howard Shaver will allow it to happen. Besides, Jason showed very poor judgment himself. He was more in the wrong than you, and that will be your salvation."

Zack held her eyes as he picked up his jacket. "Maybe I've already realized a salvation of another kind . . . or at least the beginnings of it." He gingerly pulled on the jacket, wincing with still-fresh pain in his bandaged arm.

Iris smiled. "Maybe so, Captain Myers."

He grinned rather bashfully, feeling a little embarrassed for the emotion he'd shown just a few hours before. "I was overtired," he explained. "I guess things just kind of got to me last night."

"Zack, it's all right. You know that."

He looked at her lovingly. "You're a good woman, an understanding woman. I don't think anybody else would have understood." He stepped closer. "I think I went out there to save Thomas, partly because I wanted to keep *any* of our men from suffering the tortures of a captive; but in this case . . ." He turned away to sit on the bed and pull on his boots.

"In this case it was Thomas, and it was personal," she finished for him. "In this case you truly cared about the man involved. You realized he was your friend."

He glanced up at her. "There is also a part of me that has always wanted to make up for not being able to help my family. This was kind of a vindication." He sighed. "I've put you through hell for all the wrong reasons, Iris. Now for all the *right* reasons things might get worse. I'm sorry."

"Don't be. I couldn't be more happy than I am right now, just having you back alive. Not just that, but also having the whole man, the real man, the man I always knew Zack Myers could be. I have never been more proud of you." She walked over and took hold of his hands. "I love you, Zack. You have never looked more handsome, never seemed so brave. We'll go and see Thomas after Howard Shaver's little hearing this morning."

He squeezed her hands, worry coming into his eyes. "Yeah. We'd better get the baby and head over there. It's almost time." He looked her over, appreciating the way her full bosom filled out the bodice of her dress. "You look nice."

"Thank you, Captain." She smiled, wanting to reassure him as best she could. "Everything is going to work out. You'll see." She let go of his hands and knelt over the bed to pick up little Jacob, who lay there sleeping. She cradled him in her arm and watched Zack finish dressing. He had decided to attend the meeting in full dress uniform, shell jacket with two stripes of gold cording at the end of the sleeves; blue trousers with a gold stripe down the side of each leg; polished black boots; black felt, brimmed hat with an insignia of crossed sabres at the front. He strapped on his buff-leather sabre belt, took his dragoon sabre down from where it hung on the wall and shoved it into its sheath attached to the belt, then pulled on white gloves.

"Well?" he asked. "Take a good look. This might be the last time you see me dressed this way."

Her eyes teared. "And I will always remember how you look this very moment. No matter what happens today, you can be proud."

He nodded. "I'm sure you'll remind me of it the rest of our lives," he answered with a nervous grin. "Let's go face the music," he said. He put a hand on her shoulder and led her out the door. They walked across the parade grounds, and Zack could feel some of the men staring. He didn't doubt that every man at the fort would be eagerly waiting the outcome of this meeting.

Sergeant Bailey hurried over to catch him before going into Shaver's quarters. "Captain Myers, sir!" The man saluted him. "You look damn spiffy, sir, if I may say so."

Zack grinned sadly. "Thank you, Bailey. What is it?"

Bailey nodded to Iris before answering. "Just wanted to tell you we're all rooting for you, sir, even most of Major Ward's men. They aren't real fond of the man, if I may say so, sir."

"You certainly may," Zack answered. "And thank you."

The two saluted each other, and Zack turned to go inside. A private ushered him into Shaver's office, where Jason Ward already stood at attention, also in his full dress uniform. Iris took great pleasure in the fact that his nose was bandaged, and there was a large cut on his right cheek that showed bloody stitches. He glanced back to see her standing outside the room holding Jacob, and the look in his eyes betrayed his hatred.

Zack saluted both Jason and Howard Shaver, who saw Iris standing in the outer room. "Come in, Mrs. Myers. The wives out here have to put up with whatever fate befalls their husbands. You might as well hear my decision."

Iris could feel Jason's embarrassment at her seeing him so battered. He shifted restlessly when she came into the room. Zack had thrashed him good, and Jason must have been feeling the humiliation. Zack and his men were being called heroic, and she did not doubt Jason was jealous of that. He had yet to be involved in any kind of important battle himself.

"At ease, both of you," Shaver told the men. "Sit down. You, too, Mrs. Myers."

They all took chairs, and Zack removed his gloves and hat. Iris patted Jacob's bottom. He had awakened, but seemed contented.

Shaver remained standing, facing Zack and Jason with a firm look in his eyes. "I already told Major Ward I want no new explanations or arguments from either of you this morning. I know both of you well, and don't forget that I was right there yesterday. I saw everything—heard every word that was said, so neither of you needs to clarify, rationalize, or justify your actions." He folded his arms authoritatively. "Captain Myers, you hit an officer as well as overruled an order. Major Ward has every right to bring you up on charges, but I in turn have the right to ignore those charges." He looked at Jason. "You might as well know I *am* going to ignore them, simply because, considering the situation yesterday, any man might have acted irrationally. Captain Myers went against the rules going out to save Thomas Red Hand. Agreed. However, he knows better than anyone what might have happened to Thomas if the Sioux got hold of him. I have absolutely no doubt that if it had been you lying out there wounded, Major, Captain Myers would have done exactly the same thing." He looked at Zack. "Am I right, Captain?"

Zack glanced at Jason, who stared straight ahead and said nothing. "Yes, sir, I believe I would have."

Shaver nodded. "We are not supposed to let personal feelings cause us to make irrational decisions, Captain, but I will allow it this one time. However, I will have to report it, so if such a poor decision happens again, you cannot expect some other officer to be so understanding about it. A second mistake could cost you dearly."

"Yes, sir."

"As far as hitting a superior officer, I am also pardoning that. I will *not*, however, report it, nor will I report the fact that Major Ward goaded you unfairly."

"Sir, I want no favors," Jason put in. "I feel that once I explain my side of it—"

"You behaved in a grossly immature manner for an officer," Shaver interrupted. "If I were you, I would be glad to be getting out of this with those gold leaves still on your shoulders!" The man sighed and sat down behind his desk. "I am doing this because I think you are both good officers, as long as you don't have to work together. I am attributing your little encounter with each other yesterday to frayed nerves. After all, Captain Myers had just been through a hellish Indian fight. We in turn were imagining we'd find thirty or more men massacred, and we were all nervous that the Sioux would come back. It is difficult to stay calm in a situation like that."

"Yes, sir," they both answered.

"Major Ward, I want you to take this no further. I think you realize that if you do, you will only damage yourself. Your own career is better off if you let it go. I am going to put in for a transfer for you. You mentioned once that you thought you might enjoy serving under George Armstrong Custer. Right now he is temporarily suspended for flagrantly disobeying army rules. I will write to headquarters in Minnesota and make sure they know you would like to join the

Seventh Cavalry. Perhaps in a year or so Custer will resume his command. In the meantime, I am having you transferred back to Fort Snelling and have requested you be replaced here. I will not elaborate on the reasons and nothing will go against your record. Does that suit you?"

Jason still refused to look at Zack and Iris. "It would suit me just fine, sir."

"Good." Shaver turned his attention to Zack. "Captain Myers, you will stay here through one more winter. I have been informed that next summer it is very likely this fort as well as Fort C. F. Smith and Fort Reno will be closed. The situation with Red Cloud has become much too dangerous. Until Congress can decide what to do about it, and until more talks can be conducted with Red Cloud in an effort to settle all of this, we simply must withdraw. It is costing the lives of too many men. When this fort is closed, I will be retiring and will move back east. I have a wife and family there who hardly know me anymore. At that time I will have you transferred even farther west. I hope that won't be too upsetting for your wife, but I assure you that you will have more comfortable quarters at Lapwai."

Zack frowned. "Lapwai? That's Nez Perce country, isn't it?"

Shaver nodded. "Western Idaho. I think it would do you good to get involved with a different tribe of Indians. Whoever handles these problems with the Sioux, it will have to be men fresh to the purpose, men who haven't had their nerves worn to a frazzle by Red Cloud's endless threats and attacks. It is time for you to move on to new places, and I firmly believe that now you will have a new outlook on the Indian situation. You have learned something these last few months, something you can use to deal with the Nez Perce. They are much, much more advanced and civilized than the Sioux, many of them Christian; however, the age-old problem of wanting land set aside for their hunting grounds is the same as with all the other tribes. There, too, gold has been discovered, and white men have swarmed onto their land. However, it is hoped that because over the years the Nez Perce have been basically peaceful and cooperative with whites, something can still be done to salvage the situation and ease the growing tensions. I have decided you will act as a mediator."

Zack's eyebrows arched in surprise. He glanced at Iris,

saw her own shock at the assignment. "Me?" he asked, look-ing back at Shaver. "A mediator between the army and Indi-ans?"

Shaver leaned farther over his desk. "Yes, you. Along with it, I am putting in for a promotion to major."

Iris drew in her breath in surprise and joy. Jason Ward shot up out of his chair. "Sir, this is entirely unfair! Zack Myers disobeyed orders and hit an officer! Everyone knows he is risky material for an officer—"

"Are you arguing with a superior officer, Major?" Shaver interrupted. "Questioning my judgment? I will remind you that I could easily bring *you* up on charges and have you *de-moted* for your actions yesterday!"

Jason took a deep breath and spoke through gritted teeth. "Sir, I request my transfer be made as soon as possible."

"Rest assured that it will, Major Ward. You can get back to your duties now. You are dismissed."

Jason saluted the man. "Yes, *sir*! And thank you, sir, for putting in for my transfer without blemishing my record." He turned and walked out, and Shaver watched after him a mo-ment.

"As far as I'm concerned, General Custer is headed for di-saster," he told Zack. "There isn't an officer in this army who's more irrational and careless. How he gets away with it, I'll never know, but if that's who Jason Ward would rather serve under, then he's welcome to it. As for you, I'm not sure what kind of glorious future you have at Lapwai, but I *am* sure I'm doing the right thing. Your purpose in this army has always been different from men like Jason Ward or even myself. Maybe at Lapwai you can truly find your niche."

Zack sighed. "I don't know much about the Nez Perce."

"You know what you need to know to reason with them. Thomas has helped you understand their point of view. I know it seems strange to think so, but I think you would be more fair than some others. I would hate to see the situation out there get as bad as it is here, especially considering how well the Nez Perce got along with whites up until just a few years ago. There's hope there, Zack, just like there is hope for you. It's beautiful country, much cooler most of the time than it is here. The post has been abandoned twice due to a lack of troops, but my communications tell me it will be reopened later this year. Good officers are needed. Since this post will be closed next summer, I am to suggest where my officers might best be suited to serve. I will make a specific request that decent quarters be built for you and Iris. One thing they have there is plenty of wood and easy access to it. There is no reason why you two can't have a nice cabin of your own while you're there, and you'll have plenty of heating wood, so no more cold winters."

Zack rose. "Thank you, Howard. Everything I am, every success I've had with the army, I owe it all to you. I know my actions yesterday could have cost me dearly. Nothing like that will happen again."

"I have no doubt about it, Zack." Shaver smiled and put out his hand. "I will miss you once we part, but that won't be for a while yet. You must promise to write me back east and let me know everything that's happening, not just with the army and the Nez Perce, but with Iris, future children. You're like a son to me, and I never want to lose touch."

Zack grasped his hand. "I wouldn't want that either. You're the finest man I've ever known."

Howard grinned. "I feel the same way about you, Zack." His smile faded, and a great sadness came into his eyes as he released his grip and ran his hand through his red hair, hair that was now even more heavily streaked with gray and white. "I am afraid I have some bad news for you. I wanted to wait until this meeting was over and Jason Ward was out of the room."

Zack's heart tightened at the words. "Thomas?"

"He, uh, he died just an hour or so ago. After he passed out late yesterday, after you talked to him alone, well, he never woke up."

"Oh, no," Iris said softly. She looked up at Zack, watched him pale. His lips were pressed tightly together, and his jaw flexed in repressed emotions.

"I'm sorry, Zack," Shaver told him. "I'm having a coffin built now. He'll be buried at nine o'clock with the other six who died yesterday. I thought you'd want to say something over Thomas's grave. Would you?"

Zack nodded, swallowing. Iris saw tears come into his eyes. "Yes, sir, I would. We've lost some good men but Thomas was . . . special."

Shaver studied him carefully. "I've heard it said the Lord works in strange ways, Zack. I think Thomas's death has served a great purpose."

Zack put on his hat. "May I be dismissed?"

Shaver nodded.

"Thank you, sir." Zack turned to Iris. "Take the baby back to our quarters. I'm going for a short ride. I want to be alone."

He quickly left, and Iris held the baby closer, kissing his cheek. Her heart ached with great remorse for Thomas, and painful sympathy for what Zack was suffering that moment. She well knew what Thomas's death meant to him. She met Shaver's eyes, and the man simply nodded.

"He's come a long way. I hope you don't mind my sending you farther west, Iris. I assure you you'll have decent living conditions. I have personally requested it."

"Thank you." A tear slipped down her cheek. "And thank you for everything you've done for Zack."

The man smiled sadly. "You've done much more for him. You've been wonderful, putting up with the hell of living here. He'll need you more than ever the next few days, but he'll be the better man for all of this. I'm sending him to Idaho because he needs to come full circle now. He's a good officer, and an experienced Indian fighter; but I don't feel that is how he can best serve. I think he's just beginning to understand that."

"Thank you, Colonel Shaver," Iris told him. "And I don't mind where I live, as long as I can be with Zack." She turned and left, hurrying over to the stables, where Zack was leading a saddled horse out of a stall. "Zack, are you all right?" Jacob began to fuss, and she patted his bottom. Her heart ached at Zack's red eyes.

"I don't know," he answered. "I just want to be alone for a while, think about what I'll say over Thomas's grave."

She nodded. "I understand." She followed him outside, where he mounted his horse.

"It's damn ironic, isn't it?"

"What's that, Zack?"

He adjusted his hat and looked away. "All these years I dreamed about revenge, ached to kill Pawnee Indians. Even one . . . just one. And now it tears my guts out to have to bury one." He kicked his horse into a light trot and rode toward the gate.

Iris watched him through tears, wishing there were something she could do to soothe his aching heart, but this was something he had to handle alone. She turned back toward their quarters, feeling sick at the sound of the carpenter's hammer. She prayed she would never have to hear the carpenter building a coffin for Zack Myers. She didn't know much about the Nez Perce. She could only hope things would not be as dangerous in Idaho as they had been at Fort Kearny.

Part Three

24

JULY 1868

*A*lthough they were traveling through some of the most ruggedly beautiful country she had ever seen, Iris lamented they were too far north to have taken a train at least part of the way. According to reports, the transcontinental railroad was on its way to completion. The Union Pacific was over halfway through Wyoming Territory. Few had believed such a thing could be done, but now it looked as though it would really happen. How they managed to build a railroad through country like this was beyond her imagination, and she doubted there could ever be a railroad this far north, although there was already talk of it. Trouble was, railroads brought more whites, and that created only more Indian problems. Zack had his work cut out for him.

She wrapped her cloak higher around her neck. Although it was summer, nights in country like this were always cold. She could understand why no one made a journey like this in winter. It would be impossible. The guides who'd been hired to lead them into Idaho Territory had told them some spine-tingling stories about life in these mountains, how horrific the winters could be, although the past two winters in Montana had been no better. At least in their new location it supposedly did not get quite so unbearably hot in summer.

Outside, men tethered horses and checked their gear. Every night the wagons that carried supplies were gathered in a circle because of the constant danger of Indian attack, although they were out of Sioux country now. Crow and Blackfoot Indians often roamed this country, but were mostly peaceful. Even so, Zack was taking no chances, especially with his wife and son along. They had been told that once they reached Fort Lapwai, there could be trouble with the Cayuse Indians, who were not as cooperative as the Nez Perce.

Iris looked out the back of the wagon to see Zack talking to the grizzly looking mountain man who was their guide. Sandy Bodine was one of those mysterious creatures of the mountains who seemed to come from nowhere and had no purpose in life but to hunt and trap and occasionally take a job leading others into rugged land that was as familiar to him as the back of his hand. The man had outlived two Indian wives and had children living among the Crow and Cayuse. He didn't know how many and seemed not to care. He chewed tobacco and drank too much whiskey, and Iris found it difficult to even look at him, let alone stand downwind of him; but he did seem to know his business when it came to getting them through these mountains, and that was all that mattered.

She took out her diary, glancing at Jacob, who played on a blanket. His eyes were drooping as sleepiness began to overtake him. It was refreshing to see him playing quietly. He was beginning to be quite a handful, and she had to watch the active tot constantly, for fear he would fall out of the wagon while it was moving. When he was not inside, his chubby legs sent him wandering, and the Bitterroot Mountains were no place for that.

The boy looked up at her and grinned, oblivious of the danger and hardship of their journey. He was a handsome child. To Iris's delight, he had his father's provocative green eyes and dark hair. He worshipped Zack, and Zack most certainly worshipped his son. He often carried him on his horse to relieve Iris of the burden of having to constantly run after him, but because of Zack's duties as the leader of the sixty men with them, he could not often take the responsibility of Jacob. Iris wasn't sure if she was more weary from the difficult journey and the tasks of life on the trail or from constantly chasing after Jacob.

Jacob lay down but held up one of the blocks still in his hand.

"Thank you," she said. "That's good, Jacob."

"Daddy?"

She smiled. "Daddy will come soon, but you need to sleep. Why don't you be a good boy and close your eyes?"

It took little persuasion on her part this time. Jacob had done a lot of walking today and was obviously already very tired. His pretty eyes drooped again, dark lashes against the soft skin of his chubby cheeks. Iris took great pleasure at the sight, then took a bottle of ink from a little wooden box and carefully uncorked it. She dipped her pen into the ink and began writing.

July 16, 1868 . . . Jacob is thirteen months old, and has discovered why he has legs. We are now in the Bitterroot Mountains, and getting this far with such an active baby has not been easy. We almost lost the boy over a cliff while coming through the Rockies. He got away from me, and by the time I realized it, he had wandered to the edge. My heart still beats wildly at the memory.

We have encountered many wild animals—bears, moose, elk, wolves, mountain lions. This is a wild, beautiful land, and I can see why the Indians would not want to give it up. At the same time, I cannot imagine why so many whites want to settle here in such remote country, so far from the civilization of the East, so far from good doctors, from theaters and parks and places to shop. I am here because my husband has been assigned here. Yet he would not even be here if not for the thousands of whites who insist on coming, creating more Indian problems. The smell of gold is a tantalizing scent indeed. It makes sane, settled men do very insane things. Because of them, the Indians and men like my husband must suffer.

She paused, feeling another pain, telling herself it was nothing. She wondered if she should enter into the diary the fact that she was expecting another baby. She had told no one, not even Zack. She had decided to wait and tell him when they reached Lapwai, and pray she had no problems before then, but these pains were beginning to frighten her. *Ignore them*, she told herself. *They'll go away.* She continued her diary entry.

> *I am told Lapwai means "place of the butterflies." Nez Perce country is supposed to be some of the most beautiful in the West, and I can already see that is so. This is a land of purple mountains, clear blue skies, rugged rocks in rainbows of colors, waterfalls and sparkling streams, and sprawling meadows of wildflowers. It is truly God's country, with eagles and hawks lording the skies, grizzlies, elk and wolves owning the land . . . along with the Indians. It is my own opinion that the land should be left to them.*

She put her pen down when Zack climbed up on the back of the wagon and leaned over the tailgate. "Everything all right?" he asked.

"Other than being cold, everything is fine. I hope Jacob doesn't take sick from these cold nights, after the warm days."

Zack grinned, leaning over the feather mattress spread out in the narrow bottom of the wagon. "I think our worries amount to more than him catching a cold. A real powder keg of energy, isn't he?"

Iris rubbed the back of her neck. "He certainly is." She sat on the other end of the wagon, near the seat, using a crate for a table. "I was just making another diary entry before trying to sleep."

Zack climbed inside and carefully maneuvered around the baby, picking up the edge of the featherbed so as not to step on it. His big frame filled the wagon, and because it was so small, he'd resorted to changing clothes outside, often sleeping in a tent to give Iris and Jacob more room. He sat down behind Iris, pulling her between his legs. "Things will get better," he promised. "I'm going to have some men build us a real house. It might have to be of logs, but at least you'll have room, a real kitchen, a big fireplace, at least two bedrooms, and wood floors."

She leaned her back against him. "I can't wait. After those tiny rooms at Phil Kearny, and now this awkward wagon . . ." She sighed. "I wonder how long we'll be stationed out here, Zack."

"Hard to say. We can take it only one year at a time. At least we'll have a decent place to live, and we won't be living with the constant danger we had to put up with back at Kearny."

"It all seems so unreal now." When they first abandoned the fort, they had gone north along the Bozeman to Fort C. F. Smith, and only hours later a messenger had come to tell them Fort Phil Kearny was already on fire. Red Cloud was burning forts just as fast as they were abandoned. C. F. Smith had also gone up in flames not long after it, too, was abandoned. Zack and his troops had come west, Sergeant Bailey with them. The rest of the three hundred or so men had been sent east and then south, most to Fort Laramie, a well-garrisoned post from which a new army campaign against the Sioux would be staged. "They'll send out a lot more soldiers, won't they?"

"If they have any sense, they will. It was crazy to expect us to protect the Bozeman Trail with only four hundred men, sometimes less, against thousands of Indians. The trouble is, the government will concentrate on the Sioux now, and at Lapwai we'll have the same problem, not enough men."

She sighed, enjoying the comfort and safety of his arms. "I wish Thomas could be with us."

Zack pondered the remark, feeling a pull at his heart. "Well, my guess is he wouldn't have wanted to come. He'd probably say something like, 'I don' know nothin' about them Nez Perces. I'd rather stay here and kill me some more of them damn Sioux.' "

He'd spoken the words in a raspy voice similar to Thomas's, and Iris laughed lightly. "You sound just like him!" She turned her face up to him, and Zack smiled sadly.

"Life takes strange turns, doesn't it?"

Iris leaned up and kissed him. "Yes," she said softly, knowing it still hurt to think about Thomas. She removed his hat and set it aside. "We are going to have a big family, Zack Myers, many children and grandchildren. Someday you'll retire from the army and we'll have a real home somewhere. We'll sit by the hearth at Christmas and bounce grandchildren on our knees, and life will be as good as you've always dreamed it could be again for you. I'll be a good granny, like my own grandmother was to me."

A twinkle came into his eyes. "Somehow I can't picture you old and gray. You'll always be as beautiful to me as you are right now."

"And you will always be my strong, handsome soldier, even after you retire." She kissed him again. "Can you sleep in here tonight?"

He pressed a big hand to her stomach, ran it over her breasts. "I would very much like to do that, but I'd hate to have an emergency in the middle of making love to my wife and have the sergeant have to come here and get me. Besides, out here in this clear, still air, every little sound can be heard a mile away."

"Well, we don't *have* to make love. It's too cold for you to be outdoors." They both talked in a near whisper so men camped outside would not hear them.

"Not make love snuggled into that feather mattress with you? And after all these weeks of abstinence?" He kissed her hungrily, squeezing her breasts gently as he searched her mouth. Wolves called to one another, some distant, some not so far away. Zack pulled away. "I have to be available to the men. We'll just have to wait until we reach Lapwai."

Iris sighed. "How much longer do you think it will be?"

"That's what I was asking Sandy earlier. About three weeks, he says."

"Well, just don't pick up any fleas from that man," she frowned.

Zack grinned and put his hat back on. "I keep my distance. At least he knows his business. I can't imagine finding my way through these mountains without his aid. I just hope the Nez Perces never make us have to give chase. Sandy says they know this country better than him or any man alive. We'd play hell trying to track them down and capture them if they decided to flee into these mountains. Sandy says a few

Nez Perces could probably elude a thousand soldiers out here, and they damn well know it."

He kissed her once more and climbed out of the wagon over the front seat so as not to disturb Jacob. Iris turned back to her diary, writing down what he had just told her about the Nez Perces. *I could not help feeling,* she wrote, *that his words were rather ominous.*

She set the pen aside, wincing with another cramp deep in her belly. "Please, God, don't let anything go wrong," she prayed. She leaned against a barrel, listening to the howling of wolves. She wondered if there would be any white women at Lapwai to help her with the birth. She told herself if she could just make it to Lapwai, she'd be all right. The trouble was, it was becoming more and more difficult to hide this pain from her husband.

The train of wagons and horse soldiers snaked its way along narrow roads cut from the sides of mountains, over precipices so high that Iris had never known such fear, not even the times when Sioux threatened to attack Fort Kearny. She was sure they must be high enough to find an eagle's nest, and eagles did sometimes circle closely, giving out their eerie cries of warning. Some mornings when they first left they were shrouded in fog, finally realizing they were actually in a cloud.

When the terrifying, rocky roadway began its descent on the west side of the Bitterroots, there came even more reason to fear for their lives. It was not easy to handle the mules that pulled the wagons. The heavy weight behind them made them skid and falter. Sandy suggested a group of soldiers ride behind each wagon with ropes attached to the rear axles and tied around the pommels of their saddles. The ropes were pulled taut to keep from driving mules and wagons over a cliff.

Zack tried the idea, allowing no one to ride inside the wagons. A soldier who had accidentally shot himself in the foot was carried on a stretcher by four men. Iris walked with Jacob, either carrying him or letting him walk beside her, a rope tied around his waist so he would not be able to run away and get hurt.

They passed cascading waterfalls, rainbow-colored rocks, the pungent smell of pine filling their nostrils with its pleasant, clean odor. They had once nearly reached what Sandy called the tree line, a point where it was so cold most of the year that even the pines would not grow there. Now, finally, they made their descent, and Iris was terrified for Zack, who rode ahead with Sandy, often moving to the side whenever the narrow road would allow, and watching team after team pass, soldiers behind the wagons with the drag ropes. He encouraged them as best he could.

After three days of constant downhill terror, they finally reached a plateau, coming into a lush green meadow where the animals were allowed to graze. "They've earned the rest," he told the men. "All of us have. It's a little early, but we'll camp here for the remainder of the afternoon and tonight." He rode back to Iris, who waded through the tall grass carrying Jacob.

"I'm afraid to put him down," she told him. "There could be snakes in this grass."

Zack whisked the boy up onto the horse with him. "You'd better get into the wagon and try to get some rest yourself. You've walked all day."

Iris nodded, blinking back tears. She hated to tell him the awful truth, but all day the cramping deep in her belly had grown worse. When she had gone behind some rocks earlier to relieve herself, she'd been shocked to discover she was bleeding. The long journey through wild mountains, the hard work of making and breaking camp daily, most of all the strain of walking for miles over steep country, carrying a hefty Jacob much of the way, had been too much in her condition. She had been nearly ready to cry out for help when Zack finally halted the train.

"Zack—" She stood there feeling helpless, sorry she had not told him the truth of her pregnancy, wondering how she was going to get through this with no women along to help her. There was not even a doctor among the soldiers. She bent over and went to her knees.

"Iris!" Zack quickly dismounted, shouting to Sergeant Bailey to come and get Jacob. He held the boy in one arm while he knelt beside her. "What is it! Did *you* get bit?"

Bailey charged up to him and dismounted before his horse came to a full halt. "Sir! What is it, sir?"

"I'm not sure. Take Jacob and have some of the other men watch him. There could be snakes in this grass."

"Yes, sir! Come on, little major," Bailey said, hoisting Jacob onto his horse.

Jacob laughed with delight, oblivious of his mother's distress. He knew all of the men and readily went to any of them.

Bailey rode off with the boy, and Zack leaned over Iris, taking hold of her shoulders. "Iris, honey, what the heck is wrong?"

She grasped his arm. "I think I'm . . . having a miscarriage."

His hands tightened on her shoulders. "What! Iris, why didn't you tell me!"

"I just couldn't. You had your assignment. We had to leave. I didn't want you to worry."

"I could have made better arrangements! I could have sent you to Laramie until the baby was born, had you brought out later, *anything* but this!"

"I hate being pampered. I thought I could do this. I didn't want us to be apart. Anything could happen. You could be killed and I'd never see you again."

"And what about you! This isn't any less dangerous! *Damn!*" He picked her up in his arms and carried her at a near run to their wagon. "What the hell are we going to do? I don't know anything about this, and neither does anybody else on this train." He shouted an order for his first lieutenant, Joseph Best, to help lift her inside. Iris caught the terror in his voice.

"I'll be all right," she tried to assure him, not wanting to let him know how frightened she was herself. She remembered a woman back in Washington had died from losing a baby, bled to death. She'd heard stories of other women dying the same way. If only there were a doctor . . .

Zack laid her down on the featherbed and ordered Best to take charge of the men. The lieutenant climbed out while Zack frantically began helping her undress. He took out her flannel gown, and Iris heard a horse come thundering up to the wagon. "What's goin' on, Major?" Through her pain and blurred vision Iris recognized Sandy Bodine's voice. Zack moved to the rear of the wagon.

"My wife's having a miscarriage. I didn't even know she was carrying."

Iris felt embarrassed, and angry that she had shown a weaker side. She hated weakness in others, hated holding everyone up when they were so close to their destination. Most of all, she hated losing Zack's child. She so wanted to give him a big family. She curled up in tears, most of her clothes off but her gown still not on. She pulled a blanket over herself.

"Good God, that's bad," she heard Sandy say. "I ain't much for what to do about somethin' like that."

"That's just the problem. Neither am I, and neither is anybody else here," Zack lamented.

"That ain't our only problem," Sandy told him. "Out there on the horizon, next to them foothills to the west. You've been wonderin' about the Nez Perce. Here's your chance to meet some. They ain't usually this far east, but they might be on a hunt. Got some women with 'em, probably to help gut and skin whatever they kill, clean the hides, and smoke the meat. They're outside reservation borders, but most of them don't much cotton to borders yet."

"Jesus," Zack muttered. "My wife is losing a baby. I can't go riding off to talk to any Indians right now."

Iris gritted her teeth against another pain, not wanting to cry out.

"Might be they could help," she heard Sandy say. "Like I say, they got women along. Ain't nobody knows much more about how to tend to such things than the Indians. They been takin' care of themselves for centuries without no white doctors, their women droppin' babies with just each other's help. We could ride over there, see if any of their women maybe could help."

"Dear God," Iris whispered. She told herself not to be afraid an Indian woman might have to help. This could be a godsend. The Lord seemed to have been with them this far. Still, much as she preached finding ways to make peace with them, she was not so sure about letting an Indian woman doctor her. She imagined chanting and rattles, perhaps some ungodly ritual. She knew nothing about the Nez Perce except they were supposedly a little more civilized than the Sioux. She hoped for that much.

Zack was kneeling beside her then. "Let's get your gown on," he told her. Iris managed to sit up while he slipped it over her head. "Iris, I don't know what to do. You have to have some kind of help. You can't just lie here and go through this alone. Sandy says there are some Nez Perce women with a hunting party not far away. They've been watching us. I think they're friendly. We don't have any choice but to see if any of their women can help you. Do you want me to go out there and find out?"

Iris lay back down, and Zack covered her with quilts, leaning down to kiss her tears. "Yes," she groaned. "I'm afraid, Zack ... losing blood. But I'm afraid of ... those Indian women too."

"I'm so damn sorry," he said. "Bringing you out here. I should have just quit the army and settled someplace."

"No ... no." She lay calm for a moment between cramps. "It's what you needed. There is a reason for this. I have to believe that. I'll be all right, Zack." She gritted her teeth against another pain. "Jacob. Somebody has to take care of him."

Zack breathed deeply against his own tears. "Don't worry about Jacob. The men love him, and he loves them. I hate to leave you, Iris, but I want to see these Indian women for myself before letting them come into camp. I don't know what else to do. We have to try it."

"I know," she whispered.

He leaned down and kissed her again. "Don't you die on me," he said brokenly. "I couldn't live without you."

Iris sensed his leaving. "Zack ..." Pain overcame her awareness of everything but fear ... fear of the strange Indian women coming to help her ... fear of dying in this strange new land.

25

*T*he ride across the vast meadow toward the waiting Indians seemed the longest of Zack's life. His mind raced
with fear that he was losing his wife. It would not be easy to
ask these Indians for help. In spite of what he had come to
feel for Thomas and the understanding he now had of these
people, he still didn't want to ask them for help, and he had
trouble believing it was even right to do so. Should he let Indian women tend to Iris so intimately?

How strange it felt to ride out with only one other man,
his guide and interpreter, toward a large contingent of Indians! He could not shed the sensation that there could be a
few thousand more Nez Perce farther in the hills. That was
the kind of trickery he'd become accustomed to with the
Sioux.

"You sure we're safe?" he asked Sandy once more before
reaching the warriors.

"Yup. Nez Perces ain't into runnin' in big war parties, and
they wouldn't bring women and children along if that's what
this was. Reservation meat is rotten half the time, and with
whites movin' in and killin' off so much game, they're forced

to ride farther and farther out of their territory to find good meat."

"I don't like this. I'm not used to asking an Indian for help. Where I came from, when you see Indians, you kill them before they kill you. White women live in fear of their person and their scalps. It's difficult for me to trust them."

"Hell, you trusted that there Thomas Red Hand, didn't you?"

"He was Pawnee—hated the Sioux. I'm told the Nez Perce are Sioux allies, learned the art of hunting on horseback and living in tipis from them, often trade with them."

"Not so much anymore. The Sioux have their own troubles and so do the Nez Perce—no time for roamin' across them damn mountains to hook up with each other. That's the main reason we'll win in the end, you know."

"How do you mean?"

"They'll bring it on themselves. If every Indian tribe in the country got together against the whites, we'd be in a fix; but they're too scattered, and some of them are born enemies and wouldn't think of teamin' up. Besides that, they've got no way of communicatin' like we do with the railroad and telegraph and such. These Nez Perce don't know nothin' about what's happenin' with the Apache and Comanche down in the Southwest, and them two tribes is enemies, so they won't team up down there. Up here you've got the Pawnee hatin' the Sioux, the Cheyenne hatin' the Crow, the Cayuse and Nez Perce not always gettin' along . . . same with the Navajo and Hopi. They're all broke up into their own smaller tribes, and that's how we've got to go at 'em, piece by piece. It's gonna be a long, slow campaign, but we'll do it."

Zack was surprised he found something sad in the comment. He always thought he'd like nothing better than to eliminate all Indians, but ever since Thomas died, something had changed.

A very proud-looking Nez Perce warrior rode forward to greet them as they drew close. Zack guessed him to be about the same age as he was, late twenties, maybe thirty. He was handsome and well built. His Appaloosa was adorned with a decorative collar made of red cloth, glass beads, and brass bells that tinkled with the horse's every move. He wore only a vest and deerskin leggings, but both were grandly beaded, the vest in front and the leggings down the sides. His moccasins were also beaded, and a bone necklace adorned his throat. His long black hair was pulled into a tail, and a round, beaded hairpiece was fastened into the side of it, two small feathers hanging from the hairpiece. He seemed very clean, Zack thought, and his dark eyes flashed with arrogance.

"So, the Great Father has chosen to send more soldiers," he said, surprising Zack with his clear English. He kept his eyes on Zack. "Tell me, Major, are you here to protect *us*, as you are supposed to do, or the whites who come into our land without our permission?"

Zack studied the man intently. This was no ordinary savage. This man was articulate, and his eyes showed the unnerving confidence and intelligence of a leader. "How do you know I am a major?"

The Indian grinned with genuine humor. "My people are more familiar with you bluecoats than they care to be. When you know you might someday do battle with certain men, you learn about them, who their leaders are. I know that the gold leaves on your shoulders say you are a major, and that a major has much authority."

Zack watched him silently for a moment. Here was a challenge, a true contender. "I am here for both. I am Major Zachary Myers. What are you called?"

The Indian held his chin a little higher. "I am Strong Runner."

"Strong Runner. I've heard of you," Sandy put in. "You're with Chief Joseph's bunch, over at Walla Walla, by the Blue Mountains. You're a long way from there."

Strong Runner studied Major Myers a moment longer without answering. The honesty and wisdom he saw in Zack's eyes made him wonder. He had little use for any white man, especially a soldier, but there was something about this one that rang true. He did not have the cockiness of most soldiers of rank.

He finally turned his gaze to the guide, looking him over scornfully. He disliked these white men who never bathed or shaved, could hardly bear the smell of them. "We hunt," he answered simply. "The white settlers kill or frighten away most game. Every summer we must go even farther to find meat. The meat your government sends is rotten and makes us sick." He looked again at Zack. "We saw all your soldiers, and the others were afraid you would come after us because we are not on land your Great Father gave to us. Is this so? Is this why you have come to me? To make council and tell us we must go back?"

Zack shook his head. "No. I am on my way to Fort Lapwai with these men. We have no special assignment at this time. I rode out here when I saw you because—" Could he really do this? Iris! He could lose her! "Because my wife is with me, in one of those wagons back there. She's in great pain, losing a baby. I am afraid for her. There are no other women along. I thought maybe—" He scanned the rest of them. There were eight or ten women along, of various ages, most with little children who now stood staring at him with big, dark eyes. Two of the women carried papooses. "I hoped one of the women with you would know what to do for her. I fear if she isn't taken care of properly, she could die. The death of a white woman probably means nothing to you, but she is my wife. She means very much to me."

Strong Runner looked warily past him toward the soldiers' camp. "How do I know this is not a trick to get me and my people into your camp, where we could be surrounded? I have been tricked by white men before, soldier, and they paid with their lives."

I'll bet they did, Zack thought. "I'll bring the wagon out here to you if you're afraid to go into the camp. Time is wasting, Strong Runner. My wife is in a bad way. I don't want to leave her alone any longer. I have to go back to her. Please, if you think any of these women can help, follow me."

Strong Runner detected a hint of tears in the man's eyes. The concern there was too evident not to believe him. "I, too, have a wife," he said. "I know the feeling to think she could be dying." He turned and said something in his own tongue, and a pretty, young Indian woman stepped forward, leading a shirtless little boy Zack guessed to be four or five years old. She carried another little boy in one arm, a chunky, bright-eyed child who looked about a year older than Jacob. "This is Morning Star, my woman. These are my sons, Wolf Boy and Jumping Bear."

"I, too, have a son," Zack told him. "His name is Jacob.

He is just a little over one year old. He is also with us. He needs his mother. Can Morning Star help?"

Strong Runner hesitated a moment longer. In the distance he heard a woman cry out, and he watched Zack squirm restlessly in his saddle. Yes, this man was telling the truth. "I will bring Morning Star and leave my sons here with the others. There is another woman along who is wise in these things. She is Little Bear, Morning Star's mother." He turned and again called out in his native tongue. An older man, who Zack guessed to be Morning Star's father, answered, turned to an older and very lovely woman, and said something to her. The woman hurried to a travois that was packed with supplies and took up a leather bag, which she slung over her shoulder. The older man got down from his horse, and the woman mounted up in his place.

Strong Runner reached down, and with one arm lifted Morning Star onto his horse in front of him. "We go," he said with authority.

Zack ignored the fact that an Indian had literally given him an order. He was too worried about Iris to care. He nodded to Strong Runner. "If they can help her, I will be forever grateful." He turned his horse and headed back to camp at a hurried lope, praying he'd done the right thing.

As they drew closer, he could hear Iris's cries of pain. Men scrambled everywhere, some tethering horses, others trying to start a fire. Two men were chasing after Jacob, who kept running away from them.

Zack dismounted. "Build that fire and heat some water," he told a private who had finally lit some kindling. "We might need it." He looked around the camp at the others, who stared at Strong Runner and Morning Star. Zack detected a hungry look in some of their eyes at the sight of Morning Star, who was indeed beautiful. "I want these Nez Perces with me treated with respect," he warned Lieutenant Best. "Those others out there are just on a hunt. They mean no harm. These women are going to try to help my wife, so give them whatever they ask for."

"Yes, sir," Best answered.

"And keep an eye on Jacob. Don't let him wander too far in that tall grass. Watch out for snakes."

"There are no snakes in this meadow." Strong Runner

spoke up, helping Morning Star slide off his horse. Her mother dismounted also.

Zack looked up at the man. "You sure?"

Strong Runner gave him a sly smile that reminded him of Thomas. He realized then that the question had been a stupid one. Who knew this land better than someone like Strong Runner? "I am sure," the man answered. "I often played in this very meadow when I was young. At one time there were many deer and elk here. That is why we came back."

Zack nodded. "All right. I'll take your word for it. Do these women speak English?"

Strong Runner nodded. "We use our native tongue so that the children learn it and never forget, but we also speak English. White missionaries taught us. Little Bear is Christian. She will be good to your woman. She understands."

"Follow me, then," he told her, leading her and Morning Star to the back of his wagon. Little Bear climbed inside, and Morning Star handed up the leather shoulder bag they had brought along. Zack hoped it contained something to alleviate pain, or stop bleeding. He'd heard plenty about Indian medicine, and he had always figured most of it was useless, a medicine man's chanting nothing but mumbo-jumbo. Still, these people had an amazing instinct for survival.

Morning Star hesitated before climbing inside. She looked from Zack to Strong Runner, who said something to her in his own tongue. The tone of his voice and look in his eyes was reassuring, but she still seemed wary as she looked around the camp full of soldiers. When Iris cried out again the Indian woman quickly climbed into the wagon and lowered the canvas at the back so that no one could see inside.

Zack turned away, needing to cry out from sheer terror that Iris might die. He knew he could not show his emotions here. He had to be calm and collected in front of all these men. He took a deep breath for control, put his hand on the wagon gate, and glanced nervously at the canvas.

"They will not harm her," Strong Runner told him.

Zack met his eyes, steady, honest. Yes, this was one Nez Perce he was going to get to know better.

"Zack!" Iris cried out. "I want Zack."

Zack could hear the Indian women soothing her. He walked around the wagon and climbed in through the front.

He knew Iris must be terribly confused and afraid. What he saw hit him like a fist in his gut. The blankets and Iris's gown were soaked with blood. "My God," he muttered. She would surely die!

Iris screamed as Little Bear massaged her stomach. "Make them stop," she begged Zack. She lay with her head in his lap while Zack watched in helpless terror.

"Little Bear says you have to expel the baby so we can take you to a cold stream and stop the bleeding," he answered, stroking her hair. He had no idea if the Nez Perce women were right, but he had to trust them. The older one, Little Bear, had said the only way to hope to stop the bleeding was to pack Iris with ice, but since there was none, their second choice was to place her in an icy stream. They claimed there was a creek not far beyond the west side of the meadow, where they had made camp.

"The water there is always cold," Little Bear had said, "even in summer. And it is clear and bright. Your miners have not yet spoiled that one." The last words were spoken with a strong note of bitterness.

"I don't want the baby to come," Iris lamented. "I want to keep it, save it . . . for you."

"Honey, it's too late for that. There will be more babies in time. This one wasn't meant to be."

"No! No! My baby!" Iris broke into tears that led to another agonizing groan. She wished she could see better, but her pain made everything blurry and unreal. She realized two Indian women were sitting close, touching her, talking to each other in a strange tongue. She didn't like them seeing her this way, and she was afraid their pressing hands were a deliberate attempt to bring her more pain. "Make them stop, Zack! They're . . . trying to kill me!"

"Hanging on to the *baby* will kill you, Iris. Try to relax and let it come." How he hated seeing her in such pain.

Iris gave out one last scream, then passed out.

"Iris!" Zack shook her. "She's dying!"

"She is not dying," Little Bear told him. "It is the body's way of relieving her of the pain. Put another quilt over her.

Do you have small blanket you would use for a baby? Please give me one."

Zack turned around and opened a trunk, taking out a quilt and one of Jacob's blankets. He handed the smaller blanket to Little Bear, then spread the quilt over Iris's shoulders and chest. He was not sure what the Indian women were doing until the younger one, Morning Star, handed the other blanket back to him. It was bundled and bloody, and he was astonished to see tears in Morning Star's eyes.

"Here is your child," she told him. "We think it was a boy. It is very, very tiny, no bigger than the palm of my hand. But it is still a human spirit, loved by God. You must bury your child."

Zack took the bundle with shaking hands, deciding he would not look inside. Here was a piece of his own life, a piece of Iris. How could he fight in the Civil War, fight Indians, lead men over mountains, yet feel so helpless? This had all happened so fast. He watched the Indian women working frantically now with rags and water. They packed towels around Iris.

"Go and bring a travois, Strong Runner!" Morning Star shouted. "Quickly! We have to take her to the cold water!"

Zack heard a horse gallop off.

"Bury the child quickly," Little Bear told Zack. "We will take the woman with us. She might have to stay at our village for more than a day, and you cannot leave the baby's body that long. Strong Runner will stay and wait with you, then bring you to our village." They covered Iris completely. "We need a clean gown for her, clean blankets."

Zack still held the bloody bundle in his big hands. "I can't let you take my wife to a camp full of Indians I know nothing about," he said, still stunned at the fact that he'd had to rely on these Indians at all.

"Do you want your wife to live?" Morning Star asked him.

Zack looked at her. They seemed peaceful, as though they wanted to help. This proud and beautiful young Indian woman had tears in her eyes when she handed him the baby, as if it hurt her to see the tiny life die. "Of course I want my wife to live."

"Then you must let us take her to the stream quickly!"

Already Zack heard horses returning.

"Sir, there's more coming!" Sergeant Bailey shouted from outside the wagon.

Zack looked down at the baby, back at the waiting women.

"She is losing much blood," Little Bear told him. "She will die if we cannot stop the bleeding."

He looked at Iris, lying so still, so horribly pale. "Take her," he said. "I'll come out with Strong Runner as soon as I bury my—" The words suddenly stuck in his throat. "My son."

He turned and gently laid the bundle on top of the trunk. "It's all right!" he shouted to the men outside. "They're taking my wife to their village. There's a cold stream there. It's the only way to stop the bleeding."

Little Bear opened the back canvas.

"We have the travois," Zack heard Strong Runner tell her. "Hand the woman out to me."

Never had Zack felt more confused and afraid.

"Help us," Little Bear told him.

Without thinking, Zack knelt down and reached under Iris as the Indian women climbed out. He scooted Iris to the back of the wagon. Strong Runner lowered the gate and reached for her. For a moment Zack froze. Could he hand his wife over to this Indian man who was big enough to break her neck? Their eyes locked as Strong Runner waited.

"She is dying," the man reminded Zack.

Zack looked at Sandy, who stood nearby. "It's all right," Sandy told him. "You can trust them."

He met Strong Runner's dark eyes again. "I also have a wife," Strong Runner reminded him. "If I had to give her over to you and your soldiers to keep her alive, I would do it. Yet I trust your bluecoats no more than you trust my people."

Zack nodded. "All right." He handed her over and climbed down while Strong Runner carried Iris to a travois. The women secured her on the travois, then gave an order in their own tongue to the Indian man whose horse pulled the contraption. The man turned the horse in a wide circle and left, pulling the travois at a fast pace but not a full run. Two other Indian men who had ridden in with him also left.

Strong Runner lifted Little Bear and Morning Star up onto the horse Little Bear had ridden into camp. Zack was as-

rounded at the look of love and concern in Morning Star's
eyes when she grasped her husband's hand. "I do not like
leaving you here with all these soldiers, my husband."

"I will be fine. Do not let the white woman die. I will
come soon."

Morning Star looked around the camp with fear in her
eyes, and it struck Zack that these people were just as afraid
of soldiers as soldiers were of Indians. And the way Morning
Star and Strong Runner looked at each other was no different
from the way he and Iris often did when afraid for each other.

The two women left, and Strong Runner turned to face
Zack. "You have a son to bury. I will wait for you, then take
you to our camp."

Zack didn't know what to say. He climbed back inside the
wagon, and it took every bit of strength he had to keep from
breaking down when he picked up the bundle that was his
lifeless child.

He let the tears come, but only for a minute. He held the
little bundle close, then climbed down and shouted to Bailey
as he wiped his eyes with his shirtsleeve. "Come help me
bury the baby," he said. "I have to do it quickly and get to
that camp, where they've taken Iris."

"I'm awful sorry about the baby, sir."

Zack nodded. "You men wait here. Lieutenant Best will be
in charge. I'll come back in the morning with orders. I'll have
Sandy stay here with you. I'd better go alone to the Indian
camp."

"Yes, sir. I hope your wife will be all right."

Zack glanced at Strong Runner, who stood by, silently
watching. "So do I." He looked at Bailey. "I want him treated
with full respect."

"Yes, sir. You go pick out a spot to bury the child. I'll get
a shovel."

Strong Runner watched as Zack walked over to a lieutenant and gave more orders. Then he carried his baby to a pine
tree in the distance and waited for the one called Bailey to
bring a shovel. *You are not like the other bluecoats, Zack Myers,*
Strong Runner thought. *There is something different about you.*

ack rode off with Strong Runner, realizing he could be reprimanded for leaving his men to go into the heart of an Indian village, even though his own wife's life was in danger.

But he didn't care if he was kicked down to buck private. He was not leaving Iris. He followed Strong Runner across the meadow and through a maze of rocks, then a dense stand of pine trees, their horses' hooves making hardly a sound against a thick carpet of needles. After twenty minutes they emerged upon a small, pristine lake, where approximately twenty tipis were erected at one end.

"The creek is beyond our dwellings," Strong Runner told him, pointing. "You should go there without me. It will be just women there."

Zack noticed several small children watching him curiously. A few women were working at cleaning a deer hide, while others cooked over open fires. Everything seemed peaceful. Zack realized most of the hunting party must have returned once they knew he and Strong Runner would come. A young boy was tethering horses, and the men, a few wear-

ing white man's calico shirts, stood at various locations as
though to guard their women. Most of them were young, and
most of them eyed him warily.

"They do not trust bluecoats," Strong Runner told him.
"Most of those who ride with me are young warriors who refuse to live in the small area the white man tries to tell us is
all that is left to us. They are wondering why you have come
here with so many new soldiers."

Zack ignored the stares. He dismounted and hurried past
the tipis to where he could hear the voices of many women,
mingled with Iris's groans and pleadings. He charged to the
creek, and women backed away with fear in their eyes at the
sight of him. "Iris!"

She was struggling with Little Bear and Morning Star as
well as two other women. All of them were standing in the
cold water. Iris's bloody gown was soaked past her breasts.

"Zack!" Iris looked at him in wide-eyed terror and bewil-
derment, and Zack was glad she was at least conscious again.

"It's all right," he told her, coming closer. "Here, let me
hold her," he told Little Bear. He moved behind her, wading
into the creek boots and all to grasp her under the arms. "It's
the only way to stop the bleeding," he told Iris. "These
women are only trying to help you."

"The baby! Where's our baby? They won't let me see it."

She was hallucinating now, confused from shock and
pain. "We'll talk about the baby later. Just sit still, Iris. Just a
little longer."

"I'm so . . . cold . . . hold me, Zack."

He knelt down with his knees in the water and enfolded
her from behind, feeling her shiver. He wondered if they
would stop the bleeding only to lose her to shock or pneumonia. "It's all right. I'm right here."

"Don't let go," she pleaded. "Stay with me."

"I'll stay with you as long as it takes."

"Jacob—"

"Jacob is all right. The men will look after him."

He held her tightly, his feet and legs growing numb from
the cold. The Indian women stood around watching, whispering among themselves.

"They admire the handsome soldier who must love his
wife very much," Little Bear told him.

Zack looked at her, surprised at the remark. He noticed a twinkle in her eye, realized she had said it in an effort to help him cope with his terror that Iris would die. She was trying to calm the moment. It began to sink in then how much these people had already helped when they would probably rather see every white person and every soldier on their land just disappear or die. The women around him seemed to have lost their initial fear of him and had gathered closer, most of them smiling.

He held Iris for several more minutes, until Little Bear said they could take her out of the water. Little Bear and Morning Star helped dry her off, using government issue towels, probably part of their annuities. He helped them put a clean gown on Iris, and they laid her back onto the travois and packed more towels around her bottom.

"We will wait a few minutes and see if the bleeding has slowed," Little Bear said.

"Is my husband here with you?" Morning Star asked, fear in her voice.

"He's here," he answered. "I couldn't have found my way without him."

She held her chin a little higher. "Strong Runner is an honored warrior. So is my father, Sits-In-Sun, and Strong Runner's father, Yellow Hand."

Zack suspected she wanted to be sure he knew what he was up against if he tried anything. "I am sure they are," he answered.

"You are also a warrior."

Zack met her eyes, not sure what she meant by the remark. "I suppose you could say that, but I don't go out making war on innocent people, if that's what you think."

"I suppose we will find that out, Major Myers," Little Bear said.

Zack sensed the woman was baiting him, trying to find out his purpose for being there. "I hope you don't," he answered. "I am not here to make war on the Nez Perces. I am here only in case of trouble."

Morning Star knelt beside Iris. "Get rid of all the white settlers, and there will *be* no more trouble," she told him.

He did not answer Morning Star's remark.

Little Bear checked Iris to see that the bleeding had

slowed considerably. Iris had drifted off as soon as she was enshrouded in blankets, apparently exhausted and still suffering from shock. The women put more blankets over her, and Little Bear and Morning Star put on their moccasins, which they had left on the bank of the stream. "Come with us," Morning Star told Zack. "You can remove your boots in our tipi and dry your feet at our fire."

Since coming down out of the mountains Zack noticed the weather was much warmer, although not the heavy, overpowering heat of summer at Fort Kearny. Considering the fact that they had had to set Iris in freezing water, he was glad the air itself was warm.

The travois was still tied to a horse. Little Bear led the animal back to the village and stopped in front of a tipi painted with horses and stars, and Indian men that looked as though they were running a race.

Morning Star pulled aside the entrance flap to the tipi. "Bring your wife in here," she said. "I will keep checking her. If the bleeding does not get worse again by morning, my mother thinks she will live."

When Zack picked Iris up from the travois, she groaned and nestled against him. "Zack," she said softly.

"I'm right here. You're going to be all right, Iris." He hesitated at the tipi entrance. Never in these past eighteen years did he think he would ever step foot inside an Indian tipi, certainly not in peace. He ducked inside, surprised at how roomy it was. He could actually stand up.

Strong Runner sat cross-legged to the left of a fire that burned at the center of the dwelling. "Night is coming," he said. "The days are warm, but we are still high enough that the nights are cool. Keep many blankets over your wife. Lay her near the fire." He pointed to a pile of blankets and buffalo robes.

Zack laid her on the crude bed. Little Bear followed them inside, and she held up a blanket so that Morning Star could check Iris again. Zack glanced at Strong Runner, noticing the man had turned away to talk to his youngest son, who played with an old leather rattle. He said something softly to the boy, laughed when the child banged the rattle wildly against the earth. Zack was impressed that Strong Runner had enough respect for Iris to turn away while his wife tended her, even though Little Bear stood in front of her with a blanket.

"The bleeding is normal," Little Bear told Zack. "But she should rest through tomorrow. It will take time for the blood to rebuild inside of her. You should not go on to the fort until the next day."

Zack took off his hat and rubbed his eyes. "If I don't show up by tomorrow night, they might send men looking for me. I don't want any trouble or misunderstandings over this, not after what you've done for me."

Little Bear lowered the blanket and looked over at Strong Runner. "What do you think, Strong Runner? The woman should not be moved."

Strong Runner looked at Zack. "There will be no trouble as long as you are in our camp. The other soldiers will not want to do something that could endanger your life. But I will send a messenger to tell those in charge at Lapwai why you cannot come in until the day after tomorrow. If you wish to go in on your own, you can come back for your wife. She would be safe here."

Zack sighed, looking at Iris. "I can't do that."

"You still do not trust us?"

Zack scowled at the man. "Would *you* leave your wife sick and alone in a *soldier* camp?"

Strong Runner grinned. "You are a wise man, Major Myers."

Morning Star quietly laid another piece of wood on the fire, and her mother moved to the tipi entrance. "I will let the two of you talk," she said. "You can come for me if the white woman is worse again." She left, and Strong Runner watched carefully as Zack removed his boots and wet socks, laying the socks on rocks around the fire.

"Is this all right?" he asked Strong Runner.

Strong Runner nodded. "Fire is a good thing. It has great spirit. It is a friend when a man is cold or hungry." He looked at Morning Star. "Get a blanket for the soldier," he told her. "Fix some skins beside his woman so he can sleep next to her tonight."

Morning Star obeyed, quickly unfolding and spreading a buffalo hide beside Iris. She covered that with a quilt, more government issue.

"I can rest my head on my saddle. I'll unsaddle my horse once I know Iris is sleeping all right."

"I will have someone do it for you. You stay with your woman."

Zack could not help remembering that most Indians prized horses the way a white man prized gold. He wondered if he would even have a horse by morning.

"We do not steal the horses of guests," Strong Runner said as though to read his mind.

Zack felt his face flush a little. "I never said—"

"I saw it in your eyes. You should trust us, Major Myers. Is it not my own wife and mother-in-law who saved your woman's life? Is it not my tipi where your woman now lies resting? Is it not my fire that keeps you warm, and my food you will be eating?"

Zack sighed in resignation. "I apologize, Strong Runner. I've just lost a child and nearly lost my wife. I've deserted sixty men under my command. I am not exactly thinking straight. I truly am grateful for what you've done."

Zack suddenly realized that this was the very opportunity he'd hoped to find when he'd been assigned here. He was sitting in a Nez Perce tipi, hosted by a man who was apparently a respected warrior and leader. Zack was supposed to be a mediator, and here was a man who could tell him everything he needed to know to understand the Nez Perce and help keep the peace. Maybe there was a reason he'd landed in a Nez Perce camp. Iris always said there was a reason for everything. He put out his hand as a friendly gesture.

Strong Runner just looked at him for a moment before cautiously reaching out to grasp his hand. "We have much to learn about each other," he told Zack.

"I have the most to learn," Zack answered. "I am here to try to be a peacekeeper, Strong Runner, which means I need to understand the Nez Perces as best I can. You can help me. Once I am settled in at the fort, I would like to be able to come and talk to you often."

Strong Runner nodded. "You may come. In winter I live at the Wallowa Valley with Chief Joseph. None of us agrees with the treaty. We live our own way."

Zack was not about to argue the situation just then. Iris groaned his name, and he moved onto the blankets beside her, pulling one over his feet. "I'm right here, Iris." He leaned over her. "It's all right. You're going to be all right."

Iris opened her eyes. "Where are we?"

"We're in an Indian tipi. Nez Perce women helped you with the miscarriage. They saved your life."

"Water . . . cold—"

"We set you in a cold creek to stop the bleeding."

Iris blinked, trying to remember all that had happened. "My baby—"

Zack kissed her cheek. "We lost the baby, but thank God I didn't lose you too."

Tears welled in her eyes. "My baby. I'm so sorry, Zack."

"Don't be sorry. I'm the one who's sorry. We'll have more. This one wasn't meant to be." The memory of burying the little bit of flesh that had been a part of both of them made Zack feel sick inside.

Iris felt a wave of great emptiness engulf her. "Could they tell . . . what it was?"

"Little Bear thinks it was a boy." He blinked back tears. "I buried him before I came here." He saw the agony in her eyes. "Iris, you're always saying there is a reason for everything. We have to believe there is a reason for God taking our child. Maybe it was for this, to bring us into this Nez Perce camp. There has to be something good in all of this, Iris."

Iris looked around the tipi, beginning to understand where she was. Her eyes fell on a beautiful Indian woman who smiled down at her. The woman moved closer, knelt at her feet. "I am called Morning Star," she said. "And you are welcome here. You must rest and not be afraid."

Iris looked at Zack, amazed that he had let Indians take care of her and that he was himself inside an Indian tipi. Her heart ached at the loss of her baby, yet that loss had brought them to the very heart of the purpose for Zack coming here. What a strange way to come to know these people, through tragedy. Yet what better way to reveal people's deepest emotions? She turned her head more, noticing a strong-looking Indian man sitting on the other side of the fire. He had a little boy in his lap.

"I am Strong Runner," the man told her. "Morning Star is my wife, and these are our sons." He moved his gaze to Zack. "We will leave you alone for a while." He picked up Jumping

Bear and left, ordering Wolf Boy to follow. The little boy ran out behind his father, and Morning Star turned to pick up a pail of water with a bone ladle hooked to the side of it. She set it next to Zack.

"Here is water. She should drink as much as she can. Water is life. It will turn to blood and bring her strength." She straightened. "My husband understands that this is a time when a man and woman must have time alone. I will come back to help tend your wife tonight, but Strong Runner will sleep in my sister's dwelling with her family."

Zack continued to be astounded at the hospitality of these people. "Thank you," he answered. "You aren't afraid to be alone in here with a soldier?"

"Surrounded by Nez Perce men, with my own husband, a feared warrior, sleeping in the dwelling next to this one? I do not think you are that foolish, Major Myers," Morning Star said with a sly smile.

He smiled in return. "I only meant . . . some of the other women looked at me with so much fear—"

"I understand what you meant, Major. But your eyes tell me that even if I were alone, I would have nothing to fear. Strong Runner sees this too. That is why he is not afraid to leave me here alone tonight." She looked down at Iris, brushed Iris's quiet tears with her fingers. "Your woman is beautiful, and we can see the love you have for her. This is a sad time for both of you. I will go now so that you can talk. I will not be far away. Call my name if you think she is worse again."

She left, and Iris looked up at Zack. "I don't understand. These people . . . helped us. Why?"

He pulled her into his arms. "I'm not sure about anything right now. I'm just glad you're alive, and I'm so sorry for what you've suffered, Iris."

She rested her head against his chest. "You'll take me to the baby's grave when I'm better, won't you?" New tears came then as she clung to him.

"Of course I will. And we'll have more, but first you need to get settled in and get lots of rest, let your body heal."

"We have to give our baby a name," Iris sobbed. "We can't just . . . leave it in an unknown grave . . . forgotten."

He kissed her hair. "We'll name him. I'll have a stone put

there. He won't be forgotten." He held her tightly, letting her cry.

Iris awoke to sunlight streaming through the opening at the top of the tipi. She lay still, gathering her thoughts, the ache returning to her heart at the memory of what had happened. She'd lost a baby . . .

She turned to where Zack had slept beside her through the night. He was gone.

"You are awake!"

Iris looked to see the pretty Indian woman who'd been caring for her come inside the tipi, carrying a black kettle. She set the kettle directly on the hot coals of the tipi fire near where Iris slept. "Where is my husband?"

"He is gone. He went to the soldier camp with my husband to tell the men to go on to Fort Lapwai without him. He will bring a wagon back here for you and take you tomorrow. My husband will show him the way."

Iris frowned in surprise and not a little fear. She was alone in an Indian camp? Zack had gone off with that big Indian called Strong Runner?

"You have nothing to fear," Morning Star told her, noticing the apprehension in Iris's eyes. "I know how you must feel. I would be very afraid to be left alone in the camp of many white men and women. But you should not fear. Yesterday we saved your life. Why would we now bring you harm?" She smiled, stirring something in the kettle. "Perhaps you have forgotten I am called Morning Star. I know that your name is Iris. You are a very beautiful woman. I would like to have such golden hair. I would be considered very special among my people if I had hair like yours."

Iris put a hand to her hair, realizing how terrible she must look after her ordeal, yet this woman thought her beautiful. She began to relax, seeing only kindness in Morning Star's face. "Your own beauty is enough to make you special," she answered.

Morning Star smiled bashfully. "Strong Runner has told me since before we were married that I am the most beautiful Nez Perce woman in this land. I was very honored when he chose me for a wife. Strong Runner is brave and honored. He provides well for his family. Our two sons think their father is the grandest warrior who ever walked." She spooned something into a wooden bowl, noticing the fallen look on Iris's face. "I am sorry. I have made you think about the son that you lost."

Iris blinked back new tears. "My husband and I believe there is a purpose in all things. We talked about it a little last night. Maybe the little bit of life I lost was nothing more than an angel sent to guide us here to your camp. There are things about my husband you don't know. He is no ordinary soldier, and for him to have spent last night in the middle of an Indian camp is an experience that has much more meaning than it would to another white man."

Morning Star moved closer with the bowl and a small wooden spoon. "You should eat this. It is very, very important that you eat. It will give you strength."

Iris raised herself up on one elbow to look at the bowl. The contents looked very much like a simple stew. "What is it?"

"It is a soup I make with turnips and potatoes and deer meat." Morning Star held it out.

Iris leaned forward and tasted the soup. It was quite good, and she told Morning Star so.

"I put salt in it," Morning Star answered. "It is one of the few things my husband will allow me to accept from the gifts your government sends to Lapwai. He does not like things handed to him. He prefers to hunt for his own food and take care of his family his own way. Your people think we will be happy to sit around and let everything we need be given to us, but we are a proud people."

She continued to spoon the stew to Iris, telling her some of the history of the Nez Perce and their situation. Iris was grateful for the opportunity to learn as much as she could.

"Where are your children?" Iris asked when she'd finished eating.

"They are with my mother. I did not want them to come in here and disturb you." Morning Star rose with the empty bowl. "Would you like more?"

"No," Iris answered, lying back down. "I would like to wash, though, before Zack returns. If he brings our wagon, I'll be able to put on another clean gown."

Morning Star nodded. "I will bring some heated water."

The woman left, and Iris could hear children playing outside, laughter, women talking, the sounds of any peaceful village. Thomas had always tried to make Zack understand that he must look at Indians as humans, men and women with families they felt they needed to protect against starvation because of the loss of hunting grounds and game. She had agreed with Thomas, yet had herself always had trouble seeing these people as real families with feelings. She had not carried the bitter hatred Zack did, but she also had never had any close experiences with Indians except with ones bent on fighting and killing. Was life like this in a peaceful Sioux village also?

Morning Star returned with her little boys, beautiful, big-eyed, plump children with bright smiles. Morning Star's mother also came inside, and the two women helped Iris outside to a private place where she could relieve herself. Her legs felt weak, and both women had to help her back to the tipi, where they undressed and washed her, giving her clean rags to tie around herself against the bleeding, which now was normal.

Morning Star and Little Bear put a clean dress on Iris, a faded calico hand-me-down from Lapwai supplies that one of the other Indian women had offered. They snickered over a pair of drawers they held up, hinting that Indian women did not bother with such things. They asked many questions about white women's clothing, why they wore so many uncomfortable things under their dresses. Morning Star brushed Iris's hair with a bristle brush her sister had taken from government issue. Her sister, White Bird, had joined them, and all three women fussed over and admired Iris's golden tresses, touching her hair, laughing, smiling.

Iris found them delightful. For so long she had ached for a woman's company, and it surprised her to discover she could enjoy the company of Indian women just as much as white women. In some ways they were even more enjoyable because of their wonderful innocence about some things, their insatiable curiosity, their honesty. Their compliments were genuine, but when they thought something needed criticizing, they were honest about that too. Too many white women hid their true thoughts and feelings, but these Nez Perce women did not, and she liked that.

Weakness and weariness from her ordeal, combined with repeated pangs of loss over her baby, made it difficult to visit the way she would normally have liked. She wanted to know the Nez Perce women better, hoped she could remember everything they told her. She lay back on her bed of robes, thinking how surprisingly pleasant it was inside the tipi. The day was growing warmer, but when Morning Star rolled up the tipi skins about a foot above the ground, a delightful breeze moved through the dwelling, bringing with it the sound of birds calling. The other women and the children left, and Morning Star sat down beside Iris.

"Your husband and mine will be here soon."

Iris thought about Zack riding with a Nez Perce warrior. "It's a good thing—my husband being able to talk to yours." She felt her eyes drifting closed, her exhaustion taking over again.

"You have not told me everything about your man," Morning Star said, "about why it is so important that he come to know us better. When you are stronger, we will visit. We will talk more." She smoothed the hair back from Iris's forehead, soothing her to sleep. "It is as you said. Perhaps your baby led you here. Do you hear the birds calling outside?"

Iris listened, drifting deeper into sleep. "I hear," she said, her voice groggy.

"Think of one of them as your lost son. He is a spirit now, and spirits can move into other bodies. He was small, tiny like a bird. Perhaps he is out there right now, singing to his mother. When you think of it that way, you must not be sad for him. He is happy, free . . . so free. More free than any of us left here can be."

Iris imagined her little boy out there somewhere, flying free, singing to her. The thought took away some of the sting of losing him.

27

*I*t was early evening when Zack watched Strong Runner and several other men ride in from the hunt, yipping and whooping over the fact that they'd brought back two large bucks. The arrows were still in the animals, which were slung over the backs of spare horses. Strong Runner brought one of them close to his tipi, looking proudly down at Zack. "You see? We can take care of ourselves."

He slung a leg over his horse and jumped down, then pulled the blanket he used in place of a saddle off the horse's back. The day had warmed considerably, and Strong Runner had stripped to only his leggings and moccasins, a bone necklace around his neck. His long hair was pulled into a tail and tied with a simple piece of cloth.

Zack could not help noticing Strong Runner's magnificent build. In spite of his own size, this was a man he would not care to have to fight hand-to-hand. The only mark on the man was an ugly white scar and slight indentation at his left side. It looked to Zack like a healed bullet wound, but he decided not to ask about it at the moment. Strong Runner was strutting proudly and feeling his manhood. It might not be wise to bring up something that would stir the man's anger.

Zack walked around to the deer, admiring its size and beauty, the huge antlers. "A fine kill," he told Strong Runner.

Strong Runner nodded. "This meat will taste much better than the worm-infested beef your government sends us." He grasped the arrows and yanked them out with muscled force, obviously venting repressed anger. Zack flinched, remembering the arrows in his mother and sister . . . the arrow in poor Thomas's side, how the man had suffered. A myriad of emotions continued to undulate through his soul at being in an Indian camp, old hatreds wanting to rear up, quelled by a new curiosity, by memories of Thomas, and by the simple fact that these people had saved his wife's life.

He watched Morning Star embrace her husband when she came out of the tipi to see the deer. She looked up at him with pride and delight, much the same as Iris would look at him after a promotion or after returning unharmed from an Indian battle. He could not get over the fact that they seemed so natural, like any family. He had not yet had a chance to talk for long with Strong Runner, as the man had left him to go hunting as soon as he led him back to the soldier camp. Zack had sent Lieutenant Best on to the fort with the rest of the troops, and Sandy had also gone to lead the way. Strong Runner's brother-in-law, Little Eagle, had brought Zack back to the Indian camp, along with the wagon that contained Zack and Iris's belongings. Little Eagle and a few other men, including Strong Runner's father, Yellow Hand, had stayed at the camp. *We always leave some men at the camp,* Little Eagle had told him. *Women and children must never be left alone. There is seldom much trouble anymore as in the old days, with enemy tribes attacking a camp and stealing women and children, but we must always be ready. It is an old custom. Besides, we hear many stories of soldiers attacking Indian camps and killing women and children.*

The camp came alive with men celebrating, talking excitedly in their own tongue. Women emerged from tipis and campfires and dragged the deer away to begin gutting and cleaning them.

"There will be much feasting tonight and tomorrow," Strong Runner told Zack proudly. "But most of the meat will be smoked, some pounded and mixed with berries for pemmican. Pemmican is something we often take with us on the hunt. . . ." He glanced sidelong at Zack. "Or if we will be riding far to make war." He walked over and sat down on a log near the fire outside his tipi. "It lasts many months without spoiling. Perhaps if your government would first smoke and preserve the meat they send us, it would not arrive already rotten."

Zack followed him over to the fire, noticing a boy of about fourteen take Strong Runner's horses away to brush them down. Thomas had told him that the younger boys of most tribes considered it an honor to tend the horses of a respected warrior, someone they hoped to emulate. "Who's that boy?" he asked.

Strong Runner glanced at his horses being led away. "That is Running Boy. He is Little Eagle's younger brother."

"You and Little Eagle seem very close."

"He was my closest friend even before he married White Bird. We used to race each other. I always won, but it was all in fun. Little Eagle almost beat me once."

Zack glanced at a group of men who were celebrating by passing around a bottle of whiskey. Little Eagle was among them. Every soldier knew that an Indian warrior feeling proud and cocky was dangerous enough. Fill him with whiskey, and he was uncontrollable. Part of his mission back in Montana had been to keep the firewater out of the hands of the Indians by trying to control white whiskey peddlers, who traded their rot-gut brew for hides worth much more than the watered-down whiskey, or for permission to dig for gold. He looked at Strong Runner, who had also been watching the whiskey drinkers. They all sat down in a circle then, one of them taking out some marbles. It was obvious they were going to do some gambling.

Strong Runner met Zack's eyes, read his thoughts. "Don't worry. I won't let them bet on who gets to scalp you. They know that's my privilege, if I choose." He reached over and took up a piece of wood to add to the fire, then grinned at the cautious look in Zack's eyes. "I don't feel like scalping anybody today. I am too tired from the hunt." He grinned as though he thought he was telling a fine joke.

Zack smiled. "Well, I'm glad you went hunting, then. By God, he liked this Indian.

Strong Runner laughed. He called out something to Morning Star in his own language. She came out of the tipi carrying a long-stemmed pipe with feathers tied along the stem. She handed it to Strong Runner, along with a little leather bag Zack suspected held tobacco. "How is your woman?" Strong Runner asked him.

"Sleeping again. I walked with her a while. She's feeling much stronger."

Strong Runner nodded. "Good. Morning Star will stay with her while her mother and sister and the other women clean and skin the deer. She is probably glad your woman is here. Now she will get out of some work, huh?" He packed the bowl of the pipe with tobacco, glancing at his two sons, who stood near the other women in the distance, watching them cut away at the deer carcasses. Zack watched them a moment, strong, brown-skinned boys as active and happy as any child. Most of the children in camp had run naked all day because of the heat, boys and girls alike. They seemed to think nothing of it. He wished he could have brought Jacob back with him, but he needed to give his attention to Iris, and he was afraid the active baby would pester his mother, would want to be climbing into her lap or crawling over her when she tried to rest.

"You, too, have a fine son." Strong Runner spoke up, noticing Zack watching his own boys. "There will be more children for you. Your wife seems to be a strong woman." He grinned again. "And she is beautiful, for a white woman. You will not be able to stay away from her. There will be more children."

Zack chuckled at the remark, watching Strong Runner hold a burning stick of wood to the pipe bowl. He lit the pipe, drawing on it several times. He raised it toward the sky, blowing smoke upward, then looked at Zack. "In everything we do we first thank the Creator who made all life. His Law says we must give thanks in all things, to the animals we kill for food, to the life-giving waters, all things." He handed the pipe over to Zack. "To share a pipe means to share spirits and friendship. Smoke a pipe with me, and I promise not to scalp you."

There was a twinkle in his eye that showed friendship. Zack took the pipe, raised it, and looked upward before drawing some of the smoke. It tasted good to him. He handed back the pipe, telling himself to handle this man with respect and honor. Warriors like Strong Runner could sometimes be easily insulted according to what Thomas had taught him about Indian practices. "I like a good pipe myself once in a while," he told Strong Runner.

The man took the pipe from him. "You should know I do not share this pipe with just anyone."

Zack nodded. "I understand." He glanced at the men who were gambling when they all gave out a shout. They were playing with the marbles, and Little Eagle had several in front of him, apparently having won them from someone else. He took another drink of whiskey. Their shouting and laughter brought flashes of memory to Zack . . . the Pawnee whooping and laughing as they raped his mother.

Strong Runner watched Zack shift uneasily, saw the quick flash of hatred in his eyes, watched him twist his hands nervously. "Are you afraid to be in this camp around drunk Indians?" he asked. "They listen to me. They will not harm you or your woman. Besides, we are not quite so warlike as the Sioux."

Zack met his eyes. "It isn't that, and I'm not afraid. I don't think you or the others would be foolish enough to bring me harm when the whole fort up ahead knows where I am and who I'm with." He glanced at the flickering flames of the campfire, growing brighter as dusk fell. "I wouldn't be worried about you bringing me harm anyway. The Nez Perce aren't at war with anyone right now. We're hoping to keep it that way."

Strong Runner puffed on the pipe again before answering. "So, you have come as a peacemaker. Your government has sent other peacemakers, most of them liars, men who make great promises in hope of getting us to give up our land. Some even want to send us far to the south, where other Indians are sent, where the land is open and dry, where there are no mountains. Indians die there, the same as some wild animals who die if they are taken away from where they naturally live. If I am to die, I will die right here, fighting to keep my family here."

Zack saw the look of dark warning that came into the man's eyes. Yes, he would die to stay there . . . and he would kill to stay there. "I'm not a liar, Strong Runner. My words are true, and you can trust me. My reasons for being here and for wanting to keep the peace and befriend you go beyond my job and my government. It's become a very personal thing for me."

Strong Runner studied him closely. "I saw hatred in your eyes when you looked at Little Eagle and the others. Tell me the reason for this hatred. Tell me why I should trust you."

"I've seen the same hatred in your own eyes, something just as deep as what I feel. I have also seen great fear and distrust in Morning Star's eyes. My hatred is well justified. I think your own goes further than the Nez Perce being upset over whites coming on their land to dig for gold or a treaty they don't agree with."

Strong Runner nodded. He leaned closer over the fire, his dark eyes full of bitterness. "I hardly know you, Major Myers, yet there is something about you that makes me think you would understand such hatred. If you are here to keep the peace, then I will help you see why that will not be so easy. Not long after I took Morning Star for a wife, white men came to the land where we lived in a log home I had built for her. We decided to try to live the white man's way, do some farming, keep the peace by living the way your government says we must. These white men tried to put a fence on my land. They had no right doing that, and I told them so. They scoffed at me. I tore down their fence. I had a right to do that."

He leaned back again, puffed on the pipe.

"That's it?" Zack asked.

Strong Runner held his eyes and set the pipe aside. "I wish that were all. These white men came to my home in the night, set it on fire. I tried to fight them, but there were too many. They dragged Morning Star down when she fled the burning house with Wolf Boy. While some of them were beating me, four others raped Morning Star. She was carrying Jumping Bear in her belly at the time. I heard her screams." His eyes flared with rage. "I tried to go to her, to help her, but one of the white men shot me while I struggled." He pointed to the scar at his side. "Right here. It was a terrible night, one

I will never forget, nor will my hatred ever go away. It was a long time before Morning Star could sleep or eat . . . or let me come to her bed. And she is still not over her fear of most white men."

Their eyes held in an understanding no two other men could share. "I'm sorry." Suddenly, for both men, the activity surrounding them faded to unimportance. There was only this, two men from very different worlds, finding a common bond. "I truly am sorry," Zack continued. "I understand your hatred much better than anyone else could."

Strong Runner's dark eyes bored into his own. "And how is it you understand so well, soldier? You are a symbol to the Indian of all that we hate, a symbol of war, one of a legion of soldiers sent to force us out of our beloved homeland so that your own kind can come and take it all for themselves, destroy it with the filth from their mining, cut up Mother Earth with their plows. How is it someone like you can understand my hatred?"

"Because my parents and sister were murdered by Pawnee. They nearly cut off my sister's head, tortured my father to death, raped and murdered my mother, scalped all of them. I was just a boy, and I was helpless to stop what was happening. I never forgot that helpless feeling, or the rage it gave birth to. You felt that same rage and helplessness, and it has made you hate and distrust most white men, the same as I hated and could never trust Indians. That one act was the reason I joined the army, in hopes of being sent out here so I could kill Indians."

Strong Runner slowly nodded. "And have you killed many? Did it satisfy you?"

"I've killed my share, but always in battle. I've never ridden with soldiers who attack peaceful Indian camps where there are women and children. I realized not long into the game that killing did not make me feel any better, and much as I wanted to kill women and children for what was done to my mother and sister, I knew deep inside I could never have done so. It was my wife who first opened my eyes to the uselessness of hatred, Strong Runner, and it *is* useless. I hope you will learn that. Strangely enough, I came to terms with my feelings through a Pawnee Indian who scouted for me back in Montana. I despised *him* for a long time just because he was

Pawnee, but he taught me we can't hate a whole race for what one or a few men do. I came to call him friend, and he taught me how to deal with my own soul, to look at rage for the wasted feeling it is, realize how it drained men from the inside. I've learned we have to try to find a way to come together and live in peace, or all this hatred and warring will go on forever. I don't want that for my son, and I don't believe you want it for yours."

The women cleaning the deer began building a fire to shed more light on their work as the sun sank behind the mountains to the west. Strong Runner listened to the laughter and talking, thinking how peaceful and happy this camp was. If only life could always be this way for them.

"I, too, am sorry for what happened to your family. But it is easier for you to talk of keeping the peace. We Nez Perce *have* remained at peace for many years. We once traded often with white men, befriended them. Some of our women even married them. Then more came, and more and more. Promises were made and broken over and over again. Your government promised to protect what land was left to us. They said no white man would be allowed to come there, yet now our land is full of white men who tear it up, dirty the water, kill off the game. They build whole towns, one close to Lapwai. It is called Lewiston, and to have a town so close to the heart of what is supposed to be our reservation is like hitting us in the face. They take away our dignity. If there was any hope for us to keep our land and keep the white man from destroying it, we would be glad to continue living in peace, but what you must understand is that we have no such hope. We know that we are outnumbered, that your government can send as many soldiers as are needed to force us to live on a tiny reservation, that there are so many of your kind in the land east of the mountains that they could swarm into our land like locusts, devouring everything in sight. We can see that there is only one way for all of this to end, and so for now we simply cling to what we have left and take one day at a time."

The man closed his eyes and drew a deep breath, and Zack was sure there were tears in his eyes. "It will be the same for the Sioux," Strong Runner continued. "They fight now, as we will fight someday. They have managed to chase you soldiers out of their hunting grounds, burn your forts.

But it will not last. Your government will send more. The Sioux know it is a losing battle, but for now they celebrate this little victory. All your efforts at keeping the peace with the Nez Perces will go to no avail if your government cannot stop more whites from coming here, and if they cannot keep their promises to us."

He puffed on the pipe again, and Zack waited for him to continue.

"Still, your government will have its way. They have planned it well. Part of the plan is to divide us, as they have done with other tribes. Divided, we cannot be strong. Those Nez Perces at Lapwai—Looking Glass, Lawyer, Spotted Eagle—they have fallen for your government's trickery, accepting bribes and fancy gifts. Lawyer lives in a fine cabin built by your government. His children attend government schools, and he is paid money to live quietly and cause no trouble. He forgets the Indian ways, and his children will forget even more. Their children and grandchildren will one day know nothing about our language, our customs, their own spiritual connection to Mother Earth. I do not want that for my children."

He nodded toward the drinking Indians. "The firewater your white peddlers sell us—it, too, is a weapon against us. It contains an evil spirit that makes our people weak, makes them do foolish things that can only get us in more trouble. I refuse to drink it, and I will never let my sons drink it."

He picked up a stick and poked at the fire to stir the embers. "So you see, Major, much as we understand each other, there is nothing we can do to make *all* the people understand. Whatever one Nez Perce does against a white man, all will be blamed. The only way to end it is for you to kill all of us, or so weaken us that we have no choice but to crawl onto a reservation and beg like dogs just to keep our wives and children from starving to death."

Zack felt the same oddly heavy agony he'd felt when he learned Thomas had died. He was so lost in the conversation that he had not even noticed Iris had come out of the tipi behind him and had stood quietly, listening to most of the conversation. Never had he been more impressed by an Indian, nor had it ever been more clear to him what lay ahead. He didn't want to think Strong Runner could be right, but what other answer was there? He remembered Sandy saying the same thing Strong Runner had, that the best way to defeat them was to divide them. He remembered something else, something Strong Runner himself had said . . . that white men had tried to take his land from him once before, and they paid with their lives. "What happened to the white men who shot you and raped Morning Star?" he asked.

Iris's eyes widened. She had not heard that part of the conversation. Morning Star! Such a beautiful, sweet young woman. How horrible! Now she could see that Zack and Strong Runner understood hatred between Indian and white on the same personal level. She watched Strong Runner's dark eyes narrow as his lips moved into a sneer.

"They are dead," he answered.

The two men seemed locked in a moment where nothing else existed for them. "Did you kill them?" Zack asked.

Strong Runner drew a deep breath. "I did not say that I did."

Zack never took his eyes from the man. "You don't have to say it."

"There is no proof."

Zack slowly nodded. "You made sure of that."

A tiny grin of satisfaction moved across Strong Runner's face. "So they say at Lapwai. They tried to say I killed them, but they could not prove it. It was when your government was taking all the soldiers away, and they did not want to stir up my people by hanging one of their respected warriors. They were afraid it would cause too much trouble for the whites living there with no soldier protection. They said I could go free."

Zack saw a look in Strong Runner's eyes only another man who understood revenge could read. He'd killed those men, and Zack couldn't bring himself to blame him. "And if you and I should find ourselves in a battle against each other?"

"Then I would see you only as a soldier, and I would have to kill you . . . or you would have to kill me. You would see me only as a warrior against whom you must defend yourself."

Zack tore his eyes away from Strong Runner's dark, mesmerizing gaze. He removed his hat and ran a hand through his hair, rubbed his eyes. "These last couple of days I had hoped we could be friends, that you could be a kind of mediator for me between my government and your people."

"You will learn that is not what is expected of you. You will learn your job is simply to tell us how it will be, and that we must accept your terms or die. That is your government's way of negotiating. I am surprised you think it can be any other way. There must have been a time when you would have liked to kill all Indians with your own hands. Your Pawnee friend must have taught you much, soldier. Your hatred has turned to concern, but you will find that concern is the last thing your government wants from you. I only hope your offer of friendship isn't a trick."

Zack scowled. "A trick?"

Strong Runner shrugged. "We become friends, I tell you things I should not tell you. You use our friendship to make me agree to things that cause us to lose what land is left to us."

Zack shook his head. "I would never do that."

Strong Runner picked up his pipe and drew on it again. "I believe you, soldier. I see honesty in your eyes, and I trust you. You may bring your government's offers to me and to Chief Joseph. You will always be welcome in our village. I will see to that. But I warn you, no offers will be accepted unless it means we can keep our land and the whites will be removed." He stood up and walked around the fire, putting out his hand. "We can be friends, here, alone. But we are too different to let the friendship go beyond this campfire. It would be too difficult if the day should come that we must be enemies."

Zack rose, facing the man squarely. He put out his own hand, and Strong Runner grasped his wrist. He grasped Strong Runner's wrist, and both men squeezed in a quick challenge of strength, each realizing the other would be a worthy opponent.

"I hope that day never comes," Zack told him.

Strong Runner released his grip. "As do I, but the white man has lost the spirit way. To try to find it is like chasing the sun. It can never be caught again, not without prayer and blood sacrifice, so our two worlds can never fully come together, Major Myers. It is written in the wind; and I tell you now, for all your white man's education and superior weapons and fine homes and cities, in spite of all the things you think a man needs to live well, you will destroy yourselves. One day you will see that the way we live is the right way. If you do not thank the spirits of the earth and the water and the animals, they will someday turn against you and no longer sustain you and you will die. Perhaps then this land will again belong to our descendants."

Their eyes held in deep understanding, and Zack was surprised at how moved he felt. "I don't know how to thank you for helping me and Iris."

"Perhaps someday you can help me in some way."

"I hope to get the chance."

Strong Runner nodded. "We will talk more this night. I will explain to you about our ways. Morning Star will roast some fresh deer meat for us and we will have a grand feast. Tomorrow you will return to your world, and I will stay in mine."

White Bird came over to them then, carrying a thick deer roast on a skewer, her hands and arms covered with blood. She was grinning with excitement. "Thank you for the meat, Strong Runner," she said, placing the ends of the skewer into the V-hooks of two iron posts that had been planted on either side of the campfire to hold crossbars for kettles and for roasting. Blood dripped from the meat into the fire, making spitting sounds.

Zack and Iris both watched in surprise as Strong Runner pulled a large hunting knife from its sheath at his waist and sliced off a piece of the raw meat. He promptly put it into his mouth, chewed, and swallowed. "There is nothing like the meat from a fresh kill," he said. He walked closer, holding the bloody knife up to Zack. "They say those white men who hurt my wife died by the knife," he said, a satisfied glitter in his eyes. "That is a bad way to die, but at least it is quick and quiet." He held Zack's eyes a moment longer before sliding the knife across his tongue to lick off the blood, carefully avoiding the sharp edge. He slipped the knife into its sheath and put a hand on Zack's shoulder, squeezing gently. "You and your woman will join us in feasting tonight."

Strong Runner walked over to Little Eagle, who stumbled slightly when he stood up to greet his brother-in-law. It was obvious the whiskey was already running strong in Little Eagle's blood. Strong Runner said something sharply to him and walked away. Little Eagle waved him off. Strong Runner walked over to another group of men who had formed a circle around a large drum, and they all talked for a moment. Then some began pounding the drum rhythmically with padded sticks, and began chanting songs that were obviously in celebration of the hunt. Some of the women still working over the two deer carcasses joined in the chanting, and the night air hung heavy with the singing.

A chill moved through Zack at the sound that brought memories of the sounds of Sioux warriors drumming and singing in the distant hills, preparing for war. He looked at Iris, and could see she shared his own astonishment at finding themselves there at all. "How long have you been standing here?" Zack asked, moving his arms around her for support. She looked so frail and bewildered.

"Long enough to hear most of your conversation," she answered, meeting his eyes. "Zack, you understand it all now, don't you? Strong Runner has made you see their side. I've been talking with Morning Star. Zack, she's like any other woman who loves her husband and children. She told me that the shell necklace she wears was a gift from Strong Runner when she was only ten, that she has loved him since then. She talks about him and her children the same as I would talk about you and Jacob, with the same love and pride. They're no different at all!"

Zack watched Strong Runner, could see he was getting lost in the spirit of the singing. "No different at all," he repeated, "and yet they are so different, we may never be able to come to terms." He closed his eyes and breathed deeply. "I don't think Colonel Shaver knew what he was getting me into when he sent me here."

Iris rested her head on his chest. "Maybe he knew *exactly* what he was doing."

Zack held her close. These people had saved his wife from death, and the strange conversation with Strong Runner had left him with feelings he'd never before experienced toward any Indian, not even Thomas. His task was going to be the most difficult of his career, much harder than fighting faceless Indians who meant nothing to him. Strong Runner had a way of touching a man's soul.

28

*M*orning Star held Iris's arm as she walked to the wagon to leave. She had helped her wash again that morning, and Iris wore a simple blue calico dress, her hair braided and wrapped around the sides of her head. She stopped at the wagon, turning to Morning Star. "I don't know how to thank you for all you've done," she said, looking from her to Little Bear, who had walked behind them. "This has all been such a strange experience for me and my husband, terrible in some ways, but good in meeting you. Please visit us at Lapwai at any time. I would like you to meet my little boy, Jacob."

Morning Star nodded. "We sometimes go to Lapwai for the things promised us in the treaty, but Strong Runner prefers not to accept the gifts. We may not come there until next spring."

Iris was surprised to realize she would actually miss these women. She told herself it was only because she had been so lonely for the company of any woman. "I will miss you, Morning Star. Does that seem strange? I have known you only two days."

"It is not so strange. Sometimes there is a union of soul

and spirit between two people that cannot be explained. I have never met a white woman who was kind to me or wanted to visit with me. Never has any white woman invited me to her home. You have a good heart, Iris Myers. I will remember you often, and I will try to come to Lapwai and see you. Strong Runner does not like to be near so many soldiers. He does not trust them."

"Well, my husband will be there, and he would never let anything bad happen to Strong Runner."

Morning Star stepped closer as Strong Runner came riding up to the wagon on his Appaloosa. He dismounted to help Zack finish hitching the wagon to the six mules that pulled it. "There is a colonel there who does not like Strong Runner," Morning Star said quietly. "He thinks my husband killed the white men who—" She lowered her eyes. "Who brought me harm. The colonel cannot prove it. He and the other soldiers left the fort for a time, but they are back now, with more soldiers, and now your husband comes with yet more men. This colonel, his name is Clayton Porter. He still speaks against Strong Runner. That is why we seldom go there. It is better that we stay away." She glanced at her husband, then back to Iris. "I fear for Strong Runner. He is a good man, a man of fairness and honor; but he is also an angry man, as are many other Nez Perce men. I fear someday there will be much trouble, and the first one the soldiers will blame is Strong Runner."

Iris put a hand on her arm. "Zack won't let that happen if he can help it." She turned to Morning Star's mother, admiring again her lingering beauty. Her black hair was splashed with white at the temples, but it only made her seem more lovely and dignified. "Do come and visit me. I assure you, I am not like other white women, nor do I care what the other white women at the fort might think of my associating with you. I have never cared what others think. I do as I please, and there will never be peace until we can all share our lives as equals."

Little Bear nodded, her dark eyes showing pride and wisdom. "Perhaps you can convince your government to send us what we need—cloth, good cooking pans, blankets, food that is not spoiled, skins for moccasins. It is difficult for us to kill enough game anymore to sustain all our needs for clothing, but your government sends us hard shoes. We cannot wear such things. Most are not the right size, and they hurt our feet. They send us white women's undergarments. Our women do not wear such things. They send books we cannot read, china dishes we cannot use. Tell them to stop trying to make us like white women. We are Nez Perce, and we do not want to change. Will you tell them?"

Iris smiled softly. "I will tell them." She could not resist reaching out to hug each of them.

Zack looked over to see his wife embracing Morning Star and Little Bear, then glanced at Strong Runner, who also watched, looking skeptical. He turned to Zack. "Women find peace so easy. Men are not so eager for it."

Zack grinned. "Seems that way." He buckled a harness. "That's the last one." He patted the neck of one of the lead mules.

Strong Runner scowled. "These animals are ugly. I would never steal a mule, only good, strong horses."

Zack snickered. "Lucky for me I'm using mules, then. I don't much like them either, but they're damn good pack animals and they outlast horses for pulling weight." He walked around to help Iris into the wagon. She started to sit in the seat. "Get in back," he told her. "I want you lying down, not bouncing around in the seat."

"I don't want to arrive at the fort like some weak, faint-hearted easterner."

Zack climbed up beside her, talking quietly. "Iris, I don't want you to relapse. Besides, it's better if you look as though you still aren't recovered—which, I might remind you, you aren't. Colonel Porter is not going to be pleased at what I've done. He has to understand this was a life-or-death situation. It won't help if we arrive with you riding in front as though nothing happened."

Her eyes suddenly teared. "Surely he'll realize what we've been through, losing a baby—"

"Officers like Porter don't give a damn about those things. He'll figure that's your problem, not the army's. The only way he will understand we did the right thing is for him to realize you might have died otherwise."

A tear slipped down her cheek. "You *will* bring me back to the grave, won't you?"

"I said I would."

"You did pray over him, didn't you?"

Zack felt a tug at his heart. How he hated her to suffer these things. "Of course I did. I just wish you would have told me in the first place, Iris. I would have sent you to Laramie for the winter."

She sniffed. "I've always been so strong. I didn't think the trip would cause me any trouble. I didn't know how rough it would be, or that I'd have to carry Jacob so much . . . and I didn't want to be separated."

He wiped her tears with his fingers. "I know. Lie down in back now. We'll talk after we get settled at Lapwai."

She nodded, meeting his eyes. "I asked Morning Star and her mother to visit. That would be all right, wouldn't it?" She saw uncertainty in his eyes.

"It's fine with me, but I'm not sure how it would be viewed by my superiors."

"But your job is to act as a liaison, a peacekeeper. I can help."

"I know. Let's just take this a little at a time." He looked around the Indian camp. "I'm still trying to grasp the reality of all that has happened myself." He sat down in the seat. "Go on. Get in the back and lie down. Strong Runner says we'll be there the day after tomorrow."

Iris watched Morning Star walk up to Strong Runner, touching his leg. "Be careful, my husband. Take them just close enough to go the rest of the way alone. Do not go into the fort."

"Do not worry. I will start back as soon as I can. We will go north then, do more hunting before returning to the Wallowa."

"I do not like it when you ride alone. I am afraid white men will shoot at you."

"I will keep to the forest. No one will see me."

Zack pulled a whip from its brace at the side of the wagon and snapped it over the mules. He did not exactly care to make his entrance to Fort Lapwai driving a wagon pulled by mules. He would have preferred riding in on his own horse at the head of the sixty men under his command; but if this was what it took to keep his wife alive, then so be it. Strong Runner rode out ahead of him, and Zack followed.

Iris sat up in the back of the wagon, looking out at Morning Star and Little Bear. They waved, as did several of the other women. Some of the children chased after the wagon, laughing and waving, several barking dogs running along with them, tails wagging. It should have been a happy scene, and on the surface it was; but Iris felt a heaviness in her heart she could not explain. A terrible depression enveloped her, and she blamed it on the loss of her baby.

"Good-bye, Morning Star," she whispered. She lay down and wept.

The night hung warm and soft. Zack made camp along the edge of a dense stand of huge pine trees, and a light wind made their branches sing in an eerie drone, while not far away owls hooted at each other. Even farther away wolves howled. Strong Runner warned they should keep a good fire going to keep them away.

"Are there many reports of wolves attacking men out here?" Zack asked.

The three of them sat around the fire, bellies full from more roasted deer meat that Strong Runner had brought along and warmed over the fire. In spite of her weakened condition, Iris had made biscuits, needing to keep busy so as not to think too much about the baby.

"Only if a man is alone and usually if he is weak or wounded, sometimes small children. You should never let your child run off into the darkness." Strong Runner laid a deer bone beside the fire. "Do not throw the bones to the side. The wolves will smell them and come closer to try to get them. If you keep them near the fire, they will stay away. They do not like the flames. If they do come close, they will have to move into the light of the fire enough that you will be able to see their yellow eyes and you will be warned. Tomorrow, after the fire has died, they will come in and take the bones." He rubbed his lips with the back of his hand. "Mostly wolves do not bother with humans. They are just as afraid of them as humans are of wolves. Sometimes they attack only out of that fear, not because they see men as prey for food. They much prefer the meat of a deer or a rabbit."

Iris shivered at the sound of more howling. She scooted closer to Zack, who sat on a fallen log.

"The wolf spirit is very powerful," Strong Runner continued. "The wolf is an intelligent hunter, cunning, quiet, deadly."

Just like Indians, Zack thought.

"He is also a survivor," Strong Runner continued, "a wild, beautiful thing that is close to the Great Spirit and Mother Earth."

Zack rested his elbows on his knees, realizing that after tonight he might have little chance to talk to Strong Runner again. "You said you learned our tongue and can even write and read because of missionaries. You also told me many of your people took our religion and are Christian. Are *you* Christian, Strong Runner?"

Strong Runner stared into the flames. "I called myself a Christian once. Morning Star still believes in your God, as does her mother. I suppose I do, but I think He is no different from the God we worshipped before your missionaries came. I take the *Washani* faith. To us the earth is God, the trees, the water, this fire, the animals, like those wolves out there. God is in everything and in us." He frowned. "I believe we Nez Perces understand God better than you whites, and you speak about your religion with a forked tongue, the same as you speak about everything else. You say one thing but mean another. You preach one thing, but do another."

Zack finished a biscuit and drank coffee from a tin cup. "I don't understand."

Strong Runner shrugged. "You preach forgiveness, and that God sees all men as equal; but you do not forgive, and you do not see Indians as equal. Your religion says man should not kill, yet white men think nothing of killing Indians. You say your God loves us just the way we are, yet you tell us we must change, that there is something wrong with the way we live. You seem to think all people must live as you do. Who says the white man is always right? Does your Bible say that? I remember a missionary reading to me from the Bible, and it said rich men would not get to heaven, that man should look to God, not to gold; yet your people will do anything, kill Indians, kill each other, steal land, leave their families, tear up Mother Earth, all for gold. It is like a sickness with them."

Zack looked at Iris, and she knew he was greatly impressed by Strong Runner's words. "You don't leave a man much argument," he told Strong Runner. "You sound more like a teacher than one who should be taught."

Strong Runner stared at the fire for several quiet minutes. "You are here to talk peace. We Nez Perce do not want war any more than you, but in spite of all your preaching about peace and being Christian, you continue to push us into a corner. When you do that to a wild animal, it attacks out of fear and to protect its own. For us it began with a man called Isaac Stevens. He was the governor of what you call Washington Territory, much of it our land. He decided he would steal this land, and he has done just that, through treaties and trickery. Since then your people have worked to destroy our culture, our language, our customs, our religion, everything about us that is our soul. You have killed many of us with your diseases, made some of us weak with your whiskey, turned some of us away from our trueness with your bribery of gifts, divided us, slowly, slowly destroying us." He looked across the fire at them, the whites of his eyes seeming whiter in the eerie firelight. "I will never let your people destroy me or all that is Nez Perce about me. I will die first."

Their eyes held, and wolves howled again. Zack could almost feel their spirit, realizing that same wild spirit was in Strong Runner. "And you probably *will* die then. You have given me much to think about, Strong Runner, things I never considered before. I understand everything you have told me, and I agree with most of it. The trouble is, one man alone can't stop what is happening. I can't, and you can't, and I'm damn sorry about that."

Strong Runner nodded. "Then write down what you have learned. If I am to die, then at least my words can be remembered. Perhaps someday someone who reads them will see that the Nez Perce were not so wrong and not so ignorant as your missionaries say we are."

Iris was stunned by his wisdom. "I'll write down your words, Strong Runner," she told him. "I just hope you will visit us often, or at least let Morning Star visit, so she can tell me more things to write."

He rose. "I do not like it at Lapwai. We cannot come often. If your husband has a way to come to the Wallowa, we will talk more." He looked at Zack. "You should meet Chief Joseph. It is important to meet him if you are going to be a peacekeeper. If you think my words are wise, you must listen to Joseph. He has the most wisdom. He is a very honored leader, by both Indians and white men. Your leaders will know it is important that you meet him. Bring your woman if they will let you. She will be safe." He turned and spread out a blanket. "We must sleep now. We will leave very early. I wish to get you there quickly so I can go back to my camp. Morning Star does not like me to be away."

Zack realized it was a signal that he was done talking, and what Strong Runner said, he meant. He grinned at the thought, realizing he had never felt more free of the old hatreds. He found it incredible that he would go to sleep trusting this big Indian not to sneak up and kill him in the night and violate his wife. There was a time when he never would have trusted any Indian this way. "We'll be ready whenever you are," he answered, throwing more wood on the fire because of the wolves. He helped Iris into the wagon and climbed in after her. "We might as well sleep in our clothes," he said quietly. "No sense taking the time to have to dress in the morning. You sleep in here. I'll make up a bedroll outside."

He turned, and Iris touched his arm. "Zack."

He looked at her, leaned closer and kissed her lightly. "What is it?"

"I just—I've never been so moved by someone's words. This is all so unreal. I almost don't want it to end. I wanted to stay with Morning Star and talk with her more. They have such a beautiful way of speaking. She even said something that made me feel better about our baby, that his spirit could be with us in the tiny birds when they sing to us. And I see a change in you. Strong Runner has touched you in a special way."

Zack grabbed some blankets and moved to the back of the wagon to climb out. "I admit he has, but we have to remember why I'm here and that I am still an officer in the army. I'm supposed to be at Lapwai. Maybe we'll be able to look at all this more clearly once we get back into our own world."

He climbed out of the wagon. *Our own world,* she thought. *What a far cry we are from the paved streets and fancy parties and theaters of Washington, D.C.* How long had it been since she had reason to dress beautifully, since she had attended a ball, worn glittering jewelry, laughed and dined and visited with colonels and generals? How strange that none of those things mattered now.

They moved through more pristine country, around a lake, through another savagely beautiful meadow. An eagle flew over them, giving its screeching cry. Strong Runner looked up at it and waved, as though the big bird were his friend. Zack thought the man seemed to fit right into this land, as tall and strong as the trees, as rugged as the mountains, cunning as a wolf. He was primitive but educated, ruthless yet fair, both wild and tame. With his black hair, fringed buckskins, and dark skin he could easily melt into the background of this land. The soldier in him told Zack these people would be one hell of a challenge to hunt and capture if it ever came to that. How was any white man going to capture someone like Strong Runner in country like this?

Strong Runner led them to a crude road that wound into more pine forest. He stopped there. "This path was built by the army and settlers," he told them. "It goes all the way through Oregon to the Great Waters, all of it land that once belonged to us and now we have lost." He turned to Zack. "This is one of the roads you soldiers are to protect against us terrible Indians," he added, the familiar sly grin on his face. "And this is where I leave you."

Zack removed his hat and wiped the perspiration on his brow. He wore his lightest weight army pants and shirt, but he suspected he'd have been a lot cooler if he could dress like Strong Runner in loose-fitting deerskin and moccasins instead of boots. "How much farther is it?"

"Perhaps two hours. There will be no Nez Perce between here and there. They are all at Lapwai and beyond. My hunting party are the only ones who came this way."

Iris moved to the front of the wagon and into the seat, wanting to see Strong Runner once more before they parted.

"If there is anything you need, you can come in with me," Zack told him. "You don't have anything to fear."

Strong Runner scowled. "I do not like your Colonel Porter. I never go in there alone. He would look for a reason to arrest me." He rode closer, reaching out to Zack. "We go our separate ways now, Major Zack Myers, you to your army, me to my people."

Zack grasped his wrist, thinking how ominous the words felt. "You haven't seen the last of me," he told Strong Runner. "I want to talk more with you, meet Chief Joseph."

Strong Runner released his grip and nodded. "You will always be welcome, as long as you do not bring many soldiers with you, and as long as you do not come to tell us we must leave. We will never leave. You tell your government that. We will never go to that place in the south where Indians die of disease and broken hearts. Enough promises have been broken."

Zack nodded. "I will tell them. Whatever happens, I value our friendship and honor it. I will not forget what your women did for my wife."

"It's the same for me," Iris put in. "Morning Star and Little Bear will always hold a place in my heart."

Strong Runner studied her blue eyes, fascinated by this white woman. Not because she was so pale and pretty, but because she had a strength most white women did not have, an honesty he much admired. She was like Morning Star, except that her hair was as light as the sun. "You are a woman who follows her heart and her husband. That is as it should be. But his pathway, I think, will be far from my people." He looked at Zack again. "I pray we never meet in battle. In battle we must do what is right for our own people, not what is truly in our hearts."

Iris's heart tightened at the words. It wasn't fair to have to make such choices. "We will pray that never happens," she answered, thinking how Morning Star must be just as afraid of losing her husband as she was of losing her own.

Strong Runner removed a necklace from around his neck. Its rawhide string held a round ornament at the end that consisted of a beautiful circle of colorful beads, hand-sewn to a round piece of deerskin. "I give you this as a token of friendship," he said, handing it to Zack. "It represents the circle of life. Whatever your people try to do to us, the circle of life goes on, and the Nez Perce will never die. They will survive, and they will not forget the old ways."

Zack took the necklace and studied it, touching the beads carefully. "Wait," he said, laying the necklace in Iris's lap. He climbed into the back of the wagon and emerged with his personal pipe and a leather bag full of tobacco. "You say you like to smoke your pipe. Here is a small one you can carry with you anywhere. Think of me when you use it. There's plenty of tobacco here too—good tobacco, not the cheap stuff the government sends."

Strong Runner grinned, taking the items from him. "I thank you." He reined his horse away from the wagon, looking as though he wanted to say more, but he only nodded, then turned his horse, riding off into the pines.

Zack sighed, taking the necklace from Iris's lap and studying it again. "This has all taken a hell of a turn, hasn't it?"

Iris touched his arm. "You'll miss him, won't you?"

He handed her the necklace. "Put it in the trunk and lie down. We've got to get to the fort."

She took the necklace, studying his misty eyes. "You didn't answer my question."

He turned away and picked up the reins. "Yeah, I'll miss him."

29

"*H*ave a seat, Major Myers."

Zack lowered his arm after saluting Colonel Clayton Porter, whom he had met for the first time since arriving at Fort Lapwai an hour before. It was nearly dusk, and he was not only tired but confused at being suddenly thrust back into the real world of a bustling army fort. He worried about Iris, who had been quickly surrounded by six other women who lived at the fort. They had barraged her with questions about her ordeal, about what it was like to stay at an Indian camp, what a "terrible experience" it must have been for her. Little did they know it was one of the most enlightening experiences of her life, in spite of losing a baby.

"I think I would rather stand, sir," Zack answered the colonel. He already did not like this man, and he could understand why Strong Runner disliked and distrusted him. Zack could see by the man's eyes he was in for a drumming. Lieutenant Best had told him how angry the colonel was at his decision, and that anger showed now in the man's narrow, dark eyes, eyes that glared at him over a prominent, bony nose. He was so thin, Zack could not imagine how the man could han-

dle himself if he came into hand-to-hand combat with an Indian like Strong Runner, especially considering the fact that
the man's left arm was missing past his elbow.

"Fine," Porter answered tersely. He walked around Zack
and slammed shut the door to his office. "Do you know how
I lost this arm, Major Myers?" he asked, coming back around
behind his desk.

"I've heard it was in the Civil War, sir."

"Yes. You were also wounded in that war."

"Yes, sir. I was lucky that my wound healed. There was a
time when they weren't sure I'd be able to walk."

Porter sniffed. "My point, Major Myers, is that during that
war you understood who the enemy was, did you not?"

Zack frowned. "Of course, sir."

"You had no special feelings for them. When you fought
them, you thought only to kill, not caring who they were,
what they believed, if they were right or wrong."

Zack watched him closely. "I'm not sure what you mean,
sir."

Fire came into the man's eyes. "I mean, Major Myers, that
you understood they were the *enemy*! You certainly would not
have taken your sick wife into a Confederate camp, would
you?"

Zack thought the remark ridiculous, but he knew what
the man was getting at. "If it meant keeping her alive, sir, I
most certainly would have."

Porter folded his arms authoritatively, looking Zack over
derisively. "I will remind you, Major Myers, women have babies, and lose babies, all the time. Some live and some die. I
am sorry for your loss, but you made a very wrong decision
that could have turned into a sorry mess and started a whole
damn war!"

Zack could see the man was a borderline fanatic. "I hardly
think so, sir. The Nez Perces were quite friendly and helpful.
They saved my wife's life."

"You didn't know when first going in there that that was
how it would be! For God's sake, Myers, you rode off with
Strong Runner! Strong Runner, of all people! That big buck
can't be trusted any farther than you could throw him! He
murdered three men. *Three men!* Slit their throats! The cocky
son of a bitch got away with it! We can't prove it, and he

knows it. He also knows that to arrest and hang him without proof could start a war with his people. They're just chomping at the bit for a reason to kill some whites! You went off with a man who would just as soon gut you with his knife as look at you!"

Zack thought about the necklace Strong Runner had given him just hours earlier, the look in his eyes when he did so. "I don't think so, sir."

Porter sighed, his jaw flexing. "And you are a fool, Major! You're new out here. You don't understand how it is. Just because we're at peace right now doesn't mean it will stay that way. You've just come from Sioux country. You've seen what's going on there. It's going to be the same thing here if we aren't careful and stay on top of things."

"That's exactly what I think I've done. Strong Runner and I had some good talks. I'm here to act as a mediator with the army and the Indians. I've made a big step in doing just that."

Porter shook his head. "A step *backward,* Major! You misunderstand your purpose. Your purpose is to make sure the Nez Perces understand that they must give up more land, that they have no choice. If they don't do so peacefully, then many of them will die. Your purpose is to make them understand they have no choice, not to befriend them and have long talks with them!"

Zack realized how right Strong Runner was about the forked tongues of his leaders. "How else are we going to talk them into anything at all if we can't befriend them first?"

"Befriending them is fine, *if* it's only to get them to concede. It can't be anything personal, Major, and I see by your eyes that's just what this thing became for you—*personal*! We can't have that in the army, Major!"

Zack clenched his fists in anger. "Sir, they saved my wife's life."

"Maybe. And maybe she would have lived anyway."

Never had Zack wanted so badly to hit a superior, even more than when he'd landed into Jason Ward, but this time he managed to control the urge. "No, sir, she would *not* have lived. There are some *men* who could not have survived losing that much blood."

Porter sighed, moving behind his desk and sitting down.

"The fact remains, Major, that you left sixty men without their leader."

"Lieutenant Best is a very capable man, sir."

"That is not the point. The point is, you made a very poor decision, wife or no wife. The army always comes first, Major Myers. That's why *my* wife lives in Portland. You of all people, coming from that mess with Red Cloud, should know how clever and deceiving Indians can be. How could you know Strong Runner wasn't leading you away so that a larger contingent of Nez Perces could attack your leaderless men? What you did could have cost the lives of your own men, something unforgivable for an officer."

"If it was a trick, sir, Strong Runner would have come to me with some lame excuse for me to follow him. But *I* went to *him*! They had women and children along. It was obviously not a war party. I know when warriors are out for a man's blood and when they're just minding their own business. I'm no fool when it comes to Indians, Colonel Porter. I've had plenty of experience with them, in more ways than just the army."

Porter rubbed his upper lip. "I know your record, Major. I have your papers. Colonel Shaver sent me a letter recommending you act as a liaison with the Nez Perces. I know about your family being killed by the Pawnee, but that was a long time ago, and as far as I am concerned, your personal battle over how you feel about Indians could work to the detriment of the army."

Bewildered, Zack moved to a chair and finally sat down. "I don't know what you mean."

"I mean I think you've been on a personal quest, Major, looking for some way to deal with your past. Shaver thinks that's a good thing, that it somehow makes you more capable of dealing fairly and honestly with the savages. I disagree. For one thing, we don't *want* to deal fairly and honestly with them. We only want them to understand that they must live on reservations and that to fight it is to die. For another, I think this personal problem of yours causes you to make poor decisions. I know about you risking your life in Montana, just to save the life of a Pawnee Indian scout, which again would have left your men leaderless. I find that ironic, considering it was Pawnee who killed your family. That only tells me that you don't quite know how to deal with your own feelings, and that it makes you do things that could cost the lives of your men. I think that in your search to deal with your own feelings, you've developed a soft spot for Indians."

Zack thought that a ridiculous remark. "I feel no such thing, sir. I have just come to understand them better. How are we going to keep the peace if we don't understand their thinking, the reasons we've come to this point? Understanding how they think and why they fight us helps me deal with the reasons my own family had to die. They aren't that much different from us, Colonel Porter. They laugh, they cry. They have families whom they love and want to protect. They love their way of life. They are proud and want to continue to take care of their families, provide for them in their own way. They love their homeland and don't want to lose it. Most of them are simply fighting to keep their hunting grounds, to save the game they need for feeding and clothing themselves. For most of them the land where they live is sacred, and whites are intruders. It's bad enough that we go in and take it all away from them, but what makes it worse is we keep promising not to let that happen, then turn around and do it anyway. A man can take only so many lies, Colonel, before getting fed up. That's what happened with the eastern tribes, and that's what's happening with the Sioux. It will also happen with the Nez Perces if we don't make up our minds to let them keep what's left to them and find a way to keep settlers out."

Porter shook his head. "Just as I thought," he said, leaning back in his chair. "We don't need a negotiator out here, Major. We need a man who can cajole these Indians into giving up and signing one more treaty. I don't think you're the man for the job, especially now that you believe these people saved your wife's life. Besides that, you made friends with the wrong Indian. Strong Runner is a troublemaker, make no doubt about it. The man you *should* talk to is Chief Joseph."

"Strong Runner said he would take me to meet him if I went to the Wallowa Valley."

"There, you see? He's got you going to *him*. That makes them think they have a say in this thing. You've got to make him come to you."

"Strong Runner won't come here."

Porter snorted. "Of course he won't. He's afraid of me, afraid that I'll come up with a reason to have him arrested and hanged after all. Joseph doesn't like coming here either. There's bad blood between those Nez Perces and the ones who've had sense enough to settle here and give up the fight."

"I still think I can help, Colonel Porter, and I think they can be reasoned with if we just keep our end of the bargain."

Porter sighed deeply "Well, then, you can write to the powers that be in Washington, D.C., and tell that to them. Maybe you can give some of your sage advice to whoever comes out here to replace you, because I don't like Colonel Shaver's choice of liaison. I want someone who knows how to put the army first and who isn't confused about how he feels about these hostiles. You've proven you can't always make good decisions in the field, Major Myers. I'm giving you desk duty while you're here. You'll have to sit out the winter. It's too late now to get back over the mountains. Come spring, you're going back east. I'll let them decide at Fort Snelling where to send you. In the meantime, I want you to stay away from the Wallowa and Chief Joseph and especially Strong Runner. Men like you give them hope, and that's the last thing we want them to have."

Zack couldn't believe what he was hearing. Was this man really that much of a stubborn fool? He rose, hardly able to contain himself. "Sir, I take the army *very* seriously! It's been my whole life, and I didn't earn these gold leaves sitting behind a desk! I earned them at West Point, training men at Fort Snelling, fighting in the Civil War, and fighting *Indians*! I'm good at what I do, and I would never do anything to endanger the men under my command! If I had thought these men were in any danger at all, I would not have left them. I will remind you we are *not* at war with the Nez Perces! There was nothing wrong with letting them help my wife or with leaving my men under Lieutenant Best. I'm telling you I've earned Strong Runner's trust, and that means a lot! I can use that trust to try to talk some sense into him."

Porter also rose. "I said to stay away from Strong Runner. He'd just as soon stick a knife in your gut as look at you, believe me. He's got you fooled, and he's probably laughing about it right now, just like he's laughing about getting away with killing three white men!" He folded his arms authoritatively. "For the winter you will continue to train some of these new men. I hear you're a sharpshooter. You can teach the men here how to better handle their rifles. Some of them can't hit the side of a barn, and God knows when we might have to go chasing after the Nez Perces."

Zack felt light-headed with shock and fury. "I hope you change your mind over the winter, Colonel. The last thing my wife needs is to have to make that trip back over those mountains. I promised her that once we got here, we'd *stay*, and she'd have a decent place to live."

"Your wife is the daughter of a colonel. She understands that being married to an army man means being apart for months at a time, or never living in one place for long. She made her choice, and you made yours when you decided to let her live with you wherever you were stationed. She'll manage."

You bastard! Zack wanted to shout. "I need to be excused, sir, before I do something that lands me in the guardhouse."

Their eyes held in challenge for a moment. "Fine. I don't care to get *my* nose broken!"

Zack frowned in surprise. Colonel Shaver had said he would not mention the fact that he had hit Jason Ward. "Who told you?"

"Jason Ward wrote me after he heard where you'd been sent. Jason is the nephew of a good friend of mine. You have to be careful with these things, Major. You never know whose toes you're stepping on. I thought I'd give you the benefit of the doubt. I respect Colonel Shaver's opinions. But when you pulled this little stunt, I knew I'd have to replace you."

Zack shivered with rage. "You could have asked for someone else in the first place and saved us the hardship of this trip."

"You are dismissed, Major. I think it's best you get out of here quickly."

Zack glared at him, teeth clenched. "Yes, sir," he hissed. He saluted and turned, his mind racing. All the hell of getting here all of Iris's pain and discomfort, all his efforts to get closer to Strong Runner, all for nothing. He'd promised Strong Runner he'd come and see him, meet Chief Joseph. Now he would probably never see Strong Runner again. He walked out, his back and neck so tense from rage, they ached fiercely. He stormed toward the temporary quarters that had been set up for him and Iris until he could have something better built. He realized Clayton Porter had done this on purpose, just to make life more difficult for him and Iris.

Jason Ward! He might have known Ward wouldn't keep his end of the bargain to keep quiet about their fight. The sonofabitch would do his best to blackball him from any further promotions! The strange thing was, that didn't upset him nearly as much as knowing he would not be able to talk to Strong Runner again. God, how he hated having to bring this news to Iris!

Iris awoke to the touch of Jacob's hand on her arm. "Blankie, Mommy," the boy said, his eyes droopy and his lips pouted.

She looked over at Zack, who stirred when she sat up. "Where is it?" she whispered. She glanced at the mantel clock that sat on the trunk. Lamplight showed that it was two A.M. "You shouldn't be up, Jacob, and you must be very cold running around here in your bare feet." She got up, pulling on a robe against the chilly air. She carried the boy to his small bed in the outer room of the three-room major's quarters they lived in, the best living conditions they had enjoyed so far. If not for having to go back east come spring, she knew Zack would have built her that cabin he'd promised, but there was no sense in it now.

"Blankie," Jacob pouted.

"You had it when you went to bed, so where could it be?" she chided. She searched for the ragged cotton blanket the boy had carried around with him since he was a baby. She found it caught under the feather mattress he slept on. "Here it is."

The boy grinned, a quick, handsome grin that reminded her of Zack. He clutched the blanket close as Iris tucked him back into bed, and he turned on his side, sticking a thumb into his mouth and closing his eyes.

Iris smiled, watching him a moment. It was easier now that she had a child of her own to imagine what it must have been like for Zack the day his family was killed. He had worked so hard and so long to come to terms with the loss and his feelings, to realize how he could best serve—not by fighting Indians, but by being a trusted ally. Now this.

After two months there, she still had trouble believing they would have to give up all they had struggled for and go back east. Zack belonged here now. Not only that, but she could not help wondering what Strong Runner would think when Zack never came to see him. And she had so looked forward to getting to know Morning Star better, visiting more with the woman.

She wrapped her robe tighter, walked over to the potbelly heating stove that stood in a corner of the room, and threw in more wood. At least here they could have lived fairly comfortably, without the constant fear of Indian attack, without the constant threat of freezing and starvation. Men like Zack could keep it this way if more were sent to talk with the Nez Perces, but the government seemed to think it was wrong to try to be fair with them. How could they not see that leaving men like Colonel Porter in charge would only aggravate the situation? It was almost as if the government *wanted* war.

Iris watched the wood flare up and let it burn hard for a moment before closing down the draft to reduce the flames and make the wood last longer. Maybe the government *did* want war. Whites wanted the land, the gold, the trees, everything. Manifest Destiny, they called it back in Washington— the God-given right to declare this land from coast to coast as belonging to the United States. Somehow the Indians didn't fit into that plan.

She glanced over at Jacob again to see he'd already fallen back to sleep. He lay there looking so sweet and innocent, his dark hair curled in little ringlets around his face, his dark lashes outlined against his chubby cheeks. She hated the thought of making the trip all the way back east, worried it could affect his health. Poor Zack still felt terrible about the situation. He was worried sick himself about how hard the trip would be on her and Jacob. She wondered what Colonel Shaver would think of this, but Zack refused to write him about it. He felt the man had done enough for him, and now Shaver was retired. The man deserved to be home in Virginia with his wife, and he didn't need to know about army problems.

She walked back to the bedroom to see Zack resting on one elbow, waiting for her. "Is he asleep?"

"Yes." She removed the robe and crawled back into bed. "Maybe I should have also lit a fire in the kitchen cookstove to warm it up even more."

He pulled her close. "We've stayed a hell of a lot warmer than last winter."

Iris sighed, listening to wolves howling in the surrounding mountains. "And we shouldn't have any trouble cutting a tree for Christmas." The words made both of them think of Thomas, which led to thoughts of Strong Runner. "This is all so wrong, Zack. You've come so far. There couldn't be a better man for dealing with the Nez Perces than you."

He pulled the covers around them both. "Clayton Porter doesn't think so, and it doesn't look like that's going to change. I'm just sorry for you, having to make that journey again." He kissed her eyes, her throat. "You've been so patient through all the turmoil, all the hell I've put you through. I'm so damn sorry, Iris."

"Not one thing that has happened has been your fault. I wouldn't change any of it. Staying with you no matter what was my decision." She met the eyes that had always sent waves of passion through her. "I love you. I would have hated being away from you much more than putting up with the discomforts of places like Fort Kearny." She touched his scarred cheek, thinking how different he was when she first met him, how confused and lonely and full of hate. "Make love to me, Zack. It's been so long."

He sighed, kissing her forehead. "I don't know. After you losing that baby, watching you come so close to death—"

"Zack, those things happen. It won't happen every time, and I *do* want to have more children. It's been over two months. We can't go on like this forever. I'm healed and I need my husband. I *want* another baby."

"And what if you end up pregnant when we're supposed to make that trip back east?"

"If God wants me to have another, I'll have it. Besides, do you intend to abstain for nearly a year? It will be at least that long between now and when we arrive, wherever it is you'll be assigned. I will not allow it, Zack Myers."

She leaned up and kissed him hungrily, feeling a wantonness she had not felt in a long time. She had wanted to do this earlier, but he had deliberately turned away from her and gone to sleep without touching her, as he had done every night since she lost the baby. Now she had caught him off guard, sleepy, relaxed, warm.

"Please, Zack." Everything they had been through led to a sudden need to come together, to celebrate life and the freeing of souls, even mourning the loss of their baby.

Iris moved her hand over his solid body, down to his hips, inside his woolen longjohns. He groaned at the touch. She liked touching him, feeling the proof of his magnificent manhood.

Zack could not deny her when she touched him that way. "You don't play fair," he told her.

"I don't intend to."

"Are you sure it's all right? I've been trying to let you recover."

"It's all right."

He needed little persuading. He wanted her too much to resist any longer, and he met her lips again, invaded her mouth in a savage kiss as he pushed her flannel gown up to her waist, realizing she wore nothing under it. She had planned this. Painful thoughts of what it had been like to watch her almost die were overcome by a more urgent need to feel himself inside her again, to make love to this woman who was so strong, so forgiving. He caressed that most intimate part of her, felt the moistness that told him she was ready for him. Before he could even enter her, she gasped in a sweet climax at his touch. There was no going back then. He groaned with aching pleasure when he entered her, praying this would not lead to the kind of disaster she'd experienced nearly three months before.

It was a quiet, sweet, sensual moment, a reunion of body and soul, a symbol that no matter what happened in the world outside, nothing could affect the love they shared. He thrust deep, with thrilling rhythm, and it had been so long, his life quickly spilled into her. He settled against her and grinned sheepishly. "Sorry about that," he told her. "Let's clean up and do it again."

"There is a kettle of water on the heating stove."

Zack got up and pulled up his longjohns, shivering as he

hurried out to get the hot water and bring it back into the bedroom. He poured some into the washbowl. Wolves howled again, and he remembered the night he'd talked to Strong Runner about them. He looked at Iris.

"They're all right," she told him, reading his thoughts. "Indians have been surviving winters for centuries."

"Oh, I'm not worried about someone like Strong Runner surviving the winter." He sighed, setting the kettle aside. "Some terrible things are going to happen, Iris. I feel it. I should be here when they come."

She waited while he washed. "You can't stop history, Zack, and that's what's happening all over the West. That's why I keep a diary. Someday we'll have a lot to tell our children and grandchildren."

Zack walked to a window and peeked through the curtains while she got up and washed. *Most of it is going to be very difficult to tell,* he thought. He studied a full moon while the wolves continued their nightly calling.

"Come back to bed, Zack."

He turned to study her as she crawled back under the covers, an anxious feeling making him want her with an intense passion all over again.

"They are sending him back."

Morning Star wrapped dark, silky legs around her husband's strong body, nestling against him in satisfaction. She always liked this sweet moment right after lovemaking, but tonight her husband was tense and uneasy. "Sending who back?" she asked.

"Major Myers. Little Eagle told me today after returning from Lapwai with supplies. Colonel Porter is sending Zack Myers back east."

Morning Star sat up. "But he seems such an honest and fair man. You told me you thought he could be trusted."

Disgust filled his dark eyes. "Of course he could. That is why they are sending him back. They want a man who speaks out of both sides of his mouth."

Morning Star lay back down, feeling a strange depression engulf her. "I liked his wife."

Strong Runner held her close. "I know."

"If more women like her would come, there would be hope."

Strong Runner listened to the wolves, wondering how long it would take after the whites got rid of the Indians before they also got rid of all wildlife, the trees, polluted the water. Perhaps then they would get their due. They would learn the hard way that they needed the animals, trees, and the water to live, but then it would be too late for them, and far too late for his own people.

30

June 1873

*T*he music played softly, and Zack turned his wife to a waltz, appreciating how Iris could adapt to any situation. She was beautiful, elegant, and perfectly mannered at the officers' dance this evening, yet had been strong, resilient, and uncomplaining traveling a rugged trail through mountains and forest. She had lived in the humblest fashion at remote locations without losing an ounce of her courage and patience. Much as he hated it at Fort Leavenworth, doing work that meant nothing to him, he was glad for Iris.

Life was better here than anyplace Iris had lived since they were married. They had a seven-room frame home just outside the fort, a parlor, kitchen, dining room, study, and three bedrooms, which were certainly needed. Two more children had been added to the Myers family, a little girl three years old now, Audra, and a six-month-old baby boy, Michael. Four years had passed since leaving Lapwai and coming to Kansas. Jacob was six years old.

Returning east had not been nearly as difficult as their original journeys west. By the time they left Lapwai, only a year after arriving there, they needed only to travel south to

Nevada to catch a train east, rather than traveling over the mountains by wagon again. They rode the train all the way to Omaha, Nebraska, where they were met by a lieutenant who brought them by wagon to Leavenworth. Zack had been sent to train new enlistees in firearms and various cavalry skills as well as the psychology needed for fighting Indians.

The entire trip was so much faster and easier than when they originally went west. The railroad had brought a flood of postwar settlers, and farms and towns had mushroomed all along the railway. Settlers were flooding in, commanding more and more land that some Indian tribes were still not ready to give up. The Sioux remained a mighty force to be reckoned with, and the Nez Perces under young Chief Joseph were struggling to hang on to the Wallowa Valley, still insisting that area was not part of the Thief Treaty.

"You're at Lapwai again," Iris said as the music stopped.

"What?"

"I can see it in your eyes, Zack Myers."

He studied her beautiful face, the blond hair perfectly coiffed in a mass of curls on top of her head, decorated with fancy combs. Her pink velvet dress fit her bosom fetchingly, the scooped neckline showing skin as soft as the material of her dress. She wore a diamond necklace, a gift from her father she had always treasured and had kept in the trunk that had traveled with her over prairies and mountains.

"I'm sorry. I can't help thinking about the news we heard. I wish I could have been there to see Strong Runner's eyes when the commissioner of Indian affairs told them he agreed the Wallowa Valley should remain in Nez Perce hands and that all white settlers should be removed."

They walked toward a table where punch was being served. "Do you think President Grant will agree?"

"I don't know. The secretary of the interior does, and he has a lot of pull. I've heard that in spite of his leadership and victories in the Civil War, Grant is a bit of a sap as president. They say he can be talked into anything, so I guess there is hope."

A young woman dipped punch into cups for them, eyeing Zack bashfully. Iris caught the look. Young women were mightily impressed by handsome officers like her husband, especially when they wore their dress uniforms, as he did that night. She remembered how she'd always felt about men like Zack, remembered how she'd been attracted to him the very first time she met him. She was only eighteen then, Zack twenty-three. They had been through so much since then, and Zack had changed dramatically. "You're being watched, Major Myers."

"Hmmm?" He glanced at the young girl, who blushed and looked away. Zack grinned. "Kind of reminds me of you ten years ago."

Iris raised her chin in arrogance. "I was not the blushing child. I was much bolder."

Zack laughed lightly. "There's no arguing that. You nearly got me booted back to private. Thank goodness I haven't had to serve under Jason Ward for years now."

Iris smiled and sipped some of the punch. "Well, Jason should be happy riding with the Seventh Cavalry, probably busting his buttons being top man to George Custer. I'm sure he has the same political dreams Custer has."

Zack's smile faded. "I don't like what Custer did down on the Washita in 'sixty-eight, and I don't think he's a good choice to be trying to handle the Sioux and Cheyenne. They hate his very name, and that hatred just keeps them stirred up."

Iris watched others dance, happy, pampered women who had never been west, never seen its beauty, had no idea what the Indians were suffering. She would not forget when they heard the news about Custer attacking a peaceful Cheyenne village in western Kansas, raiding and murdering, calling it a military victory. People on the inside knew differently. She supposed by now the Nez Perces knew about it. She was glad they were holding out for their land, thrilled that it looked as though they would win their cause. What a happy day it would be for Strong Runner and Morning Star if Grant agreed they should keep the Wallowa Valley.

It was too bad old Chief Joseph had died two years before, never knowing whether or not his long struggle to defy the government and keep the Wallowa Valley would succeed. Word was his son, also called Joseph, was a mighty defender of his father's fight, avidly demanding that the land where his father was buried be kept in Nez Perce hands. They had heard he was an eloquent speaker, a very noble man, almost brilliant in his reasoning. She wished she and Zack could have met him, but having known Strong Runner left them with a pretty fair idea of the kind of man young Chief Joseph must be.

Zack finished his punch and set the cup aside. "What worries me is those settlers up at the Wallowa won't take a decision to kick them out lying down. There could be a lot of trouble. Most of them don't think the Nez Perces should have _any_ of that land. How we came to the belief that it all belongs to us and the Indians have no rights to any of it, I'll never quite understand. Much as I once hated Indians, I always understood that they were here first. I just couldn't figure out why we couldn't just all live together peacefully. The sad part is we could have if our own race would have looked at them as human beings with rights."

Sometimes he still was shocked at his own words, the way his feelings had changed. He found it hard to believe that he once took great satisfaction in watching Indians hanged, that he looked forward to killing as many as he could. His closest aide, Captain Robert Willam, came through the doorway then, leaving the doors open because of the warm June night. The captain appeared to be excited as he approached him.

"Major Myers! I have good news!" He held up a telegram. "He's done it! Grant signed an executive order giving the Nez Perces the Wallowa Valley!"

Iris's eyes immediately teared at the news, and Zack eagerly took the telegram from Willam. "I'll be damned," he said. He turned to Iris, and they embraced. "There will be plenty of drumming and dancing among the Nez Perces the next few days," he told her.

Word spread among the rest of the couples in the huge mess hall, the tables having been pushed aside to make room for dancing. Some looked at Zack and Iris strangely, wondering why on earth they should care about something that was happening clear out in Oregon.

"They say Major Myers befriended a Nez Perce man when he was stationed out there," a lieutenant told a group of people he stood with. "That the Nez Perce man's wife saved Mrs. Myers's life after she . . ." He realized there were women listening. "Well, after she lost a baby, so I've heard."

"Oh, my!" one woman whispered.

"She let *Indian* women tend to her?" Another woman shivered as though appalled.

"Must not have had a choice," the lieutenant answered. "Why else would she let Indian women touch her? I don't know all the details. I haven't been here that long."

"Iris never mentioned losing a baby," one of the other women said. "All the dinners and sewing clutches we've had, and she never mentioned it."

"Maybe it's just too hard for her to talk about it," another put in. "That *is* a rather personal thing, you know."

"Well, whatever happened, I don't understand an army officer being happy for *any* Indian victory," another lieutenant spoke up. "They say that's why Myers got sent back here, away from the Indian wars. I guess he made a couple of bad decisions in the field, that he's too soft on Indians."

"Well, there must be more to the story than we've heard," one of the women said, watching Iris. "Such a beautiful, refined woman as Mrs. Myers would not willingly have allowed Indians to tend to her. And Major Myers, he's so handsome, and he looks intelligent and brave."

The music started up again, and they all watched Zack and Iris Myers move onto the dance floor, whirling to the gentle rhythm of another waltz, both beaming with happiness, both with eyes only for each other. The women sighed with envy.

Zack still held the telegram, caught between his big hand and Iris's gloved one.

"People are wondering why we're so happy about this," Iris told Zack.

"Let them wonder. We both agreed people who have never been out there wouldn't understand."

Iris frowned. "It's been good to have the company of women again, but strangely enough, since knowing Morning Star, I've never been able to get really close to any of these women. I've tried a few times to explain what it's like out there, but I could tell none of them grasped any of it. I never have talked to them about losing the baby. It just seems so, I don't know, personal, special. I wish we hadn't had to leave his little grave out there, Zack."

He pulled her a little closer. "It's in a beautiful meadow

and it's well marked. No one will disturb it. Besides, you told me once his spirit was with us, in the little birds."

She smiled sadly. "Morning Star told me that. It was such a beautiful thought. It's things like that I can't explain to these women, that rather poetic Indian spirit, the way they look at things." She smiled. "And their sense of humor. How do you explain that? A person just has to experience it for themselves."

Zack thought about some of Thomas's sly jokes, and the sharp wit Strong Runner had. "You're right," he answered. He kept an arm around her when the dance ended. "I sure would like to be the one to take the news to Strong Runner."

Iris imagined how the Nez Perces would celebrate. "Oh, I wish you could be too, Zack. You don't belong here training men. If you could have stayed out there, you could have worked with the Nez Perces and their agent and Commissioner Clum on this whole thing. You *would* have been the one to take the news to Strong Runner and Joseph."

Zack led her outside, smelling the soft summer night air. "Four more years, and I can make the decision whether to stay in the army or quit. If this is all they're going to let me do, I'm thinking of quitting. Maybe we can go to D.C. and I can get some kind of government job. I have the education and experience for it. Would you like that?"

She faced him. "I want whatever you want."

"How about what *you* want? It's always been for me. It's your turn."

She touched the gold braiding on his jacket. "It has never mattered one way or the other. It probably would be good for the children, though, to be settled in one place. I loved the army life as a child, but I was by myself. I had no siblings. I just wanted to be wherever my parents were. We have three children now, and there might be more yet. Each one will be different. For some of them it might be hard to be dragged everywhere, changing schools and friends. And I have to admit it would be a lot harder on me to keep traveling with a brood of children on my hands."

He grasped her hands and squeezed. "It's settled then. In 'seventy-seven I'll be thirty-seven years old. Jacob will be ten. I lost my father when I was that age, and I dearly missed having a father. I want to be able to give more of my time to my own children. Besides, the army has let me down, or maybe I've let it down. I don't know. I guess *I'm* the one who's changed. My reasons for joining aren't there anymore."

Iris sighed. "I've been proud of everything you've done, Zack, and I know that whatever you decide to do after leaving the service, you'll do well. Let's go home and spend some time with the children. Sergeant Kirk's wife has probably had her fill of the little hellions by now, and Michael is probably getting hungry."

They walked together across the parade grounds, enjoying the night air. Zack greeted men on guard duty, wondering what they were guarding anymore. The Indians in these parts had fled or been forced into Indian Territory long ago. Pawnee, that was who used to roam this area. How well he knew, and how strange to be back in the area where all his hatred began, and now to have that hatred washed away. Still, the one thing he had not done since coming back was go to the old homestead and see if anyone was still farming it. He had so far been unable to go back there and visit his family's graves. He still feared the images such a visit would bring him.

Maybe this decision by President Grant allowing the Nez Perces to have their dream of owning the Wallowa would prove that Indians did not always have to fight and kill to get what they wanted; and maybe, just maybe, this time the government would keep its word. "This new order could be so meaningful," he told Iris. "What worries me is that it might not be worth the paper it's written on, considering our record for keeping promises."

"It's enough to keep Joseph and Strong Runner and the others happy for now. It might be enough to ensure there will never be a Nez Perce war, and that's all that matters. In these times that's the most we can hope for."

Zack looked across the parade grounds toward the mess hall, where officers and their wives still danced and drank and mingled as though they had the world by the tail. *And I suppose they do,* he thought.

Morning Star laughed, watching Wolf Boy, nine years old now, dance proudly with the adult warriors, wearing a fox-skin hat that belonged to his father and was too big for him. Seven-year-old Jumping Bear was living up to his name, jumping and laughing, caught up in the celebrating, and the night air was filled with drumming and singing.

The news had come today. The Wallowa Valley belonged to Chief Joseph's band of Nez Perces! They didn't have to worry about being forced to live elsewhere, losing their sacred burial grounds and their precious hunting grounds! Best of all, the white settlers who had invaded this part of Nez Perce land would be removed. *White* removal instead of Indian removal! This was indeed a glorious moment for the Nez Perces!

Her four-year-old daughter ran to her playfully on bare feet, her waist-length hair damp from hard play and running. "Here is my Dancing Girl," she said, holding her close. "It is late, my little one. You should go into the dwelling and sleep, like your younger sister." She took her inside and ordered her to lie down next to two-year-old Little Turtle, a second daughter for Strong Runner. She thought how in moments like this she would like to be able to talk to the white woman called Iris, who had never even seen these last two babies. She hoped Iris had herself had more children by now, to fill the emptiness in her heart over the tiny son she had lost.

She had so wanted to get to know Iris better. She was the only white woman she had ever cared about that way, the only one she knew could answer questions about the way white women lived without looking down her nose or accusing Morning Star of being wrong or dirty. Most white women she'd met either totally shunned her or were missionaries who insisted that she change the way she lived, that she should dress differently, never wear her hair long and loose, the way Strong Runner liked it; that she should wear stiff corsets and hard shoes and fancy bonnets. They wanted her to live in a real house, cook differently, eat at a table with fancy plates.

What use did she have for such things? She was happy this way, and now no one could say she must change any of it. They were free. Free! Strong Runner could hunt and provide for them, keep his honor and dignity. They would not go to Lapwai anymore for supplies. They would need little of what the government sent. Better than all of that, Colonel Porter was gone! He had retired from the army. There was no one left to accuse Strong Runner of killing those white men such a long time ago.

She went back outside, waiting for Strong Runner, who had ridden off on his horse when the news came. She was not sure why. Perhaps he had gone to say a prayer of thanksgiving alone. She joined in a trilling noise of celebration with the other women, who all locked hands and formed a circle around the men, the women dancing sideways rhythmically in one direction while the men danced singly in the opposite direction, so that the two circles continued to pass each other. A huge bonfire lit the area for many feet beyond it. Other fires were lit throughout the village, cooking fires that roasted deer meat, even some beef, for several Nez Perces farmed and raised cattle now. She noticed Chief Joseph watching, his wife standing beside him. Surely the man was very proud of what he had accomplished, and surely the spirit of his father, old Chief Joseph, was with them this night.

She left the singing and dancing and walked into the darkness beyond the fire, wishing Strong Runner would return. Once her eyes adjusted to the moonlight, she was sure she saw someone sitting on a horse in the distance. "Strong Runner," she shouted.

The horse turned. "I am here," he answered.

She walked toward him as he nudged his horse into a slow walk, meeting her halfway. She grasped the horse's rope bridle. "Where have you been? We have so much celebrating to do! I want to enjoy this moment with my husband, and you should see Wolf Boy and Jumping Bear dancing. It will make you laugh, but also make you feel so proud!"

Strong Runner looked toward the village. "I am not so sure we should be celebrating yet."

"Why! The order cannot be changed, Strong Runner. The Great Father himself signed it! He has the power, and he has said this valley belongs to us."

Strong Runner swung his leg over the horse's neck and slid off the animal. He faced her in the moonlight. "Think back, Morning Star. How many times have promises been made and then broken?"

Her smile faded. "Please do not spoil this night, Strong Runner."

He grasped her arms. "I do not want to spoil it. I want

only to avoid the hurt of another broken promise. There are a lot of whites in this valley. They will do all they can to make trouble over this. This new order does not say what rights we have to move against them if they do not leave, nor has anyone drawn the boundaries of what is ours."

"Mr. Ordeneal, the superintendent of Indian affairs, he will make sure the boundaries are correct. He is a fair man. He and agent Monteith are the reason Mr. Clum investigated our claim that this land was not part of the Thief Treaty. They are the reason we have won this land."

He nodded. "I will still feel better once it is certain, and once I see soldiers making the whites leave."

Morning Star wrapped her arms around him. "You are too full of doubts, my husband."

"I would feel better if Major Myers had been the one to bring me the news. He would tell me what is really true and what is not."

"Yes, I think he would." She looked up at him. "Come and join the dancing, Strong Runner. For one night let your heart fly free and be glad for a victory, even if it proves to be short-lived. Come and celebrate with your sons. Little Turtle and Dancing Girl sleep now, but your sons are still dancing."

He moved a foot behind her ankle and gave a gentle kick, catching her as she fell backward and laying her down in the thick grass. "First we will celebrate another way. When a man feels victory, another feeling overcomes him and makes him want his woman."

Morning Star laughed, running her hands along his muscled arms. "Then celebrate however you wish, my husband."

He untied his breechcloth, the only thing he wore because the day had been warm. He tossed it aside, leaving his knife tied by a leather cord to his waist and thigh. He pushed up her tunic and in a moment he was inside of her, moving rhythmically with the drumming.

He enjoyed Morning Star's gasps of pleasure, grasped her hips and pushed deep until his life came forth in his own sweet ecstasy. He held himself there a moment before leaving her.

"Come with me to the stream and we will wash before we go back," she told him.

"I will come." He picked up his breechcloth and slung it

over his horse, then followed her to a nearby stream. Morning Star lifted her tunic and kicked off her moccasins, wading into the stream and sitting down in it to wash herself.

Strong Runner wanted to believe this was real, though he would rather have realized such a victory through battle; but the white man fought a different way, with writing and paper and men who were called lawyers and judges, agents and commissioners. He much preferred sinking his knife into a man to end an argument. At least then his enemy was dead and could not come back to change what had been decided.

He would go and join the dancing, and he would smoke the little pipe Zack Myers had given him. "What do you think of all this, Major Myers?" he muttered. "This could be a very good thing, as long as your people do not break this new promise."

31

JUNE 1876

*T*he grave look on Colonel Stanley Johnson's face startled Zack when he walked into the man's office after being summoned by a sergeant. "Somethin' terrible is wrong," the sergeant had said on their walk over. "I can tell. Colonel Johnson got a telegram, and I watched his face pale right there, thought he was gonna pass out. He wouldn't say what it was. Said he wanted to talk to you first, Colonel Myers."

Colonel Myers. He was actually a Lieutenant-Colonel now, one step below colonel, but most referred to the office as colonel when addressing him. In spite of his plans to leave the army, he was proud of his promotion, and he knew by the letter he had received from retired Colonel Howard Shaver that his mentor was also very proud. It seemed incredible that he had reached Shaver's classification—so many years, so much hardship and personal turmoil.

He could see by Colonel Johnson's face that the sergeant had been right. He had served under this man for seven years now, ever since coming to Fort Leavenworth. He'd learned to respect and like the man, and to read him well. Right now his white hair looked even whiter against his flushed face, and his pale blue eyes showed terrible sorrow. His tall, slender frame seemed stooped. Zack saluted the man.

"Sit down, Colonel Myers," Johnson said, not even saluting in return.

Zack removed his hat and took a chair, and Johnson walked over and closed the door. He moved back behind his desk, meeting Zack's eyes. "It's days like this that I know I'm ready to get out of the army."

Zack frowned. "What's happened, sir?"

The man closed his eyes and sighed, finally sitting down. "I know you're planning on retiring next year, but I'd like to know if you would be willing to spend that last year back out west, at Lapwai."

Zack's heart raced a little faster. Something had gone wrong. He had known it would. After the way the government botched the Wallowa Valley agreement, the trouble with the Nez Perces wasn't a surprise. Someone had completely erred in designating the boundaries of the new reservation, cheating the Nez Perces out of the best land around Wallowa Lake and the upper Wallowa River. No one would take blame for the mistake, and no one seemed eager to change it. One thing had led to another, the Nez Perce up in arms over being cheated out of the best land, the settlers in a rage that any deal had been made at all. They insisted all Nez Perces belonged on the Lapwai reservation area in Idaho. A war with the Modocs in northern California three years before had rekindled the settlers' belief that no Indian could be trusted and all must be controlled on designated lands. Agent Monteith, the trusted agent who had supported the original Nez Perce claim, was now turning against the Nez Perces because they had begun preaching and practicing their old religion again, rejecting white rule, refusing reservation life, refusing land promised to them by the president of the United States. That promise had been officially broken by the president himself last year, a move sure to set the Nez Perces on fire with outrage.

"I know it's turning into a sorry mess out there, sir," he told Johnson, "but why send me now, after all this time? I don't think there is anything I can do at this point."

"There might not be. The problem is, we need men out there, lots of men. Things are coming to a head, and more of our top men are being sent west to join Generals Crook and Terry. More men are on their way to Washington and Oregon to begin preparing for a possible war. It isn't just the Nez Perce trouble. If we're lucky and send enough men, we can probably end that problem before it explodes into something bigger. I know you had a friendship with the one called Strong Runner. Perhaps he'd listen to you. We want to avoid bloodshed, but if that is to come, then we need good leaders in charge of the men who will have to use force to keep the Nez Perces under control."

"Well, sir, if they're all like Strong Runner, that will not be an easy task. They would rather die than give up that land or go live on a reservation."

Johnson's eyes were bloodshot and misty, and Zack felt grave alarm. "What is it, Colonel Johnson?"

The man sniffed. "There has already been enough bloodshed. We've got to stop it from happening again because . . ." The words seemed to stick in his throat, and Zack could see what a struggle it was for him to finish. "Because we've just lost two hundred and twenty-five soldiers, Colonel Myers, including officers—General George Custer, his brother and brother-in-law, Major Jason Ward . . ."

Jason Ward! Custer! Zack leaned forward. "What on earth happened!"

"The Sioux." Johnson rubbed his eyes. "It happened near the Little Bighorn. I don't have all the details yet. I just got a telegram about it. General Custer and two hundred twenty-five men who had been part of a huge campaign to round up the Sioux and force them onto the reservations in the Dakotas were surrounded by anywhere from three thousand to five thousand Sioux and Cheyenne Indians and massacred. A lot of the men involved were fresh recruits who had never even been in a battle before; some hardly knew how to ride a horse." He shook his head. "No one knows how it happened, except that Custer is known to go against orders and take his men where they don't belong, thinking he's going to cut out his own little piece of glory."

The room hung silent for a moment while both men tried to grasp the enormity of the news.

"It never should have happened," Johnson went on. "There were upward of thirty-seven hundred soldiers on that campaign under Crook and Terry, let alone another two hundred and fifty or so scouts. As far as I am concerned, there is no excuse for Custer getting caught separated from the others like that, but what's done is done. This is the end for the Sioux. They've taken flight in every direction, a lot of them heading for Canada. You can bet we'll break them to pieces and they've made matters worse for the Nez Perces. They've got us mad now, and the Nez Perces will probably suffer for it."

Zack felt torn between a loyalty to the army and soldiers and an understanding of why the massacre had taken place. Jason! Much as he had hated the man, he was sorry he'd died so terribly. "The Nez Perces can't be blamed for this, sir."

"Of course not, but that won't matter to settlers and other soldiers when the word gets out. In their minds Indians are Indians, and the Nez Perces are now considered troublemakers because they're insisting we stick to our promise to give them the Wallowa Valley. Settlers are refusing to move out, and the government is reluctant to go in there and force them out. Grant's order was completely ignored by the governor of Oregon and even Agent Monteith is siding against the Indians. Now that Grant has rescinded the original order, there can't be anything but trouble ahead. Men like you are needed out there, Zack, and I'd like you to go."

Zack sighed with indecision. "I need time to think about it. I would very much like to go, mainly to talk to Strong Runner again, if that's even possible now."

"Don't take more than twenty-four hours to decide. There are already thousands of soldiers chasing after the scattered Sioux. Red Cloud's days of glory are over and he's been on a reservation for some time. It's their new leaders, Sitting Bull and Crazy Horse, who have caused the most trouble, but they've dug their own graves this time. The day of the free Indian is over, Zack, and the Nez Perces have to understand that if they want to live. Someone must convince them to accept what is and not fight it any longer. Grant is sending thousands more soldiers to Idaho and Oregon," Johnson concluded.

Zack knew this would be a blow to Iris. With four children to tend, one of them a new baby daughter, he could not expect her to go along this time. Life had been good here for her and the children, peaceful, settled, just like he'd promised. He would not uproot her again, but except for those first few months right after they were married, they had never been separated. Iris would hate this, would worry herself sick over it. Yet somehow he suspected she would think he should go. Neither of them had ever forgotten Strong Runner and Morning Star, and he had always felt something was unfinished there.

"Give me an answer in the morning," Johnson said. "You'll need to make a fast trip of it since it's nearly July already. At least now you can take a train most of the way."

"Yes, sir." A wave of sorrow engulfed Zack at the reality of what Colonel Johnson had just told him. Two hundred twenty-five men! He remembered how awful he'd felt finding the eighty men under Fetterman so brutally slain, remembered the frightful horror of the wagon box fight and how it had felt to think thousands of Indians were going to swarm over them and mutilate them. What an awful thing Custer's men had suffered! Was the same ugly fighting in store with the Nez Perces? Could he bring himself to raise a rifle against them if it became necessary? He rose from his chair. "I, uh, I'd better go have a talk with my wife."

"Certainly. She'll stay here, of course."

"Yes. I've dragged her around enough since she married me." God, the memories. Something told him he'd need Iris more than ever once he reached Lapwai and got involved in the Nez Perce situation. But he had to do this alone. "Thank you for your confidence, sir."

Johnson rose. "Well, if you're going to leave the army, you might as well have men go out doing something more useful than training and pushing paper, but what happened with Custer is one example of why our recruits *do* need training."

"Yes, sir." Zack saluted the man and left to go tell the horrible news to his wife.

Iris sat staring at her embroidery, trying to grasp what Zack had just told her. "*All* of them? Over two hundred men?"

"All of them." Zack shivered. "There just seems to be no other way to end the Indian situation, Iris, but if there is any hope of ending it differently for the Nez Perces, then we have to try."

She set the embroidery aside and stood up, walking to the brick fireplace, where at last her mantel clock had a proper setting. "I can't imagine you going back out there without me, Zack, and after this thing with Custer, I'll go crazy with worry."

"That was the Sioux. The Nez Perces aren't known to do things like that, although they will fight if confronted. There also aren't as many of them." He walked over to her. "We both know it's out of the question for you to come with me. I won't be out there that long, and even while I'm there I'll most likely be gone a lot, negotiating with Chief Joseph's people at the Wallowa Valley. With four kids to tote along, there just isn't any sense in your going. You can stay right here at Leavenworth."

She turned and moved her arms around him. "We've never been apart, not like this." She looked up at him with tears in her eyes. "You must tell Morning Star how often I have thought of her, how sorry I am we never got to know each other better. My God, Zack, I never saw her again!"

"I'll tell her, if I find her and Strong Runner. For all I know, they've hightailed it for Canada, suspecting trouble."

She shook her head. "They'll stay and fight for the Wallowa. That's what worries me about you going out there."

They embraced with a feeling of desperate longing and aching dread. Jacob walked into the parlor then, carrying his baby sister in his arms. The little girl was crying.

"Nancy skinned her knee," Jacob told his parents.

Iris left Zack to hurry over and soothe her daughter when six-year-old Audra and Michael, three, also came bounding in. Zack watched them all fuss over Nancy, Audra and Michael trying to get Iris's attention away from their little sister. Zack thought how amazing and wonderful it was to have such a big family. This was the kind of thing he could only dream about once. Would he lose it all by going back to Idaho?

He studied Jacob, close to the age he was when he witnessed his family murdered. Knowing how he felt about his own son now, how innocent and dependent Jacob was, he found it amazing he had survived such a horror and managed to find a normal life for himself. That was thanks to Howard Shaver . . . and thanks to the beautiful woman who had given him this family and had put up with so much agony in return. He hated leaving her behind. Only two months earlier she'd received word that her grandfather had died. He was all she had, and he prayed this whole thing would not end in disaster. Whatever the outcome, he knew he had to go; Iris knew it too.

Iris stood watching the busy street below. Even at night Denver did not sleep. It was gold that had first brought people there, and just like what had happened all over the West, they had stayed and built a city. This was the crux of the whole Indian problem, her own people's constant desire to breach new frontiers, find free land, expand their territory, take advantage of any wealth that could be gained. Somewhere below a few men laughed. *Yes,* she thought, *you can laugh. You've rid yourself of the Cheyenne, and soon, farther north, the Sioux will also be killed off or put onto a reservation.*

She turned and looked at Zack, lying in bed in their hotel room. They had agreed to let one of the other officers' families at Fort Leavenworth watch the children while she came this far with him. She wished she could go all the way, but this would have to be the end of her journey. She would go back to the children. Zack would take a train from there to Cheyenne, another west into Nevada, then head north to Lapwai.

It frightened and saddened her to leave this man who was her whole world. She walked over to the bed and lay back down, and a strong arm came around her. "I was wondering when you'd come back here."

"You're awake?" She turned to him.

His answer was to lean over and nuzzle her ear while he moved a hand up her leg and over her bottom, pulling at her drawers. "I've been too worried and lost in thought for this, Iris," he said softly, "but tomorrow we go our separate ways."

She needed no more explanation. She'd been wanting this too, but knew he had a lot on his mind. He was shirtless against the warm night air, and she kissed his shoulder, his neck, met his mouth in a sweet, desperate kiss. This could be the last time she shared her husband's body, felt his skin against her own, felt him inside her.

Zack, her precious Zack. Somehow amid the heated kisses and pressing hands her nightgown and drawers came off, as did his own underwear. Suddenly they could not get enough of each other. She took him with groaning ecstasy, arching against him, aching to remember every touch, every kiss, the sound of his whisper in her ear. All these years of loving and hardship came to this moment that could be their last.

He surged inside of her, feeling his own desperate need, giving, taking, making love almost savagely. He shuddered with a mixture of satisfaction and anxiousness when his life spilled forth, and he settled beside her, wanting just to hold her close, never let go. He heard a train whistle in the distance. "It's like chasing the sun, Iris."

She traced her fingers over the hairs of his chest. "What is?"

"Trying to find an answer to the situation with the Indians. Trying to find a way to make it all work. There is no end to it. Every day the sun rises and falls. A man could chase it forever and never catch it, racing around the earth to no avail. Trying to solve the Indian problem is the same thing, reaching for answers but never finding them. Strong Runner used that phrase once, and I never forgot it."

"Maybe you're chasing your own soul."

He stroked her hair. "Don't let the kids forget me."

"I would never let that happen." She leaned up and kissed his chin. "We'll all be fine, and you'll be back with us in time. You *are* coming back, Zack. God will bring you back to me."

They clung together in sleep, awoke to sunshine, washed and dressed in near silence, not wanting the day to begin. Their things were packed, and a carriage took them to the train station, where other officers and soldiers waited, all headed for Lapwai. The conductor for Zack's train shouted for people to board, and never since falling in love with Zack Myers had Iris felt so lonely and afraid.

One last embrace. How she prayed she would feel these arms again. He boarded the train, and she could see him through a window. He waved, and the train whistle blew as the engine got under way.

"Good-bye, Zack," she whispered, tears brimming in her

eyes. "God bless you, my love." She watched the train until it disappeared, then turned to see an old Indian sitting on the platform, begging. It made her think of Strong Runner, so proud and handsome and determined to take care of himself and his own. God forbid he should ever be reduced to sitting idle and broken like that beggar. No, he would never allow it to come to that. Nor would most of the Nez Perces under Chief Joseph. They would fight and die first, and that was what frightened her.

32

Z ack waited anxiously with others who had been appointed under General Howard to council with Chief Joseph and his followers. A cold November wind stung his ears as he sat on his horse, watching for the arrival of Joseph and his most important cohorts, which Zack was sure would include Strong Runner. Scouts had said they were due to arrive any moment. In a large building used for meetings and dances, General Howard waited with David Jerome, a Mr. Barstow, Bill Stickney, and Major Wood. The first three were governmental delegates who worked for the Bureau of Indian Affairs.

Zack thought that if George Custer had survived the Little Bighorn, he'd like to kill him himself. If not for his blunder and the ensuing slaughter, the Nez Perces would not be in such a fix. Ever since the Custer massacre, whites everywhere had given a general outcry for the removal of all Indians, peaceful or not, to reservation areas, where they could be guarded and controlled.

Finally the Indians began arriving, and being the designated greeter, Zack rode out to escort them. The Indian riding in front was a stunning picture of good looks, pride, and dignity. His dark eyes showed intelligence, but his rugged face betrayed a man weighed with the problems of a whole Indian nation on his shoulders. Zack knew without asking that he had to be Chief Joseph. "Welcome to Lapwai," he told the man.

Zack pointed to a building in the distance, and cavalry soldiers sat at straight attention in a double row to form a welcoming pathway to the building. "General Howard waits there for you," he told Joseph. "I am Lieutenant-Colonel Zachary Myers. You are Chief Joseph?"

The man nodded. "So. You have come back."

Zack felt pleasant surprise at the remark. "Strong Runner told you about me?"

Joseph nodded. "He said you are a fair man, with an understanding the others do not have. We were afraid that this might be a trap for us, but if you are here, I think there is nothing to fear. Strong Runner did not want to come. He holds back." He turned, pointing to a stand of trees. "There. Our families wait there too. Strong Runner is ready to come in with other warriors and save us if these soldiers here should try to arrest us."

Zack shook his head. "They want only to talk. I promise you that. I will come and sit in on the talks, but I will go out and try to get Strong Runner to come in too. You tell General Howard to wait for Strong Runner. I think it's important for him to be there."

Joseph nodded. He rode forward, followed by a contingent of formidable-looking warriors. Zack turned to his lieutenant. "I'm going out to find Strong Runner."

"Yes, sir."

He left the fort grounds, riding past the rest of Joseph's delegation as he headed for the stand of trees. Zack pulled his hat down a little farther on his forehead against the wind, and a light snow on the ground muffled his horse's hooves. He thought with unnerving foreboding how easily these people could hide. At first he hardly noticed them, but as he got closer he realized there were at least fifty men on grandlooking Appaloosas, and half again as many women and children, wrapped in blankets, huddled together.

As he got even closer, one man rode forward. He wore

heavy winter leggings and knee-high moccasins of what looked like bearskin, the fur turned inward. His coat also looked like bearskin, and his head was covered with the skin of a fox, feet and all, the head of the fox forming the top of the hat. The warrior's horse was painted with colorful circles, and the man carried a Spencer rifle.

It was Strong Runner. Zack shouted his name, thrilled to see him again, to know he was all right, alive and well. He rode closer, and he could see the same joy in Strong Runner's eyes. Zack suspected Strong Runner had just as much urge to ride closer and embrace as he did, but they halted their horses, facing each other from a few feet away.

"Zack Myers," Strong Runner said with the sly grin Zack had missed. "So, now you are a lieutenant-colonel. The gold leaves on your shoulders are now silver."

Zack grinned, always impressed by how well this man knew soldier regalia. "Don't ask me how I got the promotion. All I've been doing is paperwork and training cavalry back at Fort Leavenworth in Kansas."

Strong Runner nodded, nudging his horse a little closer. "Your woman?"

"She's fine. She's had three more children since leaving here. I have two daughters and two sons now. They all stayed back at Leavenworth."

Strong Runner nodded. "That is too bad. Morning Star would like to have seen your woman again."

"And Iris would have liked the same. She talks about Morning Star often, Strong Runner. I just didn't want her to have to make the long trip."

Strong Runner eyed him closely. "And why did *you* come, Lieutenant-Colonel Zack Myers?"

Zack's smile faded. "I think you know why. General Howard wants to talk with Chief Joseph and the rest of you. They know how I feel about the situation, that I know you. They asked me to be a part of the talks."

"They asked you to convince me to come live at Lapwai?"

Their eyes held in challenge. "I'm not so sure it has to be that way. Why don't you take me to see your family, then come to the council with me. I assure you there are no tricks to this. No one is going to be arrested. Besides, Colonel Porter is gone now. General Howard and I are in charge."

Strong Runner looked toward the fort, then back at Zack. "I will go. Come with me first and see my family. We will leave as soon as the talks are done, and I cannot say when or if we will see each other again."

Zack followed him to the stand of trees, watched a woman rise and smile. She was still very pretty, giving hint to what a beautiful young maiden she must have been when Strong Runner married her. He caught a look of relief on her face, as though she thought everything would be all right now that he was there. It made him uneasy. Morning Star apparently trusted him, could probably convince Strong Runner to trust him; but he worried that anything he or General Howard or anyone else told them would be turned into a lie by a fickle government that could not seem to make up its mind about the Indian situation.

"You have come back, Zack Myers," Morning Star said.

Others watched cautiously as Zack rode closer to her. "The army is a little short of men," he answered. "I did not expect this, but I'm glad to be here, glad to see you and Strong Runner once more."

Morning Star held a little girl in her arms who Zack guessed to be about five years old. "How is your wife? Has she had more children?"

Zack was touched that both of them had asked right away about Iris. "We have four children now, nine, six, three, and one—two sons and two daughters."

Morning Star smiled with genuine pleasure. "I am glad. This is our youngest, Little Turtle," she said, indicating the girl in her arms. She turned to three other children. "This is Dancing Girl. She is seven summers. You remember our first two sons. Jumping Bear is ten years old now, and Wolf Boy is twelve. He is learning to be a good hunter. He is very good with rifle and bow. Soon he will go off alone and fast and pray so that he can find his guiding spirit, discover what our God wants him to do with his life."

Zack studied the boy, big for his age. He looked every bit his father, and Zack caught a haughty, daring spirit in Wolf Boy's dark eyes. He knew Indians considered a boy a man at a much earlier age than whites did. It made him sick to think that if they ended up at war with these people, boys like Strong Runner's oldest son would probably fight alongside their fathers. He turned his attention to Strong Runner, who was watching him with that all-knowing, unnerving look in his eyes, as though to read his thoughts.

"We go now," Strong Runner told him. "I wish to hear what your General Howard has to say to Chief Joseph."

Zack glanced at the man's family once more. Strong Runner wanted them to be happy, to live a peaceful life, to have warm backs and full bellies, not to be in danger. Zack wanted the same thing, thinking of a time when he would have cared nothing for these people. He nodded to Strong Runner. "Yes, I think you should be there. The government representatives will value your opinion as much as Joseph's." He tipped his hat to Morning Star. "He'll be safe," he told her, remembering how she hated her husband to go to Lapwai.

He turned his horse and headed back to the fort. Strong Runner rode beside him, the biting wind whipping fresh snow in little swirls around the horses' feet. "The time of the cold moon is upon us," Strong Runner said. He stared straight ahead, saying the words with a deep, prophetic sadness.

They rode on silently for several seconds. "Yes," Zack finally answered.

Joseph spoke with such wisdom that General Howard hardly knew how to answer him, Zack wrote in his letter to Iris.

> *Howard told him he would have to give up the Wallowa Valley and come to Lapwai. He told Howard that when his God, which he calls the Creative Power, formed the earth, He did not make lines on it or divide it in any other way and say that this people should live here, and that people there. He said that wherever a man is born, and where his ancestors are buried, is sacred land, and that all the gold white men could pay for it would never be enough to make them leave.*

He stopped writing and leaned back in his chair, wondering if he would ever see Strong Runner again. He and Joseph had flatly refused to accept any offer to leave the Wallowa Valley. The entire situation was headed smack in the direction he dreaded most. The commissioners and Agent Monteith were becoming adamant that if the Nez Perces were not going to voluntarily give up the Wallowa and come to Lapwai, then they would have to be forced into submission. General Howard, called the "Christian General" by many, had become very angry at the council meeting, calling Joseph a malcontent who illegally denied the government's jurisdiction over all Indians. After the meeting Howard had carried on in private about how sinful it was that the Nez Perces had turned away from Christianity and had reverted to their own Washani faith, which he considered nothing short of devil worship.

Nothing had gone as Zack had hoped. He took up his pen again.

> It's all just as I had feared. Strong Runner, Joseph, all of them refuse to leave, and Agent Monteith is demanding that soldiers be sent into the Wallowa to drag them out. What a foolish request! He fully underestimates what a difficult task that would be. Not only that, but we would also have to deal with the Upper Palouse tribes. Now that the settlers think we're going to drive out the Nez Perces, they want us to put the Palouse on a reservation also. They are not a part of this problem, but the settlers are making them a part of it.

Zack felt haunted by the look he'd seen in Strong Runner's eyes after the talks failed. That look of tragedy, hopelessness, victory singed with the knowledge that it would be short-lived—he had seen it in Red Eagle, Thomas, the warriors who'd attacked his men at the wagon box fight.

Joseph had said flat-out that he would not leave the Wallowa until he was forced to leave. Zack shivered from a draft in the room. What a miserable, impossible feat it would be for soldiers to dig the Nez Perces out of the Wallowa in this weather, let alone the possibility they could flee into the mountains, country they knew better than most men knew their own backyards.

> I am going to try to talk to Strong Runner again on my own. I pray we can avoid bloodshed. I suspect Strong

Runner's oldest son, Wolf Boy, will also be expected to
fight like the warrior he wants to be. He has the same
pride and fire in his eyes as his father.

Don't worry for me, Iris. Worry for them. Howard is
being obstinate and arrogant. I would like to say it is hard
to believe the wonderful decision Grant made to allow the
Nez Perces to remain in the Wallowa has turned into
something so dangerous and ugly, but considering how ev
ery other peace talk and treaty with other tribes has
turned out, this is no surprise. It seems to be over for the
Sioux, with Sitting Bull in Canada, Red Cloud quietly resigned to reservation life, and Crazy Horse dead.

I miss you. You probably know I'll want to stay here
until this is solved, even if it goes beyond my retirement
date. I feel as though I would somehow be deserting
Strong Runner if I leave before we find an answer to the
problem. I love you so. I ache to hold you and to see my
children. Give them my love.

He put the pen down again, rereading the letter. How could
he have survived without her? She had taught him so much
about love and patience and forgiveness. Through all these
years Iris Gray had been his strength. Even in her absence he
could feel that love and strength, felt her with him spiritually.
"I may need that strength more than either of us knows," he
said softly.

The familiar sound of wolves howling in the distant hills
reminded him of all he'd been through to reach this point in
his life, and Iris had been with him through the worst of it.
He thought the wolves seemed farther away than they had
when he was here years earlier, their howling not quite so
pervasive.

He started to fold the letter, heard distant gunfire. The
sound pierced his heart as if the bullet had hit him. Wolf
hunters. It was a common sound now. They built fires, baited
the wolves . . . settlers, who blamed wolves for every head of
missing cattle, who were sure all wolves were out to kill every
chicken and cow they owned, maybe kill their little children.
Another gunshot . . . wildlife being slowly snuffed out, something the Indians could hardly bear. How long would it be

before the same thing happened to the Nez Perces, all in the name of settlement and progress?

He sat there alone listening . . . waiting. He heard no more howling.

The Indian camp came alive at the sight of a soldier riding in alone. Unlike the hunting camp where Zack had stayed when Iris was ill, he felt an entirely different reaction this time as he was surrounded by Nez Perces. The friendly openness was not there. Many of those who lined up to watch him ride in were young men with great animosity and challenge in their eyes, black hair hanging long in defiance of those "tame" Nez Perces at Lapwai who had cut their hair the white man's way. They looked eager and full of fire, and Zack felt rumblings of danger. If not for the fact that Strong Runner was somewhere among them, he wondered just how safe he would be.

It was a misty spring morning in the Wallowa Valley, a sudden warm spell causing the remaining melting spring snows to throw out so much moisture that it literally hung in the air. The smoke from many cooking fires also hung low, creating an eerie bluish cast all around, so that it was impossible even to see the other end of the huge village. He had come there with only a handful of men and a scout, all of whom he'd left two miles back, deciding to come into the camp alone. More and more men, women, and children filed out of tipis to get a look at him, dogs barked incessantly, more children laughed and played somewhere in the distance. He hoped that was a sound that could always be heard, except it would have to be at Lapwai. Again the government wanted to talk. It was his job to get Joseph to go back to Lapwai to speak again with General Howard.

Some of the women smiled and pointed, speaking in their own tongue; others gave him looks of derision. The younger warriors followed along on foot, taunting him, asking if he had come to tell Joseph the soldiers and government had given up and would go away now.

"We have been here another winter with no trouble," one of them shouted. "You see? We do not need your government, and we also make no trouble for the whites, so leave us alone."

"Are you afraid, soldier blue? another taunted. "You better go back where you belong. You tell the white settlers that too. This valley is ours."

"I would like to see a soldier fight a Nez Perce warrior hand to hand," another gloated. "He could never win such a fight. The soldiers are cowards. They fight from far away with their big guns; they are so afraid to get close to an Indian."

Yes, the mood of the Nez Perces was entirely different from the friendly people they had been for so many years. Zack halted his horse. "I am looking for Strong Runner and Joseph."

A tall, slender young man stepped forward. "My father's dwelling is up there," he said, pointing to a rise where the village stretched out to over a half-mile in length. "He will see you coming and come out to greet you."

Zack frowned. "Wolf Boy?"

He stepped back. "I am called Man Of Wolves now. Over the winter I found a den of wolves and I slept with them. They did not harm me. We share the same spirit."

Zack was astounded at how much taller the boy had grown over the winter. He was only thirteen, but he looked closer to sixteen or seventeen. "Well, I'm glad for you, Man Of Wolves. You've found your spirit way."

The boy nodded proudly. He turned and said something to the others, apparently ordering them to stop taunting Zack. They sniffed or shrugged and walked away. "I will take you to my father," Man Of Wolves said then. "I will show you how fast I can run. My father says I am as fast as he once was."

He sprinted away, and Zack had to urge his horse into a near gallop to keep up with him. The boy arrived at his father's camp laughing as he ran up to Strong Runner. "I made his horse run," he said. He grabbed a piece of jerked meat from a rack, where it hung to dry, and ran off again. Strong Runner walked up to Zack's horse, grinning proudly.

"Now you know what a fast runner I once was," he said. "I am not much slower now, but my son can beat me with those long, young legs of his."

Zack grinned as he dismounted. "He's turning into quite a man, Strong Runner. He told me he has a new name now."

Strong Runner nodded. "Man Of Wolves. It is fitting." His smile faded. "And what brings you to my camp, Zack Myers?

I have not seen you since the November moon. I would like to think this is just a friendly visit, but I think perhaps it is more than that." He ordered Jumping Bear to tend to Zack's horse. Zack noticed the boy had been helping his father make arrows. He set aside one to which he had been tying feathers and came over to take his horse. Zack met Strong Runner's eyes.

"Are those arrows for hunting?"

Their eyes held in challenge. "For hunting," Strong Runner answered. "Some animals have four legs. Some have two."

Zack breathed deeply in disappointment. More talks were not going to help. He could already see that. "I, too, wish this were just a friendly visit, Strong Runner, but the situation we have now leaves no time for friendly visits. I need to talk to Joseph."

Strong Runner nodded. "I will take you to him." He turned and looked toward a tipi just a few yards farther up the hill. "You see? He already knows you are here. He waits."

Zack saw the tall, dignified leader of a proud people standing in front of his tipi, watching them. He thought how much more respectable and wise Chief Joseph was than many of the officers and governmental representatives he'd dealt with. This whole thing seemed ridiculous. There was no reason to kick these people out of this valley. It was happening simply because the whites wanted it to themselves and didn't want to be "bothered" with the Indian problem any longer.

Strong Runner led Zack toward Joseph, and on the way Zack looked over to see Morning Star hanging more meat to dry. She smiled at him, her two young daughters standing beside her staring curiously. The littlest one suddenly smiled, showing dimples in her beautiful, dark face. She had the sweet, chubby look that made a person want to pick her up and hug her. Zack grinned in return, suddenly missing his own daughters terribly. Audra was only one year younger than Dancing Girl and one year older than Little Turtle. He hated missing one day of his own children growing up. Little Nancy would be almost two now. He ached to hold her, to hold their mother.

"Strong Runner," he said before reaching Joseph. Strong Runner stopped and looked at him, waiting. "I just want you to know . . ." He sighed. "I don't even know how to say this."

"That no matter how this turns out, you will always think of me as a friend."

Their eyes held in mutual heartache. "Yes. I've come to understand a lot of things. If I could change what is happening here, I would do it. I'm trying. But I am only one man. I am begging you, if this comes to conflict, please bring your family to Lapwai and give it up. I hate the thought of you and Morning Star and your children being involved in this mess. Life isn't so terrible at Lapwai, and maybe in time—"

Strong Runner shook his head. "It is not about how good or bad life would be at Lapwai. It is the fact that we would be taken care of like little children, with no pride. They will teach my children they must forget Nez Perce ways, forget their language, their customs. They will be taught to cut their hair and worship a foreign God and tear up Mother Earth in farming. They will be told that everything about their way of life is wrong, and they will lose the spirit way. I do not want that for my children. Some things are *worth* fighting and dying for, Zack Myers. And if a man must live with no pride, it is better not to live at all." He looked up toward Joseph, back at Zack. "But it is the same for me. No matter what happens, I will always think of you as my friend. I will know that your heart is good, that you sincerely tried to keep this from happening. You must find your own spirit way, Zack Myers, and follow it. You have lost the hatred that made your soul sick, and that is good."

He turned and led Zack to Joseph. Zack's legs felt heavier, as did his heart.

33

Zack did not expect a good ending to the council, but he prayed for a miracle. Chief Joseph had told him that he and his brother, Ollokot, also an honored leader, had already been discussing another council with General Howard because of rumors that even more soldiers were being sent to Lapwai. Zack was forced to admit that that was true.

"They can be here for only one reason," Joseph had said. "To force us to go to Lapwai. This piece of Mother Earth belongs to us, and we will not leave it."

Zack watched the Nez Perce representatives ride in and take their places in a semicircle, facing General Howard, Agent Monteith, and the commissioners. Strong Runner was among them, but today he would give no special indication of their personal friendship. Zack expected that. He stood facing the Nez Perce leaders, struggling with his feelings for Strong Runner. He could already feel trouble brewing because these nontreaty Nez Perces, who had reverted to their old Washani religion, had brought with them their fiery religious leader, Toohoolhoolzote, to speak for them; the Palouse brought their own religious leader, Husishusis Kute. Both were vehement in declaring the earth belonged to the Nez Perces and could not be divided up. Both were responsible for firing up the Nez Perces and Palouse to fight for what was rightfully theirs. Worse, General Howard hated both holy men and was adamant the Nez Perces should come to Lapwai and be Christianized again. In private, he had already referred to Husishusis Kute as "oily and wily," and to Toohoolhoolzote as "deep-chested, thick-necked," an "ugly, obstinate savage of the worst type, who betrays his strong hatred for all Caucasians with every word he speaks."

When it was apparent those two religious leaders were going to speak for the Indians, Zack knew trouble was at hand. Howard sat before the council in full dress uniform, his heavy beard neatly combed, the right sleeve of his uniform pinned to the side of the jacket. He was determined to control the situation with force and authority, showing Chief Joseph and the others through a show of many soldiers and his own stern countenance that they had no choice but to obey the government command that they come to Lapwai.

Toohoolhoolzote opened with the firm statement that Chief Joseph and the Nez Perces of the Wallowa never signed the Thief Treaty of 1863 and were not a part of that agreement. That had already been acknowledged once by the United States government, and the white leaders had gone back on their word in now declaring they must give up the Wallowa. It was theirs by "inheritance," and they were not ready to sell it or give it away. That land was sacred and legally belonged to the Nez Perces. To leave it would be to go against Indian law and their deepest religious beliefs.

Zack could see General Howard growing angrier with every word Toohoolhoolzote spoke. His cheeks above his beard were turning redder with fury, his eyes blazing arrogance. Finally he lost his temper with the Indian holy man. "Twenty times over you repeat that the earth is your mother!" he shouted. "Let us hear it no more, but come to business at once!"

"You white people get together, measure the earth, and then divide it," Toohoolhoolzote replied with equal defiance, "so I want you to say directly what you mean."

"What I mean is that I am here to enforce the law!" Howard answered with authority. "You Nez Perces signed a treaty in 1863 that gave you the land around Lapwai as a reservation. I am here to make sure *all* of you obey that treaty and come to Lapwai!"

"*Part* of the Nez Perces gave up their land," Toohoolhoolzote answered. "I never did! The earth is part of my body, and I never gave up the earth. What person pretends to divide the land and put me on it?"

"*I* am that man," Howard answered. "I stand here for the president, and there is no spirit, good or bad, that will hinder me. My orders are plain, and will be executed."

Zack glanced at Strong Runner, who was watching General Howard with murder in his eyes.

"You are trifling with the law of the earth," Toohoolhoolzote answered. "The treaty Nez Perces may do what they like, but I and Chief Joseph and the other nontreaty Indians will not come to the reservation."

Howard rose, eyes blazing even hotter. "This is the kind of bad advice you give the Nez Perces! For that you and the rest of them will end up in Indian Territory to the south! I'll see it happen if it takes years!"

Zack noticed Strong Runner's whole body tense. "We will never go there!" he growled.

"Captain Perry!" Howard shouted, never taking his eyes from Toohoolhoolzote, ignoring Strong Runner. "I want this man arrested!"

The entire entourage on both sides grew extremely tense. Zack prayed Strong Runner would not do something stupid and get himself shot, for he looked ready to lunge at Howard. Chief Joseph watched in silent indignation. Zack could see the man expected this, was ready for it, wisely primed to hold his temper. He said something to Strong Runner in his own tongue, and Strong Runner took a deep breath and looked at the chief, barking something back to him, his whole countenance in a rage. Captain Perry stepped forward, taking hold of Toohoolhoolzote's arm. "Come with me," he said sternly.

Toohoolhoolzote gave a last glare at Howard. "You will regret this day, General." He turned and walked off with Perry and two other soldiers, and the rest of the Nez Perces and the Palouse watched silently. The tension in the air was near stifling.

"Now," Howard told Joseph. "Will you come to Lapwai?"

Joseph folded his arms, his eyes reflecting that terrible tragedy Zack had seen before. "You are like the grizzly," he told Howard, "and we are like the deer. You leave us no choice."

"You have showed us the rifle," one called Yellow Wolf said. Zack had met him the day he went to the Nez Perce camp to talk to Joseph. He was Joseph's nephew. "We know the only thing left if we do not come to Lapwai is to fight."

Zack's heart ached at the agony in Strong Runner's eyes. He remained silent.

"If we fight, we would have to flee to the mountains," Ollokot spoke up. "I love my wife and children. I do not want to leave them to fight soldiers."

One by one the Nez Perce leaders, including a very reluctant Strong Runner, agreed to leave the Wallowa and come to Lapwai. Zack wanted to take heart in the surrender, hoping maybe this really was the end of the struggle; but the Indian resignation to settle for reservation life seemed too superficial, too easy. To see it actually happen would be another thing.

"I will give you letters to take with you," Howard told Joseph, Strong Runner, and the other leaders. "You will be moving many hundreds of Indians across the valley and the plateau leading here to Lapwai, many women and children. It might alarm some of the settlers. If any of them gives you trouble, the letters will explain what you are doing and that you mean no one any harm. The letters will help prevent trouble."

Joseph nodded. "When must we be here?"

Howard straightened victoriously. "Thirty days."

Strong Runner stepped forward. "That is not enough time! Many of us are settled there, with cattle and horses grazing over many acres. We must round up all our herds, pack everything, sell some of our things."

"Thirty days," Howard repeated.

"We have much to visit and pray over and say good-bye to," Joseph put in. "All that land is sacred to us. Our women will weep. Even some of our men will weep. We need time to say good-bye to our very souls. The bones of our parents and grandparents lie there."

"Thirty days," Howard said a third time.

Strong Runner turned and stormed away. Zack moved

around behind the contingent of soldiers, hurrying to catch up with Strong Runner. He called out to him, and Strong Runner turned, holding a defiant stance.

"I'm damn sorry, Strong Runner."

The man nodded, holding his chin high. "So am I, Zack Myers. Sorry for the earth and how she will be treated by you whites; sorry there can be no friendship between us; sorry Joseph and the others gave in so easily. I go along with this only because I alone cannot fight the whole army."

"I hate this as much as you do, but it can't be changed. To do this any other way would only mean the blood of many Nez Perces, including women and children."

Strong Runner held his eyes steadily. "And what about you? If you have to fight us, would *you* kill our women and children?"

"Would you kill *white* women and children?"

Strong Runner thought long and hard. "If I had to."

Zack nodded. "Then I guess a man just does what he has to do at the moment, doesn't he?"

"I suppose. But we have agreed to come peacefully, and soon you will leave the army and go home. It is done."

Zack prayed that was true. "I suppose it is." He felt a dull ache in his chest. "I will never forget you, Strong Runner. I will never forget what I have learned from you."

Strong Runner put out his hand. "And when you whites destroy this earth, remember that I warned you it would happen."

Zack grasped his wrist. "As you said, you are only one man. It's the same for me. I'm just glad this is ending peacefully."

Strong Runner released his grip. "At least you leave with your pride and dignity. I have lost everything." His voice broke on the last words, and he turned away.

Zack knew the man did not want him to see the tears in his eyes, so he let him go. He turned and looked across the crowd at Howard, who was still talking to Joseph. "Damn you!" he muttered. "Damn all of you!"

"This is a good place to spend a few days before we go to Lapwai." Morning Star spoke the words to Seeks The Sun, a woman widowed the year before when her husband, Eagle Robe, was murdered by a white settler named Larry Ott. As with all acts against Indians, nothing had been done to reprimand Ott or bring him to any kind of justice. It had just been another incident that had angered the Nez Perces and caused them to hold out so long in giving up their land.

The two women watched their sons riding across the prairie, racing horses. "The young ones will find life on the reservation hard," Seeks The Sun told Morning Star. "Especially my son. He is still so full of hatred over his father's death."

Morning Star could understand the young man's anger. Wahlitits hated the whites, was one of those who could still stir up trouble. She worried he would drag Man Of Wolves into that trouble, for her own son had become fast friends with Wahlitits and practically worshipped the older boy, who longed to be a true warrior. She tried to ease her own worries by dwelling on the beautiful moment.

"We must be glad for today," she told Seeks The Sun. "This place where the camas grows has always been a gathering place for our people, and for a little while we can pretend nothing has changed." She laid out more camas bulbs to dry. This was where they gathered the bulbs, which felt and tasted very much like a potato. They had decided that on their way to Lapwai they would gather the bulbs to take with them, something they could use to continue feeding themselves for a while rather than take government rations. "We can see our beautiful mountains in the distance, see the purple flowers that grow across the prairie, gather the camas bulbs. Here, for two or three days, we can still be ourselves. The men will do a little hunting, we will do the gathering, as in old times."

Seeks The Sun looked at her with sad eyes. "Always you try to see the good side. Do you not realize there is no good side? At least you still have your husband. Your sons have their father."

Wahlitits rode toward them then, chased on horseback by Man Of Wolves. Wahlitits and even Strong Runner had been even harder to contain since white settlers brazenly ran off a good share of the Nez Perces' herd of prized horses before they could gather their stock together to bring to Lapwai. Many of the warriors had wanted to go back on their promise then and there, to make war instead. The theft of the horses was just another blow to their already decimated pride, and when white authorities refused to do anything about it, Chief Joseph had had to do some fast talking to keep the younger warriors from riding against the whites.

Wahlitits gave out a war cry and rode his horse right up to his mother, deliberately riding over the camas bulbs then, smashing many of them.

"Wahlitits, why are you doing this!" Seeks The Sun screamed at her son.

He rode over more of the bulbs, then approached his mother with defiance and hatred in his eyes. Man Of Wolves rode up beside him, looking a little sorry, but Morning Star could see he was in a mood to follow Wahlitits's dictates.

"Why do you even gather the bulbs!" Wahlitits shouted at his mother. "What good will it do? For a little while we can feed ourselves. *Then* what? Then we go begging to the white man's government! I saw you weep when we had to leave the Wallowa. I saw many of the women weep! It is not fair! None of it is fair!"

"Do not take your anger out on this precious food," Seeks The Sun chastised him. "It is wrong. It took many women to dig so many bulbs. You ruin their work! If you want to show your revenge, then show it against the man who killed your father, not your own people!"

Wahlitits halted his horse. "Perhaps I *should*," he answered. "There is a better way, Mother. Going to Lapwai with our heads hung low is not the answer. Perhaps the others are willing to give up their pride, but not me!" He swung his horse around and rode off, shouting for two of his friends, Swan Necklace and Red Moccasin Tops. "I go and kill the man who killed my father!" he shouted. "Come and join me!"

"Wahlitits!" Seeks The Sun cried. "No! I was wrong! I did not mean you should do this! No! You will bring the soldiers on us!"

Morning Star watched with dread as the other two warriors, also among those eager for a fight, ran for their horses, all three of them shouting war cries. She looked up at Man Of Wolves, pleading with her eyes that he not follow.

Man Of Wolves looked at her sadly. "Father has always told me to follow my heart," he said. "My heart tells me to help Wahlitits avenge his father's death, as I would do if it were my father who was murdered."

"Do not go, my son," Morning Star pleaded. "Speak with Strong Runner first. You are so young."

He tossed his head. "I am old enough." He turned his horse. "I love you, my mother," he called to her as he rode off.

"Man Of Wolves! Do not go!" Morning Star dropped her basket of bulbs and ran toward the main village, where tipis had been erected for a stay of a few days before going on to Lapwai. She screamed Strong Runner's name, found him helping Little Eagle skin some rabbits. Morning Star breathlessly told Strong Runner what had happened. "You must go after him!" she told her husband.

Strong Runner looked in the direction his son had ridden. Already the four young men were out of sight. He turned his gaze to Morning Star, agony in his eyes. "He is a man now. He has chosen his way."

"Strong Runner—"

"To stop him now would be to destroy what pride he has left. And it would not keep Wahlitits from doing what he must do. Whether Man Of Wolves is with him or not, he will do what his heart tells him, and he will bring much trouble upon us. I have seen it coming. The young ones cannot accept what must be, and that is their right."

"But we *all* will suffer for it!" Morning Star answered, rage in her eyes. "Jumping Bear, Dancing Girl, Little Turtle . . . my sister and her children—all of us, Strong Runner! We've come so close . . . so close to peace, to settling all of this with no bloodshed!"

Strong Runner came closer, still holding a bloody knife in his hand. "Did you really think that could happen, woman?"

Her eyes teared. "I prayed and prayed that it was over, that there would be no more danger to you and our family. If the soldiers come because of this, I know who will be leading the warriors against them."

Strong Runner drew in his breath. "Tell me you would not be proud."

Morning Star turned away, the tears coming harder. A moment ago she had felt the brief wonder of peace and happiness, had experienced for a moment what life might have been like . . . once. She fell to the ground sobbing her son's name.

Everything I was afraid would happen has come to be, Iris read in Zack's latest letter, delivered by the fastest route possible. She had already read the letter once, knew that by then Zack Myers was in the middle of a campaign against the Nez Perces.

> *A young Nez Perce warrior named Wahlitits, whose father was murdered by a white man last year, apparently decided to avenge his father's death. All was going well, Chief Joseph's people on their way to Lapwai. But Wahlitits and three other young men, one of them Strong Runner's oldest son, raided several white settlements along the Salmon River, killing three men and wounding another. The whites now believe the Nez Perces have chosen war rather than peace. I think more violence could have been avoided if Howard would have first tried once more to talk to Joseph, who took his people to White Bird Canyon to wait for the soldiers they knew were coming to escort them to Lapwai. I think they went to the canyon because they knew they could protect themselves there if the soldiers were out for blood. Needless to say, General Howard wanted just that. He refused to let me go in and talk to Joseph and Strong Runner. As soon as his troops came upon Joseph's people at the canyon, they started firing without asking one question first.*
>
> *The fools! They should have known that was country Joseph knew all too well. They were dug in good and well protected. A lot of men were lost. I think the Nez Perces are pretty confused right now. They've been joined by young chief Looking Glass, whose father was among those who signed the original treaty back in '55. If not for Howard, Looking Glass would not have taken his people to join the now-hostile Nez Perces. Howard attacked Looking Glass's village with no provocation. They were among the*

*peaceful Nez Perces. Now he has riled them and made
matters worse.*

*By the time you get this letter I will be among the
troops ordered to chase down the Nez Perces. They have
headed into the Bitterroots along the Lolo Trail. You know
what a rugged, impossible route that is. I was ready to
come home, when all of this happened, but now I have to
stay in this to the end, Iris. I think you understand why.*

*Pray for me, and pray for Strong Runner and his fam-
ily. I love you. Remember that. Take care of my children.
Don't let them forget me.*

How she hated those words, words that made it sound as
though he were not coming back. "Oh, God, Zack," she
moaned. "Why did it have to come to this? Why?"

"Mother? What's wrong?" Jacob came into the parlor. "You
crying?"

She took a deep breath before turning around. "You might
as well know that I've received a letter from your father. It
looks as though they're involved in an all-out war with the
Nez Perces."

"They are? Why! Didn't the last letter say the Indians decided to go to Lapwai and give up?"

Iris nodded. "It's a little complicated, and you and Audra
have to get to school. We'll all talk tonight at the supper table
and I'll explain."

"Could Dad get hurt? I mean, wouldn't that Indian,
Strong Runner, keep them from hurting Dad?"

How she wished that could be so, but in war, men shooting at each other without even seeing each other's faces, how
could Zack be any more protected than anyone else? "We just
have to pray for your father, Jacob. He's an experienced man.
I'm sure he'll be all right." How she wished she truly believed
that. "You be a brave boy now. Your father would want that.
I'm sure he'll be home by this fall, certainly by Christmas."

Jacob frowned with worry, turning and waiting for seven-
year-old Audra to come down the stairs. "Come on, Jacob!
We'll be late!" she said, hurrying out without even noticing
the agony on her mother's face.

"Don't say anything to her until I talk to you tonight," Iris told her son.

Jacob shrugged. "Okay." He walked out with his head hanging. Iris went to the door, thinking how good life had been at Leavenworth, a decent home at last, warmth, full bellies, her children healthy and going to a real school built on the army post for officers' children. Four-year-old Michael and two-year-old Nancy played in the front yard with a stray dog they had adopted. Her children had a future. Morning Star's children did not. How sad for her. Sadder still was the fact that the very people she felt so sorry for in this mess could end up responsible for her husband's death.

"Come back to me, Zack Myers," she whispered.

34

Zack wondered if men like Strong Runner were laughing at the army. General Howard continued to underestimate the fighting prowess of the Nez Perces, as well as their determination and their knowledge of the land. For weeks they lost the Nez Perces altogether, then caught up with them well entrenched at Clearwater Creek in mid-July, approximately five hundred soldiers plus two hundred scouts, teamsters, packers, civilians, all after a like number of Indians, of which they guessed only about three hundred were fighting warriors, the rest women and children. The Indians had quickly pinned them down from higher ground, and then fled in full view of the soldiers. For some strange reason Howard did not follow right away, and because the man insisted on never fighting or traveling on Sundays, the Indians were gifted an extra day every week to flee while the soldiers camped, hunted, played games, took a leisurely day off.

It seemed to Zack that Joseph and his people should be able to reach Canada easily at this pace. Why Howard was calling the battle at Clearwater a victory for the soldiers, he could not imagine. There were only seven or eight Nez Perces killed, a few more wounded, that they could figure. The army loss was thirteen dead and twenty-three wounded.

The race was on, but Zack did not see how the army could win, especially under Howard; and he did not much care. He actually hoped the Nez Perces would make it to Canada. Chasing them through the Bitterroots had been a taxing journey through some of the most rugged country the West had to offer, and Zack felt like an experienced mountain man when they came down the eastern slopes, weary, aching, growing miserably hot as they headed into the lower valleys beyond. He was sure that by now, after Clearwater, the Indians were even more unified in their efforts to escape. Other bands of Nez Perces, encouraged by Joseph's determination and success, joined him, building their forces.

The struggle to climb the heights of the Lolo Trail had taken its toll on the soldiers, and many of them were marching in boots that were falling apart, a few even marching in stocking feet. Their only salvation was that in the mountains the weather in July was pleasant. To have had to do this in winter would have been impossible. Now many of the men were beginning to complain that they wanted to go back to Lapwai, that they would never catch the Nez Perces and that to try to do so would probably drag them back into the mountains in the rugged terrain of Montana. Howard insisted that wherever an Indian could go, so could a soldier, giving no consideration to the fact that this was Indian country, that the Nez Perces knew it well and were accustomed to survival in country like this. Many of these men were first-timers out here, finding the climate difficult enough under normal conditions.

We should be coming onto the troops under Colonel John Gibbon soon, Zack wrote in a diary he'd decided to keep. He wanted to remember everything, to be able to tell Iris all that happened. Colonel Gibbon had been telegraphed at Fort Shaw that he should be on the lookout. The Nez Perces were headed in his direction. Zack put his pen aside and exited his tent when he heard the sound of thundering horses. Scouts were riding into camp at a gallop. They dismounted in front of General Howard's tent, and Zack rushed over to hear the report.

"Joseph and the bunch of them held up at Big Hole Valley,

sir," one of them reported. "Must have figured once they got out of the Wallowa and over the mountains, they didn't have to be in a hurry anymore—figured they lost us, I guess."

"Can we catch up to them?" Howard asked.

"We have to, sir," the scout answered, a grizzly mountain man who reminded Zack of Sandy Bodine. "Colonel Gibbon went after them after he got your telegraphed message, and when we came upon his camp, it was a mess. The way they told it, they attacked the Nez Perce camp at dawn, but it had been so rough getting there that Gibbon's men were pretty wore out and beaten before they even could fight. They ended up having to make their way through cold creek water and mucky ground to reach the village. The fighting was pretty unorganized, but the soldiers managed to scare up most of them, chased them out of their tipis."

"Was it a victory?" Howard asked anxiously.

"No, sir, and they need your troops for reinforcements."

"Hell, I've already sent half my men back to Lapwai!" Howard complained. "What happened? Gibbon should have been able to take them."

"It's like we said," the second scout answered. "Gibbon wasn't too organized, and his men were in bad shape by the time they got there. They did manage to kill several women and children, but the warriors finally drove them back across the creek and into the trees."

"They *retreated*?"

Zack hardly heard the next few words. Women and children had been killed. Morning Star and Strong Runner's family were among the fleeing Nez Perces.

"Joseph and his men are damn good shots," the second scout was saying. "They zeroed in on the soldiers right good. Even got Gibbon in the hip, but he's gonna live. Drove them right back out of their village, then went in to pick up their dead and wounded. Some of the men told us it was an awful thing, listenin' to the warriors screamin' over their dead."

A sick feeling moved into Zack's gut.

"They're a good two days' hard ride from here, sir," the first scout explained. "That's how long we had to ride to get back to you. God only knows what's happened by now. You've got to get over there."

"Yes." Howard strutted, holding his chin high. Zack could

see what the man was thinking. Glory. Glory and notoriety. That was all men like Howard cared about. Gibbon must be just as hungry for it, going after the Nez Perces before securing Howard's help. The arrogance of some officers never ceased to irritate him. He had never wanted those things when he joined this army. He had wanted to be an officer only because it meant he could take better care of Iris. "We could exact a victory here and end this thing," Howard said.

"The Nez Perces have Gibbon and his men pinned down, sir. They've retreated to the pines and dug into the ground, hiding in trenches. The Nez Perces could rout them anytime and kill all of them. So far they haven't done it. We don't know if it's because they're takin' time to bury their dead, or maybe just arguin' among themselves if they should keep to the fight or move on. I think they're pretty confused themselves about all of this. It don't help, them knowin' that some people are afraid of them, even some troops. Some soldiers under a Captain Rawn had them trapped on the east end of the Lolo, a couple hundred volunteers with him, but they all backed off and let Joseph go through. They was outnumbered, but they could have put up some kind of stand. Joseph probably thinks he ain't gonna get no more trouble, especially now that he's turned Gibbon back. They even have the women fightin'. It was a woman that killed one of Gibbon's men, Captain Logan. His men shot her up pretty good."

Howard breathed deeply in rage. "Do you hear that, men? Make no qualms about shooting the women. They'll shoot you dead just as easily." He moved his gaze to Zack. "That goes for you too, Colonel Myers. I know you have friends among them, and you tried your best to prevent this, but what's done is done, and this is war! Friend or not, if they're shooting at you, you've got no choice but to fight back. Get what's left of your men organized. We're going to relieve Gibbon."

"Yes, sir." Zack left to gather his men, wondering if Strong Runner and his family were still alive.

What Howard and his men found at Big Hole Valley was enough to plant anger and vengeance in any soldier's heart, but by then the two-day march of already-weary men had left most of them with no desire to keep going. The Nez Perces had made Gibbon look like a fool, and Zack could not help thinking that Strong Runner and the others must be laughing by now—if not for the fact that when Gibbon originally attacked the Nez Perce village, the soldiers had cold-bloodedly shot down women and children as they ran screaming from their tipis. Some of the men had joked about it once help arrived, saying some of the men and women who came running out of their dwellings were stark naked.

The Nez Perce warriors had quickly pushed Gibbon's men back, then had kept them literally pinned down in a stand of trees. Because Gibbon had left Fort Shaw hastily, he had not planned his rations, which were nearly depleted by the time he first encountered the Nez Perces at Big Hole. By the time Howard came to relieve them, they were dining on horseflesh. Not only that, an attempt Gibbon had made to blow the Nez Perce apart with a howitzer had also failed. He'd had men drag the big gun up a steep hill and fire on the village across the creek. The gun had been set in a poor position and did little harm. The Nez Perce warriors had surrounded and attacked the soldiers handling the gun, sending them running for their lives. The Indians had then proceeded to dismantle the howitzer and send it tumbling down the hill.

Such was the progress of this campaign. The only thing gained so far was a new respect for the prowess and determination of the Nez Perces, and a high regard for the fighting strategy of Chief Joseph.

"He has a lot of skilled and crafty warriors doing his fighting for him," Howard told Zack at a meeting of commanders. "But make no mistake, it's Joseph himself who is making all the decisions."

"Our men and Gibbon's men are in pretty poor shape, General," one of the other officers said. "Maybe we should give up the chase."

"Give up? Never! That's just what Joseph is hoping for! We'll give all the men time to recuperate, and then we will be off again! Those savages are not going to outrun and outsmart the United States Army!"

"Might I remind you, sir, that scouts say they're headed south, toward Yellowstone?" Zack put in.

"And what if they are?"

Zack sighed with irritation. "That's damn rugged country all the way, country they know better than we know the inside of our own quarters. For a bunch of already-tired, hungry, and practically shoeless troops, it will be hellish to continue the chase."

"I repeat, Colonel Myers, we are not going to quit."

"We could head for the nearest fort first and get fresh troops."

"That is just another form of giving up. I will not do it! God is on our side, Colonel Myers. He will not let those heathens succeed. We will harass them and wear them down until they have no choice but to surrender. No Indians are going to best me, Colonel, especially those who have denied the Christian faith!"

Zack wondered how much more proof the man needed that they were not properly prepared and fortified to continue the hunt. Evidence came when they finally got under way again. The Nez Perces raided ranches along the way, stealing food and horses, killing off remaining cattle and horses so that the army could not in turn garner fresh mounts or eat fresh meat. Settlers who resisted were killed, and people were beginning to blame the ineptness of the U.S. Army for what was happening. It sickened Zack to see so much unnecessary bloodshed, when he knew damn well that originally the Nez Perces intended to come to Lapwai peacefully. If only the army had not reacted so quickly and violently to the original raids committed by Wahlitits and his friends. One soldier had joked about how the night air was full of the wailing of both men and women once the Nez Perces had returned to their village after the first attack and found their dead.

"That ought to have taught them something," the man had commented. "They make trouble, they get killed— women, kids, it don't matter. Indians is Indians."

The trail of blood continued into Yellowstone. Zack wondered why Joseph had not simply headed straight north into Canada when he first came down the eastern side of the Bitterroots. He could think of no other reason than the Nez Perces must have thought that once they left the Wallowa and made it across the mountains peacefully, they would be left alone to seek freedom someplace else, perhaps find refuge with the Crow. He tried to reason the way Strong Runner would reason. To that point they had brought harm to no one. They were gone from the Wallowa. That should have been the end of it. If Gibbon had not acted so hastily and irrationally, perhaps that *would* have been the end of it. But this was just another case of army officers trying to outdo each other and show themselves as the heroes.

All they had really done was cause more bloodshed. If Gibbon had not planned the sneak attack on the Nez Perces at Big Hole, if he had not killed women and children, the Nez Perces might have finally turned north and left the States in peace. Now they knew they were going to be pursued. What they feared more than death was being taken to Indian Territory in the south. Zack had no doubt that was why they were now beginning to put up a true fight. Lack of communication, misunderstandings, poor army decisions, had all led to this, and now the Nez Perces were truly a warring tribe on the run, which meant more innocent lives lost.

Chasing them with inept, weary, hungry troops was just another mistake, but Howard kept on, spurred by a sign that the Nez Perces were beginning to weaken. At the site of a ranch that had been raided, their old ones had been left behind with food and water. The army's Bannock scouts had found them first, and they had promptly murdered and scalped them. In spite of the fact that settlers there had also been killed, Zack could not help feeling fury at the slaughter of the old Nez Perces in return. Joseph must have felt that the old ones left there would be returned to Lapwai and taken care of. Obviously, if he had known this would happen, he never would have left them there. It seemed so senseless when anyone with common sense could tell those old ones had no part in killing the settlers.

Now came strategy against strategy, general against chief. Howard sent troops to Targhee Pass, the western entrance to Yellowstone, sure that Joseph was now headed in the same direction, back toward Idaho. Zack was not so sure Joseph would do the expected, and he argued the point, but Howard would have none of it. Zack's opinion was proved right when Howard's own camp was attacked in the night. The air was filled with shooting and war whoops. Soldiers shot into the darkness at targets they could not see, and the only result was all the army pack mules were run off and scattered.

Zack was ordered to ride after the fleeing raiders, an order he totally disagreed with but one he obeyed. Just as he feared, the Nez Perces were up to the same trickery the Sioux once used. They ambushed his men in an open meadow. Some managed to quickly retreat, but Zack and some of the others were already too deep into the ambush. He ordered those still trapped to dismount and form a circle. He and some of the others pulled their horses down to use as barriers, and bullets and arrows rained down on them from a slight rise to the east. Suddenly, unexpectedly, the ambushers ceased firing and slipped away.

"Why do you think they did that, sir?" a lieutenant asked Zack.

Zack slowly stood up. "I don't know." He was sure as he rode into the meadow and then hastily took refuge behind his horse that he'd seen a familiar Appaloosa on the distant hill, a big warrior riding back and forth yipping and calling out orders. He'd looked very much like Strong Runner. Had Strong Runner realized it was Zack Myers he had pinned down? "I don't know," he repeated.

They returned to the main camp, helped tend the wounded. The lieutenant who'd been sent to Targhee Pass returned after his allotted time there, and there was no more trouble from the Nez Perces, who, they discovered upon pursuit, had slipped quietly and peacefully through the same pass that had been guarded only hours earlier. Again they had eluded the soldiers, through skilled mobility, superior war tactics, deep penetration into enemy territory, trickery, ambush, front and rear guards, and just plain outfoxing General Oliver Howard.

It was August when Zack accompanied General Howard into Virginia City, Montana, while the rest of the troops rested from the agonizing pursuit of the Nez Perces. Howard hoped to find volunteer help there, but no one was willing. The only thing they got for all their trouble was the derision of local citizens, who all but called Howard a procrastinating, blundering fool. Zack could not help secretly agreeing. They discovered that the newspapers were calling the Nez Perces brilliant strategists with "splendid military intelligence." Howard wired Sherman, asking for more troops, as his men were tired and beaten. Zack could not help feeling Howard's embarrassment when Sherman wired back the message that if Howard was so tired, he should give his command to a younger, more energetic officer. The reply only infuriated Howard, who declared that Sherman need not doubt his "pluck and energy."

Zack thought the exchange of words between two grown men of high command was rather childish. Now Chief Joseph had caused animosity among army leaders, which would only cause them to make more foolish decisions. Joseph would be pleased to have heard the wired argument between Howard and Sherman. Just as Zack feared, Howard vowed to go on with what men he had rather than wait for Sherman, who at least said he would come into Yellowstone from the east with the Fifth Cavalry. He had wired that some of Custer's Seventh would also move in from east to west. They planned to surround and pursue the Nez Perces even more vigorously, sure that now the Indians would head for Canada.

Howard purchased shoes, clothes, and medicine at Virginia City, as well as a string of unbroken ponies and a few pack mules, one of the only good things that came of his visit there and his attempt to garner help from Sherman. The one other benefit was the fact that the men received three days of rest while they waited for their leader to return. Unfortunately, what he had managed to bring in the way of new mounts and supplies was still not sufficient for the campaign ahead. At that point Zack and others who had disagreed with his strategy and thought him a fool at least began to look at the man with a little more respect because he would not give up. In spite of his age and his inexperience traversing such rugged territory, he was determined to keep on, even though others of his rank had accused him of being too old and tired for such a venture.

The campaign was on in full force, Howard's men pushing up from the south, Sherman and part of the Seventh Cavalry moving into Yellowstone Valley and heading north, and, according to wired messages at Virginia City, a Colonel Samuel Sturgis also heading northwest with three hundred fifty men. Most important, couriers told Howard that Colonel Nelson

Miles was also now in pursuit, coming out of Fort Keogh with six companies of infantry, five troops of cavalry, and at least a hundred Indian scouts, many of them Crow, who had once called the Nez Perces their friends. Again the government had turned Indian against Indian. It was said Miles was also bringing along two field guns and several wagons of supplies to keep his troops going for weeks, perhaps months, if that was what it would take.

They pressed on, thousands of soldiers after a few hundred Indians running toward Canada . . . and freedom. By now they were surely beginning to feel the effects of constantly being on the run, and totally misunderstood. Zack felt torn between, not wanting to see any more innocent blood shed on either side, wanting to finish his last days as an officer in the U.S. Army with dignity and intelligence, yet wanting equal dignity for Strong Runner and those with him who wanted only a place to call their own.

"Colonel Myers, I am sending you north with twenty men to intercept Colonel Miles's troops," Howard told Zack. Both men sat at a campfire outside Howard's tent, where Howard had summoned Zack.

"I don't understand, sir."

Howard sighed. "I am no longer in this for the glory of it, Myers. I've missed my chance, thanks to Joseph's wily maneuvers and his resilience. I am bogged down with tired, wounded men. What little I could bring them in the way of new mounts and supplies from Virginia City can't make up for their own broken spirits. Joseph has dragged us over mountains and through canyons and thrashed us about this rugged country for close to a thousand miles, and right now I see no hope of catching him. The only one with that hope is Miles, and young officers like you should be in on the kill. You could end up earning yourself yet another promotion. I hate to see you leave the army, Myers. I hope you'll stay. Maybe being a part of the final chase will convince you that this is where you belong."

Zack did not reply right away. He puffed on a pipe the general had given him permission to light, remembering another pipe—his gift to Strong Runner. This man apparently had no concept of the real reason he would like to join Miles, if he could catch him. He didn't want any of the glory either, nor did he want to "be in on the kill," as Howard had put it. He wanted to be there for Strong Runner and his family, to protect them if they were indeed taken captive, to speak in behalf of the Nez Perces against being sent to Indian Territory if it came to that. He wished Howard Shaver were there. He would like to be able to talk to the man.

"I imagine you'll catch up to Miles, sir."

"Not before he catches up with those savages. They're on a dead run for Canada now, and Miles knows it. He'll be hot on their tail. I can't move these troops that fast, but you and twenty of the men who are in better shape than the others can reach Miles. Are you up for it?"

"Yes, sir, I think I am."

"You tell Miles I sent you because you have a special relationship with the one called Strong Runner. Maybe there is something you can do or say to influence the man to give up the fight. I doubt that anything will work now, but it's worth a try."

"Yes, sir."

Howard winced with aching joints as he stood up to stretch. "This is one chase that will be long remembered, Myers, and you can be one of the names mentioned in the history books. Take a couple of the scouts so you don't lose your way." He stared into the darkness. "God know that's easy for a man to do in country like this." He rubbed his eyes, then scratched the skin beneath his thick beard. "This Joseph and the other Nez Perce leaders, young Looking Glass, Strong Runner, they are indeed master strategists, the most intelligent Indians I have ever encountered, don't you think?"

"Yes, sir. I know Strong Runner well enough to be able to tell you he is highly intelligent, very wise, very spiritual, and there is not an ounce of fear in him. He would rather die than be sent south, rather die than give up his dignity. It's that way for all of them, sir. They don't fear death the way most men do. They almost welcome it if it means defending their loved ones and their honor."

Howard nodded. "You should get some rest. I want you to leave at first light. You pick the men. I know this is not in conformance with protocol, but I am sure Miles won't mind the extra soldiers, and since you are so close to your retirement date, doing something a little out of the ordinary won't matter much."

Zack rose and faced him. "Thank you for the opportunity, sir." He held his pipe in his left hand and put out his right hand to the general. "You will receive new honors yourself, sir, I'm sure."

The man snickered as he shook Zack's hand. "They're already calling me the 'day after tomorrow' general because I predicted back in Virginia City that we'd capture the Nez Perce the day after tomorrow. That was several days ago. No, I won't get much credit for this one, Colonel Myers, if, indeed, we capture the Nez Perces at all. If anyone does, it will be Miles. He wants the glory, for more reasons than one. He's married to General Sherman's daughter, you know. Sherman is bound to be close behind all of us. Miles will want to make a big impression on his father-in-law. You probably understand the feeling. You married a colonel's daughter when you were just a lieutenant, did you not?"

Zack let go of his hand, grinning, feeling a deep ache for Iris. "Yes, sir, but I never needed to make an impression. Iris's father had already been killed in the Civil War."

"Well, once we get all Indians settled onto reservations, our work will mostly be done, except for areas where things are still pretty lawless. This whole West will eventually be civilized, though, you watch and see."

"Yes, sir." Zack did not like the way the Indians would have to pay for that civilization, but it seemed there was no stopping it. "Good evening, sir." He saluted and left the man, feeling a little sorry for him in spite of his bad judgment. He had good intentions, truly thought in his own mind that he was doing the right and Christian thing.

Zack rousted some of the men, picked those he would take with him, all cavalrymen. Some were irritated that they had to make the hard ride, others were excited to be among those who finally bagged the Nez Perces after so many weeks of chasing them. *I hope none of you gets the chance,* Zack thought. He bedded down for the night, but he knew sleep would not come to him. His thoughts were too full of Iris and the children, the trouble he could be riding into . . . and of Strong Runner.

35

"*D*o you think he is out there?" Morning Star walked up to Strong Runner, who stood outside the light of their campfire, looking into the blackness to the south.

"He is there," Strong Runner answered. "But not for the same reasons as the others. And he has one good advantage."

"What is that, my husband?"

He looked down at her in the moonlight, thinking how this woman was still as beautiful to him as the day he took her for a bride. "He can fight without the worry of his woman and children being hurt. Army men do not bring their families to battle, but since we flee with our families, we have no choice." He took hold of her arms. "I am sorry it must be this way. You could take the children and go to Lapwai, but what would life be for us apart?"

She touched his strong chest. "I would never leave you. You know that."

Strong Runner pulled her into his arms. They had lost little Dancing Girl at Big Hole Valley. The pain of it was almost too much to bear, let alone the added sorrow of losing Morning Star's sister, White Bird, and her husband, Little Eagle.

Little Eagle—his good friend since boyhood. Morning Star's mother and father, Little Bear and Sits-In-Sun, had also been killed at that place of slaughter; and his own father, Yellow Hand, had died from the effects of the hard journey. That was part of the reason other old ones had been left behind at the place of the bubbling waters. Scouts told them those old ones had been murdered and scalped, another dagger in Strong Runner's heart.

"So much bloodshed. So much death," he groaned. "If they would just have talked to us after those raids Wahlitits and our own son visited upon those settlers. We might still have kept the peace."

"But our son might have been captured and hanged. He is only thirteen."

Tears filled Strong Runner's eyes. "I cannot blame him for what he did, and we could not have let the soldiers capture him. But how many more lives will be lost, Morning Star?"

"No more," she reassured him. "We are so close to being free now. Those soldiers cannot catch us. Just a few days of rest here, and we will make a last dash for Canada and be free. The scouts say there is no sign of soldiers being close behind. Howard's men are tired and beaten. Surely they have given up the chase."

Strong Runner wanted to believe that was true, but he understood too well the pompous arrogance of some of the soldier leaders. He supposed he was not so different, but he also had not chosen to make war against them. It was the white man who had made that decision. The Indians still would have been willing to talk, but the soldiers had come on fighting and had not stopped since.

"I would like to think so," Strong Runner answered. "My heart is so heavy, Morning Star. I am afraid for you and the children. So often I think about what it was like once, when we were first married, how free we were then. They had not yet discovered the gold. There were no treaties binding us. It was a good time, a time we hoped would last. I did not think it would all come to this so soon. We have not even had the chance to grow old together."

"We will grow old together in Canada, where we will be free again."

How he missed Little Eagle. How they both ached to hold

their little Dancing Girl, but she was buried back at Big Hole. At least she lay in Mother Earth's arms, with her grandparents, her aunt and uncle. Poor White Bird had died without ever having children. It had broken her heart to never be able to give Little Eagle a son or a daughter, but now Strong Runner wondered if perhaps it was better that way, no children who had to see this, no children who had to learn to live a new way.

"I am so tired, Morning Star."

"We are both tired, my husband. It is having to carry such heavy hearts that makes us feel this way."

They stood there listening to wolves, a sound that was becoming more and more rare. Joseph had chosen to make camp there. They had something to celebrate, and that was another victory over the army. They had roundly beaten troops that numbered at least three hundred fifty back at a place called Canyon Creek. They were not General Howard's men. They were not even sure who it was, but they had taken the life out of them, for now it seemed neither those men nor General Howard's men were in close pursuit. Unfortunately, the last battle had left the Nez Perces in a bad way. They had lost many men, and close to three hundred horses, shot down or rustled away by the soldiers before the warriors beat them back.

Every such skirmish took its toll. They could not withstand much more, that was certain. "I do not like stopping here to rest. I think we should keep running," Strong Runner told Morning Star. "We think they have given up, but instinct tells me they have not. I would hate to think we have come this far, so close to freedom, to lose it now."

"That will not happen, Strong Runner. We have to believe that, and we cannot go on without killing fresh meat to sustain us, without treating the sores on our horses and without cleaning and repairing our weapons. Come and sleep, my husband. You will need your strength for the last of our journey."

He kissed her hair, loving her as deeply as ever. He fingered the shell necklace he had given her so many years before, when she was just a little girl. She had worn it constantly since then. "You go. Hold the children so they will not be afraid. Send Man Of Wolves out to me. I want to sit out here for a while with my oldest son, feel the night air, listen to the wolves, watch the stars, talk about what life was like for us and our mothers and fathers, our grandparents. The children should know these things, and remember."

Tears trickled down Morning Star's face. "Do come later. I treasure the nights that you still hold me in your arms."

"I will come." He watched her leave him, thinking how much he loved her. He sat down in the tall grass, looking up at the stars. Such a big universe up there, and such big country down here. Why was there not room for everyone? Why did the white man have to have it all?

Zack carried a letter from General Howard as he approached Nelson Miles on legs weary and a little shaky from many hours in the saddle. "Lieutenant-Colonel Zack Myers, sir," he greeted the colonel, noticing Miles was quite a handsome man, with blue eyes and a heavy mustache and sideburns. "Pardon my rather ragged appearance, but I have been with General Howard's troops for weeks now. The men I brought with me are pretty battle-weary too, but we'll help however we can. General Howard thought I might be of some assistance. Here's a letter with his orders for me."

Miles looked him over, took the letter. He read it quickly, met Zack's eyes again. "So, Howard has given me the final victory, has he?"

"I suppose so, sir, if we do manage to catch up to Joseph."

"We will, Colonel Myers," the man answered firmly. "We already know they decided to make camp near the Bear Paw Mountains. They have made a grave mistake taking time to reconnoiter and rest themselves. I suppose they think we have given up, but they have a surprise coming."

"Sir, I happen to be rather closely acquainted with the one called Strong Runner. I dare say I could ride into their camp without fearing harm. I would be willing to do that, to talk to them first before—"

"And warn them that we are closing in? No, Colonel Myers. We have a chance to catch them, and we will give no forewarning. As far as more talks, they've had their chance and they broke their word. The time for talking is over. Are you experienced at fighting Indians?"

Zack checked his anger. "Yes, sir, I was stationed at Phil Kearny during the Fetterman massacre and was involved in the wagon box fight."

"Good. Then you shall come in handy, I don't doubt. I intend to ride these men hard, putting on many miles a day until we are close. We have no time to waste, since Joseph could decide to break camp and continue the run at any moment. I will send men around the rim of the valley in which the Indians are camped, set up a blockade against a northern escape. The rest of us will charge hard and fast, no warning, no talks first. It has come to the point where we cannot pussyfoot around them the way Howard has done. We cannot take too much time letting men and horses rest. That is what Joseph is doing now, and that will be his downfall. I don't doubt he does not even know yet of our approach. He is probably watching to the south for General Howard, whom he has already dodged and defeated more than once, so he is not too worried about him. I will give him something to worry about, except that I will give him no *time* for that worry."

The man threw the letter on a table inside his tent, where Zack had gone to meet with him. Zack found it incredible that Miles had managed to lug along a table and chairs, but he supposed he thought an officer of his caliber should have such things. He sat down behind the table but did not offer Zack a chair. "I will remind you, Colonel Myers, that it is already nearing the end of September. This tag game has gone on long enough. Winter will be setting in soon, and I don't need to tell you what that means in regards to chasing Indians through mountains. If we don't get our hands on Joseph's band quickly, we never will. That means they will get to Canada, where they cannot stay forever. The Canadian government is not thrilled about putting up with the Sioux who have already gone there. They will not want more to come. The Nez Perces will eventually have to return to what they think is home, and what will happen then? The trouble will start all over again, and we'll be doing this kind of thing for years to come. It has to end here and now, Colonel Myers. I'm sure you agree with that."

Zack thought about how tired he was, how tired Strong

Runner and his family must be by now. "Yes, sir, I suppose we don't have much choice."

"It's the Nez Perces who don't have any choice, Colonel. I'm glad you could join us. We can use experienced men. Many of these troops are new to this, but then, what better way to learn than in real action?"

"Yes, sir."

"Use the rest of today and tonight to rest, Colonel. We'll be leaving early, and we'll be pushing hard."

"I'll tell my men, sir."

"Sorry you don't have more time to rest. I expect by the time we reach our destination Howard will be close at hand, and perhaps even Sherman. The Nez Perces won't escape this time, and we'll end this thing."

"I hope so, sir." Zack saluted and left, feeling an anxious need to have it over with. He just wanted to know Strong Runner was all right. He walked back to his own camp and gave his men the news, feeling sorry at the look of weariness in their eyes. He unpacked more of his own gear then and went inside a tent his men had put up for him, taking out pen and paper. They were getting so close. He needed to keep his journal for Iris updated.

We are very close, he wrote. *In just a few days this might all be over.*

Zack's written words turned out all too true. All the while he rode at an agonizing pace with Miles and his troops, he prayed the Nez Perces would be gone by the time they arrived. Why the Indians had camped for so long he could not imagine, except that they must have thought the army had given up, or perhaps they felt they were close enough to their destination that a few extra days could not keep them from reaching it. One thing was certain, their delay was a sign that they, too, were feeling the effects of the grueling journey, made worse for them by the fact that women and children were along. Rumor had it Joseph's wife had given birth not long before they originally agreed to come to Lapwai.

It was the end of September, and Miles's troops were worn to a frazzle, their horses dispirited, everyone approaching total exhaustion. Scouts said the Nez Perces were camped

only three miles away near Snake Creek, and Miles immediately deployed several cavalry troops to circle around behind
the hills to the northwest exit from the bowllike valley in
which the Indians camped. They were to block their escape
should it be necessary. The men were given no time to rest,
something Zack considered a grave mistake. Miles intended to
attack the main camp at a hard gallop, giving the Nez Perces
little time to organize themselves. The trouble was, such an
attack meant riding up a steep ridge of hills first, then gallop-
ing tired horses across three miles of open land at a run. He
had no doubt some of the horses would collapse before ever
reaching the camp, but Miles kept his confidence, strutting
about like an already-victorious commander.

Miles planned to surprise and scatter the Nez Perces, who
would then run right into the northwest blockade. Zack argued the decision, to Miles's anger. "Sir, so far the Nez Perces
have shown no inclination to ever run from a fight," he
pointed out. "And if we're going to go charging in over two
or three miles of open land, we certainly won't be surprising
them. It will take a good twenty minutes to reach the camp,
and that's a lot of time, considering their skills at hurriedly re-
sponding to battle. We're also allowing ourselves to ride right
into a valley where there is nowhere to run for cover if necessary. Once we're down in there, we'll be fighting them on
their turf and on their terms. We don't know what's really
waiting for us down there, and we have to remember that
many of those warriors are crack shots with rifles, and they
have plenty of those as well as plenty of ammunition."

"I don't need a colonel I hardly know coming in here and
telling me how to plan a battle, Myers," the man replied. "The
point is, they don't know we're here. It most certainly *will* be
a surprise to them, and they're tired and most likely low on
ammunition by now."

Thunder rolled ominously as a storm brewed in the
mountains to the west. It was early morning, and the blockade of troops had already left. The men were restless and
frightened, none of them wanting to attack in their present
bedraggled condition. Some even had trouble controlling
their horses, since the weary animals wanted nothing more
than to graze peacefully. The horses had only one night to

rest, but even then they were left saddled in case the Indians should turn on them and be the ones to charge.

Men were ordered to mount up. The storm moved closer, as though to vent its anger in tune with the conflict about to be met. Zack gave up arguing with Miles. It was obvious the man was not going to allow anything to stop him. He was close to capturing the famous Chief Joseph, Looking Glass, and Strong Runner, a feat which would earn him a place in history. The Indians had trekked nearly thirteen hundred miles, and Zack had followed them nearly all of that way. It seemed to him that Colonel Miles would get the message that so far the Nez Perces had managed to evade and defeat the army in every moment of conflict. Why would it be any different today, especially when they were riding right down into the heart of their camp and could easily be surrounded?

With rolling thunder and an increasing wind whipping at them from the west, by early afternoon the charge was on. Rain began to pour down on the troops, the weather turning colder by the minute. Its misery made the charge even more difficult, tired men on tired horses now soaked and chilled to the bone. Zack's predictions were soon proved right. Miles waited and watched while his troops, led by Zack and other officers, thundered toward the Nez Perces, only to be halted in their tracks by a volley of gunfire that mowed down the front line. Horses reared and men fell screaming. More men came on, and more were shot down by Indians who could shoot as well or better than the soldiers. Zack was as vulnerable as the others, and a bullet slammed into his left shoulder, throwing him right off his horse. He landed with a thud that knocked the breath out of him, and he lay there stunned for several minutes while all around him men turned and fled back to the base camp.

Rain beat against Zack's face and drenched his uniform, mixing with the blood that poured from his shoulder. He lay waiting, watching black clouds roll across the sky, thinking how strange it was to lie there watching a thunderstorm when just beyond was a camp full of murderous Nez Perces. He could not be positive Strong Runner was still among them, or even what Strong Runner's temperament would be. For that reason he lay still, deciding it might be better if the Indians thought he was dead. Help would surely come soon.

He waited, the rain turning colder, the wind growing wilder. He could hear war whoops somewhere not so far away, the cries, mixed with his dazed condition, bringing on memories he thought were finally buried, never to be resurrected. Instead, it all came back to him in that moment of cold misery and shouting Indians—another time, a ten-year-old boy, a family murdered by painted Pawnee. All he'd been through, it had all come to this then, to die himself in a rain-soaked valley somewhere . . . nowhere . . . killed by Indians. They were coming for him, weren't they? They would scalp him, mutilate him, steal his weapons. Iris. This would be so terrible for her. What about his children? If only he could see them once more.

A horrible cold settled into Zack's bones. He waited for what seemed like hours, not even sure anymore for what. He wished he could move to look at his pocket watch, but he still feared the Nez Perces were now in a murderous enough mood to come and scalp him. He still could not quite dispel the memories that had come so alive for him again.

Finally he heard them, rebellike yells to his right. That would be the direction of the soldiers. Miles was sending in the infantry now, probably backed by more cavalry. As soon as they were close enough, he would get up. He *had* to get up. He had to live for Iris, for the children. If he wanted to live, he had to get back to the base camp for help.

They came closer, and now he heard the Nez Perces charging toward the soldiers, the air filled with war whoops and wind and snow. Soldiers ran past him, and with one great effort he rolled to his knees, pain ripping through his left shoulder. Quickly he found himself caught in the melee of guns and knives, swords and hatchets. He could barely see for his pain. He managed to get his revolver from its holster, heard the scream of a warrior close by. He turned, saw a big man coming at him with hatchet raised, his torso bare in spite of the cold.

It all seemed to happen in one instant, each of them recognizing the other too late. Zack's pistol was fired at the same time the warrior literally froze with his arm in the air. A bloody hole opened in his throat. Zack stared, first in amazement, then in horrible dread and sorrow. "Strong Runner!" he gasped.

"Look out, sir!" The words were shouted by a private who stood near him with a bloody bayonet in his left hand, a pistol in his right. A woman was running toward them. Zack saw no weapons on her. Everything happened as though in a strange dream, more a nightmare. She was beautiful. Morning Star! She had seen her husband shot down.

"No! Wait!" he shouted to the private who had raised his pistol. The gun fired even as Zack yelled the words. A hole exploded in Morning Star's chest, breaking a shell necklace she wore. The shells fell and scattered across Strong Runner's body as she fell over her husband.

All around the fighting continued, but Zack was momentarily oblivious of any of it. He stared in shock at Strong Runner and Morning Star. "No!" he cried. He went to his knees.

"Murderers!" he heard a young man scream. Zack looked up to see Man Of Wolves coming at him now, hatchet raised. He had no choice. No choice. He fired his pistol again, catching the boy in the head. Man Of Wolves fell near his parents.

"My God! My God!" Zack moaned. He crawled to Strong Runner, saw that his eyes were still open, realized he was still alive. The man looked at him in that way Red Eagle had looked at him. "Strong Runner! My God, I didn't know!"

A tear slipped down one side of Strong Runner's face, and Zack threw himself over the man.

"Save my son . . . daughter . . ." Strong Runner whispered. "Friend . . . it is over."

Zack felt the man's last breath against his cheek. He felt for a pulse, found none. The fighting continued, but moved in another direction so that he knelt there alone amid dead bodies. He could not stop a sudden convulsion. He turned away and vomited, shivering from his wound, pain, the awful cold, mostly from the horror of what had just happened. He groaned, convulsing again, this time into wretched sobbing. All the hatred left in him seemed to well up and gush out of him through the vomiting and the tears. "It *is* over," he sobbed. "It *is* over."

"Sir! Here! I'll take you back!"

Zack looked up to see a mounted soldier, in too much pain even to recognize what rank he was.

"Hurry, sir! I can save you! We're being driven back again. Hurry!"

Zack looked down at Strong Runner once more, Morning Star, Man Of Wolves. Nothing seemed real. He reached down and picked up some of the shells of the broken necklace, vaguely remembering Iris telling him once that the shell necklace Morning Star always wore was a gift from her husband when she was just a little girl.

He managed to get to his feet, put the shells into his pants pocket. The soldier helping him dismounted and gave him a shove up onto his horse, then mounted up himself and headed the animal back toward camp, bullets whizzing past them. Zack suddenly didn't care if one of those bullets hit him.

"We've attacked twice and have been soundly thrashed twice!" the soldier complained.

Zack was not surprised.

Badly beaten, Miles's troops settled in to wait out the Nez Perces. They had been unable to defeat them in battle, so now they would simply keep them surrounded and starve them out, or simply wear down their resistance. Zack did his waiting in the medical tent, where the bullet was removed from his shoulder, his agony made worse by the knowledge that he had killed Strong Runner and Man Of Wolves himself. He could not forget Strong Runner's last words. *Save my son . . . daughter.* Was that all that was left of the man's beautiful family? One son? One daughter?

Days passed. His pain became more bearable. He waited with the rest of them, wondering if the siege would ever end. More men died from belly-down snipers on both sides. The high winds forced the snow into a high-country blizzard. The cold was miserable for the wounded, including Zack, whose heart was as wounded and tired as his body. Badly needed supplies that were supposedly on their way to Miles's troops still had not arrived. He had sent for General Howard to make haste in coming to his aid. A few Nez Perce scouts managed to sneak through the lines, and Miles suspected they were headed into Canada to ask Sitting Bull for help. They all hoped the man would not oblige, as it was guessed there were at least three thousand Sioux just across the border. None came to the aid of the Nez Perces.

Miles knew the Indians had to give in sooner or later. The soldiers could continue to get supplies from outside their ring of imprisonment. The Nez Perces could not. Their supplies would run out. Most of their horses were already dead, and they were encumbered by women and children. "They won't let their families freeze or starve," Miles remarked more than once.

"No, they won't," Zack muttered. Strong Runner had died for that very cause, but he didn't know most of his family would die with him. Zack was as eager as anyone now for this to be over, but for a different reason. He wanted to be able to go among the Nez Perces and find what was left of Strong Runner's family.

Scouts rode back and forth with messages, attempts to talk peace, news from each camp. Looking Glass had been killed, shot in the head by a stray bullet. That meant that all of the Indians' most ardent leaders but one were dead. The only one left was Joseph, and he had once said he would continue the fight only as long as he felt there was a chance of saving the women and children. Now many of them were also dead. It was only a matter of time.

Word finally came that Joseph was ready to surrender. By that time General Howard had arrived, and after a rather stiff reception by Colonel Miles, things relaxed when Howard assured Miles he had not come to steal the glory of the moment. Miles could receive Joseph's surrender.

Through it all, Zack took care of his own men but kept relatively silent. Some of the men knew he'd once been friends with Strong Runner, and Zack knew it was probably evident that he was suffering from more than a bullet wound. He'd seen his own haggard face in a mirror. He'd kept quiet, talking to no one about what had happened. It was something he had to suffer alone. How could any of them understand? Only Iris would know how he was feeling.

He ached to be with her, to tell her all of it. Most of these men didn't even know he'd shot Strong Runner himself, and it was not something he cared to boast about. It did not make him proud. He wanted none of the notoriety, and he doubted one man among them felt the way he did when Joseph gath-

ered his people and then rode forward, into the open, to surrender to Miles and Howard, who rode out to greet him.

Zack and other officers sat mounted behind their commanders, watched Joseph take a rifle from under the blanket
he wore around his shoulders, and start to hand it to Howard. Howard motioned for him to give it to Miles instead,
which he did. Zack couldn't miss the sad, tragic look in his
eyes that he had seen in Strong Runner's, in Thomas's, in Red
Eagle's.

"Tell General Howard I know his heart," Joseph told
Miles. "What he told me before in Idaho, I have in my heart.
I am tired of fighting. My people ask me for food, and I have
none to give. It is cold, and we have no blankets, no wood.
My people are starving to death. Where is my little daugh-
ter? I do not know. Perhaps even now she is freezing to death.
Hear me, my chiefs! I have fought. But from where the sun
now stands, Joseph will fight no more forever."

The words struck deep. To Zack's relief, Howard and
Miles treated Joseph with the respect and kindness the brilliant war chief deserved. The survivors were allowed to bury
their dead. Zack made sure to watch Strong Runner, Man Of
Wolves, and Morning Star buried, wanting to know where
their graves were. He said a prayer over them, not caring that
some of the soldiers stared and whispered. Technically, as of
the day of the burial, he was no longer in the army, an ironic
fact that tore at his insides. He had joined this army to kill Indians, and he had done just that. There was no satisfaction in
it. He had just buried one of the most honorable men he'd
ever known.

Iris waited at the train station, her heart pounding harder
with anticipation, joy, dread, curiosity. Jacob, Audra, Michael,
and Nancy all waited with her, as excited as their mother. Michael turned five that day, January 10, 1878. They were
dressed in their finest, longing to greet the daddy they had
missed. All knew they would have to accept two new children
into the family, both of them Nez Perce Indians, a twelve-
year-old boy named Jumping Bear, and a six-year-old girl
named Little Turtle. Iris had told them they could help pick
Christian names for their new siblings after they arrived, and

she explained they would be very lonely and confused for a while. She did not know herself what had actually happened to Strong Runner and Morning Star and all the others, how and when they had been killed. Zack had written only that these two were all that were left and that he wanted to bring them home with him. He had received special permission from Agent Monteith, and he had received his honorable discharge from the army as a full colonel rather than a lieutenant-colonel.

Iris's emotions alternated from happiness and relief to sorrow for Strong Runner and Morning Star. Such a waste of a handsome, intelligent family. Like most citizens all over the country, she had heard the story of the Nez Perce flight, how they had almost reached Canada, Chief Joseph's chillingly poignant words at his surrender. It made her sick inside to read that General Sherman had not kept his promise that Joseph and his people could go back to their homeland and would have a reservation there. The government was instead sending them to the one place they hated and dreaded most, Indian Territory. She had no doubt many would die there of broken hearts, and she knew Zack wanted to keep Strong Runner's children because that was the one thing Strong Runner never wanted for them, to go to the hot, dry land to the south and live like beggars. This was the least she and Zack could do to repay Strong Runner and Morning Star for saving her life.

So, it was over. Over. She could not even imagine men like Joseph and Strong Runner as prisoners. Maybe Strong Runner was better off dead after all, but it must have been so hard for Zack. He'd mentioned he had been wounded but promised he was all right. How she wished she could have been with him.

Finally the train rumbled into the station, steam billowing from its boiler. The older children ran along with the engine a little way, their breath also coming out in steam because of the bitterly cold air. Nancy jumped up and down with excitement at seeing her daddy again. Iris waited on the platform, not sure which car Zack rode. She looked in both directions, and finally saw two Indian children dressed like white children climb down the train steps. A man was holding the little girl's hand, while the boy climbed down first, looking bewildered at the new sights and sounds.

"My God," she whispered. He stood there in full uniform, handsome as ever, but in spite of the woolen army coat he wore, she could tell he had lost weight, and there was a look in his eyes that spoke of a tragedy worse than Strong Runner's death. "Watch your little sister," she told Michael. She ran to her husband, her Zack, home, alive! He let go of the little girl's hand and swept her up into his arms, pressing her tight against him, both of them trembling from the cold and from sheer relief and joy.

"God, Iris, you don't know how much I wished you were with me."

"I'm just so glad you're home. Oh, hold me, Zack. Don't ever let go, and don't ever leave again!"

"Never again. I've resigned."

Iris started to pull away, just to have a look at him, but he clung to her.

"It was me," he said quietly in her ear so that Jumping Bear could not hear. "I killed him," he groaned. "I didn't even know it was him until it was too late." He took a deep, shivering breath. "I killed Strong Runner and Wolf Boy both."

Iris clung to him in shock. "My God, Zack!" She kissed his cheek, reached her arms around his neck. "My poor Zack."

"I've never experienced anything like it." He pulled away, his eyes wet with tears. "I got sick to my stomach. It was as though all the old hatreds just poured out of me. Strong Runner's last words were to ask me to help his son and daughter. Morning Star was shot by another soldier. She died right beside her husband. I don't even know what happened to Dancing Girl. I think she was killed in the battle at Big Hole Valley." He sniffed and breathed deeply. "We have so much to talk about. I hope you don't mind my bringing Little Turtle and Jumping Bear. I want to keep them, Iris, raise them. It might be hard, what with the way some people think about Indians—"

"Have I ever folded against a challenge?"

He smiled through tears, and Iris felt old desires at the sight of his handsome green eyes. "No," he answered. "You sure as hell haven't."

"They will become part of our family. Together we can help them adjust. I've already told the children—"

Before she could finish, all four children were clamoring around their father, peppering him with questions. Zack protested, telling them he only wanted to look at them, see how much they had grown. He'd been gone well over a year. He hugged each of them, relishing the feel of his children in his arms, thanking God they were well and happy and alive. Children like these had hope for their future. The Nez Perces and so many other tribes did not feel that hope. He introduced them to Little Turtle and Jumping Bear. The beautiful Little Turtle smiled brightly, showing her dimples. She was hardly aware of the gravity of what had taken place, probably did not even realize her mother was never coming for her. Jumping Bear was more belligerent, very quiet. He missed his father. He was going to be a challenge, but Zack was determined to love the boy, and that the boy would one day love him. He would never tell him he'd killed Strong Runner and Man Of Wolves.

He turned to Iris while the children talked to Little Turtle and Jumping Bear. "Iris, I feel like I've come full circle. All the way home I thought about what we should do now that I'm out of the army, and I thought . . . if you'll agree, I'd like to go back to the old farm where my life began. I want to see my family's graves. Maybe we can convince whoever owns the place to sell it, or maybe it's never even been worked since. I don't know, but I think I'm ready to face those graves. I'd like to go back and maybe settle there, farm the place again."

She grasped both his hands. "If that's what you want, we'll go. I'm so sorry it happened, Zack, but I can see that this has done for your soul. I can see it in your eyes. You've chased the sun and you've caught it. You've found your spirit way. That's how Strong Runner would have looked at it."

He nodded, remembering the look in Strong Runner's eyes. "I hope he would have." He leaned down and met her lips in a warm kiss. "Let's go home," he told her. He gathered the children together, and Iris noticed two older white women staring at the Indian children and whispering. She picked up Little Turtle, put an arm around Jumping Bear, and walked over to them.

"What are you looking at?" she asked the ladies boldly.

They both looked flustered and embarrassed. "We were just . . . we've never seen Indian children dressed like that before. Who are they?"

Iris smiled proudly. "They are my adopted son and daughter. Their father was a great Nez Perce warrior, and their mother saved my life once."

Both women looked taken aback, left speechless. Iris marched off with Little Turtle and Jumping Bear to the carriage where the rest of the children were waiting. Zack stood there smiling the smile that had always melted her heart. "You haven't changed a bit, Mrs. Myers."

She placed Little Turtle into the carriage. "Did you think that I would?"

He shook his head. "No. That's why I knew you could handle two more children, Indians at that. You're one hell of a woman, Iris Myers."

"And it takes one hell of a man to handle me, wouldn't you say?" She drew something out of her handbag, handing it to Zack. "I thought I'd bring this for you to give to Jumping Bear."

Zack looked down at the circular beaded necklace Strong Runner had given him once, telling him it represented the unending circle of life. His heart tightened at the sight of the necklace, the memory of his talks with the Nez Perce warrior. He turned to Jumping Bear, who still had not gotten into the carriage. He reached out and placed the necklace around his neck. "It was your father's," he told the boy. "He gave it to me as a gift. Now I give it back to you."

Jumping Bear looked down at the necklace, fingered it gently. "I know this sign," he said. "It is the circle of life."

Zack nodded. "That circle will continue, Jumping Bear, through you and Little Turtle and other descendants of Joseph and men like your father."

The boy watched him with a hint of hope in his dark eyes. "I hope this is true."

"It is true, Jumping Bear. Wherever your people are sent, I promise to take you to see them whenever possible. I want you always to remember their ways, their language. I will never take that away from you." Zack turned to Iris, reaching into his pants pocket and pulling out a handkerchief tied into a little bundle. He handed it to Iris. "Keep this in a safe place.

Give it to Little Turtle when she's older and understands its importance."

Iris took the little package. "What is it?"

"Seashells. They're from the necklace Morning Star always wore. You told me once it was a gift to her from Strong Runner. It broke when . . . when she was shot. I grabbed up some of the shells before I left."

The tears in his eyes tore at Iris's heart. She put the bundle of seashells into her handbag. "I'll make sure Little Turtle gets them someday." Oh, how it hurt to think she'd never see Morning Star again, to realize the beautiful young woman was gone from this earth.

They climbed into the buggy together and were off. The train gave out three long blasts of its steam whistle, signaling for the boarding of people who were headed even farther east, on tracks that now spanned a continent fast filling with settlers from all walks of life. They had room to grow now. The Indian situation was well under control.

From the author ...

I hope you have enjoyed my story. If you would like to know more about me and other books I have written, just send a legal size (#10) self-addressed and stamped envelope to me at 6013 North Coloma Road, Coloma, Michigan 49038–9309, and I will send you a newsletter and bookmark. Thank you so much for your support!

About the author ...

An award-winning romance writer, ROSANNE BITTNER has been acclaimed for both her thrilling love stories and the true-to-the-past authenticity of her novels. Specializing in the history of the American Indians and the early settlers, her books span the West from Canada to Mexico, Missouri to California, and are based on Rosanne's visits to almost every setting chosen for her novels, extensive research, and membership in the Western Outlaw-Lawman History Association, the Oregon-California Trails Association, the Council on America's Military Past, and the Nebraska State Historical Society.

She has won awards for best Indian novel and Best Western Series from *Romantic Times* and is a Silver Pen, Golden Certificate, Golden Pen and Reviewer's Choice for Excellence Award winner from *Affaire de Coeur*. She has also won several Reader's Choice awards and is a member of Romance Writers of America.

Rosanne and her husband have two grown sons and live in a small town in southwest Michigan.

DON'T MISS THESE FABULOUS
BANTAM WOMEN'S FICTION TITLES